REST OF MINE

B. RAMONDA

First published in 2026 by Radici House

Paperback ISBN: 979-8-9936794-2-6
Ebook ISBN: 979-8-9936794-3-3

First edition

www.bramonda.com

The Diamond Guide interior illustrations by Rachel Sierra
www.rachelsierraart.com

Cover design by Maria Barbara Ramonda
Cover image © Canva, used under license

To my brother David,
whose existence first made me a sister.

And to my brother Giuseppe,
who taught me how to be one.

"The mystery of love is greater than the mystery of death."

—Oscar Wilde

The Diamond Guide

by Leo Sartori

CARAT

Weight isn't everything, but it does set the scale.

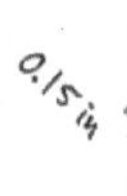
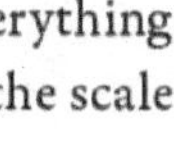
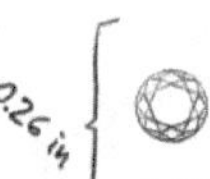

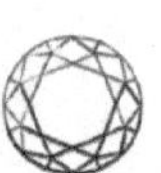
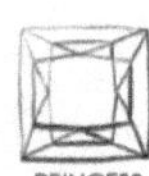

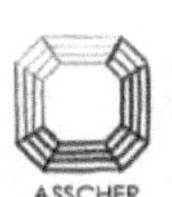
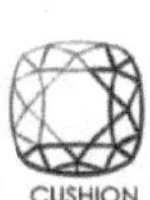

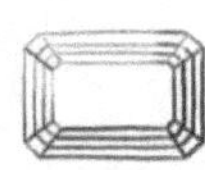

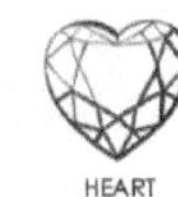

CUT

Where math meets magic. An ideal cut flashes brilliance with every angle.

COLOR

Perfect is supposed to be colorless, but that's not always where the value is.

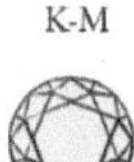

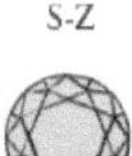
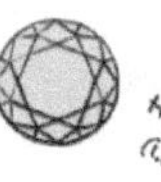

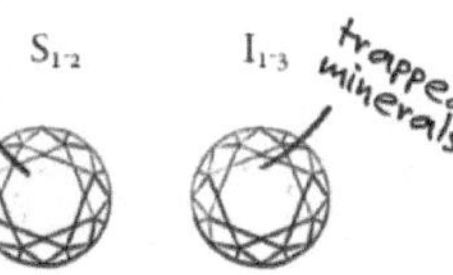

CLARITY

The clean ones are rare, but the ones with marks survived something.

Prologue

Did you know the Inuit have dozens of words for different kinds of snow, and the Scots over four hundred distinct words for rain?

That's what happens when something is everywhere. When it lingers, shapes your lifestyle, becomes the landscape itself.

And still you can't quite grasp its grandiosity, so you keep naming it. Searching for the perfect term that might finally do it justice.

But it never really works. So, you're left with a reduced abstraction—a word doing its best but failing miserably at describing this all-encompassing thing around you.

Do you know the kind of love I'm talking about?

The kind that's everywhere. Even when he's nowhere.

I never had to search for new words when it came to love.

I just knew the gentle kind. The one that never asks to be chosen first. That doesn't demand grand gestures or heroic sacrifice. Because it simply is.

The kind that lasts a lifetime, or just long enough to feel like it could've.

And when it's gone, it doesn't take anything with it.

It won't fight for you. Not because it doesn't care, but because it was never trying to win.

Then there's something else.

Something, someone, somehow I still don't have a name for.

The kind that takes up so much of your chest there's no room left for yourself.

The kind that feels like walking barefoot through a forest of splinters or crossing 7th Avenue blindfolded, because what if they're late because they misread your text and are waiting for you on the other side?

The one you'd set yourself on fire for, just for the chance they might finally look your way.

A reckless kind of love. Like a drunk driver flying down the road on a school morning.

It makes you bold. Makes you dizzy. Makes you think freedom and danger are the same thing.

And when it finally fucks off, all that's left is a door slammed shut, because he took the keys.

So yeah, I do believe there are unnamed loves out there. Or right *here*. Through you, across you, within you.

Ones that overtake everything. Even language.

You know exactly the kind of love I'm talking about.

But which one is your favorite?

And tell me—just between us—were the views worth it during the freefall?

1
Isadora

"You know he'll be there, right?" Jamie says, flipping through a magazine on the armchair.

"What?" my best friend Allie yelps. I don't even flinch.

Jamie shrugs. "Everyone with a name is attending tonight."

"But it's her brother's event," Allie argues.

He raises an eyebrow. "You really think Kathy's triple-checking the guest list for exes?"

Jamie's mother is Kathy Ellington—New York's most sought-after event planner. But you probably already knew that. Especially after the last Whitney Gala made it into *Architectural Digest.*

"Actually," I cut in, "the guest list is always my father's domain. And no one knows Milo and I ended things. Well—except you two."

Jamie's phone rings. "Speak of the devil. It's my mother. Back in a sec," he says, already halfway out the door.

A distant honk echoes through the open window of our dressing room as I drag a comb through my hair.

It's late March and still freezing in New York City, but Allie has a strict no-sealed-air rule. If a window can open, it must. I've stopped arguing. At this point, I think she's rewired my internal thermostat.

She's balancing on one foot, naked save for a half-zipped silk dress and a string of French profanity.

"This zipper is personally victimizing me." She twists around.

"Hold still," I say, kneeling behind her. "You're wearing architecture."

The fabric slips through my fingers like water. Her perfume—vanilla, laced with something woody—mingles with the scent of heat and hairspray.

"Remind me why we're doing our own glam again?" she asks.

"Because we always do. You hate people touching your face, and I hate anyone going near my hair."

"Right. I forget that's a thing."

She exhales with relief as I fasten the final inch, then twirls away like she's on stage—humming off-key, mascara wand clenched between her teeth like a dagger. The dress clings in all the right places. Champagne silk, plunging back, the kind that slips if you so much as breathe. Which, of course, is the point.

I turn to the mirror and smooth the black fabric over my hips. My hair's too long and unruly for tonight, so I slick it back with both hands.

The dress I chose is backless, liquid satin, the kind that feels like stepping into ink. It dips low between my shoulder blades, held by delicate straps knotted at my neck.

"Earrings?" Allie asks while rifling through my velvet-lined drawer like it's a candy box.

"Pearls. Grandma's."

She passes them over. I put them in. Cool against my skin. Weightless, until they're not.

"Adore. Shoes?"

"Black satin Choos. The ones with the crystal ankle strap."

"Bold. I think I'll go with the Valentinos, the red suede ones."

"Are you sure? Last time you wore those, we left after thirty minutes, and you asked Rami to take us to the nearest police station so you could report, and I quote, 'an assassination attempt.'"

She snorts.

"I don't think Rami found it funny. He made us hand over our phones and do a full security sweep."

"That's because your bodyguard doesn't understand sarcasm. Also, he hates me."

"He doesn't hate you. He's just... a tough nut to crack."

"Like, armored tank-level tough."

I look at my phone screen. "We're late."

Right on cue, Jamie's head pops in.

"Our chariot awaits. And by chariot, I mean the government-issue Escalade downstairs that doesn't tolerate lateness."

Allie groans and grabs her heels. "Ugh. Democracy awaits."

"And Kathy, who's *not* happy we're late."

I slide the pink Chanel bullet—*Mademoiselle*—into my clutch and snap it shut.

My hands are steady. They always are. Until they're not.

In the lobby, the air shifts to something cooler. Sleeker. It smells like marble polish and orchids.

Outside, the SUV idles like a panther. Rami opens the door without a word, his expression carved from stone. I smile at him. He doesn't return it.

Allie pulls down a window and kicks off her heels the second she's in.

"Someone please escort me directly to the champagne tower the moment we arrive," Jamie says, adjusting his cuffs.

"I was against it, for the record," Allie says, eyes on the window. "I suggested Krug, poured from a mirrored staircase by a harpist playing real glassware. Didn't fly."

I still can't believe my brother convinced her to help him with this. Allie adores all things design, and she does run the most exclusive showroom of her family's heritage design house, *Granite & Grove*. But politics isn't exactly her canvas. And working with Hadrian's team, especially with my father circling, is something we usually avoid like the plague.

At least I do.

"Yeah, well, my mother still said you did a flawless job," Jamie says. "She was genuinely impressed. And you know she doesn't hand out compliments for sport."

"I haven't seen it yet," I add, "but jaw-dropping is the bare minimum where Allie's involved."

"Thanks, babe," she sighs, leaning back. "But this was a one-time exception. I'm officially retiring from event design after tonight."

I catch a flicker of a smile on her lips before she turns away.

"My mom will be disappointed," Jamie says. "She was already scheming to poach you."

"She'll get over it." She looks at me now, concerned eyes out. "Is, we don't have to go. Your brother won't mind. We could skip the whole thing and head to Soho. Or that place in Chinatown with the glowing koi and those absurdly theatrical cocktails—"

Jamie gasps, scandalized. "Excuse me? We're already late, and now you want to ghost the whole thing? This tux demands its moment."

I squeeze Allie's hand. "Thanks, Als. But you know I can't miss a Carter-Bello gala. I'd never hear the end of it. Plus, it's important to Hadrian."

"RSVPs closed weeks ago. If he's on the list, he's coming." Jamie checks his watch for the millionth time tonight. "Then again, we're late. Maybe the universe is doing us a solid."

Allie bumps his shoulder. "Alright, hopeboy. You saw the guest list, who else is coming? Come on, spill."

I flash her a grateful smile.

Truth is, I'll always be happy to see Milo.

He's been my best friend since before we could spell our names. And then one day, he just became more.

We were fourteen, walking our usual path through Central Park while Allie was off watching Hadrian and his best friend Blake play frisbee.

It was a difficult year. My parents were fighting constantly. My mother was gone more than not. Our house felt like it had been built out of cards, and we were bracing for the wind.

Milo and I were wandering toward our favorite spot near the fountain, where a cart sold peach iced tea so sweet it made your teeth ache.

Out of nowhere, a blur came barreling toward us on a skateboard. I still don't know how he moved so fast, but Milo's hand found mine and pulled me close. We stumbled, just a single step.

Some moments arrive so suddenly, and mark you so deeply, they burn into your memory with impossible clarity.

Like the way he smelled faintly of sunscreen and something clean. Dryer sheets and wind, I think. Or how his hand lingered around mine for a beat too long. The way his eyes caught the light, warm and golden like honey pots.

Whoa. I've never seen that before, I remember thinking. Even his smile—tilted slightly to the left, like it hadn't quite decided whether to be shy or bold—struck me.

The scent of linden trees. The single cloud drifting across the sky. A little boy crying near the pond. The book in my backpack—*Como Agua Para Chocolate.*

That moment was one of those.

And if you haven't read that book, truly, do yourself a favor.

Here, let me share my favorite passage. Consider it a nudge.

'(...) lloró y tejió, hasta que en la madrugada terminó la colcha y se la echó encima. De nada sirvió. Ni esa noche ni muchas otras mientras vivió logró controlar el frío.'

Funny, jocular really, how words can shift shape over time without changing at all. Same quilt, same useless attempt at warmth, just a different type of cold.

I've translated that line, sat with it, reworded it a hundred ways while I was in college. If you're curious, I kept the notes. I'll make sure they get to you somehow.

"WHAT?" Allie's scream yanks me out of the memory like a slap of cold air.

From the front seat, I catch a glimpse of Rami's shoulders tensing slightly.

"You're telling me *the queen* is going to be there?"

"Uh-huh," Jamie mumbles.

I blink. "Which queen?"

She gasps. "Brielle Warner, *obviously*. There's only one queen in New York, and she doesn't wear a crown, she wears vintage Mugler."

Milo

You're still coming, right?

Yes

Should I say hi?

If you want to

I always want to ⊠

Then you always should ⊠

2

Leo

I HATE THESE EVENTS. Always have.

The lights, the flashbulbs, the small talk that tastes like ash.

I landed in New York four hours ago. I was meant to be in bed by now—my bed, my sheets, my place.

Not here, blinking under chandeliers while strangers tell me things I couldn't give fewer fucks about.

Six months in Europe, and I'd almost forgotten what this city feels like when it closes in.

But here I am. Tux pressed, jaw tight, shaking hands like I give a damn.

"Smile, Leone. Some of these bastards are worth keeping happy," my father murmurs just for me, as some overfed relic in a velvet blazer snaps his fingers at a waitress.

"Have you met Hadrian?" the man asks, nodding toward a guy around my age weaving through the crowd, shaking hands like he was born doing it.

"We haven't had the pleasure," my father replies.

"Hadrian! Come here, let me introduce you to a dear friend of mine." His voice booms—too loud for the room, too loud for me. He clasps the young man on the shoulder and steers him toward us.

"This is Lupo Sartori, from the—"

"Sartori Group, of course," Hadrian cuts in.

"A pleasure, Hadrian. I voted for your grandfather, he was one of the good ones. We don't get many like that anymore."

Lupo Sartori is already in full performance mode. The offensive charm, the easy laugh, the way he leans in just enough to make you feel seen while silently taking your measure.

I've watched him close deals over caviar and blackmail. I've watched him do worse.

"And this is Lupo's son—"

"Leo," I cut in.

"Nice to meet you, Leo."

"My pleasure." We shake hands too, and he holds my gaze a beat too long, waiting for something more. I don't give it.

"Second! There you are."

A woman cuts in, voice warm, rehearsed. I swear I've seen her before—in a movie, maybe?

She slips her arm through his like it's second nature. "I heard there's a cellar under the garden dome where they keep the donor gifts before they're raffled off. You'll have to show me."

I don't recognize her, but I sure recognize the piece she's wearing.

A collar necklace composed of alternating pear-shaped canary yellow diamonds—Zimmi origin, GIA-certified, VVS1 clarity—and elongated baguette-cut D-E color white diamonds, set in graduated spikes across the collarbone. Each yellow diamond is individually haloed in colorless pavé, enhancing saturation and fire.

Total diamond weight exceeds ninety carats, including over fifty-eight carats of natural canary yellow diamonds.

Sartori provenance. Crafted in 1998 as a bespoke commission.

Not for sale. Not anymore.

"Apologies, gentlemen. Looks like I've got a tour to give. Enjoy your evening."

Smiles are exchanged, and they all walk away, including the man whose name I can't remember. Figures.

"Quite the rock on her neck." I nod toward where they disappeared.

"Yeah. Probably on loan. No one in this room's actually paying full price for that." My father tips the glass back for the last sip, then lets it hang loosely from his fingers as he lets out a small grin. "If she only knew the path those stones took to reach her collarbone."

He gestures toward the bar with his empty glass before walking off.

And here's the thing about me—I learned what this business entails before I even knew how to spell my last name.

My father never bothered to hide it. And even if he had, I was too mesmerized by the man on the fucking high horse to miss it.

So, yeah, I was always well aware of the ugliness of the industry we are in.

But see, diamonds are like people. They don't show you the ugly right away.

They're forged in the heart of the Earth under unimaginable pressures that could crush a human body in seconds. Molten lava flows like rivers, reaching temperatures over 2,200°F, a hellish inferno where only the fiercest minerals can survive.

Did you know that?

I do. Not because I'm obsessed with diamonds, that came after.

I know it because it was the first real conversation I ever had with my father.

I was ten, and he was gone most of the time.

But that night, he came home early, smiling in a way that didn't belong in our house.

"*Figlio mio*," he called. "Come say hi to your Papa."

I didn't run, I flew.

I used to live off his love in trickles. Not anymore. Now I tame my thirst in lesser evils.

He scooped me into the air, and I laughed through the spin.

"Why are you so happy, Papa?"

He knelt, pulled a paper envelope from his coat, opened it, and dropped a diamond into his palm.

It caught the hallway light like a tiny, caged sun.

"This," he said, "was born in the depths of the earth—crushed, burned, torn through chaos just to get here. You don't get brilliance without pressure, Leo. Today was brilliant."

I should have known back then that the fire I could see in his eyes was indeed diamond-like. So mighty it held the earth's power to crush you. A heat so fierce it promised brilliance, but also the high chance of leaving you in ashes.

"Can I hold it?"

He hesitated, then placed it in my hand.

"Careful, Leonello. It's worth more than our house."

It was smooth and sharp. Small but heavy. I couldn't believe its weight.

"How do you know which ones are special?" I asked.

His eyes sparkled like he'd been waiting years for me to ask that exact thing.

"Ah, that's the art of it, *figlio*. It takes years to train your eye, to understand the subtle differences in clarity, color, cut. But more than that, it takes instinct. A feeling in your gut, a whisper in your ear, a tickle on the back of your neck. One day, you'll know."

I was completely in awe.

"And where's it from?"

"This beauty comes from a place as magical as the stone itself. It's from Brazil, deep in the heart of the Amazon rainforest."

Today, I know that the complexities of diamonds aren't just in finding them. It's so much more than that. But in that fleeting moment, the course of my entire life was set. A life like a rainforest, full of mazes so tight you can't pass through, air so thick you feel the world's weight on your chest, trees so tall you can't see the sky.

"Here! To your left!"

The shouts rip me out of my reminiscing.

I'm halfway to the exit, slipping past the velvet ropes while the paparazzi lose their minds over whoever just pulled up. I move through the shadows and make it past them.

"Isadora! Look this way! Give us a smile!"

"Just one shot, darling!"

The shouts are followed by a storm of clicks. They swarm her, flashbulbs firing like they're trying to set the night on fire.

I reach the end of the carpet and glance back, mostly out of curiosity. All I catch is the back of a young woman and—based on his rigid posture and crowd scanning—definitely an ex-military bodyguard heading inside.

Whoever that was, they're in.

And luckily, I'm the hell out.

OG

Where are you?

Out

You can't just walk out mid-event.

Watch me

Your father wants you back in the room.

Not happening

You're making it harder than it needs to be.

Apple doesn't fall far from the tree.

3

Isadora

"WHAT'S THIS GALA FOR again?" I ask, catching up to Allie and Jamie.

"Road safety," Allie murmurs.

Jamie nods toward the street. "Because nothing says road safety like a Chiron parked out front."

"Thank God." Kathy grabs Allie by the arm as soon as we step inside. "I need your help."

Allie shoots us a helpless look over her shoulder.

"Good luck," I mouth as they walk away.

Jamie lets out a short laugh. "Hi to you too, Mom."

I spot my father across the lawn, standing beneath one of the patio heaters with two other men.

"I'll be right back," I say to Jamie, and head toward him.

He greets me with that familiar warmth, perfectly measured.

"Isadora." A nod, a half-smile. Just his usual affectionate but contained self. Then he turns to the two men beside him. One of them I recognize immediately—New York's current mayor.

"This is my daughter," he says. "Isadora Carter-Bello."

"A pleasure," the mayor replies, offering his hand. "Do you have the political gene too?"

"That depends on how you define it," I smile as candidly as I can manage. "I'm a permanent translator at the United Nations headquarters here in New York."

"That's impressive." His interest is clearly piqued. "What language do you specialize in?"

"Languages," my father cuts in before I can answer. "Besides English, she speaks Spanish, Portuguese, French, Polish, Italian, Russian... and what's the other one? I always forget."

I let out an internal sigh, knowing what's coming. He tends to oversell me. Portuguese hardly counts—I'm not ATA-certified yet.

"Occitan," I say, smiling. Which also barely counts, by the way. There isn't even a standard certification for it, just a few regional institutions in France that offer academic exams.

"Occitan?" The mayor blinks. "Now that's unusual."

"It's a dying language," my father answers for me again. "She's made it her mission to only learn endangered ones moving forward." He chuckles softly, like it's a charming eccentricity he tolerates.

"Remarkable," the mayor says, turning back to him with a smile. "You've done a fine job with both your kids, Victor."

My father nods, absorbing the credit like it's owed. I figure I've done enough to keep him content. A part of me is satisfied—probably the one that always seeks his approving nod, the one I never quite managed to outgrow. The other part is just...sad, mostly. Though that's probably not about him at all. Or not entirely.

"See you around, gentlemen." I excuse myself and weave through the crowd. Jamie was right, this really is a masterpiece of an event.

It spans both the outdoor gardens and Ross Hall. The grounds themselves are impossibly curated—hedges trimmed to perfection, floral arrangements that look hand-painted, guests meandering across flagstone paths as if choreographed. The breeze carries hints of jasmine and something green and clean, like rain on new leaves.

Inside, the hall is pure fantasy. Crystal chandeliers hang like frozen rain from a vaulted ceiling, casting fracturing light across marble floors and sequined gowns. Waitstaff weave soundlessly between clusters of guests, balancing flutes of champagne glowing like liquid gold. Somewhere, the string quartet has switched to Billie Eilish, though you wouldn't know it from the cello's slow, aching drawl.

The crowd is eclectic, to say the least. Politicians, venture capitalists, society darlings. I think I just saw Marcus Kessler—yes, definitely Marcus—the tech mogul Hadrian's been close to lately.

But Hadrian himself? Nowhere. And neither is Brielle Warner.

I glance down at my phone. *E! News* posted her arrival an hour ago. Alone. Something tells me she's not anymore.

I come to a stop as someone steps directly into my path.

It's Étienne. We've crossed paths before at the French Embassy.

He leans in now, eyes glinting with mischief, his breath tinged with rum.

"*Vous êtes encore plus radieuse la nuit.*" His voice has the smooth cadence of someone accustomed to getting what they want.

I laugh—quick, a little forced—but cut it off before he can savor the effect.

"Careful, Étienne. You're dangerously close to being predictable."

His smile only widens.

"Ah, but some *clichés...*"—he switches to English now, thick accent coating every word—"are only *cliché* because they work."

I guess this would be the easy way, wouldn't it? Just hooking up with someone else. No big deal.

Except even the idea of being with another man makes my stomach twirl.

"*Je vous prie de profiter de votre soirée, Étienne,*" I say, wishing him a pleasant evening in the most formal way possible, and step away before he can follow.

The stem of my champagne flute is still cool between my fingers. The music swells and I let myself drift along the edge of the crowd, just out of reach.

I'm not looking for him. Not exactly. But I feel it before I see it.

A shift in the atmosphere, almost like I'm floating now. A bit adrift. But someone's telling me it's time to return to Earth. To re-enter orbit. To come back home.

And then, there he is. Camilo Valencia. *Milo.*

Across the room, he's half-caught in the soft flicker of chandelier light. A little undone, as always. His bowtie sits askew. His hair looks like it's been tousled by the wind or maybe by someone's hand. The suit is perfect, but he wears it like he'd rather be in something else. Like he always has.

He's laughing—head tipped back, the sound almost visible—and then, as if something brushes against his skin, he turns.

Our eyes meet.

And everything else dissolves—the chatter, the string quartet, the sound of glass on glass. It all recedes, as if the room knows better than to intrude.

He doesn't smile.

Neither do I.

I was the one who ended it. So, if anyone's meant to approach, it should be me.

And so, I start to.

Hands shaking. Because how else is one supposed to feel in moments like this?

He doesn't come toward me. Just subtly shifts a step to the right, enough to separate himself from the group.

"Hey," I say, softly.

"Hey back." He exhales, more sigh than breath. "You look... unbelievably beautiful, Scout."

"Thanks." I offer a small smile. "You don't look too bad yourself."

He nods, then glances down for a second. "I hope it's okay I came. I just—I wanted to be here. For Hadrian. And, you know... for you too."

His voice is raspier than usual, like he hasn't spoken much today.

"Milo," I say gently. "You don't have to explain. I meant what I said. I don't want to lose you. I still want you in my life."

"Just not as your boyfriend." He's quieter now. "Yeah. I got that."

I sigh because I don't know how to answer that.

The silence that follows is clumsy, stretched thin. But it's not empty. It's full of everything we haven't figured out how to say yet.

I glance down at my glass. The champagne's gone flat.

Beside me, Milo shifts his weight like he's about to say something, then decides against it. He just looks at me, really looks, and it does something to my chest I wish I could ignore.

"Do you want to get some air?" I ask, barely above a whisper.

He nods, almost instantly. "Yeah. I'd like that."

We don't excuse ourselves from anyone. Just move together toward one of the side exits that leads into the garden.

The night air hits soft and cool. The scent of jasmine still clings to the breeze.

I don't know what this is. What I'm doing. But his hand brushes against mine, and I don't pull away.

We walk in silence, side by side beneath the string lights, past the edge of the tent and into the garden. Behind us, the hum of the party fades, replaced by the hush of rustling leaves and the echo of distant laughter.

Milo slows near a marble bench, and I follow. We don't sit. Just stand there, close, but not touching. Rami lingers a few feet behind.

The stillness between us feels fragile—like if we say too much, it'll all crack open.

"Oh, thought that was you two!" a familiar voice calls.

I turn, and there she is: Aunt Honor.

Hair swept up, heels somehow steady in the grass. Her gown is black and impeccably tailored, minimal jewelry, not a hair out of place.

"Milo!" she says, beaming, already reaching to kiss him on the cheek. "So handsome, as usual. I haven't seen you since... what, Christmas?"

"Hi, Honor." His voice softens into something almost shy, but I can hear the sadness in it. "You look great."

"You two always disappear during these things," she says, amused. "Still sneaking off like you did at one of The Andromeda Trust fundraisers in Montauk? Remember that? You must've been—what—fifteen?"

I smile, but it's tight. Milo shifts beside me.

"You disappeared for half the night," Honor continues, laughing now. "I asked where you'd gone and you said—oh, what was it?" She tilts her head, searching. "Right. You said you went out to 'watch the sky move slower.'" She chuckles. "God, I loved that."

My throat goes tighter.

I remember that night. Bare feet in the dune grass. The salt on his lips. His jacket around my shoulders. How I thought, just for a moment, that time might actually stop if we wished hard enough.

"I always thought that was the loveliest thing." Honor reaches for my arm and squeezes it. "You two—back then—you had this... I don't know. *Softness.* Like the world hadn't touched you yet." She pauses, pulling at the memory. "Your grandfather kept pacing, asking where you'd run off to. Said if you weren't back by dessert, he'd send the Secret Service *and* Coast Guard to find you."

I open my mouth, but nothing comes out.

"I remember that," Milo steps in. "Hadrian Sr. pulled me aside when we got back and asked what my intentions were with his beloved granddaughter." He smiles faintly. "I was properly terrified. Pretty sure I blacked out the second I heard the Vice President of the United States calling me 'son.'"

Honor chuckles, eyes softening. "He adored you both. Said there was something rare in the way you looked at each other. Something... gentle."

She lets go of my arm. "Anyway, come say hello to your grandmother before she heads out, if you get the chance."

She turns and starts walking away. The silence settles again.

This time, it stings.

I don't dare look at Milo.

"I'm so sorry. You know her. She doesn't—"

"Don't apologize," he says shaking his head. "I'm just wondering why you haven't told your family yet. I mean... I haven't either, but *I* know why."

I force myself to stop staring at my heels and look at him instead.

Hands in his pockets. Eyebrows slightly furrowed. His face is softer in the garden light. The angles are a little less sharp, the dimple near his mouth more visible. His eyes—tired, steady—hold mine like he's waiting for something I don't know how to give.

"I guess..." I let a breath out. "I'm also not ready for it to be truly over."

I know he's about to kiss me before he even moves an inch.

He lifts a hand and places it gently on my cheek. And when he gets closer, I don't stop him.

Because I've been kissing that mouth for almost a decade. And right now, I can't remember a single good reason I ever asked it to stop.

4
Hadrian

I'VE BEEN HALF-LISTENING TO an art historian hold court on post-Romantic symbolism—whatever that's meant to imply—when a hand lands lightly on my shoulder, drawing me back into the room. Marcus.

"Second." He tips his chin.

"Marcus." I return it.

"Back from the private tour?"

"Still standing," I say, lifting my glass. "Barely." I glance at him. "Have you seen my sister?"

"I saw her leave with Milo," he says, voice nearly swallowed by the string quartet. "Allie just slipped out too. The other one's still orbiting somewhere."

I exhale, quiet. "Of course."

My phone is already in my hand. I scroll to her name. The message is brief.

Come back. Please.

If hope had a currency, I went bankrupt in seconds when the reply popped up.

No.

Of course.

"Beautiful but so stubborn," I whisper mostly to myself, hitting the call button. The dial tone is like the ticking of a judgmental clock, counting down the seconds I don't have.

"Hadrian?" Her voice is the first wave after a drought, but there is an icy edge to it.

"Listen, Allie—"

"Hadrian, my cab is here," she interrupts. "Isa has already left, and Kathy is driving me insane."

"Please," I plead, leaning against the marble pillar to steady myself. "I need you here." *In ways I can't even begin to articulate*, I add silently.

There is a pause long enough for regret to seep in, but then she sighs. "Fine."

I'm standing with a clear view of the entrance when she walks back through those ornate doors, and my heart skips not just a beat, but an entire measure. The gala could be a ghost town for all I care, because Allie's presence fills every inch of space around me. She approaches with an elegance that makes my palms sweat, her blonde hair catching the light.

And it hits me—this is new.

Not her. The way I see her.

"Hi," I say, voice hoarse with emotions I couldn't distill into words.

"Hi." Allie's smile doesn't quite reach her eyes, but it is enough to ignite something within me.

We stand there, close enough for me to memorize the pattern of blue in her eyes if I hadn't done so already, yet miles apart in everything unspoken. My gaze drifts to her lips as they so often do lately. And she pretends to not notice like she does lately.

"So... how's the fundraising going?"

Better now that you're back, is what I want to say.

"Same as usual—deep pockets, shallow conversations."

"And your usual fan club, I see," she says, tilting her chin toward the cluster of women eyeing us from across the room.

I don't want to explain it, but if I did, how could I make her see that every woman who isn't her might as well be a shadow?

I snort, but it's hollow.

"Perks of the job," I say, smirking. "The real part is right here."

She rolls her eyes at me, and as we stand there, the world around us fades into a watercolor backdrop. Allie is the only thing in sharp focus, a masterpiece among sketches. Her eyes, those pools of cerulean that have drowned my resolve so often, sparkle with a mischief that makes my heart stutter.

Did you know that every night, the Earth reaches its coldest point just before sunrise? I've been thinking that Allie is that first ray of light after the coldest night of the year.

Scratch that.

She's the first break of dawn at the North Pole's spring equinox.

I wonder how it would feel to tell her that she's the owner of every laugh of mine that isn't forced for the sake of social niceties. That in this endless sea of faces, hers is my North Star. But I can't, can I?

So instead, I clear my throat and say, "Dance with me?"

I hold my hand up to her and she grabs it, her pale skin contrasting mine.

"Until I Found You" by Stephen Sanchez plays in the background, and now we're in the middle of the dance floor. The chasm between us is filled with longing. I know she feels it too. How could she not? It's crackling with electricity that threatens to either bridge the gap or burn us both to ash. Standing there, inches apart, the whole room fades away until it's just her piercing blue eyes locked onto mine.

"Stop looking at me like that," she urges, her hand brushing against my arm. The touch is light, but it sends a ripple of shivers down my spine, awakening every nerve I've tried to keep numb.

"Allegra, you know the drill. Tell me to stay away from you, and I will," I breathe, my voice rawer than I intended.

"We're friends. And you're Isa's brother. I'll never tell you to stay away."

That should've settled it. It used to. But now... it's like it's gone from platonic to just simply out of reach.

I look at her. Same as I always do. The same way you look at sunsets—a little heartbroken but still holding onto hope.

Without another word, we continue dancing, though it's slow, barely movement. The music swells around us. Her hand rests lightly on my chest, heat bleeding through the fabric like it's not even there. Her eyes—those beautiful, wide-open blue eyes—are steady, unguarded.

"Hadrian," she breathes, and I know it: the sound of my name on her lips will one day be my undoing.

"Second!"

The voice cuts through the moment and the spell breaks. Of course it does. It always does.

Brielle Warner stands a few feet away, the actress I just exercised poor judgment with in some underground cellar, her perfect pink lips curled into a smile that feels more like a warning than a greeting.

"Brielle." I try to keep my cool, but her name catches in my throat anyway.

Allie's eyes go wide, a flush rising to her cheeks, and Brielle gives her a once-over.

"Thanks for keeping him busy while I was gone." It's sugarcoated, but the dig lands because Allie stiffens and her hand slips from my arm like I burned her.

"I—sure. Okay." She smiles. But I know her eyes too well not to see the crack forming. I wish I didn't.

"Brielle, now's not the time." I try, but I already know we've crossed the point of no return.

"It's always the time." Allie's voice has gone glacial. Her eyes dart between Brielle and me, piecing together a puzzle she clearly has no desire to complete. Without another word, she offers a polite smile to her, then to me, before spinning on her heel and disappearing into the crowd.

"Right," I mutter under my breath, staring at the space she'd vacated, my chest tight and my mind blank.

"Relax, Second." Brielle slides a hand down my arm.

I shake her off and step back. "Excuse me," I say, offering a polite smile.

Brushing past her, I make a beeline for my father, who's been giving me warning glances from across the room while deep in conversation with Senator Hayes. Maybe playing his game for a bit will distract me from the self-loathing gnawing at my insides, or at least numb it for a hot second.

"Hadrian, there you are!" My father's tone is brisk, businesslike. "Senator Hayes was just discussing the upcoming vote on environmental policy. What's your take on it?"

"Frankly, sir," I force my mind to switch gears, "we're prioritizing short-term gains at the expense of long-term sustainability. If we don't shift our focus to practices that yield enduring value, what kind of legacy are we leaving for future generations?"

It's smoke and mirrors, and I hate how easily I play my part. Don't get me wrong, I'm not a fatalist or a skeptic. I truly believe there are people fighting for environmental causes with genuine passion and viable solutions. But I've been with my father in rooms when these laws are still embryonic, and trust me, there's nothing genuine or honorable there.

"Ah, the idealism of youth." Senator Hayes chuckles, though his eyes hold a glint of respect. "Perhaps you should consider running soon," he says as he winks at me. "We need that young blood with passion like yours."

I give a forced smile in reply.

"Hayes, do you mind giving us a moment?" My father offers one of his practiced smiles. The Senator nods, already half-distracted, and shouts at a passing waitress to refill his glass before striding away.

"What now, Dad?" I ask, not even bothering to hide my annoyance.

"You tell me. First you vanish for an hour, and then this? Optics, son. We can't afford to have you be seen with someone so... *off-message*. It risks alienating our base and undermining our voter support."

I exhale slowly, only half-listening to this tired argument. Allie isn't the problem, her last name is. But of course, that distinction doesn't matter to him. Or anyone else, for that matter.

And just like that, the autumn equinox hits, and the Polar Night descends again. My feet hit the ground, my future splinters before me, and I can't decide which path hurts less. Each of my father's words adds another brick to the wall I've been building around my heart. Except I don't have one right now. Allie takes it with her every time she walks away.

Hadrian Carter-Bello for the Second District of New York.

Welcome to my ghost town.

Isa

Is it true?? You and Brielle?

Don't start.

Wasn't planning to.

But is it?

Define "it"

Hadrian…

If you're asking whether I left with her, yes.

Voluntarily?

I was escorted by her security team, technical-ly.

So that's a yes.

Stop being nosy.

Then stop being an idiot.

Good night

Love u

Me too

5
Isadora

It's Beauty and Bagels Day, so I'm getting ready while Allie rearranges our living room furniture for the second time today. Mind you, it's only ten a.m. On a Sunday.

She and I moved in here right after college a couple of years ago. It's a bright, upper-level apartment on the Upper East Side, tucked between Madison and Park in one of those prewar buildings with a doorman, wrought-iron balconies, and an elevator that sighs like an old soul.

Her family owns it, which meant she was firmly against us moving in at first. She ended up caving eventually. I mean, the location is unbeatable, and the Montroses don't even live in New York. It's just her.

Allie's family comes from the timber industry in Williamsport, Pennsylvania. Her great-grandfather, Robert Montrose, founded Montrose Timber Co. in the early twentieth century. It's one of those legacy companies that started as a modest lumber operation and quietly grew into one of the region's most successful enterprises. Today, if you are in America and own a hardwood dining table, a cello, a cutting board, or even the floors beneath your feet, there's a high likelihood the wood came from them.

The door opens just as I'm pulling on a black turtleneck.

"Almost ready," I say, fixing my hair.

I hear Allie's steps cross the room, then the soft click of the window opening.

The cold breeze drifts in, oddly relieving.

She drops onto my bed and starts scrolling through her phone.

When Allie turned twelve, her parents sent her to the boarding program at Dalton. I was a day student.

I remember her walking down the hallway that first day. She moved through the chaos like none of it touched her. Composed. Unbothered. Like the noise was just static she could tune out.

Then one afternoon, in Mr. Hawthorne's English class, she slid into the seat beside me like it was the most natural thing in the world.

"You're always writing," she said, eyeing my notebook.

I shrugged. "Guess I am."

"Any chance it's about a shipwreck? Treasure? A girl who disappears at sea?"

"Uh... no. It's about my mom. We visited Argentina over break. She was born there."

She nodded, like she was filing that away. "Cool. But if you ever want to write about a runaway girl turned pirate queen, I've got ideas."

I smiled. "Do they involve sword fights and bad weather?"

"Obviously. And betrayal. Always betrayal."

I laughed. "Heads up—I get seasick. Like, tragically."

She gasped.

"Still think we could be friends, despite my landlocked ways?"

She gave me a small smile. "Yeah. I think so."

The next week, she asked to borrow my book. A few days later, I found a warm sesame bagel on my desk with a sticky note that said: *for the pirate in recovery.*

And just like that, we stuck.

"Where are we going today?" she asks, eyes still on her phone.

"Brunch at Buvette, then Valmont Spa at The Carlyle."

"Heck yes. I've been dreaming of their signature regenerating collagen mask since the last time we were there."

She puts down her phone and looks at me like she does when she means business.

"So, how many more nights do I have to pretend I don't hear Milo sneaking in and out of our flat before you actually tell me what's going on?"

I freeze. I knew today was the day she'd say something, I just thought she'd at least show me mercy with brunch first.

"Yeah, take a moment. Think it through."

"Maybe I was waiting for you to bring it up first?" I ask, buying time.

Her eyebrows practically hit the ceiling.

"Okay, okay. Does it help if I say I don't know what I'm doing either?"

"No. It doesn't. Most importantly, it doesn't help *you.*" Her arms are crossed now, and she's sitting on the edge of my bed.

"I don't know, Als. Nothing actually bad happened between us."

Truth is, whatever stereotype you've got in your head about the perfect guy, Milo's all of it. Stellar kid, straight-A student who grew up to become a doctor. Now he's in his orthopedic residency, runs marathons for charity, flips killer pancakes. An amazing friend. He's been in my life longer than he hasn't.

"Nothing bad needs to. It still doesn't change reality."

"The reality is, he's all in—the written-in-your-eyes kind of way. I don't think that's common, Allie. I don't think taking it for granted is the right way forward. I mean... really, what else could a girl ask for?"

I give her a pleading smile.

"Love."

Allie's shortest answers always land the hardest.

That feels... unfair. I do love him. He's my first love. My first everything, really. How could I not?

"You know I love him."

"Loving someone and being *in love* with them aren't the same. And you know it. You're just trying to forget that."

I'm not entirely sure I agree. Though I don't think I could explain it to her even if I tried.

Loving someone is a choice. Isn't it?

Choosing the one person who's always been there. Who's seen every version of you and stayed. Who's weathered the ugly parts, the quiet parts, the growing pains.

What does a preposition change, really? *In* love, *with* love, *for* love.

Isn't love still love? Just a word. A hinge so small it barely registers. And yet hinges are what doors turn on.

I know better than most that language is rarely decorative. That the wrong preposition can tilt a sentence, soften a promise, undo a confession.

Still, I pretend the difference is negligible. Safer that way. If I flatten it, if I convince myself it's all the same, then I don't have to admit that something has shifted. Because if "in" and "with" are not interchangeable, then maybe neither are feelings.

And I know this spiral is my doing. I started it. All these questions I started having about Milo and me, I could've kept them to myself. I could've protected us from the fallout.

But now it's out there. And I have to be consequential. Even if I'm still not sure what I've done. Or why.

My phone rings, and I'm literally saved by the bell.

I glance at the screen. It's my father.

"Sorry, it's Dad. Gotta take it."

Allie points a finger at me and sighs wordlessly as she stands up and leaves the room.

"Hi, Daddy."

"Morning, sweetheart." His voice is warm, but with that clipped undertone he saves for busy days. "Sleep okay?"

I sink into the armchair across from the window.

"Yep. How about you?"

"Well... you know I'm not much of a sleeper. Especially when there's this much going on."

"Yeah, I figured. How's Hadrian handling the announcement?"

My brother has officially decided to launch his political career—he's running for Congress in New York's Second District. And, as expected, he and my father are not exactly seeing eye to eye.

"Hadrian is... Hadrian. Determined, ambitious, and utterly convinced he knows what's best."

Sounds like him.

"So, not much has changed then?"

"Oh, things have changed," my father says, a sigh tucked just beneath the words. "He's sharper now. More strategic. But sometimes I wonder if he remembers why he wanted this in the first place."

"And what, pray tell, were those reasons?"

"To survive a legacy."

A brief silence follows.

"Anyway," he says, brisk again. "Just a reminder—dinner next Wednesday. Your mother wants us all there. Usual place. Six sharp. Don't be late."

And the line goes dead.

Milo

Your father texted me time and address for tonight. Should I come?

Stop typing and deleting.

I'll tell him I have something else tonight.

Don't worry.

Thank you

And sorry...

6

Hadrian

I LET MY GAZE sweep over the table at Gramercy Tavern—our family's culinary sanctuary in New York.

Isa catches my eye over our mother's shoulder and immediately stands. She crosses the room with the kind of purpose you only develop after a childhood of diplomatic dinners and dodging our parents' moods.

"Finally," she says, pulling me into a quick hug.

"That bad?"

She exhales through her nose. "Dad keeps asking if I'll come to that Madrid conference with him."

Isa hates working with our father. Though sometimes I suspect that sentiment applies to me too.

"You mean... the NATO Summit?"

She nods. "That's the one."

"I hear the new U.S. envoy's making their debut," I say, matching her stride toward the table.

She gives me a look. "I think you're confusing me with you."

"Hadrian!" My mother greets me as though I've just come back from a war zone, except it's she who's returned from her annual trip to the Argentine Patagonia. She does this every year with her side of the family, same time, same remote estancia. She's from there, by the way. I don't know if I've mentioned that before.

I hug her back. She smells like fresh roses, same as always. And it steadies me.

We take a seat, just the two of us across from the architects of our existence.

"So, Isadora, back to our discussion," my father starts.

"Hadrian," she interrupts. Can't be good. "Humor me—aren't hosts supposed to greet their guests at their own galas?"

My mother's brow pinches slightly, confusion flickering across her face.

"Hilarious." I lean back in my chair, all feigned calm. "Because I thought guests were supposed to be on time. You know, protocol?"

She started it. Fair's fair.

"Actually, a queen is never late. Everyone else is simply early," says a voice to my right.

Allie.

She takes the seat beside Isa. Her perfume drifts in just as I fight the urge to close my eyes.

"Allie!" my mother beams.

"Hi, Elena. I'm so glad you're back. Beauty and Bagels days just aren't the same without you."

My mother nods sympathetically, and dinner unfolds much as expected. Isa and Allie nudge her for every last detail of her trip, while my father tunes out the way he always does when she talks about Argentina, his blank expression barely concealing his boredom.

Sometimes I wonder how a man like him came from someone like my grandfather. The kindest man I've ever known. He held one of the highest offices in the country and still showed up for the small stuff. Like Parents' Day in my first year at Dalton. My parents didn't come—I don't even remember why—but I remember the moment Grandpa walked through the classroom door.

"Grandpa?" I grinned so wide it hurt. "What are you doing here?"

He looked genuinely offended. "What do you mean, what am I doing here? It's my day."

I scrunched my nose, confused. "No, it's Parents' Day."

"Good thing I'm a *grand* one, then," he said, pulling me into a bear hug. "There's no you without me. Now show me your locker. And you better have a picture of me in there."

I haven't gone anywhere without a passport-sized photo of him since. It's in my wallet right now.

The waiter fills my glass. I take a sip. It's oddly warm inside. April in New York is finally softening—mid-fifties today, still jacket weather.

"I suppose Milo isn't coming?" my mother asks.

Isa turns to me for the briefest second, just long enough for me to catch that something's off. Not long enough to figure out what.

"He couldn't make it," she answers. "Sorry. Forgot to tell you."

"Let's order, then," my father cuts in.

He calls the waiter and rattles off our usuals: roasted chicken with wild mushrooms and polenta for my mother, the dry-aged duck breast for him, Isa's fennel risotto, my hanger steak, rare, and seared scallops and a side of spring greens for Allie.

I allow myself a glance at her.

Nothing has happened between us, by the way. Or, well—barely anything. But we made a promise not to tell anyone. I'm afraid that includes you.

Whatever this is, it's not mess-around friendly. I have no interest in getting off on the wrong foot when the circumstances are already a minefield. One wrong step, and there's no coming back from it. Not that I'd want that, coming back from her.

"So, Hadrian Sebastian." My mother turns to me, and so does everyone else, because of course she dropped the full name. "I'm still unclear. Why weren't you greeting your guests at your own gala?"

How does one explain to their mother that they were momentarily tangled up with a very demanding actress in an underground cellar?

My father is watching me with that look that I could do without. So I rummage for a passable answer.

"That guy—I forget his name, velvet blazer—he pulled me over to meet Lupo Sartori and his son. Leo, I think? And then I got swamped. You know how it is, one handshake turns into ten."

"Wait—Leo Sartori was there?" Allie asks, her tone light, too light. "I must've missed him. What a shame."

Water boils at 212°F. I'm at a thousand. You do the math.

"Lupo Sartori has a son?" my father asks, brow lifting.

"And why is it a shame?" my mother adds.

"Yes, he does. He's not one for the spotlight, but it doesn't matter. His looks don't go unnoticed," Allie replies breezily.

Two thousand.

"I've barely seen him around," Isa chips in. "Can't remember his face. Show me a picture."

"He doesn't have social media that I know of," Allie says, pulling out her phone. "But let's try Google."

"Because that's exactly what this dinner needed," I mutter.

My mother and Isa both give me the same look.

“Stay away from that family,” my father says. “We need all the positive press we can get right now, and those companies thrive in the gray areas.”

And for once—shockingly, disturbingly—I agree with him.

“Gladly,” I mutter. Though from the looks I’m getting, I must’ve said it louder than I meant to.

“Jealous?” Allie tilts her head. “You’re handsome too, Hadrian.”

Isa rolls her eyes. “Please don’t tell him that. He’s been insufferable ever since *GQ* called him ‘New York’s most eligible heir.’”

“Isadora,” our mother warns.

Allie flashes her phone at Isa, whose eyes widen before she schools her expression.

“Oh, yeah. Sure.” She gives a little nod, approving. “He's definitely not hard to look at.”

Allie snorts. I pretend not to hear it, which is useless.

“You have a boyfriend, remember?” I say, turning to Isa.

She looks up from her drink, lips quirking around the straw. “He’s not even my type.”

“Your type?” I shoot back. “You’ve only ever been with one person. You don’t have a type. You just have Milo.”

I lean in a little, voice sharper now, because, at the very least, this is all getting on my nerves. “And you can’t take it back. Words are permanent, remember? Your rule.”

“Enough,” my father interjects. “The three of you are acting like children.” He turns to me. “Hadrian. You might want to learn how to better handle pressure. It’s a skill most leaders develop early.”

“Victor,” my mother’s gentle voice breaks through the tension. “Perhaps we should—”

“Stay out of this, Elena,” he snaps.

Before I can stop myself, I’m on my feet, leaning across the table.

“You will not speak to her like that.”

The silence that follows is deafening. I can hear my own heart pounding in my ears, feel the weight of everyone’s eyes on me.

I’ve just drawn a line in the sand.

History suggests he won’t resist crossing it.

Mom

I hate the way he speaks to you.

Don't worry, darling. I'm used to it.

You shouldn't be.

Why do you put up with it?

It's fine. The campaign has him wound too tight.

Marrying a politician… not your brightest moment.

You're one too now.

Exactly… why not leave us?

I'd never, in a million years, leave you.

Plus, someone has to keep you both human.

You do.

7
Leo

THE SCANNER HUMS BEFORE I'm even at the door.

A discreet camera locks onto my eye, and a red beam slices across my retina.

The black glass gates part without a sound, and I step into the lobby—silent, gleaming, obscene. Everything in here reflects something: the marble, the walls, the people.

And there, as always, sits *The Sartori*.

A cushion-cut, D-colorless, VVS1 diamond. So flawless that when you see it from afar, you only catch sparkles. It's encased in bulletproof glass, a testament to its value and the lengths my father goes to protect what's his. It catches the morning light and throws it back in fractured flashes like it's alive. Or trying to be.

My father had it placed dead center on purpose. You can't walk in without seeing it.

I head to the front desk. New face. Blonde. I can't see her legs, but I'm telling you, they're long. Smoking hot. Young, but not *too* young. Just how my father likes them.

"Mr. Sartori." She nods, smiling. "I just heard on the internal comm—they're seven minutes out."

"Got it. Thanks."

I make my way to the elevators.

This place is the opposite of old, cranky, or abandoned. And yet growing up, I always thought it was haunted.

I step inside, press thirty-seven, and lean against the wall as the doors close.

First floors are surveillance and security. Cameras, scanners, threat response teams watching every inch of this place. Not the safe rooms, though—those are underground.

Then the public-facing levels. The diamond gallery. The museum. The press lounges.

Next, the machinery: legal teams, logistics, gemologists, engineers. People with quiet jobs but loud NDAs.

Family-only access now. Private elevators only. The suite—my father's. All blackout windows and imported stone. I've only been inside twice.

The elevator slows.

Ding.

Floor thirty-seven. The helipad.

The doors open and I step outside.

The air is sharp up here, cuts right into you. Wind rushes across the landing pad. The view—Manhattan laid out like a blueprint, Central Park a neat rectangle of green, the East River shining like a blade in the sun—it never gets old.

I find the silence of distant chaos the most relaxing.

Right on time, the sound of the chopper cuts through the air, and the wind shifts, less steady now, more chaotic.

It makes a soft landing, and the door swings open almost immediately. OG steps out, followed by my father. No security, as usual.

He pulls off his aviators, scanning the pad. OG shouts something at him, but I can't hear it over the rotor.

Then he sees me, and heads straight over.

"You're here," he says, already walking past me toward the elevator.

OG and I follow.

"He's in a mood today," OG mutters under his breath.

"I heard that," my father snaps.

"What happened?" I ask as the elevator doors close.

"Nothing that concerns you."

OG throws me a shrug.

He's been with my father forever—two bullets in his arm and shoulder to prove it. More than a right hand. Sometimes the brother my father never had. The man who built the system that kept him untouchable once things got big enough to draw fire. The first line of defense. The last man standing. The fortress we live in, he built it with his own hands.

Us two, we've had our fallouts, more than I can count. But when it counted, he showed up in ways my father never did.

We reach the family lounge. OG heads straight to the bar.

"Three whiskeys. Rocks," he tells the bartender.

"A bit early, don't you think?" I settle into one of the leather chairs.

"For you maybe," my father edges in as he takes the seat across from me. "Let's get to it. What do you have?"

"Some movement." I accept the glass from OG. "His circle's locked down tight, but I found a crack. His daughter, Irina Mikhailov. Lives in London. Dating a model guy from New York. Ivy League, weak backbone, always trying to prove something. Way easier getting to him."

My father nods, thoughtful.

"How did you play it?"

"Met him in St. Moritz. January. Made it look accidental. Kept it casual. Didn't mention the family name straight away."

"Smart," OG approves. "And now?"

"Built some trust, got invited back to London. Met Irina. Once, twice. Just enough to be familiar. Now they're in New York. Which is why I'm back."

My father leans back, glass in hand.

"Good. Speed it up. I want her father on our side before Q4. He controls half the Siberian output contracts and three shipping corridors through Kazakhstan. If we don't move now, the Belgians will."

"On it," I say, rising to my feet. "Anything else?"

"Yeah, actually." He doesn't even blink. "Don't fuck it up. Or I'll fuck you up."

"Easy, Lupo," OG cuts in. "Told you—bad mood today."

"Sure," I mutter, turning away.

What I really want to say is:

I'd love to see you try.

8

Isadora

THE SOUND OF SHATTERING glass startles me.

On instinct, I reach for the small black device Rami gave me—it looks like a car key. He calls it the *Dot.* Hold it down for three seconds, and it sends a silent alert straight to him.

I set down *Kamara: A Life in Stones and Silence*, one of the books I've been reading in preparation for my next translation engagement at the summit next week.

The sound came from the home office.

I move, barefoot and careful, and peek inside.

It's nothing, just a fallen frame.

Allie had ordered these "non-damaging" adhesive strips to test for her clients. "Can't recommend them if I haven't tried them myself," she said. We're not renting, but she treats our walls like experiments—especially in here, where the rules are looser.

Only one fell—Milo and me at the beach. My favorite. We're tangled in each other, sun-drunk and laughing, my face tilted toward him like I'm a sunflower and he's the sun.

It was taken in Watch Hill, our usual summer spot. Also the place we met when we were three. Our families have vacationed there since long before we were born, houses side by side, summers stitched together by habit.

His parents are retired now—off chasing sunsets, mostly in Europe. Same as we will.

Or so that was the plan.

The year we took that picture was different. It was the first trip we spent there alone. We returned to New York with everyone in September, as always. And then, a week later, we snuck back just for a few nights. No parents or siblings. No dinners we couldn't say no to. Just us.

I crouch to pick it up, the frame cracked but the image intact. I remember the day clearly. I got us completely lost trying to find my car.

"You have the worst sense of direction," he said, hands on his hips like a disappointed dad.

"I do not! I knew it was this general direction."

"You led us into a private yacht club."

"An exclusive detour," I shrugged.

He just shook his head, grinning. "Alright, *Scout*. Lead the way."

It took me forty-five minutes to find the car. We stick to valets now.

When it comes to Milo, I don't think it's flashbacks that I get. It's rather a never-ending chain of memories, all linked and mixed and overlapping, and I never seem to be able to find the final stop to it.

"Scout, are you okay?"

I snap up. Milo's standing by the doorframe, hands in his pockets.

"Sorry. Didn't mean to scare you."

I offer him a smile and swallow the lump in my throat. Not now.

"I'm fine. Our frame, not so much."

I set the picture gently on the desk and make my way toward him. I kiss him on the cheek and head straight to my bedroom.

"Hey, you sure you're okay?" His voice is softer now, almost cautious, scared. So unlike him. So unlike us.

"Yes. Just tired. All the prep for next week."

"Right, the summit." He pauses. "What's this one for again?"

"Global Gem Summit." I yawn.

He watches me. His honey-colored eyes—warm, steady—never lie to you, never try to.

He doesn't say anything at first. Just stands there, trying to read between the lines of everything I'm not saying. And lately, there's plenty of that.

"How was dinner on Wednesday?"

He steps closer, close enough that I catch the scent of clean linen and something distinctly him.

"Well, the usual drama. But nice overall. You didn't miss much."

"I missed *you*."

"Mils—"

"I know. I know." He lifts his hands in surrender. "We're just hanging out. Figuring it out." Then he tilts his head, eyes catching the light. "You gonna take that off?"

His fingers graze my shoulder where the sweater has slipped just enough to let the night air in.

"Skincare first," I say, already slipping into the bathroom.

His footsteps follow, unhurried. He leans against the doorway, watching as I reach for a rosewater-soaked cotton pad. The first swipe leaves a comet trail of mascara across my cheek.

"I've seen you do this enough times to do it blindfolded," he muses.

"You? Please." I meet his gaze in the mirror. "You once used my peel-off mask thinking it was just a serum. Your face was bright red for hours."

"I was innovating," he counters, grinning.

He steps closer, his hand trailing down my arm.

"Let me help."

I swat him away, laughing. "Absolutely not."

He feigns offense, tilting his head against the wall, and I take him in for a second, capture a mental black-and-white film still. Because he's plenty of good things, but he's also undeniably handsome.

I toss a cotton pad at him. It sticks to his cheek like a drunken starfish.

For a beat, there's silence. Then we both break into laughter, and it spills into the space like it's lived here all along. And I figure it has—alongside the other million little pieces of us stitched into the walls of every room of our hearts.

Milo straightens. His thumb finds an errant smudge beneath my lashes, brushing it away with his usual care.

"There she is," he says, his voice softer now.

"Who?"

"My girl."

His fingers trace the softened edges of my face—the micellar water, the half-peeled layers of the day, and whatever honesty seeps out in moments like this.

"The one who steals fries off my plate after swearing she's done with fried food. And the one who's had my heart for as long as she's known it."

"How?" I ask, almost as a reflex.

His expression twists, puzzled.

"How can you be so sure?" I add.

His shoulders drop slightly. "About us?"

"About everything," I say. "But yeah, mostly us. We've been together since we were kids. We've never really dated anyone else. How do you know this is it?"

"I just do."

I sigh, mostly at the frustration of how lonely this feels. We used to feel everything together. Now it's like I've stumbled into some hidden room inside me and he can't seem to find the door.

"I'm okay in the in-between while you figure it out," he says. "As long as you're here. As long as we're trying."

And I want to mean it when I nod.

I want to reach across the space between who we were and who we are now and stitch it shut.

"I... I just feel like I've spent so long following one storyline. And now that I've reached the part where everything's supposed to fall into place it feels... foreign."

He steps closer. "We'll figure it out."

I try to smile back. I even lean into his touch when he brushes a damp strand of hair behind my ear.

"I love you," he mutters.

I kiss his shoulder and rest my head there.

And I hope—pray, even—that it'll be enough again.

9
Hadrian

HAVE YOU EVER SAT through a campaign meeting?

If you haven't, let me give you a glimpse: a cacophony of voices, each one competing for dominance, while the air is thick with the scent of stale coffee and the clacking of a dozen laptops. The room pulses with tension, everyone waiting for the next word to tip the scales. And then, of course, the endless parade of statistics—charts and numbers, all presented with the kind of gravitas that makes you wonder if they're trying to sell you something or bury you in the weight of their own importance.

Today's meeting is no different, save for the fact that it's centered on two things: my upcoming announcement about running for Congress in New York's Second District and the delicate, often precarious, subject of funding.

You'd think the former would be the priority. But this is politics. Money always speaks first.

After the last census, NY-2 was redrawn to account for population decline in Long Island and growth in lower Manhattan, swallowing SoHo, Tribeca, even Greenwich Village. Our arena. Grandpa always said it would happen.

"Urban sprawl. Population shifts. Political realignment—it's inevitable," he used to say. "And when it does, that'll be your moment. New map, new faces. Clean slate."

So here we are. Running the district he saw coming before anyone else did. Tossing out names like chips at a poker table. Some are legacy donors—old money, big names, the kind of people who could buy a Senate seat if they wanted to. Others are long shots.

"What about Leo Sartori?" Marcus asks, tilting his chair back.

That name again. It's getting old, if you ask me.

Marcus leans forward, sensing he has the floor. He's always the sharpest mind in the room. The guy coded his first data-scraping tool before most kids learned long division. We met a couple of years ago at an event. He walked over, said he'd found an old betting alias tied to one of my shell cards, and that he'd already wiped it. Didn't ask for anything. Just thought I'd want to know. He's the first call I made when it was time to build the dream team.

"I saw him at the last gala," he adds, "he's around our age," nodding in my direction. "Hasn't backed any politician before, not publicly anyway. Doesn't carry the weight of his father's name yet—not fully. Might see this as a way to change that."

He pauses just long enough to make the room lean in.

"And the Sartori Group could be a game-changer. With everything unfolding, their backing could give us exactly the kind of reach we need."

A beat.

"Let me be perfectly clear." My father's voice slices through the room and everyone stills.

"We will not accept money from extractivists. I don't care how much they offer. Their wealth is tainted, and I won't let it stain this campaign."

He scans the room slowly, with that deliberate coolness only he can pull off. Everyone nods, or pretends to.

"Any confirmed scandals?" Lydia, my campaign manager, asks. She was my second call. Lydia worked with my grandfather during both of his terms as Vice President, then joined his team years later when he launched his presidential campaign, before he pulled out of the race, that is.

You know what happened. Hell, you probably tweeted about it.

"Do you remember the Peterson campaign?" My father proceeds. "They took money from a mining firm with full environmental certifications. The paperwork was perfect. But no one cared. All the public saw was blood. And just like that, the campaign collapsed. Their candidate never recovered."

A chill spreads through the room. Peterson is still the cautionary tale no one wants to be.

"We can't afford that," he continues, his voice ice-smooth. "We move forward on clean money. No compromises. No associations with those who profit from the ruination of anything. If we win, we win untarnished."

A few murmurs of agreement follow. But I know better. It's not about morals. It's not even about optics, though that's what he'll claim. It's about control. His control. Who gets to be in the room. Who gets to owe him and who doesn't.

"Winning a campaign requires a very delicate balance. It's about precision. Timing. Discipline. Knowing exactly when to pivot and when to hold your line. Candidates forget that. They get caught up in the emotion and their newfound power. That's when they lose."

That's what does it.

"Says the man who's never actually run," I mutter, not meaning for anyone to hear.

But heads turn. Silence ripples.

He looks at me. Smiles. That practiced, polished smile he uses when the cameras are rolling. It used to send chills down my spine.

"I did help put someone in the Oval no one thought would ever get there," he says lightly. "Didn't I?"

"Okay, next topic." Lydia's attempt to defuse the tension. "Hadrian, have you finally decided to get your own security detail?"

I shake my head at once. "Not happening."

"But—"

"That's final. I can handle myself. I'm not adding another layer between me and the district neighbors."

"Well, well, well."

A very familiar voice cuts in, and everyone snaps their heads toward the door. "I leave for a few months and come back to find you in full JFK mode?"

Blake's leaning against the frame, arms crossed. My best friend since forever. Same cocky grin, same god-awful habit of showing up without warning.

"Blake! What the hell are you doing here?" I cross the room and pull him into a firm half-hug, back-slap.

"What—you thought I'd miss your political coming-out party?" His grin grows wider.

"Hi, Blake. Good to have you back." My father joins me, his hand already extended.

"Happy to be back, sir."

"This is Marcus Kessler," I say, gesturing toward him as he steps over.

"My replacement, huh?" Blake offers a handshake. "Kidding. Appreciate you taking care of this one."

"Not the easiest task," Marcus jokes back.

"Alright, everyone," I say, turning back to the room. "Thirty for lunch. Be back here after."

Chairs scrape, people scatter, and the buzz of conversation trails out behind them.

We've barely sat down next door at Rosemary's for a quick lunch when Blake grins and leans across the table.

"Second—please, for the love of God, tell me the rumors are true and you're actually shagging Brielle Warner."

I laugh, shaking my head. "You're a dick. I'm so glad you're back."

"Missed you too, buddy. Now spill—how'd you meet her?"

"Her uncle's a donor."

"Oh right, the producer guy?"

I nod. "Yeah. He's also... somewhat close to my father. He introduced us at the last gala."

He gives me a proud smile. "Feeling ready? When's the big moment?"

"As ready as I'll ever be. Announcement's next Tuesday."

"Drop the coordinates. I wouldn't miss it for the world."

"You know my father. He insisted on City Hall Park—and I quote—'a site that stands as both a historical beacon and a nod to the civic heart of the Second District.'"

Blake snorts. "God, he really doesn't break character, does he?"

"Never."

"You nervous?"

I shrug. "Wouldn't be human if I wasn't."

"Well, lucky for you, I'm back to reintroduce some chaos. You've gotten way too polished without me."

I shake my head, still smiling.

He lifts the menu with purpose. "Wine?"

"Not tonight. I'm keeping things clean. More or less."

“Right.” A slow, knowing smile. “In that case, guess I’ll go powder my nose solo.”

He gets up and disappears toward the bathroom without waiting for a response.

I’m tempted. No point denying it. But I need to do this clean.

I made a promise I’m not ready to break.

10
Isadora

I'M NOT EXACTLY THE poster girl for punctuality. But when it comes to work I don't mess around.

Rami and I arrive at the Gemological Institute of America a full hour and a half before my shift begins. I've always preferred it this way. I like to ease into a new space, get a feel for the energy. Acquaint myself with the building's tech. Double-check the microphone frequencies in the interpreting booth. Make sure the translation software isn't glitching like it did last time in Geneva. I even test the backup headset, just in case. If something can go wrong, it will. And I'd rather it do so while I'm the only one here to witness it.

"Rami, please wait in the car."

"No."

"It's a secured building. I have the Dot. And there'll be plenty of international officials here with their own security."

"Exactly." His Balkan accent wraps tightly around the vowels. "*Their* security. Not yours. They don't give a shit about you if things go bad."

"Nothing bad is going to happen. I promise."

He exhales through his nose, already tired of this argument. Then he steps out of the car and holds the door open for me.

"Rule number one." He pauses. "Never trust a room just because it has a nameplate and metal detectors."

I sigh. "Do I even have a choice?"

"That would be a no too."

We head toward the entrance of the International Gem Tower. It's my first time here, but I've seen it before. Hard not to. A stark, modern structure of mostly steel-frames, glass walls, and guarded like a bank.

The security guard gives Rami a nod, me a quick scan, and buzzes us through without much fuss.

I glance at him. "Wait—what, is there a bodyguard club I'm not aware of?"

"Something like that," he says, flat.

"Do you guys swap stories or just flex silently across rooms?"

"Depends on the room."

I laugh a little. He rolls his eyes at me and finds his spot against the wall.

I walk to reception, give my name, and flash my badge. I'm early, which means someone has to call someone who has to call someone else to confirm I'm supposed to be here. Bureaucracy at its finest.

I take a seat, pull *Lettera a un bambino mai nato* from my bag, and sink into the pages. The lobby is chilled and sterile. A few voices murmur by the elevator bank, but I tune them out. It'll be just Fallaci and me now.

"*Non si muore per amore*," a male voice cuts in. "*Si vive per amare*."

"*Ed è molto più difficile*," I add, almost instinctively.

A tall man stands in front of me, casting a shadow under the flat white lights. His hair is dark and slightly unkempt, jaw defined, features carved clean. But it's his eyes that stop me. Stormy gray, steady. Unflinching.

"My mother used to read that book to me," he says. "That line's always stuck."

"Do I know you?" I ask.

"Leo Sartori," he replies. "Pleasure to meet you."

Right. Lupo Sartori's son. The one Hadrian mentioned.

Safe to say, the photos online didn't do him justice.

He studies me, like he's also trying to place something.

"And your name is?"

"Isadora." I clear my throat. "Carter-Bello."

"Right. Isadora. Are you here for the Summit?"

"Yes. I'm with the French interpreting team. And you? Something tells me you're not a tailor."

He lifts a brow, faintly amused.

"Sartori. That's what it means," I offer.

A quiet laugh escapes him—dry, almost to himself.

I give him a confused look. He must catch it, because he shrugs.

"Nothing. Just wondering what life would look like if I were one. Maybe simpler."

"Maybe," I say, tilting my head. "Or you'd be a tailor with a very complicated life."

That gets something out of him. Not a smile—just a flicker of something... worn.

"Well," he says finally, "it was a pleasure meeting you, Isadora."

I give him a polite nod. He takes a step, then half-turns.

"Will you be at the closing remarks and drinks tonight?"

I meet his gaze. "Yes."

"Then I'll see you there."

He walks away, and the space he occupied feels abruptly vacant.

"Ms. Carter-Bello?" the guard says from behind the desk. "You're good to head up."

I check my schedule and head toward the main Auditorium, where I'm assigned for the morning block. Each summit room is equipped with its own interpretation booths—glass-paneled and elevated at the back, just above the audience.

I enter the French booth, set up for simultaneous interpretation. The others are labeled Spanish, Mandarin, Arabic, German—each with a pair of headsets, microphones, and a row of thick briefing folders stacked.

A few interpreters are already settling in. Some I know. Some I don't. There's a polite nod here and there. But the air feels like it always does before a major summit—still yet charged with expectation. Almost electrified.

It's a known hierarchy in simultaneous interpretation—Team A and Team B. Something like first chair and second. The first does the live translation. The second listens in, ready to jump in if anything goes wrong. It's collaborative on paper, competitive in practice. Especially in high-stakes summits like this one.

I'm Team A today. But for me, this has never just been about performance.

Did you know that in some countries, a translation is considered a creative work in its own right? Not a reproduction, but more like a rebirth.

Translators are bridge-builders. Quiet architects of understanding. We don't just swap one word for another. We interpret rhythm, subtext, breath. We decide what to keep, what to let go. What must never be lost.

We are all islands, drifting in our own cultures, humor, and unspoken codes. And translators are the ones who learn to swim across. Soul-readers, if you ask me.

It's almost time.

I slip on my headset and glance through the glass toward the audience. The seats are nearly full. Everyone's here for Dr. Stefan van Oost—the keynote speaker, a respected name in the world of mineral ethics. I remember from the prep notes I read last night: he's a stiff academic type, very into certification systems. Not exactly riveting, but technical enough to require precision.

I adjust my headset and glance down at my glossary one last time.

A quiet hush spreads through the auditorium.

The house lights dim slightly as the introducer steps onto the stage.

"Good morning, everyone, and welcome to the opening session of this year's Global Gem Summit..."

I flick on my mic.

"Bonjour à tous, et bienvenue à la session inaugurale du Sommet Mondial de la Gemmologie..."

My voice is even, calm. Behind the glass, no one sees how tightly I'm holding the mic stem. The words come easily. Still, I weigh them—commitment or obligation, evolution or reform. In my world, a single word can tip the scales.

"Whether you're representing government, industry, or advocacy, your presence signals a shared commitment to transparency, sustainability, and evolution in this ever-changing landscape."

A polite ripple of applause moves through the auditorium. I use the pause to roll my shoulders back and reset my posture.

"As many of you may know, Dr. Stefan van Oost was scheduled to lead this keynote, but due to unforeseen delays on his flight from Cape Town, he won't be able to join us this morning."

I frown slightly, glancing down at the printed schedule again, just to double-check. Still Van Oost.

"Fortunately, we are honored to welcome a speaker whose name and legacy resonate deeply within the industry. Someone whose background blends technical expertise with lived experience, and whose insights challenge convention while demanding integrity."

My words catch for half a beat. The interpreter beside me shifts, ready to jump in. But I keep going.

"He is a gemologist, mineralogist, and strategic consultant. He has advised private collectors, corporate boards, and international regulatory bodies—including our very own Certification Process—on ethical sourcing, lab-grown markets, and black-market intervention."

I keep my voice measured.

"But beyond his professional achievements, he comes from one of the oldest family-run operations in the diamond world and is also one of the youngest experts to ever brief our committee."

I sit up straighter.

"Please join me in welcoming... Mr. Leone Matteo Sartori."

I blink.

"Veuillez accueillir..."

A pause.

"Monsieur Leone Matteo Sartori."

He walks onto the stage, and just before he speaks, stormy eyes look up—right through the glass and into mine.

Allie

Guess what

Sorry babes, just read this. My new client is a handful.

How was the summit?

And what am I guessing???

Never mind.

I'm at the post-summit drinks, but leaving soon. It's predictably tragic.

Are you home?

Yes! Just got in. I'll cook us dinner.

Leaving now!

11
Leo

Irina Mikhailov is throwing a party tonight.

Her douchebag boyfriend texted me the invite. I'm headed there now.

I need to make some sort of move. After getting roped into the Global Gem Summit, I haven't had time for any of this.

I pull up to the address he sent—some new glass monstrosity on 57th. One of those ultra-skinny towers that looks like it might snap in the wind but somehow costs a hundred million a floor. I had OG dig around. Irina's father owns the trust that owns the company that owns the building.

I'll never get the obsession with penthouses. All that height and nowhere to run. A nightmare for security.

I give my name to reception and they point me toward the elevators.

The doors open before I even press anything. It shoots up—silent, fast—and I'm hit with chaos the second they slide open.

A wall of floor-to-ceiling windows opens onto the skyline—Manhattan in full burn. Chrome and gold, the Chrysler to the left, glittering like it was staged. A DJ's remixing Tchaikovsky into something that vibrates through your ribs.

The ceiling is dripping with a brutalist chandelier—metal, spiked, probably custom-built. Smoke curls from fat cigars. There's a tiger-patterned rug beneath a glass piano. A girl in red stilettos does slow splits on a Lucite table. A guy in a velvet robe hands her a stack of hundreds. Someone else is yelling in Russian, wearing a fur coat and nothing underneath. Vodka's being poured like water. But truly, it's the lack of imagination that baffles me.

I scan the crowd and catch Irina's face on the far side of the room. She's a model. High-end. The kind that walks for brands people can't pronounce and never smiles in photos. She moves like she's always being watched, and she probably is.

She sees me and waves, and I head towards her.

"Hey, Leo! So nice of you to come!" she slurs, voice pitched too high to be sober.

"There you are, man. Wasn't sure you'd show," Blake says, cracking a grin. He slings an arm around someone next to him. "This is my best friend—"

"Hadrian," I cut in. "Nice to see you again."

He looks... pissed? Definitely not my problem.

His eyes flicker toward Blake, then back at me. "I didn't know you two were friends."

"We met a few months ago in Europe," says Blake. "Come—have something to drink."

We move through the crowd. Or rather, they move around us.

"What do you want?" Blake asks, already making his way to the bar.

"What do you have?"

He grins. "Come on, shoot for the stars. There's nothing we don't."

"Yamazaki 55." If I have to be here all night, might as well make it worth my while.

He jerks his chin toward the back shelf. "Third row, left."

I grab the bottle. "You want one too?"

"Nah. Running on chemistry tonight," Blake says, almost proudly.

Shame, if you ask me. Not that I say anything. Not my place. And I couldn't care less.

"See you later. Mingle. Have fun," he calls over his shoulder, already drifting toward the DJ, who's a guy in a latex bodysuit and mirrored gas mask.

I stay behind the bar. Just curious.

Some of these bottles belong in a museum. 1945 Macallan. Pre-war Armagnac. A Louis XIII. What a waste of good liquor.

"Can I please have a vodka martini? Extra dirty."

The voice is familiar.

I turn.

Isadora Carter-Bello.

Hair down, longer than I'd pictured. Her skin has that kind of gold you only see in Sorolla's women—sun-warmed, effortless, like she belongs to a different latitude. A full mouth. Brown eyes that hold firmly on whatever they land on. Not soft. Not sharp. Just steady, like she doesn't need to look twice to know what she's seeing.

She looks a lot like Hadrian but completely different at the same time. His hair's lighter, eyes green. But you can tell. They're cut from the same place.

"I know you," she says.

"Guess I went from tailor to barman in under a week. Career's really taking off."

She laughs, and for some reason it sounds better than I thought it would.

"Vodka martini it is. Extra dirty."

I grab the vodka. Beluga Gold. Dry vermouth. Olive brine. Ice.

She's still looking at me like she's trying to place something deeper than my face.

Her posture's loose, but not careless. One hand resting on the bar, fingers relaxed. Nails short. No rings. Nothing performative.

"I met Blake and Irina a couple months ago in Europe."

"That's not what I was wondering," she says.

I say nothing, hoping she'll keep going.

"You didn't show."

"I didn't show?" I echo, but I already know what she means.

"To the cocktail. After the summit. You didn't show."

"How much have you had to drink?" I ask.

"Not much. This'll be my second."

Lightweight. Of course.

I glance around for her bodyguard—same guy, same threatening look from the corner. I nod at him. He doesn't nod back.

Honestly, I get it. If I were him, the idea of someone trying to hurt her would make me feel a bit murderous too.

Hadrian's nearby too, watching in our direction. Same pissed off expression as before.

"There you are." A blonde girl grabs her arm.

"Allie," she hesitates for a split second. "This is Leo. Leo, Allie."

"Nice to meet you," I offer.

She just stands there staring at me like I've come back from the dead as another guy walks up behind her.

"This party's getting weird," he says.

"And this is Jamie," Isadora adds.

"And that is *definitely* not my brother," Jamie says, nodding toward Blake, who's now standing on the piano and pouring tequila straight into people's mouths.

I can see the resemblance. Though less obvious. I guess in this crowd, everyone's someone's something.

"Are you all friends with Irina too?"

"Not really. We just met her," Isadora says, taking a sip.

She winces slightly after—barely noticeable, like she hates the taste but won't admit it.

"Not exactly a fan," Jamie says, eyes scanning the room.

"She's fine," Allie speaks up for the first time.

Isadora shrugs. "I've seen worse."

I nod toward Blake. "So, are they staying in the city long?"

She follows my gaze. "No idea."

Jamie sneers. "Pretty sure he'll go wherever she does."

"Sounds about right," Allie chips in.

I swirl the glass in my hand. Then look at Jamie. "Has she met your parents?"

"Not yet. But it's gonna happen soon."

Allie snorts, and we all shift toward her. "Oh, nothing. Just picturing it. Kathy'll have a feast with her."

Both Isadora and Jamie start laughing now too.

"I'm sure Blake meeting Irina's parents will be something else too," I say nonchalantly. A bit bold, but they're drunk enough not to clock it.

Isadora raises an eyebrow.

"Yeah, that's happening soon too," Jamie says. "Heard her father's flying in. Supposed to be this scary Russian czar who doesn't even speak English. Maybe we'll have to hire Isadora."

I turn to her. "You speak Russian too?"

"Too?" Allie echoes.

A hollow thud breaks through the music, followed by a scream.

We all turn.

Blake's on the floor, nose bleeding, and Hadrian's being held back by two guys I don't recognize. The DJ kills the music mid-beat. Glass shatters somewhere behind us. Someone laughs like they think it's part of the show.

Irina's shouting in Russian now.

Allie stiffens.
"What the—" Jamie starts.
Isadora bolts. No hesitation.
I follow.

12

Hadrian

"SECOND, WHAT THE FUCK man?" Blake shouts, hand pressed to his face, blood slipping through his fingers.

I don't answer. Can't. My vision's pulsing at the edges, heat boiling up from the inside out. I jerk forward again, trying to break loose from whoever's got me by the shoulders.

I see Isadora first.

"Hadrian. You need to calm down."

Her tone is urgent, but I'm not looking at her. Not really. I'm staring just past her at Blake's face and at the way he wipes the blood like he didn't deserve it. My fist clenches again. My whole body does.

My pulse is spiking. I can feel it in my ears.

What the hell did I take?

"Calm. Down." Isa's voice cuts through the noise insistently. Still her voice, but different now. Closer. Like we're not in a memory, but here.

I blink. Finally meet her eyes.

"We are surrounded by people. With phones."

That lands. I start to hear the static around us. The murmurs. The cameras.

I glance around. Faces turned in our direction. Phones raised. A brunette whispering something to a man in a robe. Someone else laughing, like this is entertainment.

Sartori steps in from the side. He's already reaching for Blake, lifting him by the arm. Blake shrugs him off but ends up taking the help anyway.

I catch a flash of blonde in the corner of my eye. I don't need to see her face to recognize that profile. Still, I turn. Allie. Completely still. Watching me like she's trying to figure out if I'm still me. It presses down on me, so I turn away.

"Let's get out of here," I say to Isa, jaw tight.

"Rami," she calls over my shoulder, calm as glass. "Get the car."

Guess it was Rami holding me back.

"I can drive you," Sartori offers, already stepping in.

"Yes. You drive us. Rami, stay with Marcus. I don't want a single recording of this night still breathing." I'm back in my skin, able to order my body what to do, my mouth what to say.

"No." Rami's voice is even, just for us. "I already broke protocol dragging your ass out of that mess. I'm not leaving Isadora exposed again."

I glare at him. I'm not in the mood for this. Not now.

Sartori steps in, leans toward him, and says something too low for me to hear.

Rami doesn't argue. Just nods once.

"Go."

Isa moves before I can even look back at her.

We move through the crowd. Mostly blank stares. Except a guy in a robe who hasn't even noticed the music's stopped.

The elevator doors open. Sartori, Isa, and I step in. Allie too. She's there in my periphery, but I don't look. Can't.

The ride down's a blur. I'm fighting to shove the rage back down but it's burning up my chest like it's forcing its way through bone. Every ounce of strength I've got goes into it. *Compose yourself, for God's sake.*

"Wait here," Sartori says as we move through the lobby.

I ignore him and follow out.

The valet's already rushing to get the car.

It's just Sartori and me out here. I start pacing.

"What the hell did you tell Rami?" I turn to him. He's just standing there, watching me like he's got all the time in the world. "I've never seen him agree to anything. Let alone that fast."

Sartori says nothing.

"Whatever," I mutter under my breath, dragging a hand across my jaw.

"I'll tell you," he says finally, "if you tell me what Blake said that made you lose it."

"Not your concern."

He doesn't back off. Just holds my gaze. Long enough to register something, but I can't tell if it's pity or warning.

He lets out a short breath, almost... disappointed. "I just told Rami I'd keep Isadora safe."

I stop walking. Run both hands through my hair, gripping the back of my neck like it might keep my head from splitting open.

"I wouldn't count on it."

Sartori doesn't flinch.

"Stay away from my sister."

The car pulls up beside us. The valet steps out, holding the door open.

I turn on my heel, start walking away.

"Just get in the car, Hadrian."

I spin, ready to tell Sartori to back off, but all I see is Allie, standing right beside the open door.

It didn't even register they'd come out too.

"What's happening?" Isa cuts in.

I don't answer. Can't. Because Allie's eyes are on me, steady and unblinking, and I know that look. I've seen it before. Didn't, for the longest time. But now it's back. And I know exactly who put it there.

I breathe in and open the back door for them. Then I slide into the front seat.

The car ride starts off quiet in the worst kind of way. I keep my eyes on the windshield, watching Manhattan blur past like it's trying not to look at us either.

"All good back there?" Sartori's voice breaks through the silence.

"They're fine," I cut in.

No one corrects me.

Blake

Second

We're cool right?

Don't know what the hell that was bro

But just so you know, all good here.

...

Hello?

Allie

Are you okay?

Yes

Are you?

I'm fine...

But it wasn't me doing the punching tonight.

He deserved it.

Still, you scared me a little.

I know…

I'm sorry.

Don't be.

Just don't do that again.

I won't.

Night, Als

Goodnight

13
Isadora

It's Tuesday morning, just hours before Hadrian's big announcement, and let me tell you, the tension in the air is thick enough to slice clean through.

"Distract me," Hadrian says, adjusting his tie.

"How distracting are we talking?"

"Anything, really."

"Have you seen Brielle's new movie?"

"Not Brielle. Please."

"Okay, then Allie. Maybe you'll finally get inspired and admit it?"

"You suck at this." He gives me a sidelong glance while keeping his head still. "And I have no idea what you're talking about."

"I'm talking about your little platonic game blowing up in your faces like I always knew it would."

He shrugs. "Still no clue."

"Boring. Seriously, Hadrian—do you think I'm stupid, or are you just lying to yourself? You're twenty-nine. Isn't it time you started owning your feelings?"

"It's more complex than that, Isa."

"How?" I shoot back. "You like her. She likes you. The only obstacle is your shared refusal to admit it—to yourselves, or to me. Which, by the way, is both rude and exhausting."

"It's not that simple." His voice is sharper now. "You know what her family represents. What they stand for. And I'm about to launch a congressional campaign that's going to put me under every microscope in the city. Or did that little detail escape you?"

"You've got to be kidding me." I roll my eyes. "Bipartisan couples exist—Daniel Carrigan and Sarah Mathers, for one."

"That's not the same," he snaps. "They're established. They've got the political capital to survive controversy. I don't. I'm just getting started. And the voting pool's more divided than ever. This isn't about love, it's about optics."

"Did you just quote our father?"

"Yeah, you're definitely not helping." He straightens his tie for the tenth time in the last ten minutes and stalks back to his campaign manager Lydia and the team.

The prep spirals after that—two heated wardrobe debates, a missing lapel pin, and someone almost crying over the wrong color tie. By the time we're ready to leave, everyone's spiraled through the full emotional range of humankind at least once.

My mother and I go with what she calls understated elegance—nothing flashy, just enough to say we belong. Coordinated, but nothing too on the nose. She triple-checked that.

And even though City Hall Park is practically walkable, we take the car.

My parents sit across from us and Hadrian's beside me, staring straight ahead.

His fist is closed, knuckles tight. A faint curve of gold peeks between his fingers, rounded and worn at the edges.

Grandpa's coin. A South African rand, given to him by Nelson Mandela in 1994. One side bears the crest. On the other it reads, *'Liberty belongs to the brave.'* He used to call it his anchor. He said he kept it close whenever the stakes were high. Then, one day, I think after he stepped down from the presidential race, he just gave it to Hadrian. Passed him the torch.

My chest tightens. I don't know why it's only hitting me now, how brutal it must be for him, doing all of this without Grandpa. The man he admired most. The one who shaped him. Who believed in him before anyone else did.

I catch a twitch in his other hand. Barely there, but I see it. Without thinking, I reach over and take it.

He doesn't look at me, but he doesn't pull away either.

"Remember that time I had to fly alone for the first time?" I say quietly, eyes still forward.

"No," he lies.

"To Turks and Caicos," I whisper, just for the two of us. "You were already at Columbia. Mom and Dad had ditched us to go early. I'd just finished my SATs. I called you from the airport—freaking out, obviously—and you said, and I quote, 'Just pretend I'm the seatbelt. You'll be fine.'"

He bites back a laugh, mouth twitching. "Wow. Inspirational."

"Honestly? It worked," I say. "Except you weren't just the seatbelt. You were also the oxygen mask. And the pilot trying to stabilize the plane. And the random lady next to me giving me that reassuring smile right before takeoff."

That gets half a smile out of him.

I nudge him lightly with my elbow. "You've always been that for me, Hadrian. The one who somehow takes the hit so I never get the worst of it."

Soda Stereo crackles low through the speakers—*Tratame Suavemente*—a subtle cue from my mother, who doesn't say a word but is absolutely trying to soothe him.

"You're about to do something terrifying," I whisper. "And amazing. And I know you're scared. But I'm not. Because you're the one doing it."

He finally looks at me, eyes a little too shiny to pass off as allergies.

"If you need a co-pilot up there—"my throat grows thick—"I've logged a few miles."

He huffs a quiet laugh, then squeezes my hand. "Thanks." His voice is still low, but steadier now.

The car comes to a full stop, and we step out of it as spring air rushes to greet us. The city sounds like it always does, except today it feels like it's holding its breath.

Cameras click from every direction, the staccato clatter of shutters building a frenetic rhythm. Flashes pop like lightning, and the air is filled with murmurs, microphones, and the electronic hiss of live feeds going up.

Hadrian stands at the entrance of City Hall Park, framed by the black iron gates that have watched this neighborhood grow and fray and bloom again. My parents flank him—two quiet pillars of pride. I hover just to his right, close enough to catch the faint crease forming between his brows.

He steps up to the podium.

"Good morning," he begins, voice rich, fully steady now. "It's an honor to stand here, in the heart of what is now the Second District—a place that's more than just my home. It's the soil that shaped me, the air that taught me how to breathe, and the people who showed me what it means to care."

He pauses. Lets the silence settle.

"This district isn't just where I grew up, it's where I became who I am. It's the corner store that always knew your name, even when you didn't think anyone noticed. It's the night shift nurse who sees more pain in one week than most do in a lifetime and still shows up. It's the high school teacher who bought snacks for kids who didn't have lunch and stayed late to help them apply to college."

He speaks like someone born to this moment. But I can still see it—his fingers tightening on the edge of the podium, like he's holding himself together by instinct.

"And for me, it's also where my grandfather stood before me. He taught me that public service doesn't start with power. It starts with proximity. With listening. With showing up."

Then he falters. Just a second. A pause too long. I follow his gaze to the back of the crowd.

Allie.

She's standing still, bathed in morning light, her gaze fixed on him with the quiet awe of someone witnessing a passing star for the first time. Like he's about to become something luminous.

Hadrian blinks. Once. Twice. Draws a breath. Refocuses.

"This district deserves leadership that sees it not as a stepping stone, but as a cornerstone. A place that doesn't just endure but flourishes. I'm here today to officially announce my candidacy for the United States House of Representatives, because I believe in this evolving Second District. Not just for what it already is, but for what it can become."

A swell moves through the crowd. Applause breaks like a wave against the line of cameras. The park fills with motion—flashes, scribbled notes, voices rising, journalists jostling for a better angle.

It doesn't take long.

"Mr. Carter-Bello," a reporter calls from the front, cutting clean through the noise. "Some critics say your platform is too moderate. What do you say to voters who feel you're not aligning with their values?"

"Let me be very clear." Hadrian doesn't hesitate, his gaze firm and his voice steady. "I'm not here to serve a party or a donor list. My focus is on the people of this district—on rebuilding trust, restoring fairness, and making sure opportunity isn't reserved for a select few."

He holds their gaze.

"This platform was built on principle. I won't be bought or steered. I'm here to earn your trust. Trading in favors is not the job. And call me a dreamer, but I believe politics should work for the public. Never the other way around."

The applause is immediate, a wave of sound that swells and crashes. Hadrian steps back for a moment. His eyes meet mine for a split second, and in them, I see what he didn't say aloud: something almost fragile. And I get it now. They simply won't let him exist on common ground. He isn't just seeing the support he's earned or the momentum he's built, he's also seeing the one thing he's just given up: Allie.

"Any further questions?"

14
Hadrian

Seeing her standing there with those eyes knocked something loose inside me.

So as soon as the questions wrap and we make our way past the reporters snapping their last pictures, I lean toward Isa.

"Please. Go find her. Bring her to my place."

She looks at me like she's searching for something. I guess she finds it, because she nods, then turns and walks back into the crowd.

It's not far—still rooted in the Second District—but just removed enough from the family home to feel like mine.

I trust her with this. Still, I text Allie.

Please.

The message reads like a plea, even though I know I can't afford for it to sound like one.

The car winds through familiar streets, past elegant townhouses and trees heavy with spring blossoms, petals scattering like confetti across the pavement. I loosen my tie, fingers trembling at the knot. My mind won't stop racing. I keep checking my phone like looking at the screen might conjure her name.

Just as we turn onto my street, it buzzes. It's Isa.

On our way.

Relief washes over me but it's edged with something heavier.

What, exactly, am I doing?

I'm soaring. The view is spectacular. And still, there's a quieter part of me waiting for someone to pull me back to earth. To steady me. To remind me where the ground is.

Today was everything my grandfather and I had always dreamed about and more.And now, somehow, still not enough.

My thoughts start racing, looping, folding in on themselves. And now I'm back at Isa's and Allie's place. A few years ago. Maybe more. Time behaves strangely around her.

I'd dropped by like always. No reason. Figured I'd find Isa half-asleep, complaining about deadlines. But Allie opened the door barefoot, swallowed by one of those oversized sweaters she favors, the hem barely brushing her thighs. Her hair was down, soft waves catching the lamplight. And I remember stopping. As if I'd stepped into a memory that hadn't happened yet.

"Hey," she said.

"Hey," I echoed, stepping inside. The TV was on—an old black-and-white movie flickering in the background.

"Since when are you into silent films?" I asked.

"I've always been into them. Isa definitely isn't."

That made sense. Isa needs dialogue like oxygen.

"It's called *The Artist*," she said. "There's something beautiful about it—how it leaves space for imagination but still lets us feel everything. They're in love. They're in pain. Sometimes eyes say more than mouths ever could. Don't you think?"

I do now.

The whole place smelled incredible—lemon, garlic, something warm and rich clinging to the air. She said Isa was out with Milo. Said she'd made enough for two. So I stayed.

Somehow, dinner turned into hours of conversation—well, mostly her—wandering into theories about the ocean's depths. Atlantis. Underwater UFOs. The Bermuda TriangleBut her favorite was what she called the Great Oceanic Abyss. A portal. A bridge between worlds. She explained that in some cultures, the sea is believed to connect the physical realm with the spiritual one—a place where gods and ancestors drift just beneath the surface.

I remember thinking I'd never really understood people's obsession with the ocean. The way they spoke of it like it was divine, sacred, alive. I never cared for the beach, never bought into all that mystery.

But in that moment—staring into her eyes, deep and dark and endless—I got it. I finally understood the pull.

Because I swear, hand to heart, those eyes hold the oceanic abyss.

I know they've arrived before the door even opens—I'm standing at the window like an idiot, watching their car pull up. Isa doesn't bother knocking, she has keys and no concept of boundaries.

I hate that from anyone. But a little less from her.

She steps in first. "Sorry. The only way she'd come was if I did too. Don't worry, I've got a book. I'll be in the guest room."

She disappears before I can reply, leaving just the two of us.

"Anything to drink?" I ask, stepping into the kitchen. She shakes her head as she leans her forearms on the island that separates us, her gaze steady.

"Congratulations, Hadrian. Your speech was flawless."

I walk over and rest against the opposite side, mirroring her.

"Thanks. And thank you for being there. It meant a lot."

She shrugs slightly. "I couldn't miss it. You've been talking about this moment for months."

"Listen, Allie..." I start, because pretending this is casual would be yet another lie neither of us can carry.

"You don't have to say anything..." Her voice trails.

"Except I have to. And I need to."

The adrenaline's still in me, burning hot, making it impossible to hold anything back.

"I'm sorry it took me so long to say this."

I shift my weight. My throat tightens, jaw right behind it.

"At some point these past years, I started falling for you. Properly. I should've stopped it then. And when I realized I couldn't, I should've told you straight, no games. Not just let it live in the things I didn't say, in how I looked at you."

I glance down, then back up, because I want her to see this. All of it.

"The truth is... I'd jump ship for you, Allegra. I'd let it all sink. I'd paddle to whatever deserted island we could find—just the two of us—so we could figure out what this is. What we could be."

My hands curl into fists at my sides. I take a breath so deep it almost hurts.

"But this sea... is just too big for us. If I leave this boat now, we won't make it anywhere."

It's out there now. No taking back. The big fat truth. Just sitting between us, staring us down, waiting to see who flinches first.

I silently beg that she'll be all the brave I can't be. That she'll ask me to jump anyway, tell me we can find the ocean's portal into a different dimension where we are not bound to other people's ideologies, just us. Just once. Just say it. Tip the scales, and I'll follow you into the deep end.

She doesn't. Instead, she looks at me with a quiet sadness, like a child who's just been told Santa isn't real. And my heart sinks, heavy as an anchor.

"You do what you have to do, Hadrian." Her tone comes out flat, but it doesn't quite match her face. "I don't judge you for it. I actually respect you for it."

I nod, swallowing hard.

"But I won't give you my heart in return." She turns away. "Because if I do, I don't think I'll get all of it back. And I need it whole if we're going to stay in each other's lives."

This is it. The death knell. The quiet, devastating end to something that never even had the chance to begin. Call the morgue, let them know we're on our way. And while you're at it, call the doctors too. Tell them you *can*, in fact, die of a broken heart.

"I'm sorry." My voice is rough. My heart is too.

"You're not to blame," she whispers.

Blame needs a body. If it belongs to no one, it dissolves. I can't let that happen. I need it lodged somewhere inside me—something to hate, something to draw from. Cocaine works the same way. It erodes you, but it sharpens the edges just long enough to convince you you're in control.

"I won't ask you to wait for me to find tamer seas but... please, do? Somehow. Anyhow."

She exhales and like in a silent film, her eyes say everything her mouth won't. She fell too. She understands why this won't work. And she won't wait.

"Sorry, guys. I need to bounce." Isa's voice slices through the stillness. "Als, do you need a bit longer? I can ask Rami to wait for you."

"No," Allie says without a second's hesitation. "I'm ready to go now."

They move in sync, like they've rehearsed this exit a hundred times. And I let them.

"See you both around," I manage.

Isa throws me a look—half pity, half fury—before turning away.

Once they're gone, I turn on the speakers. Gustavo Cerati's voice floods the silence. *Nací para esto.*

And I let what I just did settle in.

Lo terrible del mar, es morir de sed. The line twists in my chest. The sea itself, endless, and still dying of thirst inside it.

And I know I will.

15

Leo

"Yo, Leo. What's new?" Blake's voice slices through the speaker.

I guess he's been feeling the void since whatever went down with Hadrian. Must not have many friends in New York, because he's been orbiting me like a lost satellite.

"Hey, man. All good. Just heading out. You?"

"Not much. Watching Irina do an infrared sauna on the terrace," he says. "In heels."

I blink. "Sounds... healthy."

"She said it aligns her chakras."

A beat.

"Also looks good on camera."

"Right." I keep walking, letting the silence stretch. "So, talked to Hadrian yet? Killer speech he gave."

"Yeah, saw it too. Haven't talked to him though. He's pissed." A weary sigh follows. "Still."

I swipe open the door to the car waiting at the curb. "What the hell happened between you two?"

"Who the fuck knows, dude. I think it was something I said about Allie. A joke—but whatever. Didn't land."

I pause. "What type of joke?"

Blake chuckles, which I'm quickly learning is never a good sign. "I was hammered. Can't remember the exact wording."

"Right. Just thought you two were tight."

"We are." He sounds more serious now.

"Then whatever you said must've hit a nerve. Hadrian doesn't seem like the type to throw punches for fun."

Honestly, I can't believe I'm out here playing therapist for this guy. He means well, sort of, but he's got the emotional range of a Central Park squirrel.

"I didn't say anything I haven't said before. I mean, have you seen her? She's unreal. The shit I'd do..."

"Yeah," I say, sliding into the backseat, "that'd do it."

"Bit dramatic, no? I've said worse."

I let that one slide.

"Look, you wanna take your mind off it or what?" I ask, eyes on the city sliding past the glass.

"Obviously."

"Meet me at Sotheby's."

I half-regret it the second the line goes dead. But the kid needs to blow off some steam and there's no place like this one to do it.

Sotheby's has always felt like a sanctuary to me. Not for peace. For precision. A place where the chaos of the world fades and something more primal takes over.

For most, it's about the hunt—artifacts, jewels, relics laid bare for the highest bidder. For me, it's something else. This place doesn't just hold objects. It breathes history. Whispers secrets. It's alive in a way most people aren't.

The building itself is a contradiction. Sleek glass reflecting Manhattan's restlessness, guarding treasures older than memory. Inside, the lobby is an exercise in quiet dominance: marble floors polished to a mirror shine, towering vases of lilies scenting the air, and walls lined with discreet plaques that don't beg for attention. Everything about it is deliberate. Calculated. Just unsettling enough to remind you exactly where you stand.

But the main auction room, that's where the real games begin.

My phone buzzes. It's Blake.

Bro, this place is sick

Where u at?

Main Salesroom.

Leather seats. Soft lighting. A stage where fortunes change hands in minutes as the auctioneer commands the room like a conductor. The audience is usually a predictable mix of old money, new money, and the kind desperate to be mistaken for either. The main event revolves around a sale, yes. But truthfully, it's a spectacle. A battlefield where wealth is flexed, calibrated, and, when necessary, weaponized.

My name's already on the back of the second-row seat. Aisle, as usual. Easy to get in and out. Easy to watch the room without being watched.

I sit. The lights dim slightly. Voices hush.

Blake arrives just in time for the show. No tie. Shirt slightly wrinkled.

He scans the room, then spots me and makes his way over, sliding into the seat next to mine with that half-smirk, like he thinks we're about to start some shit.

"Hey," he mutters. "What are we doing here?"

"Watch." I nod toward the stage. "You'll see."

A woman in black gloves steps onto the stage, carrying a velvet case the size of a shoebox. She opens it slowly—dramatically, even—revealing a cushion-cut blue diamond the size of a nickel. I've seen less bring down governments.

Blake leans in. "Is that… real?"

"Very."

The auctioneer clears his throat. "Lot 47. A 17.8-carat fancy vivid blue diamond, unmounted. GIA certified. To be offered for sale at auction. Ladies and gentlemen, this is Royal Rain."

The opening bid flashes: Eight million.

Blake makes a sound somewhere between a scoff and a choke.

"Jesus."

Nine million.

Ten.

Ten-five.

Eleven.

Hands keep rising like they're playing with Monopoly money. The tension is surgical—precise, controlled, but one inch away from madness.

Twelve.

Thirteen.

"Are they out of their minds?" Blake hisses. "It's a rock."

Fourteen.

Fourteen-five.

"Dude. I could buy a skyscraper in Lisbon."

"Nah." I shake my head. "Wouldn't shine like that."

Fifteen.

The room holds its breath.

Three... two... one.

The gavel slams.

"Sold for fifteen million dollars to paddle seven."

The room exhales.

And that feeling just now? That spine-prickling surge, that chemical snap behind your eyes. That's why I don't do drugs. This is the hit. Everything else just chases it.

Blake turns to me, wide-eyed. "Who the fuck just dropped fifteen million on a single diamond?"

I glance one row ahead, then nod slightly. "Guy in the navy Brioni, on the phone. Balding. Looks like a retired Bond villain."

Blake leans forward to see.

"He's Valentin Azarov's bidding agent," I say. "Oligarch money. Moved half his portfolio into stones after the sanctions hit. Divorce settlements, offshore vaults, bribery. It all looks cleaner when it glitters."

Blake stares like he just found out fairies are real.

"Phew," he exhales. "What a fucking rush."

I let out a short laugh. "Wanna know the best part?"

Blake swallows. "What?"

"That diamond?" I keep my voice low. "I rescued it myself. Northern Angola."

His jaw practically hits the floor.

16

Isadora

"I BROUGHT US A blanket and some tea," I say, handing a cup to Allie as I settle beside her on the rooftop bench.

I glance sideways. She hasn't said much since we came up. Or for the last few days, for that matter.

The wind tugs on my sleeves. Below us, the city simmers—yellow taxis, distant sirens, flickers of movement that make it feel alive, even from up here.

I grew up in a brownstone in Greenwich Village, and rooftops there were more rusted ladders and tar paper than skyline views.

But this place is twenty-five floors up, clean lines, glass railings, and a view that makes the whole city look like a diorama. Allie says it calms her.

"What are we looking at?" I ask, pulling the blanket tighter around my shoulders.

"There." Allie points across the rooftop, her finger steady. "Tenth floor, third window from the right. The one with the pale curtains."

I follow her gaze. Across the gap, in an older version of our building a woman sits alone on a green sofa. Still. No TV on. No book in hand.

"She's been there every day this week. Same time. Just... sitting. Almost like she angled the whole sofa so she can watch the entrance." She tilts her head. "Who do you think she's waiting for?"

From here, the woman looks like she's in her late forties, maybe early fifties. Her hands rest on her lap, still.

"I don't know, Als..." I turn to her. "Maybe she's just... contemplating."

Allie closes her eyes like she always does when she's enjoying the fresh air or having a deep thought.

"I don't think so," she says eventually. "She's definitely waiting for someone to walk through that door."

I glance at the woman again. Still as stone.

"Well… I hope she's not."

Allie opens her eyes and looks over at me, brows drawn together.

I shrug slightly. "I hope she's not just sitting there, day after day, waiting for someone who's not coming."

She rolls her eyes like she's trying to shake something off.

"How do you even know he's not coming?"

I raise an eyebrow. "He?"

She doesn't answer. Just takes a sip of tea and stares back at the window.

"That's not the point," I say softly. "Maybe 'he' is, maybe he's not. It doesn't matter. She still shouldn't be putting her whole life on pause."

Allie exhales hard through her nose. "Of course you'd say that."

"What's that supposed to mean?"

She turns her face away, voice tighter now.

"It's easy for you to believe that. You're not the one waiting around for someone else."

That stings. More than I want it to.

But I know her. And that right there—that wasn't about me.

"Sorry." Eyes still fixed on the skyline.

"It's okay. Maybe you're right."

She shifts, fiddling with the rim of her cup.

"Not just that. I'm sorry I didn't say anything sooner."

Allie's always been the kind to keep things in until they curdle. Like that one time in ninth grade, when she didn't say a word about not having anywhere to go for Thanksgiving break. I had this horrible pit in my stomach. Woke up that morning and went straight to her dorm. She was there, obviously, sitting cross-legged in bed, eating a boiled egg off a paper towel, skimming through some glossy magazine like it was just any Thursday.

"I didn't feel like traveling," she said with a shrug. But her voice cracked on traveling.

I shift towards her too. "Allie, you've had a crush on Hadrian since day zero. I highly doubt you befriended me just because I was his sister."

My best friend laughs, and I swear a star twinkles right on cue.

"You didn't have to tell me," I say plainly. "I always knew. And I always figured that if it ever turned into something more, it wouldn't change a thing between us. Not one damn thing."

A brief silence, then she looks at me, eyes glassy.

"I'm in love with him."

"Yeah. You are."

I take a breath.

"But you can love someone and still decide not to wait for them. Those things aren't mutually exclusive."

A tear slips down her cheek, and I brush it away.

"Listen, Allie. I'm not going to sit here and call Hadrian an idiot—though, let's be honest, he absolutely is. And I'm not going to waste our night railing against politics or last names or all the crap. You already know all of that."

She doesn't look away. Just listens.

"But I will say this: it's not your job to make it easier for him. Or to prove you're worth the risk. You are. That's not on you. That's on him."

Allie exhales, and I nudge her shoulder gently.

"Now chin up. Crown's slipping."

She smiles at me, and we sit in silence for a few minutes, letting the spring night wrap around us.

The air smells like our neighbor Pippa's lemon rosemary chicken, laced with something floral, maybe jasmine, or whatever's in bloom along the fire escape. Somewhere nearby, music escapes through an open window—something jazzy, barely there, and a soft laugh echoes from a balcony a couple of floors down.

The season's turning, whether we're ready or not.

"So... you speak Russian *too*?" Allie's teasing tone is dialed all the way up.

"Hell no. We're not making this about me."

"Too late. There are some serious plot holes I need filled immediately."

I take the last sip of my second cup of tea and set it down.

"We met at the Summit. Super briefly—like, blink-and-you-miss-it. I was waiting in the lobby, and he came up and introduced himself."

"He just... walked up to you and said hi?"

"Kind of."

"What?" She narrows her eyes.

"What what?" I narrow mine too.

"You're making a face."

"What face?" I shrug nonchalantly "I'm literally just sitting here."

"Nope. That's the face you make when something's bugging you."

I laugh. "It's nothing, seriously."

"Mm-hmm."

"Now *you're* making a face."

"What face?" she mimics, full sass.

"The one you make when you think you know better."

She shrugs, not even pretending to deny it.

"He sounds even hotter than he looks. Which, frankly, should be illegal," she says, deadpan.

I snort just as the rooftop door creaks open, and we both glance over.

Jamie steps out, hands stuffed in his pockets.

"I knew I'd find you two up here."

"Hi, James."

He settles beside us, tugging a corner of the blanket over his lap.

"What'd I miss?"

"Oh... not much." I nod towards the building in front of us. "Just spying on a woman who won't be waiting around anymore."

He lifts a brow. "Am I supposed to know what's happening here?"

Allie and I both laugh.

He settles and lets out a breath. "This is nice."

"It is," Allie mumbles.

"Any plans for the weekend?" he asks.

"Actually..." Their eyes lock on mine. "How does Bedford sound?"

"Life-changing," Jamie declares.

"You read my mind," Allie adds almost instantly.

My family has a place in Bedford. It's Allie's favorite spot in the world. Ours, really. Tons of memories. The kind where the moment you step through the door, you're back in the best of it, weightless and eyes full of sunshine.

"Should we leave Thursday or Friday?"

"I could leave now." "Let's do tonight," Allie and Jamie say in unison.

I offer them a mischievous little grin. "Alright, then. Time to pack."

Rami

Rami, we're heading to Bedford.

Could you drive us please?

Yes. Provide departure date and time so I can plan accordingly.

We were thinking now…

Not possible. Need to sweep the route, vehicle check must be logged, comms test required. Earliest is tomorrow.

Rami, this is Allie. No worries, I'll just ask the guy whose penthouse I'm remodeling in the Meatpacking District to drive us. You know, the one who wanted bulletproof windows. He's got a limo and said he loves long drives.

See you in thirty.

17
Hadrian

THE TRILL OF MY phone slices through the stillness.

Isa's name flashes across the screen. I answer on the second ring.

"Morning, Isa," I say, aiming for casual, keeping the rough edges out of my voice.

"Morning. How's it going?"

"Good," I lie, one hand braced on the kitchen counter. "I'll be at Second Front soon. Wanna grab breakfast before the circus kicks off?"

"I... can't. I've got plans with Allie."

I pause, a quiet frown tugging at my mouth. "How is she?"

"Ground rule." Her tone sharpens. "I'm not giving you information about Allie. But..." A brief pause. So unnecessarily dramatic. "I can't promise the reverse is true."

"Noted." I aim for casual again. It's not convincing.

"Any plans for the weekend?"

"What, besides running a campaign? Not much. You?"

"You know... the usual, just hanging around. Anyway... good luck with that."

She hangs up before I can say goodbye.

I stare at the screen for a beat, then toss the phone onto the counter.

I don't have the bandwidth for whatever that was.

As usual, I take my bike to Second Front. It's a short ride—ten minutes, tops—and usually enough to clear my head.

Not today. Today it loops back to what I shouldn't be thinking about.

Personal matters have a way of getting louder when I need them quiet.

I grip the handlebars tighter, forcing myself to focus. Campaign mode. No distractions.

I park my bike in front of the restaurant I always do. Ivy-covered façade, too carefully charming. Fleetwood Mac's already playing, they never miss a morning. I used to find it comforting. Now it feels like nostalgia that doesn't belong to me.

Second Front is next door, two floors we're renting above what used to be an art framing shop. Marcus found it. Named it too.

"You're Second, it's the Second District, and we're going offensive. So—Second Front," he said. I wasn't sold. It stuck.

The stairwell groans as I push through the side door and take the steps two at a time.

Inside, the space is already humming—laptops open, cords taped down, campaign posters curling slightly at the edges. My favorite is pinned above the coffee station, a vintage print of Bobby Kennedy's "Ripples of Hope" speech.

It's not a home. It's not quite an office. It's something in between, like it's still figuring out what to be. Like me.

"We need to lock in dates for the town halls." JJ, my campaign strategist trails behind me. "And we're hearing whispers about a few names throwing their hats into the ring."

That makes me stop in my tracks. "Like who?" I start walking again.

"Jonas Mercer." Meet Ava Patel, my communications director.

"Mercer?" I scoff. "He's a legacy candidate. No substance."

"And Linda Park." That's Nate Holloway, my policy advisor.

"Smart." We reach the main meeting room, and I sit. Everyone else follows. "But too niche. She won't land outside her base."

JJ flips a page on his clipboard. "Then there's the usual background noise—Spencer Myles is making calls again."

I roll my eyes. "Didn't he tank his last debate because he quoted Elon Musk?"

"Yep. Still polling under two percent," Rachel adds, deadpan.

"Amanda Cho is testing the waters too." Ava again. "She just launched a podcast."

"Great," I say under my breath as I sink deeper into my chair.

"And Elijah Burr." Nate. He doesn't look up. "If he announces again, that'll make five runs in twelve years."

JJ leans back. "At this point, he should just lease the campaign office year-round."

A few chuckles ripple around the table. I just shake my head. "We'll keep an eye on Mercer and Park. The rest... noise."

We spent the last hour dissecting these names and potential appearances. The primaries loom like a thundercloud on the horizon.

As the team disperses, I catch Marcus lingering by the coffee station.

"Got a minute?" I ask.

"Always," he replies, following me into a smaller meeting room.

The room smells faintly of coffee and something sweet.

"What's on your mind?" Marcus gives one of his complicit looks. "Besides a hangover."

I let out a short laugh.

"Current trends." I lean against the desk. "What's working, what's not."

"We need to get ahead of the algorithm shifts," he says. "The platforms are favoring short-form emotional hits right now, not long-winded policy posts. And public sentiment? It's turning faster than usual—people are reacting, not thinking. We've got to stay ahead of the curve."

He has a way of cutting through the noise, finding the pulse beneath the spin.

"If we're smart, we'll own the narrative before Mercer or Park even get a chance," he adds.

"Then let's be smart," I say, clapping him on the shoulder.

The door creaks open slowly. A second later, Blake's head pops in, looking like he spent the night somewhere he shouldn't have. His eyes flick from me to Marcus and back again.

"Hey, man." He steps inside. "Sorry to interrupt." He clears his throat. "Can I—uh—talk to you, Second?"

Marcus gives me a look that says, *Your call.* I nod, and then he slips out.

I cross my arms. "What's up?"

Blake shifts his weight, scratches the back of his neck.

"I don't know." He's struggling to find the words. That much is clear from the look on his face. "I guess I just... wanted to apologize."

I lift a brow. "You *guess*?"

He lets out a dry laugh. "I mean—I still don't totally know what I said that crossed the line. I run my mouth constantly and you usually just call me an ass."

He pauses.

"So yeah. I was clearly out of line. I'm sorry. I'll keep my mouth shut about Is. Or Allie. Whichever one got me clocked."

For a second, I'm back at that stupid party, out of my mind furious all over again. Then I look at him, standing there with that wide, sorry grin.

So I give him a tight smile. "All good. I'm sorry I punched you, too."

"Yeah... what the hell *was* that right hook?" he says, eyes widening slightly. "You've been holding out on me."

I brush past him toward the door.

"You *are* an ass."

"Lunch?"

"Can't. Busy week. Trying to squeeze the most out of this momentum."

"Well... congrats. For what it's worth, you've got my vote."

"You don't vote in the Second District."

"Oh, fair. I'll buy a flat here so I can." He follows me into the war room. "Anyway—see you soon?"

"Yeah. Let's catch up this weekend."

He nods once and disappears.

I barely have time to exhale before Lydia waves me over from the far side of the room. She's tossing a paper coffee cup into the trash as I approach.

"Victor wants to see you."

"What now?"

"Hadrian..." She rolls her eyes. "Just remember—he speaks from a different place than where you listen from."

Lydia—ever the wise one.

I make my way to my father's office. The door is ajar. He's leaning back in his chair, flipping through a thick dossier with that same air of casual detachment he always wears like a veil. Sometimes see-through. Sometimes thick as cement.

"Wanted to see me?" I ask, stepping inside.

"Come in." His tone is as perfunctory as the smile he offers, setting the folder aside. "How's the team holding up?"

"Focused. We've mapped out the next two months. Mercer's name came up."

"Jonas Mercer is a puppet. If he's our competition, we'll crush him."

"I don't want to underestimate him," I reply, steady. "Even puppets can pull strings if the right hands are behind them."

He leans forward, fingers steepled. "Don't waste time second-guessing. This campaign isn't about Mercer. It's about you. Your voice. Your story. Stick to that. And we win."

It's meant to sound like confidence. But it lands like a warning dressed as praise.

"Understood." I turn to leave, start walking to the door, but I can feel he's not done.

"Remember." His voice stops me. I turn back to him. His facial expression tells me I'm going to regret it. "Our name carries weight. Don't let anyone forget it. And don't let me regret putting it behind you."

Funny how his words always land just far enough to seem harmless, but deep enough to get under my skin.

"You only gave me half my name." I make eye contact with him. "I'm not just a Carter. I'm a Carter-Bello. And you can rest assured I'll honor that 'til the day I die."

18
Isadora

"RAMI'S STAYING AT THE pool house for the rest of the weekend," I say, sinking back into the deep linen cushions of the great room sofa—a custom Pierre Paulin *Dune* Allie chose when she refreshed the space in 2020, one of ten projects she somehow took on while the rest of us were just baking banana bread. The room smells faintly of cedar and lavender, framed by old beams and mullioned windows that still catch the last of the light. "You know... to prevent any further incidents of nakedness."

Allie yawns. "I can't control my bladder. Especially at four a.m."

"Well, you can control what you wear to sleep, can't you?" Jamie counters, yanking the tartan blanket off his legs.

It's cooler here than in the city. Crisper. Nights in Bedford always feel a little more cinematic—air like apple skin and stone, trees that hush the world into stillness. Everything feels easier here. Like the hard edges of real life don't quite reach past the gravel drive.

"Not really." Allie helps herself to a dramatic fistful of popcorn from the coffee table. The legs are wood, but the surface is an almost unreal, looks-like-a-cloud marble—creamy white with soft, branching veins in beige and pale gold. She's very specific about her marble, loves to remind us every so often that cracks mean it wasn't sealed right, uniform veins usually mean it's fake, and real Carrara stays cold no matter the season. "Sleeping topless is sort of a medical necessity. Something about... regulating core temperature. And also, boobs deserve freedom after a long day. It's a human rights thing."

She tosses a piece of popcorn into her mouth. "Who in their right mind would sleep with anything but Comporta cotton against their skin?" She swallows. "Honestly? The worst misuse of free will I can think of."

Jamie and I both laugh because our best friend is ridiculous. And possibly correct. And definitely perfect in the exact way that makes me feel like I'm home.

I grab the remote and hit Play.

The Butterfly Effect flickers to life on the screen, that moody grain lighting up the wide-paned windows like the start of something dramatic. It's my favorite movie of all time. And I earned the right to pick it after winning *Dead or Fictional*—our long-running, deeply stupid game from Dalton where you name three outrageous personality traits, and everyone has to guess whether the person you're describing is dead, fictional, or both.

Allie once insisted Jack Dawson was a real historical figure. Jamie swears Cleopatra is fictional.

Today, Jamie tried to trip me up with "mood swings, owns a falcon, smells like gin." I said Ernest Hemingway. I was right.

Allie guessed Christian Grey. She was also right. Which was terrifying.

The movie goes on—Evan walking down that sterile hallway again, fluorescent lights buzzing above him, the camera slightly off-kilter like the world's already started tilting. He opens his childhood notebook, flips to the page, and the screen flashes white.

I've seen this scene a hundred times, but I still feel that strange pull in my chest when it happens—like something's being rewound inside me too.

Outside, the sky's gone charcoal, the kind of almost-summer evening where the clouds hang heavy, swollen with a storm that hasn't fully formed yet. There's that hush before rain when even the birds go quiet. A few cicadas still hum at the edges, and a breeze stirs the tall trees lining the property, brushing their leaves against the glass from the open window like fingers tapping. From where I'm sitting, I can just make out the golden halo of the garden lights glowing through the mist. The hydrangeas are bent from the weight of the air.

An hour and fifty-three minutes later, the credits roll, the screen fades to black, and outside, it's fully night.

Jamie's already half-reclined, phone in hand, scrolling with the vacant look of someone deep in a dopamine spiral.

I wipe a tear from the corner of my eye.

Allie catches it and sighs, reaching for the wipes without even looking. "Every time, Is. Every single time."

Jamie glances up. "Jesus. Again?" He shakes his head. "You really need to get that checked. It's *The Butterfly Effect,* not *Schindler's List.*"

I gasp, hand on my chest like he's just insulted a family heirloom. "Excuse me?"

He gives me an apologetic look. "I mean... maybe it's not meant to be *that* deep?"

I sit up straighter. "Actually, it *is* that deep. It's about sacrifice, and timing, and how love sometimes means letting go instead of holding on. He chooses a world where he never gets her, just so she can be safe. That's—" I break off, shaking my head. "That's everything."

There's a beat. Jamie blinks.

Allie tosses a piece of popcorn at my head. "Okay, *Professor Pathos.*"

Jamie smirks. "And here I thought you just liked it 'cause Ashton Kutcher's hot."

I wipe my face again. "I mean. He is. But he's also acting his little heart out. Give the man some credit."

Allie stands in one swift motion and drags the blanket off both Jamie and me without a second thought. "Okay. This is getting a bit depressing. It's also Friday night. Time for drinks."

Jamie's up immediately. "Finally. To the Carter-Bello reserves." He lifts both arms, gaze to the ceiling, theatrical as ever. "May the labels be French and the damage irreversible."

"Do *not* touch the Margaux or my dad will actually murder us," I call after them.

"We'll say it was Jamie," Allie calls back. She's already halfway down the hall.

They return a few minutes later, smug and victorious, with a bottle of Château Léoville Barton—a 2005, no less. Jamie holds it like it's a newborn.

"Good choice," I say, eyeing the label. "That's the one my mother saves for people she's trying to impress but secretly doesn't like."

Allie giggles. "Perfect. Let's drink to carefully curated tolerance."

Jamie uncorks it and starts pouring. The wine settles in the glass with a quiet weight. It's dark—almost opaque—with a slow swirl and that faint, unmistakable scent of age: a mix of graphite, old wood, and something like dried herbs pressed between book pages.

Outside, the wind shifts, and a storm cloud still lingers, though most of it has already drifted off. The air smells like rain and something sweet I can't name. Inside, we laugh and dance to Talking Heads like we're sixteen again—barefoot, reckless, hearts a little lighter than they were a few hours ago.

Jamie picks up his phone, flicks it open, and raises the camera toward us.

"Hey—no photos." I shrink away from the lens.

"It's one shot. For the 'gram. We look fab."

"No social media."

He lowers the phone, confusion written all over his face. "Okay, but why are we acting like we're in witness protection?"

"I haven't told anyone we're here."

"Still not getting the secrecy vibe."

"It's just... we don't want unexpected guests."

He stares at me, brows fully furrowed now.

"What... like us?" A masculine voice cuts through the room.

I jolt and my wine sloshes over the rim. Allie lets out a scream so sharp I feel it in my ear canal. Jamie hurls a pillow straight ahead so forcefully it knocks over a vase on the console. It crashes to the floor, water and tulips spilling across the wood.

"Well, thank God no one overreacted." Blake's standing in the doorway, mouth twitching with amusement. Hadrian's next to him, arms crossed, clearly less thrilled with the whole situation. And someone else behind them—half in shadow, hands in his coat pockets, gaze fixed.

Leo.

19
Hadrian

"What's wrong?"

Rami storms in like he's expecting a body on the floor, shoulders squared, already blocking Isa with his whole frame.

She looks at me. Then at him. Then back at me.

"Umm... that was me." Allie holds up her hand, clutching the Dot like it's a grenade she forgot she was holding.

Rami doesn't move. Still tense.

"Sorry," she adds quickly. "They scared the shit out of me, okay? But... coast is clear. Situation neutralized. Or whatever the tactical lingo is." She tries a sheepish smile. "Sorry?"

Rami's jaw ticks. "The Dot is not for you, ma'am." He plucks it from her hand and places it back in Isa's.

"Hey—rude," Allie shoots back. "What if she's knocked out or something? I need to be able to call you too, don't I?"

He exhales. Sharp. Borderline growl.

"They weren't expecting us," I step in before we have an international incident. "That's on me."

I meet his eyes. "We've got it."

He gives a grunt that may or may not be a goodbye, then walks off, muttering something in Serbian.

Allie blinks. "Did he just insult me in another language?"

"No idea," Isa lies. She absolutely knows.

"What are we drinking?" Blake's already reaching for the bottle on the console near the back wall. "Not really feeling wine. Second?"

"Whatever you want. I'm staying clear."

I glance at Allie. And once again for what feels like the millionth time, my chest does that impossible thing where it tightens and expands all at once.

"Scotch. Neat." Right. Sartori's here too. Great.

"Same." I turn to join Blake at the liquor tray. It's set up on a long sideboard across from the couch. Cut glass decanters, heavy tumblers, no shortage of options.

"Excuse me—"Isa's trying to blot the wine off her sweater—"will someone explain what you're all doing here?"

"It's my house too." I pick up a glass.

She looks at me, exasperated. "Sure. Great timing lately. You should teach a class."

Jamie lets out a quiet "oof" from the couch. "Sorry?"

"Jamie!"

"I just told Blake we'd be gone for the weekend," Jamie shrugs halfheartedly. "He asked where, so I answered. Again—I didn't realize it was classified."

"Let's not pretend we didn't just upgrade your weekend." Blake's already pouring himself a second glass.

"Cute." Allie now. "Where's Irina?"

Blake shrugs. "She had to fly back to Russia with her father for a few days. Something business related."

"And your campaign?" Isa turns to me, settling on one end of the couch.

"All under control. A night off was overdue." I sit on the armrest beside her. "I'm back first thing."

Sartori crosses the room without a word and lowers himself onto the opposite end of the couch.

"Let's play something," Blake announces. "Dead or Fictional."

"We already did." Jamie takes a sip. "Is won. As usual."

"That's because I wasn't here," I throw in.

"Exactly." Blake grins. "So let's up the stakes."

Jamie groans. "Here we go."

"This time"—Blake turns toward the group—"it's someone you'd kill or someone you'd fuck. Fictionally, of course."

"Blake." There's a warning tucked beneath my tone.

"What?" He bites back a smile. "It's efficient. And honest."

He downs what's left of his probably third drink like a shot. "Allie, you start."

Allie doesn't miss a beat. "Fine. Ryan Gosling in *The Notebook*—dead. But Ryan Gosling in *Drive*? Fictional. Hard fictional."

Jamie chokes on his drink. Isa hides a laugh behind hers.

"Nice," Blake says as he scrolls through his phone just as M.I.A.'s "Bad Girls" crashes through the speakers. "But that's not how it works. You don't answer your own. You pick someone else. That's the fun."

He exhales a thin stream of mango-scented vapor. "Sartori. You're up. Princess Diana or Mother Teresa."

Now he's fully in his element.

Everyone lets out a collective ugh.

"You're beyond help." Isa laughs, half-amused, half-horrified.

Blake winks at me. God help me.

Sartori doesn't flinch. Just sips his scotch, watching us like he's studying us.

"Guess the old lady'll have to go," he finally says. "She's probably headed straight to paradise anyway."

Jamie fakes a shudder. "You're both sick."

A few more rounds in, and it's already so far off the rails we're essentially free-falling.

We've now learned that Allie would kill the Dalai Lama but fuck Batman—specifically Christian Bale Batman. Information I could've absolutely lived without.

"Not Robert Pattinson?" Jamie asks.

Allie shakes her head. "Too emotionally available. Total turn-off."

Blake looks over. "That says way more about your taste in men than you think."

She tilts her head, her expression tighter. "Excuse me?"

"Nothing personal," he adds. "Just... the truth."

"Careful, Blake." I don't smile. "You're starting to sound like someone who thinks he gets a vote."

His smile flickers, but only slightly.

"Right," he says. "Let's keep going then."

He takes a long sip of his drink. Waits just long enough.

"Second. Your turn."

I glance up. "Already gave mine."

"No, no," he retorts, all serious now. "*Real* one. Since you're so clear about who gets a vote." A brief pause. "Allie or Brielle."

The shift is instant.

Isa stills. Jamie stops mid-pour.

Allie doesn't move. But she's listening. So is everyone else.

I look at Blake. "No."

"Why not?" Blake says coolly. "Come on. You're a politician. Pick a side."

I don't notice my fists are clenched until my nails bite my palm.

"Isadora." Sartori doesn't raise his voice, but everything stops like he did.

"What's your boyfriend's name again?"

She blinks. "Sorry?"

"For the game."

"Milo," Blake answers, a bit too quick.

Sartori lifts his glass, eyes steady. "Right. Milo... or someone else in the room."

Silence.

Isa lets out a nervous little laugh. "What?"

"It's your turn, isn't it? Dead or *fictional*. Your boyfriend, or someone else in the room."

Jamie shifts on the armrest. Blake lets out a wicked laugh.

Isa stares at Sartori like she's not sure she heard him right and I can't tell if I'm holding my breath or holding myself back.

"All right." Allie breaks the tension. "That's enough existential crisis for one round."

She grabs the wine bottle and refills her glass like it's the only thing that matters.

"But sure." She looks at Sartori. "Points for dramatic tension."

His expression remains in its usual unreadable form.

Isa exhales.

"Speaking of," I say, grabbing my phone and finally checking the text I got a few minutes ago. "Milo's ten minutes out."

Heads turn.

"What?" Isa snaps.

"Great. More unexpected guests," Allie says to no one in particular.

"I'm not giving up the blue room," Jamie declares. "Just so we're clear."

"Hadrian." Isa pushes to her feet. "Can we talk? Alone. Now. Please."

"Uh-oh," Blake murmurs into his drink.

I follow her down the hall and into the library, her space. Floor-to-ceiling shelves, paperbacks spilling from side tables, a throw blanket still draped over the corner armchair.

She turns on me the second the door closes.

"Did you seriously not only invite yourself, but also invite Milo?"

I drop into the armchair across from hers. Lean forward.

"You'll thank me later."

She shifts her weight and crosses her arms. "What's your problem?"

"You want a list?" I look up at her. "Fine."

"One, this." I gesture toward the house.

"Two, Blake inviting that smug prick."

"Three, you... pushing away the one man who actually shows up for you."

She flinches—barely—but I catch it.

"I'm not going to watch you torch something real just to win an argument with yourself."

Her mouth presses into a thin line, eyes fixed on some spot over my shoulder, probably one of those framed ocean prints Allie picked herself.

When she finally looks at me, there's something behind her gaze. Not anger... or shock. Just hurt.

She nods once. "Got it."

Then she stands too, heads to the door, and leaves.

20
Leo

It's already five a.m. and I'm still lying awake. Again. In a bed that isn't mine. In a house I don't want to be in.

The room faces east. Light'll hit soon. One window, one door. Thick walls. Heavy silence. Too still. It's the kind of place designed to make people feel safe. Doesn't work on me.

The mattress is soft in the wrong way. My back's already pissed. I've been staring at the ceiling for over an hour, counting the rotations of the air vent, listening for anything that might shift.

Nothing does.

Blake threw up three times in our shared bathroom before I shut the door on him. Tequila, or rather the fact that he thinks he can drink like he's still twenty. He cried on the second round. Called me his "emotional anchor" or some shit like that. I didn't stick around for the third.

Didn't help my mood. Not that I had much of one to begin with.

Every time I sleep somewhere new, my body treats it like enemy territory. A matter of habit. I was taught to clock exits before I was old enough to ride a bike. It never turned off. Probably never will.

I sleep fine at home. Triple-secured building. Top-floor. Nobody above me. No one gets in unless I say so. There, my head shuts up. Here? No chance.

Eventually, I sit up. Hoodie. Wallet. Keys. Phone. Shoes by the door—didn't bother unpacking. I grab my bag off the chair and head out.

I open the front door, and I know someone's out here before I see them.

"Leaving already?"

Her voice comes from the left.

I turn my head.

The sky's clear—no clouds, no light pollution. Just an expanse of blue-black. The moon's doing enough to light the stone terrace in front of the house.

Enough to show Isadora sitting on a low garden wall near the column, elbows on her knees, hoodie pulled up, book in hand.

I set the bag down and walk over.

"I don't do well with borrowed beds."

She doesn't move as I take a short jump up and sit beside her. The stone's cold through my sweats.

For a moment, neither of us says anything.

"Can't sleep either?" I ask, eyes on the night stretched out in front of us.

"Not quite. And I didn't want to wake up Milo."

There's a pause. I nod once.

"I probably shouldn't have said his name earlier. During that stupid game."

She doesn't answer. Doesn't look at me.

"I wasn't trying to be a dick." My voice comes out quieter this time. "I was just trying to—"

"Make sure Blake didn't end up with a black eye," she cuts in. "Again."

"Yeah, I guess so."

I glance out toward the lawn. The morning dew's already settling. The smell of wet grass reminds me of our house back in Italy.

"Anyway." I nod at the book. "What are you reading?"

"Kafka." She holds up the cover. *Letters to Milena.*

"Figures."

She raises an eyebrow. "What's that supposed to mean?"

"Just... doesn't surprise me."

She waits, silent. The night breeze comes in cool, and I get this weird urge to grab a blanket inside and wrap her in it. I, of course, don't.

"You like when things hurt a little, don't you?"

She flips a page but doesn't read it.

"Not sure *like* is the right word. We all hurt. I just don't shy away from it."

I stare out at one of the trees near the edge of the property. Its silhouette looks almost painted—blacked out against the sky, blurred at the edges, like something out of a Turner nocturne. Still, but not quiet.

"Well, Kafka definitely didn't shy away from it either."

She glances over at me, eyes curious.

"Just saying—not everything needs to be bled into a letter."

"You're missing the point. Milena wanted to translate him. She was trying to understand him through his words. Which is how eventually they fell in love."

I let out a short laugh.

"What now?" she asks.

"I don't know. I guess I just don't see it."

"You don't see how someone could fall in love with someone else after they've poured their heart out and reached that level of understanding?"

She's kind of a literary snob. It's... oddly charming. I get why she and Milo make sense.

"You're definitely one for language. Words," I say. "You must really hate abstract art."

That makes her look at me. Really look. Then her eyes lift like she's catching a thread of thought.

"I never thought about it like that." A beat. "But yeah... I guess I need words to really feel something."

"What about words that don't mean anything to you?"

She bites her thumbnail. A small tell.

"You mean like a language I don't speak? That's what translators are for. Like Milena. Like me. That's kind of the whole point of us."

"I meant more like the Voynich Manuscript."

Her head tilts. "The what?"

"The Voynich Manuscript. It's this book—five or six hundred years old. Nobody's ever been able to translate it. I've seen a few facsimiles at auctions."

Her brows draw in, eyes narrowing slightly.

I pull out my phone. The screen lights up between us. "Here."

She leans in. Her shoulder brushes mine, barely. Her hair falls forward as she looks.

For a second, all I hear is her breathing.

I scroll through a few images—those dense pages of symbols, the strange drawings of plants that don't exist, the diagrams no one's ever decoded.

She's closer now. Close enough that I can see the reflection of the screen in her eyes.

"Someone spent years writing that. And no one's ever figured it out."

She leans back a little, but not far.

A few seconds go by. May as well be minutes.

"It's a love story," she finally declares.

"What?"

"It's a love story." She repeats it, not louder, just more sure.

I almost laugh, but something in her face keeps me from it.

"I don't think that theory made the shortlist," I say instead. "Pretty sure the main one is coded herbal remedies."

She just shakes her head. Once.

"It doesn't matter. You don't invent a language unless you're desperate to connect. You don't write about remedies unless you want someone else to hurt less. That's love. Whatever this book is, it came from that place."

"So let me get this straight. Everyone hurts, and everything comes from love." I glance at her. "That's quite the predicament you've built yourself."

"Exactly." She says it simply. "You'll get it."

The phone on her lap lights up between us. Milo's name flashes across the screen.

where are you?

come back to bed

I look away before she can catch me reading it.

She hops down from the wall, brushes off her hands.

"It's late. I should head back."

I hand her the book. She tucks it under her arm.

"Yeah. Good night."

"Thanks. You too." She starts toward the door. "See you in the morning, maybe."

She doesn't look back. I don't answer.

And just as the door clicks closed, the first ray of light breaks through.

21
Isadora

THE DRIVE BACK FROM Bedford to New York is always shorter than the journey there.

Probably something to do with how eager we are to arrive and how reluctant we are to leave once it's time. Have you ever noticed that too?

Rami's driving Allie and me to my family house for brunch with my mother. Jamie rode back with Blake. Leo and Hadrian left early yesterday morning. Separately, of course. Hadrian had Marcus pick him up under the excuse of needing to discuss "pressing matters."

Milo took his own car, he's solo.

I'm still not sure how I feel about him just... showing up like that. I know Hadrian invited him, but it feels slightly intrusive that he didn't check with me first.

It's like we've slipped right back into old rhythms, except this time, I'm uncomfortable with how easily he moves through this new space between us.

There's something unfamiliar about it all. Like returning to a city you've visited a hundred times—same streets, same corners—but something's off. And you can't explain what's changed. Only that it has. Not that I'll act on it. Last time was enough of a lesson.

We're driving past Bronxville, and Allie and I are planning Double Day—also known as my birthday, June 20th.

"It needs to be exclusive." Allie taps her fingers against her knee, "but not pretentious."

"What about that new place on Fifth? The one with the rooftop garden?"

"Too public. If we're trying to keep it low-key, we need somewhere with private dining." She grabs her phone. "Let me make a few calls."

Of course, it's not just my birthday. Hence the name. It's Hadrian's, too. Four years apart, born on the same day. I have the theory that we were meant to be twins but some cosmic glitch in the universe separated us by those four years.

"Four years of blissful silence," he likes to say.

"I needed the time. It's a big decision, being related to you," I like to answer.

Double Day was born when we were kids. But it wasn't really a celebration, it was a jailbreak. I was turning seven, Hadrian eleven, and we were both in a state of righteous, full-body fury.

It was our birthday, and instead of spending it with our friends or doing something fun, we were trapped at one of Dad's charity galas. I remember the tightness of the dress, my hair pulled back too sharply, and the nauseating pit in my stomach. The night felt like an endless parade of boring adults who didn't even know our names.

The evening dragged on, and after yet another lady pinched Hadrian's cheek with a saccharine smile and cooed, *"Such a handsome young man,"* Hadrian leaned over to me, voice barely a whisper.

"We're not staying here. Not for one more second."

I shot him a confused look.

"What do you mean?"

"We're going to have some fun," he said, a mischievous glint in his eyes. "Follow me."

I didn't need more convincing. Hadrian always had a way of turning the mundane into a game. We slipped out of the ballroom unnoticed and found a storage room tucked at the back of the venue.

His eyes lit up when he spotted a rack of costumes. Without a word, he tossed me a feathered hat and a velvet cape.

"We're going to make our own party," he declared.

We changed—me in a feathered hat slipping over my eyes, him in a velvet cape he kept tripping on—and got to work. We dumped an entire box of confetti over each other's heads, dragged drapes across the floor like capes, and stacked chairs into a wobbly fort that collapsed twice before we gave up and just crawled under a table. We found an old box of plastic cups and used them to build a tower taller than me, then knocked it down on purpose just to hear the crash. At some point we stole a tray of leftover pastries and dared each other to eat the ones that looked the oldest. We laughed so hard I snorted soda through my nose.

I don't know how long we stayed there, but at some point, we drifted off in our linen fortress. By the time they found us, the gala was over, and several police officers were already looking for us.

We awoke to our grandfather's voice at the door.

"There they are."

"What happened, Grandpa?" Hadrian's voice sounded as sleepy and confused as I was.

"Nothing, you little troublemakers," he said with a laugh. "We just couldn't find you. But now we have, so all's well."

"It was my idea," Hadrian said immediately.

Grandpa scooped me into his arms, eyes twinkling.

"You're not in trouble. I'll have a word with your folks. They're just scared is all. It'll pass."

Then he looked around for the first time—at the confetti on the floor, the crooked tower of chairs, the curtain we'd pulled down and left in a heap—and let out a deep, belly laugh.

"Well, would you look at this mess," he said. "You two really are double trouble, aren't you? Don't worry, it'll be our little secret. I'm glad you got to have your day."

And just like that, Double Trouble Day was born. Eventually, for maturity purposes, it was shortened to Double Day.

This year, it feels especially worth celebrating. Hadrian's turning thirty. And if everything goes according to plan, it'll be his last as a private citizen.

"Done." Allie puts her phone down with a triumphant smile. "The Beekman Hotel it is."

I gasp, wide-eyed. "No way. You actually got the Beekman? That place books forever in advance!"

"A good magician never reveals her tricks." She cracks the window a little further down.

I look out and realize we're driving down Hadrian's street.

As we pass by his building, the main door opens and a tall, fur-draped woman steps outside. Despite the oversized sunglasses, there's no mistaking her. Brielle Warner. The massive coat hangs dramatically off her shoulders, completely unnecessary for a mild spring morning.

She doesn't rush. Just glides toward the sleek car idling at the curb. Every step is perfectly placed, her long legs peeking out with each stride.

The silence that follows is the deafening kind.

Allie drops her gaze, her fingers fidgeting in her lap.

"Is he unable to—"

"He's single, you know. He can do whatever he wants." Her eyes are fixed forward. Then she glances at me and gives me a warm smile.

She's mastered the art of camouflaging pain, my best friend. Not to me, of course. But to everyone else. And I get it, truly—even Allie's weakest smile could light up an entire house. It's no wonder men have worshipped the ground she walks on year after year, with absolutely no success.

A few moments later, we pull up to our family house.

It's a red brick townhouse on a quiet, tree-lined street in Greenwich Village. Cast-iron lacework wraps around the balcony, intricate and dark against the facade. Two white double doors, tall and carved, sit at the top of the stoop, flanked by oversized planters with manicured shrubs. It's old New York, Greek Revival, 1840s. According to Allie, anyway.

A few steps in—past the entryway and the formal sitting room no one uses unless there's press—the hall begins.

It's long and symmetrical, the floors tiled in black and white, the walls lined with photographs in gilded frames: my grandfather with dignitaries, my father shaking hands with Obama, another with Clinton. One that I've always found weird, a blurry candid of him and Madeleine Albright, caught mid-laugh with a glass of wine.

Below them, a row of marble plinths holds bronze busts—Carter men, mostly. Broad shoulders, stern mouths, identical jawlines.

Farther down, the frames shift to wood instead of gold. The photos are less vivid, more sun-faded: my mother speaking at a high-altitude observatory opening in Salta, my aunt beside a polo horse, my great-grandparents outside a stone farmhouse in Córdoba. A saddle rests on a carved bench. Leather reins looped neatly on the wall beside an old pair of stirrups.

Same family. Different soil.

We head toward the breakfast room just past the kitchen. The long oak table is already set, and it smells like blueberry pancakes.

"My girls." My mother walks over with open arms. She pulls us both into a hug. "How was Bedford?"

Allie and I exchange a look.

"Uh oh." She pulls out chairs for us. "Tell me everything."

"We had some unexpected guests." Allie takes a seat.

"Yeah. Hadrian, Blake, and Leo crashed our peaceful retreat." I seat myself too.

Allie squints at me. "And Milo."

My mother raises an eyebrow. "Leo—as in the Sartori heir?"

"Ugh. I hate that word," I complain.

"That's exactly who." Allie's voice has gone up a notch.

My mother giggles. "Maybe don't tell your father you're all hanging out with him," she whispers. "We won't hear the end of it."

Allie and I burst into quiet laughter.

She's always been our biggest ally. Except for that one time she wouldn't let us go to the One Direction concert at Madison Square Garden. Alone. We were fourteen. Still a sore subject.

"So—" Allie turns to my mother, her voice still amused. "Any ideas for Double Day's dress code yet?"

My mother looks up, her face suddenly bright. "Cocktail. Elegant, nothing over the top. And absolutely *no* sequins before sunset."

From the living room, a door creaks open, followed by the sound of Hadrian and my father's voices.

A second later, they slip into the kitchen, probably following the smell of blueberry pancakes. It's a house favorite.

From the doorway to the breakfast room, Hadrian stops short the moment he sees Allie.

My mother either doesn't notice or pretends not to. Probably the latter. She picks up the tray with a bright smile.

"Good morning, you two. Pancakes?"

"I was just leaving," Hadrian says quickly. "I need to head back to Second Front. Marcus is expecting me."

"Yes, Hadrian already had breakfast anyway. We were unfortunate enough to witness the aftermath of it."

The words leave my mouth before I can stop them, and the room stills. My father—already mid-bite—shoots a confused look toward my mother.

Hadrian's expression changes instantly. His eyes narrow at me, and I see the exact moment it clicks. Then his gaze shifts to Allie.

What happens next is a conversation in silence, one only they can understand. His eyes are apologetic, almost pleading. Hers are softer, resigned.

They're both sorry. Just for entirely different reasons.

Hadrian glances back at me, jaw clenched. "Thanks, Isa."

He moves toward the door, his hand lingering on the handle for a beat.

"You are so very welcome."

Hadrian

I'm sorry…

It's fine.

You were just looking out for your best friend.

And who looks out for you?

Don't be dramatic.

Okay

But just so you know, Brielle definitely won't.

You don't even know her.

Trust me. Girl intuition and all that.

22
Hadrian

First stop of the listening tour today.

Laurel is a sliver of farmland and coastline tucked between town lines, where NY-2 starts to stretch into quieter territory. It's where conversations turn from subway lines and rent caps to soil quality, flooding, and who'll keep the post office open.

And in a district this redrawn—where SoHo rooftops and old potato farms now share a ballot—showing up here isn't optional. It's the whole point.

The team and I pile into the SUV, laptops and notepads balanced on our knees. Marcus, seated up front, rattles off social media metrics. My father flips through a folder of prepared remarks across from me.

"Hey." Lydia shifts to the seat next to mine. Her voice is quiet, clearly meant just for me. "I know today's tricky. These anniversaries always are." She waits a beat. "Your grandfather would be proud. He was very proud, actually. He used to say so all the time. Even back then, when you were just a kid."

I nod, forcing a small smile as I look around to make sure no one else is listening. "Thanks."

I drop my gaze back to my notes, pretending to read while a tight knot forms in my throat. I don't like talking about him because I can't do it the way he deserves. It always comes out hollow, edged with something I don't want to name. Can't, either.

I wasn't meant to be doing this without him. He wasn't sick. He wasn't fading. He was full of life, always moving forward. And now I move through it without him.

Maybe I only loved it because I shared it with him. And now that he's gone—that he's been gone for two whole years—I can't figure out if there's anything left of it that belongs to me.

The weeks after he died were rough.

I'd wake up tired and go to bed exhausted from doing nothing. Days bled together. I didn't leave the apartment for days at a time. Barely ate. Drank too much.

One day, Allie got Isa's keys to my place and showed up unannounced.

"What are you doing here?" I asked.

"Bringing lunch. You've canceled on us twice, and I know you—you're not eating."

Without a word, she set the food down, let me eat in silence, and then—when I had no choice but to listen—she said what she'd come to say.

"Hadrian, I get it. Losing someone you love, someone you look up to, is brutal. It's messy. And grief doesn't move in a straight line. It's rather circular." She paused, and when I didn't argue, she added, "But you need to pull yourself together. Feel it. Shut the world out—except me, if you can help it—for as long as you need. And then, you put on your best suit, walk out that door, and live for him. You don't get to disappear into yourself. I won't let you."

She squeezed my hand, and I knew then—there were two hearts in that room. And God help me, they both belonged to her.

Grandpa liked her in that matter-of-fact way he liked people who made sense to him.

"She's such a bright young woman," he told me once, a few years back. "One day, she's going to make some man so happy, every other man around her will wonder how the hell they missed it."

I suspected there was a message in that back then. I know for certain now.

The car comes to a full stop, and I swallow the lump in my throat.

We step into the venue, which is already bustling—a community center filled with folding chairs and locals milling around with coffee cups in hand. This is where the campaign feels real, where the polished ads and carefully crafted tweets collide with the raw, unfiltered voices of the people.

Pale yellow walls are covered with flyers for bake sales and after-school programs. The faint aroma of freshly brewed coffee mingles with the scent of old linoleum. Rows of folding chairs are arranged neatly in the main hall, facing a small podium with a microphone stand. The crowd is a mix of young families, retirees, and local business owners, each holding onto notecards or phones where their questions are likely typed out.

I roll my shoulders once and step toward the podium, scanning the room. The faces looking back at me seem eager. Keen to listen.

"Good morning," I begin, my voice steady. "Thank you all for taking the time to be here today. Listening tours like this are the backbone of any campaign worth its salt. Your concerns and ideas are what will shape our future together."

A smattering of applause ripples through the room—polite, but not overzealous.

I glance at Marcus, stationed at the back of the room with his ever-present tablet, monitoring God-knows-what. He gives me a thumbs-up.

My father is beside him, arms crossed, his usual air of detached authority intact.

Lydia gives me a warm smile. I nod and face the public.

An older man in a plaid shirt raises his hand first. JJ hands him a mic.

"Hi Hadrian. Thanks for being here. My name is Tom. I'm a retired teacher now. But worked at the local school for over forty years." His hand shakes a bit, but he steadies it. "I wanted to ask you about funding for local schools."

I lean forward slightly. "Thank you for that, Tom. And more importantly, thank you for your forty years in the classroom. That kind of dedication shapes communities in ways we can't always measure."

I pause, letting the moment settle.

Then I go on to explain our plan for improving public schools. But really, all I can think about is Grandpa. And how much better he'd be at saying this.

He would've known exactly how to explain the importance of trusting—and equipping—the people shaping the minds of the next generation.

And he would've connected with every single person here, no matter what walk of life they came from.

"A wise man once told me that if you want to measure the strength of a country you should walk into its smallest classroom."

"Thanks," Tom says. His smile looks genuine.

He passes the mic back to JJ just as a piercing screech cuts through the room, followed by the crackle of a megaphone.

"Hadrian Carter-Bello is a fraud!"

Heads whip around. A woman steps into the hall through a side door, holding a bold red-and-black sign that reads: *NO MORE NEPO POLITICIANS.*

Another protestor appears behind her, hoisting a cardboard sign over his head that reads: *DYNASTIES AREN'T DEMOCRACY.*

"We don't vote for last names!" the amplified voice rings out. "We want policy, not pedigree!"

There's a brief silence. Then room erupts into noise—shouts, phones lifted, chairs scraping. A few attendees begin clapping in support, others try to quiet them down. Security steps in quickly, but not fast enough to stop the commotion from building.

Marcus is at my side in seconds.

"We need to go. Now."

We're ushered out the back, the noise behind us swelling like a tide—voices rising, someone shouting my name, a sudden jolt of motion near the mic stand.

JJ pushes the door open, and we spill into the alley behind the building, the warm air intensifying the heat of my skin.

Within minutes, we're back in the SUV. Doors slam. The city begins to move around us again.

No one speaks at first.

Marcus breaks the silence. "Well. That unraveled fast."

I exhale, pressing my fingers to my temples. "How bad is it?"

"It's already trending. TikTok first, now Instagram reels. Local outlets are starting to bite. And the signs? They were made for the cameras."

I stare out the window. "We need to get ahead of it."

"Already drafting." Marcus again. "But this isn't just noise. Those two protestors were the tip of it. Based on the online traction, this was coordinated."

"Nonsense. It was bound to happen." That's my father. "You're a Carter. Of course they're going to weaponize the name. It's lazy." His tone is dismissive, but I catch the flicker in his expression. He's not as calm as he wants us to believe.

Marcus hasn't looked up from his screen. "This isn't lazy. It's calculated."

"It's a local campaign. We're not running for the Oval Office."

"Then explain why we're seeing coordinated posts, identical language across different platforms, burner accounts boosting the original video." Back to Marcus. Voice clipped now. "This isn't organic. It's astroturfing."

"Define astroturfing." That's me asking, though you probably guessed that.

"It means they're manufacturing outrage," Lydia cuts in. "Looks like grassroots, but it's paid, planted, or bot-driven."

Marcus nods in agreement. "They want to make *that* the whole story. Turn his background into a weapon before anyone looks too closely at Mercer's connections."

My father scoffs. "You think Mercer has that kind of operation?"

"I think we'd be idiots to underestimate him," I say. "He's ahead in donor contributions. If he's cozy with big money, this is exactly the kind of tactic they'd bankroll."

"We can't afford to react emotionally," Lydia says matter-of-factly. "The story's already out there. Now we have to decide. Do we correct the record, or do we shift the spotlight?"

Marcus's eyes come off the screen and he looks at me. "They're trying to set the narrative. If we don't move fast, we'll just be responding to it."

I lean back in my seat, the weight of it all pressing down hard. The car feels too quiet, like the silence after a bomb goes off.

"Alright," I say finally. "Do what you need to do. Keep it clean."

My father stays silent. Lydia clicks her pen closed. Marcus swipes a cable from his bag and connects it to his tablet.

Not another word is spoken.

Allie

Isa just told me what happened at the event. You okay?

Better now

Are we okay?

Of course we are.

You think I'd waste mascara over you?

Als…

Hadrian

Say something real

Fine. This sucks. But it's fine. We're fine.

Good

I wouldn't be able to do this otherwise.

23

Isadora

"DID YOU SEE THE pics DeuxMoi just posted of Brielle?" Jamie's eyes are glued to his phone.

Allie and I glance at each other.

We started at this bar near Lexington and 59th, close to where Jamie works. Yeah, you guessed it. He's a finance bro. And proud of it.

Somehow, a drink turned into three, and now we're sprawled across my living room, shoes off, jackets draped over chairs, half-eaten takeout on the table and open wine somewhere nearby.

He turns his phone toward us.

She's walking out of some place downtown. Impossibly tall, striking, effortless. Skin like sunlight on bronze. White cropped tank with *nepo baby* printed across the front in small black letters. Low-rise jeans. Gold belt. Straight hair, long and sharp. Glossed lips. No smile.

That print is no coincidence, let me tell you that much.

"Apparently, she's dating someone. But DeuxMoi is double-checking the data before she confirms it."

I roll my eyes. "Well, let's hope they don't confirm shit and she can keep her private life... private."

Jamie looks up from his phone. "Uh oh. What's with the mood?"

"No mood. Just... fair, you know? It's not nice to have your life dissected online."

"Did they publish something mean about you?" He tosses his phone on the table. "I'll personally take care of it."

I shake my head. "Not sure Hadrian can say the same."

"Bullshit." He grabs his phone again. "He's America's sweet boy. Have you even read what they wrote about him lately?"

Allie sits up straighter. "Like what?"

Jamie holds up his screen again. "Here. *Civetta Confidential* this morning."

It's Hadrian, biking along the West Side Highway. Helmet hooked to his backpack, sunglasses low on his nose. Tan arms, rolled-up sleeves, that annoyingly photogenic smile he only ever pulls in motion. I read the caption.

America's golden son—okay, technically grandson—rides again. Clean politics, a jawline that could pass legislation, and just enough scruff to seem relatable. Do we even deserve him?

His hair's tousled from the wind, short and sun-lightened at the tips.

"Gosh. Is he reading this? No wonder he's been insufferable."

"Here, check this one." Jamie swipes to another screenshot.

It's a close-up from the same day—Hadrian mid-laugh, head tilted slightly, sun catching the exact green of his eyes as if the light was in on it.

Those eyes could fix the economy. Green like money, incisive like judgment. If you're not in love with Hadrian Carter-Bello, you're lying.

Allie and I roll our eyes so dramatically it deserves its own entry on DeuxMoi.

Jamie smirks. "I mean, the guy's good-looking. I get the appeal."

I glance at Allie. Her face is cold as stone, but there's the slightest flush blooming across her cheeks. With her pale skin, it's impossible to miss.

"Come on. He looks like someone *playing* a politician, not actually running."

I gag, loud and theatrical. "Enough about Hadrian. Can we please discuss something else?"

Silence.

"Like... the book translation proposal I got yesterday and have no clue what to do about?"

"What?" Allie's head snaps toward me. "That's amazing! What kind of book?"

"It's this Argentinian indie author. She wants me to translate her debut novel. It's a thriller. She's hoping to publish in the fall, so it's a bit of a rush, but doable."

"So Spanish to English?" Jamie asks. "You could do that in your sleep."

"Thanks, Jamie. But honestly, it feels kind of out of my depth. I've never done fiction before—not officially, anyway."

Allie rolls her eyes. "Please. You've been side-eyeing fiction like it's the hot guy in our building."

I try not to laugh. Fail. "I guess. But now that it's real, I kind of forgot why I wanted to dip my toes in to begin with."

"I can tell you why," she fires back. Because you love fiction. Like, a concerning amount. Because you're a language genius. And because you've been feeling itchy about your life for a while now." She tilts her head. "Career-wise, I mean."

"Does that mean we get to go to Argentina again? I've been dreaming about that steak we had our last night there," Jamie practically moans. "Charred edges, buttery center, chimichurri dripping down the side... I swear I can taste it if I think hard enough."

"You're unwell, but honestly? Valid. I'd kill to be back at your family's finca in *Las Sierras de Córdoba."* Allie let's out a sigh. "Such a dream. The hills, the air, the way everything smells like pine and dust and wild oregano."

"That was probably *peperina,*" I say, smiling at the memory.

Life is definitely... different there. Slower. Kinder.

The buzzer goes off, cutting through our reminiscence.

I cross the room to the wall panel.

"Hey, Felix," I say into the speaker.

"Good evening, Miss Carter-Bello. I have a flower delivery here for you."

"Who is it from?"

"The note isn't visible, ma'am."

"Please, Felix. Call me Isadora. And sure, send them up."

The only person I can imagine sending me flowers early for my birthday is my grandmother Genevieve. She loves getting ahead of herself. She gifted me my first car, months before I could even drive it.

"We should leave," Allie says, rising from her seat. "Kathy will be here any minute."

Jamie follows, brushing invisible lint off his sleeve. "Thanks again for coming. I wouldn't survive an entire dinner with my mother solo."

Someone knocks on the door. I open it to find a delivery guy holding a bucket. Not a vase. An actual white metal bucket, with a red ribbon tied around the handle.

The flowers are enormous. Roses, sunflowers, lilies, all jammed together like they're fighting for space. There's even baby's breath.

Jamie lets out a low whistle. "Subtle."

Allie steps in for a closer look. "Oh my God. Are those carnations and orchids in the same bucket?" She recoils, hand to her chest. "Yeah, no. I can't unsee this. Jamie, let's go. And pray Kathy didn't catch this coming through the lobby."

Jamie snorts. "Fair. See you, Is."

They head out, leaving me alone with this floral fever dream and a confused frown.

I set the bucket on the counter and pull out the note wedged between two stems.

> *Ten years ago today, you kissed me for the first time. Well, technically, I think I kissed you. But you didn't pull away, so I've been counting it as mutual ever since. We were kids. I didn't know anything. Except that I wanted that moment to last longer. Still do.*
>
> *Happy us day.*
>
> *M*

I set the note down, eyes wide in realization. Did I seriously forget our anniversary?

I mean, we're not technically back together. Yet. But still.

I grab my phone instinctively, about to send him a thank you text, then stop myself.

Ten years. That's almost half my life.

And I keep falling short. Or back? Not sure. But it's like I keep reducing us to less.

Have you ever noticed how candle wax holds a memory? If you blow it out too early the first time—before the wax reaches the edges—it never burns right again. I feel like I'm doing that with Milo. Messing it up. Burning it wrong.

And now our candle will only ever reach the edge of these missteps, where I let it falter. Again and again.

24

Leo

I DON'T BELIEVE IN friendship.

Figured we should get that out of the way straight off.

And it's not cynicism. Not looking for a debate, either. I just don't. That's it. No further clarification required.

I understand that most people do. That they see their friends as sacred fixtures in their lives. Something unshakable, irreplaceable. A die-on-that-hill kind of belief. Like they need them to navigate life. Maybe even to understand it?

It's just never been me.

I don't think people are worth that kind of trust. Or vulnerability. I guess I'm what you'd call a lone wolf, though not in a poetic, misunderstood-genius sort of way. Just... a logistical one.

I was homeschooled. Tight personal security at the time. Paranoid father. In other words, the kind of childhood that doesn't exactly foster lifelong bonds.

And now, as an adult, all the traveling to remote places, the dealings with people who have the wrong interests. Same story.

I just don't believe in it.

Which is why this little social experiment with Blake and his inner circle has been... well, interesting to say the least.

Exhausting, if I'm being honest.

I don't know how they handle so many emotions all at once, all the time. How they remember who's mad at who and who's dating who and who cried in someone's bathroom last week. The dynamics are a bit... much.

They've got the most packed social calendar I've ever seen. It's been something close to my personal hell, considering I normally wouldn't show up to these things even if I were getting paid. But duty calls.

Tonight's event is the Frick Collection's Spring Garden Party, hosted at their Fifth Avenue mansion. At least it's the kind of thing with no paparazzi, no flashes, barely even a whisper in the press. Perfect for the kind of people who like to relax just enough to accidentally give one or two secrets away.

My phone starts ringing. Speak of the devil.

"Hey."

"Yo," Blake says, followed by a loud screech—metal on glass or something—and then the sound of something shattering. Then silence.

"You good?" I ask.

"Not exactly... Irina's losing her shit."

"YOU FUCKING BASTARD!" Irina's screams detonate in the background—like, full banshee-mode. "YOU THINK I WON'T FIND HER? I *WILL*, BLAKE, AND I'LL SHOVE THAT PHONE UP YOUR CHEATING ASS!"

"Babe, I'm on the phone." Blake's voice is actually shaky. No grin this time, I can tell you that much.

There's a crashing sound. Another scream. Something slams shut.

"You in trouble?" I ask coolly, though I'm actually a little concerned.

"Yeah, kind of. Something about me accidentally liking some girl's photo on Instagram." Emphasis on the word accidentally like it's his legal defense.

"Brutal."

Moronic, really.

"Yeah... anyway, don't think I'll make it to the Garden Party. Just told the others. Hadrian's out too."

"All good. I'm already headed there."

"You sure? Those chill parties are always the worst. That's why I invited you, so I wouldn't suffer alone." He pauses. "Shit. Something's burning. Gotta go, dude. Later."

The line cuts.

Well. Hope he makes it.

I grab a set of keys and head out, taking the black Range Rover Autobiography—armored, bulletproof, and quiet as a ghost.

A short drive later, I pull in by the side entrance. I hate the main-door moment at any party.

"The party entrance is around—"

The security guard clocks me, pauses, then just nods.

I walk straight in.

Inside the mansion, the air shifts. Cool, dry. The foyer opens into a long gallery. Stone floors, dim light. Paintings on every wall. Nothing contemporary, nothing abstract.

To the left, Rembrandt's self-portrait—dark eyes under heavy shadow, worn fabric, expression unreadable. Next to it, Van Dyck's portrait of Frans Snyders, dressed in black with one hand over his chest like he's guarding something.

Farther down, Vermeer's Mistress and Maid, lit just enough to catch the yellow of the silk dress. A sealed letter in the maid's hand. Both women paused mid-thought.

The walls are lined with more: El Greco, Gainsborough, Goya. Gilded frames, thick as bricks.

In the center of the room, a marble table holds a pair of Sevres vases, blue with gold accents, lids perfectly centered. Behind them, a Titian Madonna, softer in tone but heavy in presence.

On the far side, a wood-paneled reading room. Leather-bound volumes in glass cases. A globe. A long, green-shaded lamp left on.

I keep walking past a set of bronze busts. Past Holbein's portrait of Thomas More—searching eyes, pressed lips, red velvet sleeves.

I enjoy a good art moment as much as anyone with taste. But linen from Flanders and oil from Florence don't hold a candle to gems forged underground by earth itself. And you can quote me on that.

The music drifts faintly now from the garden. A shift in tone. The scent of jasmine cuts through the stone and varnish.

I push through the tall glass doors.

Outside, lanterns swing above tables in perfect rows. The gravel path is swept. The hedges trimmed to the inch.

I adjust my cuff, then step into the night.

25

Isadora

"Milo, please—"

"It's fine, Scout. I just thought we were doing better. Guess not. Or at least not enough to be your plus-one."

I sigh and press my fingers to the spot between my temple and cheek, where a headache is starting to bloom.

"Just... have fun, okay? Love you."

He waits for me to say something. I don't. Then the line goes dead.

I think what gets me most is knowing we've hit that place where being with him hurts just as much as not being with him. And that kind of defeats the point, doesn't it?

I walk out of the bathroom and Allie's waiting, holding both our drinks.

"That sounded tense."

"He's mad."

She hands me mine. "Because you forgot your anniversary?"

"That, and because I didn't ask him to come tonight."

"Right."

"There you are." Jamie pops up, just on the edge of tipsy. "That blonde from the Cartier Foundation board? She's got that whole rich-divorcee thing going. Absolute menace."

I let out the kind of laugh that, if my mother were here, she'd already be shaking her head at in disapproval.

"At least someone's winning tonight," Allie murmurs into her drink.

"Come on." Jamie grabs us both. "Let's go dance."

Jamie links his arm through Allie's, nudges me forward with his shoulder, and we head toward the garden.

I recognize some of the faces. Theodora Lynn stands near the reflecting pool, deep in conversation with someone from the MoMA board. I haven't spoken to her since she was seeing Hadrian, if my memory serves me right. She's laughing now with a woman I know I've seen before, though I can't quite place her.

Ray Dalio hovers just off the path, scanning the crowd the way he always does. Two men I'd met once at an art benefit drift past mid-conversation, champagne glasses in hand, nodding politely as they go. There's something missing from the scene. Not a face, more like a weight that usually steadies a crowd like this.

Everything is softly lit—trees glowing from underneath, candles flickering along the stone balustrades. It's humid out here. Not enough to call it sweat, but enough to make the back of my neck feel... dewy. Not quite damp. Just close.

I glance up. Are those—?

"Mother. Six o'clock," Jamie says out of the corner of his mouth.

"Allie, Isadora, darlings," Kathy Ellington beams, already mid-approach. "So glad you could make it."

"Hi, Kathy." We both smile.

She turns to Allie. "Tell me—what do we think of the suspended lemons?"

Allie tilts her head, glancing up. Dozens of real lemons—some whole, some sliced—are hanging from fine golden threads above the terrace, like a floating orchard. The scent is faint but sharp, citrus cutting through candlewax and perfume.

"They're... unforgettable. Like if Sofia Coppola directed a fever dream set in Amalfi."

Kathy laughs, delighted. "You're hired."

Allie keeps her gaze upward, smiling softly.

"Oh, come on. How much are your parents paying you to run their store? I'll double it."

Allie's smile widens.

"Triple?"

"Thanks, Kathy. Maybe one day."

"Well, don't wait too long. I need someone who gets the absurdity *and* the assignment." Then she turns to me. "Isadora, help me talk some sense into her?"

"I'll do my best."

She touches my arm lightly. "How's your brother holding up?"

"He's good," I say. "Focused. A little wired. But he's good."

"Tell him I'm proud. He looked already elected. And you know I only speak the truth when it comes to compliments. Or the lack thereof."

"That," Jamie says, "I can vouch for."

She lifts a hand to her earpiece, something I hadn't even noticed until now. Pauses. Then breathes out.

"False alarm. All handled." She turns to Jamie. "Anyway, James—where's your brother? I haven't seen him."

"Caught up in some Irina drama. You know Blake."

Kathy rolls her eyes. "I do. That girl makes everything about her—even when it isn't."

She lifts a hand to her earpiece again and holds up a finger toward Jamie. Her expression shifts. Her eyes widen.

"Okay, this is certainly not a false alarm." Brief pause. "The pianist just fainted into the koi pond." She stares at Allie with horror written all over her face, already going a little pale.

Allie nods. "Let's go." Then turn back to us. "Wish me luck."

"You've got this," I say.

And then they're gone, Kathy striding ahead like she's crossing a runway, and Allie jogging behind.

Jamie's gone still beside me, his posture suddenly tight. I follow his gaze and see the blonde woman from Cartier—who just so happens to be Ava Sterling, as in Greg Sterling's wife—walking straight toward us.

I lean in slightly. "Jamie," I whisper. "That's Ava Sterling. She's definitely not a divorcee."

Jamie shrugs, unconcerned. "Yet."

He doesn't stop smiling. Neither does she, who walks straight up to him, stands close—very *close*—and leans in to whisper something in his ear.

Jamie's eyes go wide. "You good if I disappear?"

I grin. "Totally. Have fun."

He kisses me on the cheek and vanishes with her through a side arch.

I glance around, spot Theodora across the garden, and start walking toward her.

My phone buzzes in my clutch. It's Allie.

Might be a while. The pianist is threatening to sue.

Apparently the koi staged an attack on his God-given hands.

And what did Kathy have to say about that?

"Please. I've seen better on a Starbucks barista."

LOL

See you at home

I slip past the terrace's edge, careful not to draw attention to myself—shoulders back, pace steady. I don't look too fast, don't check my phone again, don't make eye contact with anyone.

My mother would faint if she knew I was breaking protocol. *You never leave without thanking the host, Isadora. It's rude, it's obvious, and it makes people talk.*

I keep walking.

"Leaving already?"

His voice comes from behind.

I freeze. And I can feel it—the collision of two instincts slamming into each other, hard and fast. One telling me to turn around. The other telling me I should know better. Probably even run.

For a moment, I don't move.

But the stronger pull wins, and so I turn.

The suit fits like it was built onto him—midnight black, sharp-shouldered, not a crease out of place. His shirt cuff stark against the ink curling over the back of his hand. Hair just as dark.

Eyes, stormier than ever.

"I don't do well with borrowed smiles," I say, flashing him one anyway.

He laughs, low. And it sounds better than I thought it would.

The music cuts suddenly. The lights follow. Power outage? Great. Kathy's going to *love* this.

A strange hush settles over the throng of guests. I can't tell if it's clinking glass, a cough across the lawn, or just the murmurs thinning out, but something makes my stomach drop. I look for Rami somewhere in his usual silent radius, but he's nowhere to be found.

Leo's eyes shift past me. His jaw ticks.

I turn, just in time to see two waiters break from formation near the hedge line.

One lunges. For a split of a second, I think he's coming to me. But he pivots toward Sophie Dumas, the Belgian ambassador's wife.

He grabs her. She jerks back. A beat of confusion. And then a scream. High, sharp.

Leo's hand clamps around my wrist.

"Don't look. Walk."

"What's happ—"

"Now, Isadora."

He pulls, and I follow.

The lawn blurs as we weave past stunned guests and frozen waiters. Someone shouts. A chair scrapes violently against stone. Glass shatters.

I glance over my shoulder—just once—and see Sophie being dragged off, her face fully panicked.

"Faster," he orders.

We reach the hedge wall. There's a narrow slit between branches where the catering staff cut through. My heels catch in the uneven ground. I stumble.

His hand grabs my arm, steadies me in one swift motion.

We slip through the gap.

A side gate stands ahead, half open, the guard station empty.

"Where are the guards?" I gasp.

"Gone," he picks up his pace. "Move."

We push through the gate and out onto the side street. The sudden quiet feels wrong in more ways than one. I bend forward, catching my breath, head spinning.

I look up at him.

"Was that a kidnapping?"

He doesn't answer.

"Oh my god. It was. It was, wasn't it?"

My breath spikes. My ribs are tight.

"Leo." My voice splits in half.

"I know. Allie."

"I'm calling Rami."

I dig into my clutch for the Dot.

"That won't work now."

"What? Why not—"

"Just—hold on." His voice is taut. "Give me a second to think."

"I'm going back in." I turn toward the gate.

He grabs my arm. "No, you're not."

"Are you insane? My best friend is in there!" I rip my arm free. "Try and stop me."

He catches me again—this time, firmer. Less careful.

"You're absolutely not going back in there."

His grip stays locked as he pulls out his phone. One word in a language I don't recognize, clipped and urgent. Then he's already moving, guiding me down the bloc, relentless.

"Let me go right now!" I twist against him, breath catching.

He stops short. Turns to face me.

"I'm taking you to my car. It's armored and signal-blocked. Don't worry, you're safe—"

"Safe?" A sound slips out of my throat. It's a laugh, but closer to a choke. "This is not what safe feels like."

"You *are* safe. Because I say so."

My pulse is a drumbeat.

"I'll go back for Allie myself. You have my word. But you are not going in there again." His voice is calm. His face, too.

I nod once. My fingers are trembling as I fumble for my phone. I can barely hit the screen.

"I'll call the police—"

"They already know."

I look up at him.

"Then I'll call Hadrian."

I scroll. Find his name. Press call.

One ring. Two. Three.

"Isa."

"Hadrian." My voice barely makes it out.

"What's going on? Where are you?"

I open my mouth, but nothing comes. My throat clenches. I can hear my own heartbeat but not my thoughts.

Leo takes the phone from my hand.

"Hadrian. There's been an incident at the Garden Party. Isadora's safe, I got her out. But Allie's still inside."

Silence. Then muffled words I can't make out.

"Yes. See you there."

He hands me my phone back and opens the passenger door. I slide in without thinking.

"Lock it from here." He points to a flat button set into the door panel. "Do not open it. Not for anyone but me or Hadrian. Understood?"

I can only nod.

26

Hadrian

"THAT'S WHAT WE PAY you for! To take care of her. At all times." I stop walking in circles and take a step towards Rami. "Where the hell were you?"

He just stands there, taking it. Blank.

"Where is she?"

I swing toward him, jaw tight. "She's home. Safe. No thanks to *you.*"

"I'll go back to my post." He doesn't make eye contact. "To her."

I take another step forward. My hand's already in the air, finger pointed.

"She trusts you. If anything had happened—if anything had *happened,* Rami—"

"Hadrian," Allie's voice cuts through my tirade.

"You can yell all night and it still won't change the fact that she's okay."

I want to look at her. I can't. My eyes are locked on Rami.

"I swear to God—"

"*Hadrian.*"

I breathe hard through my nose. My throat is tight, voice on the edge of cracking.

"Just leave. Now."

Rami nods once and walks away.

I stand there, chest heaving, fists curled tight.

"You're not mad at him," Allie says from behind me.

I turn to her. "Don't."

She just looks at me, kind in that maddening way only she can manage.

"Go home," she says. "You're shaking."

"Als—" Nothing comes out at first. I swallow. "You were in there too."

I pause again, jaw tight. "Allie, if something—"

"Nothing happened," she cuts in. "We were just locked in a room for a while. That's all."

I nod toward the FBI agents. "A woman was taken, Allie."

"Yes. And Isa and I are fine."

"I think it's time you had your own security detail."

She actually snorts. I don't move.

"Oh—you're serious."

"Why wouldn't I be? This can't surprise you, Als."

"Well, it does a bit. Especially coming from the man who refuses a bodyguard and used to ditch the Secret Service for sport when Hadrian Sr. was in office."

I almost smile at the memory, but it's not enough to pull me off course. "You know my reasons. And this isn't the same."

"Why?" The defiance is instant. "Because I'm a woman?"

"That's not—" I exhale, shoulders down. "I just want you safe."

"I get that. I do." She pauses. "But I can't have someone tracking everywhere I go, everyone I see, like they get a say in it. That's not something I'm willing to surrender. That's exactly why I left home."

I know what she means. But it hits like a blow. Freedom shouldn't be the tax of our lives. Least of all hers. I'd trade anything to spare her that.

"And what if it happens again? What's the point of so-called freedom if it leaves you exposed?"

She folds her arms. "And all those security details tonight? What good were they?"

"So you admit it." I step closer, eyes fixed on hers. "You were in danger tonight."

Her shoulders sag, breath catching on the exhale. She's tired, hair loose, eyes rimmed red, and somehow it only makes her more arresting. It's almost scientific, the way weariness distorts everyone else yet refines her into something more beautiful.

"Okay," I say quietly. "I'll let it go. For tonight. Just promise me you'll think about it?"

She gives me a tired smile. Then a small, reluctant nod.

We're standing just off the Garden Court. Red and blue lights flash through the glass dome, washing the marble statues in something almost unreal. Inside, FBI jackets fill the space.

Kathy's pacing in circles near the East Gallery. Her heels click unevenly against the mosaic floor, one broken strap dangling. She keeps asking the same questions in different ways, not waiting for answers. No one's answering her anymore.

Someone's crying softly. I think it's the same someone who threw up into a fern earlier.

"Let's get out of here. I'll take you home."

She shakes her head. "I need to stay here with Kathy. She needs me."

"I need you." I let out a breath. "To be safe. Please. Let's just go."

"I really can't. I mean, look at her. She's about two seconds from trying to fight a statue."

I glance over. Kathy's gesturing wildly at a guard now, mascara halfway down her face, her clutch on the floor that she dropped twenty minutes ago.

"I can call Blake."

"Don't. He'll just make it worse."

Fair.

"Jamie?"

"He left with someone, still not answering his phone."

I press my palm against the edge of a column, rolling my shoulders back like that might settle something in my chest. My jaw's still clenched. I force it to loosen.

"Okay then. I'll go bring you some coffee."

"I'm fine, Hadrian. Really. And also, whatever they're serving in paper cups by the main entrance doesn't qualify as coffee."

"I'd never dream of making you drink that coffee." I pull out my phone. "Ordering you Sant Ambroeus. Postmates is still running."

She tries not to smile. Fails. "Flat white, extra hot?"

"With a pistachio croissant."

"You're the best."

Her words hang there. So does she. Like this whole situation made her forget about everything else, and her own words just reminded her.

She blushes. It's the softest shade of pink. And it goes right through what's left of my anger and evaporates it.

"Thanks," she says, softer now.

"You're so welcome." I offer a little grin as I tap in the order, including a note for the driver to drop it off at the service entrance.

"Now," I say, sliding my phone back into my pocket, "tell me how I can help."

She hesitates, then looks toward Kathy, still pacing erratically, a lost shoe in one hand now.

"Can you arrange transportation for the high-profile guests? Discreet. Back entrance. Once the questioning's done."

"Consider it handled."

27
Leo

I SHOVE THROUGH THE doors of my father's place. Full fury, tunnel vision, pulse spiking hard enough to choke.

The air hits first: sweat, skin, smoke. All of it cloying. Rotten with excess.

Low music thrums, bodies are spilled across the room, draped over chairs, slumped in corners like discarded coats. Couches too soft to hold anyone upright. A woman in lingerie and pearls leans into a man twice her age, her mouth slack, eyes glazed. Another sways by the fireplace, barefoot, holding a champagne flute and nothing else.

No one even flinches when I storm in.

I find him in the middle of it all. Of course.

He's just standing there, flanked by two women who are barely pretending to whisper in his ear.

One of them I recognize instantly. The new receptionist.

I don't stop walking. I don't speak.

I go straight for him, hand to the collar, then higher, fist to the base of his throat.

I shove him back hard, dragging him toward the nearest wall.

"Was that you?" I snarl.

He blinks sloppily. Eyes glassy. Pupils blown. He's high out of his mind. Probably on one of those untraceable blends he has flown in from Geneva that doesn't even have a street name.

Pity he won't feel a thing of this. Not today, at least.

He coughs. Still smiling.

"Leonello?" He looks at me and smiles. Really, *smiles* at me. like I've just come home for Christmas.

"What are you doing here?"

I tighten my grip.

"Was it you?" I snap again, voice rough.

He huffs a laugh. His breath reeks of stale cigars, whiskey, and something chemical.

I can feel my patience fracturing. Hairline cracks, splitting fast.

"The kidnapping," I say through clenched teeth. "Was. It. You?"

His pupils twitch. His eyes land on mine and actually stay there this time. But there's still that haze, like he's watching me through a thick glass window.

Someone grabs me from behind, an arm locks across my chest.

I drop low. Twist hard.

My elbow drives into his ribs. He chokes on impact.

I pivot, hook my foot behind his ankle, pull him off balance, and take us both down.

He hits the floor with a thud. My knee lands on his chest. Fist cocked, ready to drop.

Then I see his face.

OG.

"Fuck," I mutter, pulling back before I crack his jaw.

He rolls onto his side, coughing hard. Tries to speak but chokes on his words. One arm wrapped around his ribs.

"I was just trying to get you off him," he gasps. "Not start a fucking brawl."

Another breath. He struggles up to one knee, still catching air.

"You can't just walk in and go for his throat, Leone."

I stand, heart still racing. My father hasn't moved. He's watching now, mouth twisted somewhere between amusement and disdain. Funny thing is, no one else is.

"I asked him a question."

"What question?"

"The kidnapping. Was it him?"

OG's face shifts instantly. A muscle twitches. His jaw tightens. No words. Just a glance toward the left-hand door. He moves. I follow.

We step into my father's studio. Opposite of white and sterile. And yet, to me, this place will always be a madhouse.

OG closes the door behind me and locks it.

He pours two whiskeys and hands me one.

"Dumas's wife?"

I nod.

"How do you know about it?"

I scoff. "How do I *know*? I was *there*, goddammit."

His grip on the glass tightens. Eyes widen.

"You weren't on the guest list."

I stare at him.

He gives me nothing.

"I swear to God, OG, if you don't talk right now—"

He raises both hands. "Still doesn't explain why you thought it was *us*."

"Do you think I'm fucking stupid? Or are you just stalling?"

He sinks into the leather couch.

"We had to make a move." Takes a sip. "The Belgians are gaining ground."

I stand there, silent. Waiting.

"Mikhailov's the corridor. Kazakhstan moves through him. Whoever gets him gets Asia, plain and simple. And he's being courted hard. The Belgians sent in diplomats, deals, state dinners."

He pauses. Still don't say anything.

"So we decided to test the waters. See what shakes loose."

"And no one thought I should be looped in?" I ask, eyes on the bookshelf behind him, lined with hardcovers no one reads.

"You know how this works. Fewer people, lesser risk."

I let out a dry laugh. "Right. My father shielding me out of love. Touching."

His brow twitches. "Why do you care? You were never in danger. You know that."

"There were other people there."

"There are *always* other people. Since when does that bother you?"

"It doesn't," I snap. "I just don't like being kept in the dark on operations I'm actively involved in."

"Then maybe do your job and land Mikhailov. Time's running out."

I set the glass down—untouched—and rise to my feet.

"I'm working on it. Hard to do when there's a kidnapping at the fucking party and I have to play hero."

He angles his chin, watching me now.

"Irina was there too?"

I'm already at the door, unlocking it.

"Just keep me in the loop. For fuck's sake."

28

Isadora

"Mom, I'm fine. I promise," I repeat for the third time since we sat down.

She shakes her head, visibly deflated. "I still don't understand why Milo wasn't with you."

"He couldn't make it." I place the napkin on my lap, avoiding her eyes.

We're at BG Restaurant, our usual table by the window. White lilies in a low vase. The same waiter who's been here since I was at Dalton. She ordered the grilled asparagus and zucchini and the crispy burrata. I didn't answer fast enough when he asked me, so she ordered for me too.

She hasn't stopped calling all week. And now, face-to-face, the questions are multiplying.

"Have you been reading what I sent you on PTSD?" She cuts a piece of bread into precise little squares. "You know it can manifest weeks after the incident. Flashbacks, sleep disruption, memory issues, low appetite, panic—"

"I'm not panicking."

She narrows her eyes, searching my face. Whatever she's looking for there, she won't find it.

"I mean—I'm fine. I haven't had a single... anything."

"Sometimes the body doesn't register trauma right away. You might not even notice what's shifted until something triggers it."

"Mom," I sigh. "You're not a therapist."

"No." She stirs her consommé. "But I did raise two kids in a very high-profile family, through three campaign cycles and two near-scandals. That has to count for something."

I take a slow sip of water, trying not to snap at her, which requires a lot of reminding myself that she's just trying to help.

She pulls out her phone. "There's a doctor in SoHo. He runs a private practice—quite reputable, actually. I already forwarded you his details. He specializes in EMDR, somatic therapy, tapping—whatever it takes."

"Tapping?"

"It's more effective than it sounds. Kathy swears by it."

"I'll keep it in mind," I lie.

She sets her spoon down and folds her napkin. "How's Allie holding up?"

"She's... busy. Mostly with Kathy. I think this whole thing finally got her what she wanted: Allie caving in."

She gives me the look she always used to when I was on the verge of trouble.

"That came out wrong," I add.

She dabs the corner of her mouth. "Don't be tasteless, Isadora. A woman is still missing."

"Any news on that?"

She gives a small shrug. "Not quite. Your father says it will be resolved, but it's turning into something of an international matter now."

I don't say anything.

"They may need additional translators. The Belgian ambassador in question is an old-guard Walloon—only French may be spoken in his presence. Shall I put your name forward?"

"No, thank you. I've got my hands full at the moment."

She tilts her head. "Really?" A hint of a smile. "Doing what?"

"It's a little outside my usual comfort zone."

One eyebrow lifts.

"I've taken on a book translation."

The other eyebrow joins it.

"I wasn't aware you were switching careers."

"Switching careers?" I lift my napkin to the corner of my mouth, even though my plate's untouched. "It's still translating."

She reaches for her lemonade, takes a slow sip, then sets the glass down with delicate precision.

"If you say so." Her voice drips with condescension. "It just seems rather... different from what you're trained for."

I breathe out, already fully regretting telling her about it.

“But then again, I suppose literary fiction is just as relevant as nuclear treaties these days.”

I glance up from my plate to meet her eyes. There was a time—back when I was a kid—when my mother and I fought almost daily. I haven’t felt that kind of anger toward her in a long time. Until maybe now.

We make eye contact, and her expression immediately softens. She feels it too.

“Excuse me,” she says, gathering her handbag. “I need to freshen up.”

We lock eyes again, and I give her a small nod. Her eyes are the exact same impossible green as Hadrian’s—the kind that shift with the weather, or whatever it is that makes them flicker from sea glass to sage to moss. The rest of her face is me. Or mine is hers. Which used to make it worse, honestly. Mostly because every time I was mad at her, it felt like I was actually mad at a mirror.

Our worst stretch was when I was fourteen.

My parents were going through a rough patch, filled with loud, relentless arguments over the smallest things. Whether to repaint the study or leave it. The “correct” way to stack dishes. The music played at dinner.

They wouldn’t stop fighting. And I wouldn’t stop taking my father’s side. No matter what the argument was about, I always aligned with him. It was like my mother and I were speaking different languages. English and Spanish—the two we shared—suddenly felt useless. She’d say *red*, and all I heard was *blood*.

Once, I even went as far as telling her that I wished I were like Allie, living in a city far away from her.

“You have no idea what you’re talking about,” she said, her voice shaky. “And don’t you dare say that lightly ever again.”

Shortly after my grandmother took a bad fall—shattered her hip—my mother flew to Argentina for a few months to help. Maybe a year?

I was relieved at first. Then I started missing her, which confused me. Then the guilt came, all at once. Then the missing again.

I truly hated that year. It’s my least favorite one. I think it’s Hadrian’s too. He was out every night, coming home when the sky was already light, his eyes bloodshot. He stopped eating. Stopped speaking unless he had to.

It all unraveled the night Blake called. He said things were bad. That I needed to come get him before someone called our father.

Luckily, Allie was staying over that night. We were about to sneak out when we found Rami in the hallway—already tense, already sensing something was off. When we told him where Hadrian was and that we needed to go, he said no immediately, and in a way that made it clear it wasn't up for debate.

Allie—calm as ever—just looked him in the eye and said something along the lines of, "Fine. I'll go by myself. You can explain my father why you let me go alone. And just know, if something happens to me, I've already decided I'll be the haunting type of ghost."

He just swore under his breath and told us to stay close at all times.

Allie handled the rest. She talked us past the doorman with a lie so smooth I barely registered it. Said her father was on the board, or the advisory council, or something equally threatening. Then we were in the elevator. Rami stood right behind us the whole time, silent and alert.

We knocked once. A big guy—tall, broad—opened the door, took one look at us, laughed, and started to close it. But then Rami stepped forward, placing his hand firmly against the door. The guy looked at him, then nodded and let us in.

Blake was standing against the wall in the back room, arms crossed, not moving. The lights were low. Music and smoke filled the air. Hadrian was slouched over a poker table, too limp in the chair, too pale under the light, too young to be surrounded by men who looked... older. Ruthless. His shirt was wrinkled, half untucked. A lowball glass was tipping sideways near his elbow, the edge of the felt damp with whatever he hadn't finished. Crumpled bills were balled in one fist. Poker chips stacked like towers in front of him.

He didn't even notice us come in. I froze the moment I saw him like that. Allie didn't. She stepped forward without hesitation.

"Hadrian," she said, almost shyly, but off-key enough to make everyone else pause and turn.

He didn't move.

"Hadrian," she said again, louder this time. Steadier. "Look at me. Now."

He blinked, slowly. His head turned like it took effort. He saw her. Then he saw me. His pupils were wide, too wide, and his expression was blank. Like whatever was inside him had gone out for air.

"We're leaving," Allie said. "Get up."

He didn't argue. He didn't even speak. He stood up, pulled a wad of bills from his pocket, dropped them on the table, and walked out.

Rami stepped aside to let him pass. He swept the room with a single glance, then waited for Allie and me before following us out.

In the car, Allie sat forward, arms crossed tight. "Why would you let those gross older men take advantage of you like that?" She wasn't yelling, just deadly serious.

He didn't answer. Just kept staring out the window, face blank, his knuckles white against his knees.

"Those aren't friends, Hadrian. They were using you. And you let them."

"Fuck you," he said, barely above a whisper.

My eyes widened. Even Rami's shoulders tensed.

"Fuck you too. And honestly? Fuck Blake. You're both morons."

I thought that was it for them. I still do, every so often. But somehow, it never is.

"Sorry," my mother's voice pulls me back. "Your father called. Dessert?"

"I'm fine, thanks."

I place my fork and knife diagonally on the right side of the plate.

"Lovely. I'll have them bring the check."

29
Hadrian

"THE WHAT?" I ASK, locking my bike outside Second Front.

"Post-Mortem party. Tonight," Blake says. "Abingdon Street. You know, the place I bought to singlehandedly save democracy."

I can hear the grin in his voice.

"I don't know, Blake. I've got a ton to do."

"Come on, Second. Just a few people. Everyone's been on edge. We need it. Is and Allie already said yes. Right, Jamie?"

"Yep. Just texted me." Jamie's voice comes through the phone.

I start walking toward the entrance.

"Yo?" Blake insists.

"Sure. See you later."

I hang up as I make my way in.

Ten minutes left of lunch, so the war room is nearly empty.

Marcus is still at his desk, shoulders hunched, fingers moving fast. The look on his face makes my stomach knot.

I spot JJ by the whiteboard, rearranging precinct pins and muttering into a headset, probably scheduling another round of local interviews. I give him a quick wave and head straight to Marcus.

"What's happening?" I ask, trying to sound casual. Calm.

He snaps his head up. "Hey—Second, didn't see you come in. Nothing major, just running diagnostics. Making sure your engagement metrics hold through the next cycle."

"Marcus."

He exhales hard, runs a hand through his hair, or really yanks at it.

"I just didn't want to worry you. You've got enough on your plate."

I don't wait for a reply. I walk toward one of the smaller offices. "Come with me."

He follows, and we both sit at the cramped meeting table.

"Talk to me."

He hesitates. "You sure?"

"Yes," I lie.

"I've tried every trick. Bot dampeners, reputation scrubs, even soft astroturfing. Your image has definitely improved, but honestly, I think most of that's organic. You've got a fanbase now. Think they're calling themselves the 'Hadrianists' or something."

His eyes are red-rimmed, the bags beneath them darker than usual.

"Media coverage is fine too. But the attacks haven't stopped. Negative comment waves keep hitting every couple of days, and I can't block them fast enough."

"How bad is it?" I know I have to ask, but I really wish I hadn't.

"You're trending on TikTok right now," he says, voice low. "And some of the comments are—"

"Show me."

He pauses. Narrow his eyes at me.

"You sure?"

I nod.

He pulls a cord from his bag and plugs his tablet into the ceiling projector. A second later, the wall flares to life with a white background, black text, nothing softened.

The first comment appears. I blink.

Hadrian Carter-Bello couldn't lead a lemonade stand, let alone a district.

Great start. Another fades in:

Why does he always look like he's on the verge of crying? Pathetic.

I feel it in my chest. That one's been going around.

Just another trust fund kid playing politician.

Right. So we're recycling the classics.

Hadrian Carter-Bello? More like Hadrian Carter-Blah-blah. Zero substance.

I huff a laugh. That one's almost impressive, in how aggressively unfunny it is.

If mediocrity had a face, it'd be his.

Okay.

This is what privilege looks like: failing upward.

"Enough."

My voice cuts through the room harder than I mean it to. Marcus freezes. The tablet stays in his hand. The projector hums softly in the silence.

His lips press into a thin line, he feels sorry for me.

"And that's just the first few hundred," he says quietly.

I breathe in. Out.

"How am I supposed to focus on the campaign—on actual policy—when I'm busy fighting TikTok trolls and comment section carnage every day?"

"Ideally? You shouldn't be." Marcus adjusts his glasses, fingers already flying across his screen. "Get off socials now. I'll take over monitoring. You don't need that poison in your bloodstream."

I nod. He's right. I've spent more nights than I care to admit doomscrolling through "Hadrian Carter-Bello fails again" edits.

"Here. Hand me your phone."

I pass it over. He clicks through a few settings, swipes, taps a passcode I never gave him, and hands it back.

"Done. You're officially locked out of your own spiral."

I half-smile. "Thanks."

He looks up now, serious. "But, Second—look, I can only work with so many unpaid interns, half-broken bots, and good intentions. If you want this shit handled properly, I need real budget."

I exhale. Loud. "How much?"

"Minimum fifty grand. Seventy-five if you want it fast."

I blink.

"That covers a private digital defense firm I know out of Berlin—ex-cybersecurity guys. Used to handle cleanup for government contracts. They're discreet. Surgical. And they'll remove what doesn't belong."

He scrolls again, calm as ever.

"I'd also bring in two freelancers I trust. One's a sentiment analyst, the other's a platform strategist. They'll amplify the right narratives, push accurate coverage to the top, and intercept smear loops before they trend."

He glances back up. "They'll work their magic and make sure the truth doesn't get buried under noise."

That's nearly what we'd budgeted for voter transport across the district. Or a month of community grants. Or expanding canvassing teams in the lower precincts.

"Okay. I'll see what I can do."

His expression settles, clearly pleased. Just as Lydia opens the door and peeks in.

Marcus stands, taking the tablet I've grown to hate with him.

"I'll be making some calls."

Lydia lets him pass through.

"Can I have a second?"

"Of course."

She closes the door behind her.

"You okay?"

I shake my head. "We need to pivot. Enough defense. I want offense. Precision hits. No more playing nice."

She studies me for a moment.

"It's a different tone than you started with."

I lean back. "Good."

"What exactly do you want to change?"

"Messaging. Soundbites. I want moments that land like punches. No more soft-focus hope and unity, we've tried that. Let's stop hoping they'll listen. Let's make them."

She shifts her weight slightly.

"That's a sharp pivot, Hadrian. We built this strategy around your grandfather's tone—measured, dignified, above the noise. That was the plan."

Her eyes are on me. I can feel them but don't return it.

"You were the one who wanted to follow his model, his steps. Statesmanlike. Principled, not reactive."

I glance at the projector wall, still faintly glowing.

"Yeah, well—he's not here to show us, is he?" I stand up, ready to leave. "This one's on me."

She nods. But I already know she wholeheartedly disagrees.

30
Isadora

"Blake and James Ellington. Aren't you a sight for sore eyes," Allie declares as we walk through the door.

"You're here!" Jamie gets to his feet. "Finally."

"Hey, Face Card Duo." Blake lifts his glass toward us with a half-smile.

Allie pauses mid-step. "Is that a thing?"

"Always was," Jamie answers, already nudging us toward the bar.

The flat opens wide with tall windows cracked for air and curtains pulled back just enough to let the city glow in. Music pulses from a speaker tucked into a bookshelf, something bass-heavy but smooth. People are already talking over it, glasses in hand.

A long wooden table near the far wall is crowded with bottles, cups, and half-finished drinks. Someone's tossed a jacket over one of the dining chairs, and a record sleeve lies face-down beside a plate of untouched olives.

Then there's the sofa. Massive doesn't begin to cover it. It's shaped like a horseshoe, maybe even a full circle if you count the two extra extensions curling at the ends. Deep green velvet, or is it charcoal?

Allie stares at it, visibly horrified. "The sofa... not a sight for sore eyes. More like a sore sight, period."

Apparently, Blake bought this flat just so he could vote for Hadrian. A ridiculous, oddly on-brand gesture.

Maxwell and his twin brother Archie are near the bar. For a while, they were everywhere, same year as Blake and Hadrian at Dalton. Same energy too. Now they play pro soccer for NYCFC, which somehow made them even louder. Their parents—Silvana and Gregor Harrowby—built their empire by securing premium water rights in the Alps. They're the ones behind that bottle, shaped like a glass teardrop, no label, just a silver cap. Now they also own half of Long Island's wine country and most of the Hamptons social calendar.

Marcus stands by the window, saying something that makes Hadrian laugh. Irina's stretched out on the far end of the sofa, scarlet slip dress, stiletto heels, a long-stemmed glass untouched in her hand.

Rami finds his back corner as we make it to the drinking table. Allie pours herself a dirty gin martini—extra olives, no vermouth.

The front door creaks open, and a collective gasp cuts through the music. I turn around.

It's Brielle Warner and Lyric... something. That model from the last Jacquemus campaign, the one with the floating runway in the middle of the sea.

They look... how do I say this nicely? Completely out of place. Like they thought they were coming to a red-carpet event and ended up in a frat house.

Brielle's in a body-hugging sequined mini, metallic gold, paired with stilettos that do not belong on hardwood floors. Lyric's wearing a feathered corset top, low-slung jeans, and a vintage Dior saddlebag.

It's over the top, sure. But let's be honest—they look incredible. And every guy here knows it. It's written all over their faces.

The open space unfolds like a movie scene from where we stand. Brielle locks eyes with Hadrian—who, judging by his expression, had no idea she'd be here tonight. Still, he doesn't flinch as she glides toward him, unwavering.

She reaches him, kisses his cheek, and leaves a perfect imprint of lipstick behind.

"Is Milo coming?" Allie asks, turning away from Hadrian and Brielle.

I shake my head in response.

Blake claps his hands once, loud enough to re-center the room.

"Group therapy, let's go."

That's all it takes. People start folding into the massive sofa, forming a loose, uneven circle. Cushions shift, limbs tangle. Glasses clink against side tables. Maxwell ends up sprawled sideways. Archie takes the floor unnecessarily, considering how big the sofa is.

Irina settles into the crook between the armrest and Blake. A second later, she's fishing a velvet pouch out of her bag, unfolding it like origami. Blake pulls out a black Amex and smooths a line across the back of his phone like he's done it a hundred times.

He leans in, takes a quick sniff. She follows suit.

He offers it to Hadrian. He shakes his head—barely a motion—and passes. I breathe out.

Marcus leans in, one fluid line, and goes right in.

Then the front door creaks open again.

Allie's elbow hits my ribcage. I turn around. It's Leo.

And the sight of him sends something strange flickering up my neck and down my spine. And this is not happening. I'm certainly, logically, not having physical reactions to other guys.

That would be... well, it simply isn't.

Blake whistles low.

"Well, look who decided to show up."

He doesn't smile. Just walks in, dark eyes scanning the room before landing on the sofa circle next to Lyric, who's now practically glowing, her lips parted, eyes wide.

Blake hands him a whiskey glass as someone changes the music—warmer now, a little grimy.

Maxwell leans back. "Alright—what's the most unhinged thing you've read about yourself. Or someone here. Bonus points if it made *Page Six.*"

Archie laughs, already halfway through his drink. "Someone said I faked a hamstring injury to fly to Ibiza with... a certain pop star."

Maxwell nods. "You did, though."

"Allegedly."

"I once saw a Reddit thread claiming I'm the product of a fertility clause in my grandfather's will," Allie says.

"Wait—are you not?" Jamie asks.

She gives him the finger and keeps drinking.

Jamie turns to Brielle. "Be honest—your *Golden Hour* co-star. The food thing. True?"

Brielle barely blinks. "Only on press tours. Otherwise it's coke and gummy bears."

Laughter rolls through. Someone coughs. Someone spills.

Marcus leans forward, his glass tracing a slow circle in his hand.

"Actually—urban legend that can be clarified real quick..."

He looks at Leo.

"Sartori—truth or myth: the ledger exists?"

"The what?" Brielle says as she drops her head against Hadrian's shoulder. Allie flinches.

"The Sartori Ledger."

"Wait." Max straightens, eyes locked on Leo. "Are you Leo Sartori? Like... Lupo Sartori's son?"

Allie's gaze flicks my way, intrigued. I meet it.

Max exhales sharply, a low hiss through his teeth. "Jesus."

"Hello?" Brielle insists. "Someone explain?"

Marcus leans back and lets the moment stretch. The rest of the room has gone unusually quiet.

"It's supposed to be a list. Handwritten. Coded. Passed down like scripture."

He pauses, glancing at Leo, probably looking for permission to continue.

"Names of everyone who's ever touched the blood trade. Not just dealers—presidents, oil heirs, monarchs. Uncut conflict diamonds. Smuggled. Hidden. Empires built off invisible stones." His voice deepens. "A whole laundering network—art collections, offshore mines, private airstrips. All of it."

Archie shifts in his seat. Brielle leans forward, eyes wide. Lyric has stopped scrolling her phone. Even Blake's stopped grinning.

Marcus glances around.

"Some say if it ever went public, it wouldn't be a scandal—it'd be collapse. Hiroshima-level. Lights-out for half the world's power structure."

No one says a word. All eyes are on Leo.

Irina snorts, breaking the spell. "Americans. You sure love your little conspiracies."

Jamie leans forward. "Some have to be true. Moon landing, Denver Airport, the whole birds-aren't-real thing—pick your poison."

Irina flicks her hand, bored. "I don't say they're all false. I say the way you obsess over them is childish. Where I come from, power isn't a riddle for dinner parties. It exists. You don't poke at it. Unless you're the bigger bear."

Marcus tips his chin toward Leo. "Well?"

Then Leo glances around the circle. A dry smile tugs at the corner of his mouth. "Total myth."

"Sure." Marcus laughs coolly. "But hypothetically, if something like that *did* exist... would you tell us?"

Leo smiles again. For the first time tonight, stormy eyes flick to me, then back to Marcus.

"Most certainly not."

31

Leo

"My Papa works with diamonds too," says Irina, eyes on the skyline, not on us.

That's the understatement of the year.

Blake's mouth twitches. "Does he?"

The party's louder now. A new wave of people rolled in, some familiar faces. You'd recognize a few. Especially that one pop singer. Phones are out, music's up, the whole thing turned glossier in seconds. But out here, on the balcony, it's cooler. Sharper. Easier to breathe.

Irina exhales a ribbon of vape smoke. "The other night he's watching some ancient film—men in bad suits, no one remotely attractive—and suddenly he starts talking about India. At first I think he's lost his mind. Then I realize he's not watching the film, he's on the phone. Very serious. Talking about cutting this new diamond in ten."

She pauses for another hit, eyes half-lidded.

Blake's brow furrows, then he turns toward me. "What would that even mean?"

"The India thing?" Irina cuts in. "That's easy. Good labor, cheaper too."

"But why would someone cut a diamond in ten?" Blake asks.

It's the right question. Just not for the reason he thinks.

"To control it," I say. "A large rough stone can be cleaved or sawn into smaller pieces to optimize yield, minimize risk, and simplify transport. Big stones draw attention. Smaller ones are easier to certify, insure, move across borders. And they sell faster."

Ten, though... Maybe there's one diamond I can think of that came close. Most of it ended up in the Queen of England's crown.

A brittle crack slices through the air, glass or porcelain, maybe both. The balcony goes still for half a second. Then the glass door slides open and the noise pours out with Jamie.

"Blake—someone just broke the bathroom sink."

Isadora's behind him. "It's Archie. He's completely lost it. You need to send him home."

"Jesus Christ." Blake's already moving by the time the words leave him, disappearing back into the chaos. Irina follows, unhurried.

Isadora's attention settles on me. I hold it.

"Um—I'll go help him," Jamie says, already backing toward the door.

She steps beside me, facing the city.

It's a stupid question. I ask it anyway. "How are you?"

"I'm fine, thanks." Her voice is soft, and it clashes with the crispy air. Softens it. Don't ask me how. I had no clue voices could do that either. "I just wanted to thank you for the other day. I didn't get the chance before Hadrian showed up and sent me straight home."

I check her from the corner of my eye. She's focused on the skyline. Her hair's up. Lips pinker than usual.

"You don't have to thank me. I did what anyone would've done in my place."

"I'm still grateful. And for making sure Allie was safe too."

The silence stretches and so does the city ahead of us.

A soft wind stirs. Her perfume reaches me. It smells like a garden I've never been to.

She's close enough for me to notice a small scar just above her right eyebrow, and the thought of her bleeding sends something cold down my spine.

"You're good at that," she says suddenly.

"At what?"

"At pretending you're not looking when you certainly are."

I huff a laugh, shake my head.

She shrugs. Her mouth curves, barely. "Guess I misread that."

I force my gaze up from her mouth, tighten my hand around the glass.

"You didn't."

She gives me a half smile. It's mad what even half of one does. Knocks the air clean out of me.

"There you are." Hadrian's voice cuts in from behind us, and we both turn to him.

"I need you and Rami to help me get Archie home."

"Nope. Not my shift," she says, flat.

Hadrian's expression shifts, almost desperate. He jerks his chin toward the house.

Through the glass doors, Allie's trying to steady Archie, who's wearing a toilet seat around his neck and looks seconds from face-planting. Brielle and Lyric are doubled over, phones out, probably filming.

"Please?" Hadrian forces a smile.

She glances at me. I'm already watching her.

A few seconds pass. Might as well be hours.

"Sure," she sighs. "Lead the way."

32
Hadrian

I'M WAITING FOR ISA to drop by mine as she promised.

She lets herself in as usual as I'm plating the leftovers from the night before.

She wrinkles her nose. "Let me guess." She slides onto a stool at the kitchen counter. "You haven't eaten anything today except maybe three espressos and one almond."

"A protein bar," I say.

"Living the dream."

I take a seat next to her.

"So?" She leans forward. "Shoot."

I stretch across the counter and snag the marked-up draft of my next speech.

"It's for the South Shore Leadership Forum next week. Donors, press, the party machine. Every word's going to be dissected. I need it to hit hard, without giving anyone an excuse to call it a meltdown."

She nods once and starts reading.

"Tell me what you think."

Isa's always been unnervingly good at this—structure, pacing, delivery, subtext, the whole anatomy of a message. She dissects languages like they're frogs on a middle school biology tray.

She skims the first half fast. Then doubles back. Slower now. Her brow starts to knit by the second paragraph, and I know that look, it's the same one she used to give me when I returned her books with the spines cracked.

She stops reading. Then looks up.

"Hadrian, you're leaning too hard into fear." She sets the draft down. "You're framing the Second District like a war zone."

"It kind of is," I reply, mouth full of cold rice.

"That's not the point," she says, already gearing up. "You don't build order by stoking panic."

"You sound like—" I stop myself.

"He said that. To you. Over and over."

I set my fork down. "Isa, you know what this city's like right now. People aren't voting from a place of hope, they're voting from exhaustion. From fear. From barely keeping the lights on."

"But if you meet them there—if you only ever speak to the fear—you'll never remind them what else is possible. What they deserve."

She says it like she still believes in deserving things. I study her—my sister who spent her whole life translating other people's words but never quite learned how to name what she wants. And yet somehow—annoyingly, even—she always seems to know exactly what I do.

"You're not wrong," I say. "But the system we're in doesn't reward speeches that dream, but rather those that don't make the donors nervous."

She stiffens. "So you are playing the game."

"I'm protecting the campaign," I say, voice a little sharper now. "That's not the same thing."

"You sure?"

I stand, move to the window. A kid rides past on a bike, laughing like the world still makes sense. Must be nice.

"You think I wanted this? To spend half my time putting out fires I didn't start? To waste budget on digital defense?" I glance back at her. "They were already setting the tone with false narratives, coordinated outrage, protests that somehow line up with my calendar to the minute."

I walk back to the table.

"The conversation was being hijacked before I even opened my mouth. So yeah, I'm going offensive. If I don't, I'll be letting everyone else define me before I ever get to show up."

She doesn't answer right away. I glance back at her. She's not angry. Her lips are pressed tight, somewhere between a smile and disappointment. Which somehow makes it worse.

"What happens when you win?" she says quietly. "And there's nothing left of you to lead with?"

I laugh under my breath. "Great. Will everyone just stop quoting Grandpa at me?"

She blinks rapidly. "Since when do you hate that?"

"Since you're all using it against me." I shake my head. "No one gets to decide what he wanted for me. That was between me and him."

"Sorry." Her eyes are shinier than before. "Sometimes I forget how hard this must be for you."

It hangs there, unspoken.

"I miss him," she adds.

"I miss him too." I swallow. "But that doesn't change the fact that it's just me now doing this. And I'm doing the best I can."

She smiles, but it doesn't quite reach her eyes. She picks up the speech again, scans it like she might find some lost part of me buried in the footnotes.

"Anyway." I clear my throat. "You're asking the right questions. I just don't have the answers. Not easy ones, at least."

She leans back in her chair. "I think you do. Somewhere deep down, you do. You've just forgotten how to trust them."

I nod. Not because I agree. Because I don't want to keep arguing with her when I know she's speaking from the same history I am. Just on a different timeline.

"Thanks for the notes," I say. "I'll rewrite some of it."

She stands and smooths her skirt. "I have to get back to work. I'm kind of on a tight schedule."

"The book?"

She nods. "Proving even harder than I thought it'd be."

"You'll be fine."

She gives me a small smile. "You will too. Just... don't forget who you are in the process, okay?"

"I'll try."

She's halfway to the door when she turns back. "And eat something real today. Please. Or I'll tell Mom you're not. Maybe then she'll stop sending me articles about trauma therapy and finally redirect that energy onto you."

She shuts the door behind her.

Silence returns. I stare at the draft, hearing her voice in every line. Not judging, just reminding me that we were raised on ideals, even if we didn't always live up to them.

My phone buzzes.

Brielle.

She called last night. Came over. We slipped back into something easy.

The sex is good. The cocaine is better. And that, I know, is the problem.

I tell myself I'll say no this time. I even mean it.

But then again... why not.

Same time tonight?

Sure

Bring the good stuff

If this sky lacks its North Star, I might as well savor the passing ones as I drift hopelessly lost at sea.

33

Isadora

Big day tomorrow.

I'm standing outside the pop-up showroom Allie threw together at one of her favorite boutiques in Tribeca, just for the Double Day gala. Her word choice, evidently. It was supposed to be a surprise. Emphasis on *supposed to*.

From the street alone, I can already see the movement inside. Light flares against glass, shadows flickering across walls. I brace myself and push the door open.

The showroom is exactly what I expect, and somehow more.

A grand, glittering chandelier hangs overhead, its crystals cascading like frozen fireworks onto a floor teeming with motion. Assistants buzz around in what can only be described as perfectly organized chaos, arranging velvet swatches on display tables.

Allie stands atop a stepladder at the far end of the room, adjusting the angle of a gold-framed mirror shaped like a sunburst. Her pale blonde hair swings as she shouts instructions with military flair.

"No, the Chesterfields go *under* the arch, not through it. Shall we go over spatial reasoning again?"

A store assistant scurries past me, nearly tripping over what I'm fairly certain is a $10,000 rug.

This—*this* is Allie's element. Herding chaos into something aesthetic. I've seen her do it since we were teenagers. She turned our high school cafeteria into a passable prom venue with just string lights and fabric drapes. She also helped Kathy throw her divorce party and even turned it into a branding opportunity. *"Because love is temporary, but copper accents are forever."* Her parents hated that one. Kathy, on the other hand, adored it.

She spots me and her eyes immediately go wide. "Is, close your eyes. Right now."

I don't.

"This is supposed to be a surprise!"

"I don't recall a surprise being part of the plan."

"Which is usually how surprises work," she mutters, rolling her eyes as she descends the stepladder.

"Was it Elena?" she asks, scanning me like she can read the answer off my cheekbones. "Jamie?"

I say nothing.

She groans. "He truly can't keep a secret, can he?"

I smile. "I'm neither confirming nor denying that one."

She starts walking toward me, assistants parting around her like she's the Miranda Priestly of interior design.

"Your mother had some concerns when I pitched the idea," she says breezily. "Said she thought we were being low-key about the party."

She bends to pick up a stray crystal napkin ring from the floor and twirls it between her fingers.

"But no one outside us actually knows what Double Day is. So I say—let them wonder." She flashes a mischievous smile.

"Clearly it worked," I mutter, nodding toward the long line forming outside. Judging by the velvet ropes and the countdown clock displayed on the entry screen, I'm guessing there's some kind of blink-and-you-miss-it time slot.

"All right, since you're already here..." She grabs my elbow. "You're on duty. Let's go."

Before I can protest, she's steering me toward a cluster of mood boards.

"Tell me which of these says *lavish but approachable*."

I squint, arm outstretched, trying to figure out which specific swatch or sketch she's referring to, when a martini appears in my hand.

Allie gets one too, handed off wordlessly by a passing assistant.

"Do all the clients get this five-star service?" I ask, raising an eyebrow.

"Only my favorite ones."

We clink glasses. Sip. Mine's on an empty stomach, but I'm not complaining.

"Tablecloths," she declares, already marching toward the samples. "We're deciding now. I'm between the triple-stitched linen or the handwoven Belgian cotton. The latter has a better fall, but the stitching on the linen is practically couture."

"I'm vetoing all the beige ones."

"It's *ecru*," she snaps, scandalized. "And it's timeless."

"It's the color of unseasoned chicken."

She gives me a long, exasperated look. "Here. Let me show you the sketch."

She pulls a tablet from under a stack of mood boards and swipes it to life like she's opening a portal. On the screen are floor plans annotated in looping gold calligraphy. Floating florals. Hanging glass orbs.

"Here." She zooms in. "The ice sculpture will melt *tragically* into a bed of orchids. And here's where the jazz quartet will play loud enough to drown out small talk. Over here, we'll have vintage armchairs to make the influencers feel like they're sitting in someone's Upper East Side parlor, circa 1963."

"Allie—" I blink, looking around. "This is just... wow."

She gives me a proud little grin.

"I know. And there's more, but I'll keep those up my sleeve."

An alarm goes off. Allie grabs her phone and silences it with a sigh. "Everyone—lunchtime. Twenty minutes."

The room empties in seconds as Allie collapses onto a sample sofa (Italian leather, *forbidden to sit on*, according to the small but deeply threatening sign attached). I follow, dropping beside her.

The buzz fades as everyone drifts off, and we're left behind. Just the two of us, finally still.

Allie sinks deeper. "So..." she starts, swirling what's left of her drink. "Maxwell stopped by earlier. He's persistent, I'll give him that. He showed up at the gym yesterday too. 'Accidentally.' During my Pilates class. Wearing a shirt two sizes too small."

I laugh. "Classic Max. Forever allergic to subtlety."

"To be fair," she says, holding up a finger, "he looked good. Like, annoyingly good."

Which, to be completely clear, he always does. Max was the hot one at school—athletic, tan, that Baywatch look that drove us all a little insane.

I shoot her a complicit look. "I say you go for it."

She shakes her head. "Don't think so."

"He's hot," I press. "Tall, broad-shouldered, annoyingly symmetrical."

"I'm just not into him. There should be a vibe. And there's no such thing."

"I still think it's worth a shot. You never know. And it'd be so easy. We've known him since forever."

She glances over. Tilts her head. The air between us shifts, light talk gone.

"Is, I can't go there just because it'd be easy." Her eyes meet mine. "Or because I don't know where else to go."

"But—"

"I love you. You know that. So I'm just going to say this one more time. For the record, okay?"

I nod. A little scared, not much point denying it.

"You've convinced yourself that easy is good. And you're right, easy can be good. Safe. Cozy. I get that. If that's what you want—an easy life—then well done, babes. Because that's what you have."

I exhale something that feels like solid air.

"But if you ever feel even the smallest flicker, like I *know* you've had before. An itch, let's call it. Please, Is. Just—don't settle."

She grabs my free hand and squeezes it. "I'll be here. We'll figure it out together."

I smile at her. And it's more than just acknowledgement. Because now, today, like every day for the past few months, I can feel the truth of what I need to—want to—*must* do creeping back up. And once again, I physically shove it down. Straight from the knot in my throat to somewhere deep enough to give me a break from it. Even if it's just for twenty-four hours.

"I'll make you a deal," I say. "If you let me choose the playlist, I'll take back my beige veto."

She narrows her eyes. "It's ecru."

I hold out my pinky. "Deal?"

She looks at it. Then at me. Her smile grows sideways and just a little sneaky.

"Deal."

34
Leo

MY FATHER SLIDES AN envelope across the desk.

"Use this."

I open it. Glance once.

Then tear it down the center without blinking.

"You sick fuck."

He doesn't flinch, just leans back and lights his cigar like we're discussing quarterly reports. Smoke curls around his face, softening nothing.

"Oh please. You think I'd give you the original?"

I step forward. The carpet muffles my feet, but OG still shifts beside him like he senses the danger.

Fuck him.

"You listen to me, real close."

I jab a finger toward the envelope's remains.

"I'm not doing this. Not for you. Not for anyone."

He exhales, amused. Cheeks puff. That greedy, satisfied look that turns my stomach.

"It's just a little skin, Leone. Don't be dramatic."

My hands clench at my sides, nails carving half-moons into my palms.

My chest burns. My pulse pounds so hard it drowns out the air.

One more word. Say one more fucking word.

"She took the pictures." He shrugs, unbothered. "She can live with the consequences."

Then he kicks his legs up on the desk—Italian leather shoes crossed at the ankle like this is all a game.

"Just rattle her a little. Ask for a meeting with his father. Nothing heavy."

I breathe in through my nose. My jaw locks so tight it pops. A muscle flares in my cheek. I taste blood.

And still, I don't look at him. Because I know his face too well. The slight raise of his left brow when he's bluffing. The way his lips twist—not quite into a smile, but close—when he thinks he's won.

I know every line. Every crease of that rotten face. And that's what sickens me most. Not just what he's capable of. But that I know—without a doubt—he'd do it. He'd release those photos. Violate her privacy to make his point.

"In no world." My voice is low, shaking from the weight of everything I'm not letting explode. "Do you understand me? In no way—no timeline, no version of reality—will you use something like that as leverage. You'll have to climb over my fucking grave first."

OG half-raises his hands like I'm a ticking bomb he's trying to defuse. "Easy, Leone. You're overreacting." His tone is cautious.

"You stay the fuck out of this." I glance from OG back to my father. "You're both disgusting. Sick to the bone."

My father lets out a low laugh. "All these new lines you're suddenly drawing—in this business, they get you killed. Just so you know."

I spin toward the door, chest heaving. Rage has too many edges, this is my least favorite one.

"I'm out."

My shoulders shake with the force of holding it all in. My hands—still fists—hang heavy at my sides.

"A week," my father calls after me. "Or those pictures get to see the light."

35
Hadrian

"I THINK SOMEONE TIPPED the paps," Marcus says as we approach the SUV.

"How do you even know that?"

"I hacked—" He stops walking. "Actually, never mind. Plausible deniability and all that."

"Great. Makes me feel great."

We step into the car.

Blake's already in, legs stretched, suit flawless: midnight-blue and open collar. His hair's slicked back just enough to signal effort, and he's nursing a glass of probably whiskey. He lifts it in my direction. "Double Day, baby."

Next to him, Irina lights a cigarette, of course without asking if anyone minds. Silver-grey dress. There's a knife tucked into the band of her heel—I know because she showed me once.

Marcus slides in beside them, already checking something on his tablet. No tie, sleeves pushed up. He's not smiling, which means he's working—probably cross-checking crowd reports and threat levels.

Jamie's wedged between Irina and Isa, knees stiff, eyes wide, trying to look unfazed. I can tell he's trying not to flinch every time Irina exhales in his direction.

I must be feeling brave because I look at Allie next.

Her blonde hair is swept up, loose strands falling softly around her face. Her neck and shoulders are bare. The soft curve of her collarbone catches the low light, and just for a second, I let my eyes linger.

Her dress is deep navy. Fitted at the waist, clean lines, fabric pooling at her ankles. A shade darker than her eyes, which are locked on mine now. Steady but razored enough to cut through me.

Her lips are a darker shade of pink tonight. And all I can think of is that color smudged against my shirt collar.

I'd wear it like a badge of honor.

She doesn't say anything. Just looks.

I nod once. She nods back.

"Hi," I say as I clear my throat.

"Hi." Her gaze doesn't waver, though there's something else in it. Calm on the surface, but deeper waters underneath.

"Happy birthday, Second," Jamie offers.

"Thanks, Jamie."

Blake lifts his glass again. "To us. And to the glorious fucking mess waiting on the other side—may it be loud, slightly criminal, and worth every headline."

I snort. "No headlines tonight. For Marcus's sake."

Marcus smirks without looking up. "Appreciated."

Rami pulls away from the curb, and a muffled swell of music fills the car. It's something smooth, with just enough bass to make it feel like the night hasn't quite started yet.

I lean back in my seat, trying to focus on anything but Allie, but it's like trying to ignore a train coming at you at full speed.

"So," Marcus says, eyes still on his screen. "Press is definitely camped outside. Someone tipped them off."

"What?" Allie's voice jumps. "I made everyone on staff sign NDAs."

"Then it was a guest," I say, shrugging. "Don't stress. We'll walk in. No stops, no quotes."

"We could slip in through the back," Jamie offers.

"We're not sneaking into our own damn party," Isa snaps.

Blake downs the rest of his drink and sets down the glass. "Yeah, that's fucked. Let them get their shots. We clean up well anyway."

Irina exhales smoke. "If one of those bottom-feeding worms tries to photograph me from the wrong angle, I swear on my country I will bury his camera—and his balls—in matching coffins."

Silence.

Jamie shifts closer to Isa.

Allie bursts out laughing.

I glance at her again. That face. That smile. You can try to describe it—go ahead. Try. Start with the eyes, move to the nose, land on the mouth. I dare you to get it right. You won't.

And maybe I'm out of line—but right now, I want the world to know. To see me holding her hand and lose their damn minds. Let the flashbulbs blind us. Let them talk. Let them come to the quiet realization that at the end of the day, it's her laugh lighting it all up. Blinding them, for once. Blinding all of us. Gladly. I'd go blind a thousand times just to hear it again.

You know that feeling? The one that makes you a little too brave and the next thing you know you are running into a house on fire because she's in there and nothing else matters.

And maybe we could figure it out. Bend the rules. Rewrite the stars. Because right now, looking at her like this, God help me. I feel like I could take on the whole world.

She glances back at me. And the truth just... hangs there.

I'm in love with her. And it's killing me. Because my hands are tied. And these chains were never about bravery.

She looks away.

I do too.

That's what it's come to. My life is now reduced to stolen moments. Flash frames I hoard like a starving man rationing scraps, not enough to satisfy, just enough to survive.

We finally pull up to the entrance of The Beekman Hotel. The stone steps are lit by warm lanterns, the awning taut above the double doors. Two doormen stand by, nodding at guests as they disappear into the glow of the lobby.

Across the street, the photographers are already waiting—maybe twenty, maybe more. Not quite a mob, but enough to set your nerves on edge. The second our car slows, lenses swing toward us like a pack of rifles cocking in unison. Flashes start firing. Names are called out, and they are not even close. Odd.

One of them edges forward, elbow raised for a better shot, before security pushes him back with a low warning.

Rami steps out from the driver's seat and opens the door on Isa's side.

That familiar, invisible pressure builds behind my ribs. My chest tightens the way it always does when I stop feeling like a person and start feeling like a target.

I try to breathe in, but Allie's perfume clings to the air wrapping itself around my neck like it's trying to strangle me.

Marcus catches my eye. "I got you."

I nod. My voice wouldn't come out if I tried.

Isa steps out first with Marcus and I follow, heart pounding.

Blake and Irina are already pacing inside. Jamie is ushering Allie forward. I slow, giving them a second to clear the line of fire.

I force a smile toward the cameras, just long enough to be usable. Then I turn, and freeze.

Brielle's already outside, walking straight towards me.

She's in a red slip dress that moves like poured wine. The neckline is deep, the slit deeper, and the fabric catches every flicker of light. Hair sleek on one side. Face done to perfection.

"Second, there you are!"

My stomach flips. The air thickens. Every camera swings toward us.

I walk toward her knowing exactly how this will look. Flashes explode. My ears ring.

"Happy birthday, darling!" she beams. Before I can say a word, she grabs my arm, pulls me close, and kisses me full on the mouth.

My brain short-circuits. One beat. Two. Three.

"Brielle! Who's the lucky guy?"

"Is he a model or what?"

"Seriously, where do you find these men?"

Laughter. Clicks. Too much light.

She laughs, dazzling. "Stop it, you'll embarrass him. This is Hadrian Carter-Bello. He's running for the second district in New York. So if you live in the area, vote for him. Let's put that pretty face to work for the people."

Flashes explode again.

I manage a tight smile. "Thanks."

I steer us toward the entrance as fast as I can without it looking like a retreat. She leans in, lips brushing the edge of my ear.

"You're welcome, darling."

36

Isadora

"WHO ON EARTH INVITED her?" I murmur, barely moving my lips.

"I did," Allie deadpans. "Your father asked me to."

"Als..." I tilt my head, searching her face. "Why didn't you say anything?"

She waves at someone behind me instead of answering. I turn.

My father stands beside my grandmother Genevieve. She's in pale lilac, a shade too delicate for how formidable she's always been. Her silver hair is perfectly swept into a chignon, but her posture isn't what it used to be—there's a faint tremble to her wrist as she clutches her cane, and her left shoulder has started to slope inward.

"Because it's not my place to second-guess the host," Allie whispers as we get closer.

"Happy birthday, sweetheart." My father pulls me into a hug.

"My little princess." Grandma's voice is paper-thin. She leans in, and there it is—gardenias and cold cream. The hug is brief but lingering, her hands cool and birdlike around my arms.

"I still remember the day you were born. You looked nothing like your brother. Screamed like you were outraged to be here."

She smiles, but it doesn't quite reach her eyes the way it used to. Grief has aged her, subtly but unmistakably. A slight fog in her gaze, as if part of her is gone somewhere else.

"Thanks, Granny." I press my cheek to hers. Her skin is soft as parchment, thinner than I remember.

I catch sight of Hadrian and Brielle greeting my father. They're all smiles and handshakes.

"Let's go." Allie shifts beside me. "Everyone else is waiting for you."

She gestures toward the corridor, and we begin walking. The hallway stretches long and hushed. Velvet ropes have been pulled aside.

Candles flicker from wall sconces, casting honeyed light over the chevron floors. A string quartet plays something soft and familiar.

"Wait. Is that—"

She smiles at me. "Skinny Love? Sure is."

I can feel the vibration of it in the soles of my heels.

As we round the final turn, the room opens in a slow, deliberate reveal.

I freeze.

The atrium glows with a kind of golden hush. The Beekman's iron balconies rise above us like opera tiers, each lit softly, as if the room itself has paused to watch. But it's the ceiling that steals the breath from my lungs. Above us, suspended like petals caught mid-bloom, dozens of lamps open and close in a silent, choreographed rhythm. Pale glass blossoms unfurl and fold again, like breathing flowers, casting shifting patterns of light across the floor.

It feels like stepping into a dream someone else had on my behalf.

"Allie," I whisper, barely able to take my eyes off the ceiling, "this is..."

"I know," she says, lips twitching.

The room is dressed in creams and soft metallics, petals spilling from towering vases, small golden place cards folded like origami on white linen. Champagne sparkles from crystal flutes.

It's... sublime.

A cluster of guests gathers near the entrance.

"Happy birthday, my sweet girl." My mother's voice is soft, breath warm against my cheek. She holds me for a beat longer than usual, and when she pulls back, her eyes are bright.

Next is Aunt Honor, crisp in navy silk. She kisses the air beside my face. "Look at you. So poised. So lovely. Happy birthday, darling."

Then Kathy Ellington and her boyfriend Brett press in from the left, handing me a tiny gold bag with tissue spilling like tulle.

"Isadora, darling." It's Juliette Anslow, her fuchsia lipstick already grazing my cheek. Her husband, Martin, offers a cheerful nod, swirling a glass of red in his hand.

The Whitlocks follow—Eleanor glowing in soft feathers, her son Jasper next to her. Behind them, the Wexlers wave from a few steps back, already mid-conversation with someone I don't recognize but feel like I should.

A light tap lands on my shoulder.

"Bryony Deighton," I smile before she can say a word. She kisses the air beside both cheeks, bracelets chiming. "We must catch up soon," she says.

"Isadora, how are you holding up?" someone asks—Mrs. Goldstein, I think, from the Foundation Board.

"Hi, Mrs.—"

"Mrs. Halberstam." Hadrian steps in beside me. I flash him a grateful smile.

"Thank you all for being here," he adds with practiced warmth, already shaking hands, easing the pressure around us. "We've just arrived, but I hear Allie outdid herself with the food. Please—don't let us hold you up."

There's a ripple of movement as the crowd begins to drift toward the atrium's central hall, where the music swells a little louder and the lighting softens into a golden haze. I start to follow.

An arm wraps around my waist, familiar and easy, pulling me gently back a step.

Milo.

"Happy birthday, Scout," he says, voice just for me. "You look beautiful."

I lean into his touch, because I always do.

"Hi," I say, barely above a whisper.

He kisses my temple like it's muscle memory. "You really do look beautiful."

I nod, but it's harder to smile now. I can feel it again—that quiet ache that starts in my throat and sinks just beneath my ribs.

He reaches for my hand. I let him take it.

"Can we sneak away for a second?" he asks.

"Right now? We just got here."

"It'll just be a second."

I glance around—the room is still swelling with arrivals—and nod.

He leads me down a narrow hallway, past velvet curtains and paneled doors, until we reach a small room tucked quietly behind the main floor. One of the hotel's private screening rooms, dimly lit and empty, except for the two armchairs and the screen already glowing to life.

"I asked them to set it up earlier," he says.

The screen flickers. And then there we are. Milo and me. Over the years, in fragments.

Ski slopes. Beach trips. A blurry video of our first New Year's kiss. That one afternoon in Positano when we accidentally crashed a wedding and I somehow ended up as the flower girl.

I shake my head, grinning.

"I was thinking... maybe someday soon, there could our wedding photos in there too."

I look at him. At the boy I've loved so long it feels like breathing. At the man I no longer see a future with. The love of a life I no longer want to live.

It's finally clear now. Like a film sharpened into focus after too long squinting at the blur. As if all the parts of me that had ever settled down suddenly stood up.

The thing I've been trying to soften, to sidestep, to bury, to name as something else—it's here now.

The elephant in every room of our hearts. His already broken, patched up with Band-Aids we've been too afraid to take off.

He wants us to go back to what we were. But I don't live there anymore. And Allie's right. I can't keep him close just because I don't know where else to go.

"Milo—"

"Please, don't." He swallows. "I already know what you're going to say."

"Then let me say it." My voice catches. "We can't keep doing this. It's not fair to you."

"Yes, we can."

"No, Milo. You're not listening to me. I don't *want* to do this anymore."

The second the words leave my mouth, I see it—the Band-Aid finally gives. His face doesn't flinch, but something under it does.

"What do you mean you don't want to?"

I look at him. Pleading, maybe. Because I don't have it in me to do this again.

His eyes soften. And then, something in him settles.

He looks at me like he's soaking in the last of me. Eyes traveling all the way up to mine.

"You really are the most beautiful girl in every room." His voice is barely above a breath. "I love you, Scout. Always will."

Then he turns off the projector, turns around, and walks away.

37
Hadrian

RAMI EXHALES, LONG-SUFFERING AS Irina leans forward again.

"Stop the car." *Gag.* "I'm going to be sick. Again."

That's the third time.

The night was good. Mostly.

Who am I kidding? It was a nightmare.

I stayed sober. Against my better will. Now I get to be the only one actually experiencing this chaos in HD.

"Is she okay?" Brielle asks, dragging the last syllable like it's on designer drugs too.

Blake leans out the window as Irina tugs at his shirt. "If I help you I'll end up throwing up as well, babe."

"Jesus," I mutter.

"I'll go." That's Allie offering. Of course.

I turn to her just in time to see Maxwell grab her thigh to keep her next to him.

Can you hear that? It's my composure cracking.

Allie peels his hand off, not unkindly enough if you ask me, and slides out to help Irina.

Isa's next to me. Her head is heavy on my shoulder. She's as drunk as I've ever seen her—maybe more. Which, for the record, is still somewhat collected.

She hiccups quietly. I shift just enough to see her eyes flutter half-shut.

"Isa, you good?" I ask.

She nods once, solemnly. Like even that took effort.

"Maybe we should all go home?" Brielle offers.

"No," Jamie and Blake say at once.

Unison. Look at that. The Ellington brothers finally found their one shared opinion. It's about not leaving a party.

I look out the window. We're parked in some alley just off Bowery, streetlights flickering over Irina, who's hunched near a pile of trash bags, making dry heaving look somehow theatrical. Allie's crouched beside her, holding her hair.

Blake's got his phone out.

"Dude, are you filming your girlfriend throwing up?" Jamie asks.

Blake grins. "Just for Close Friends."

"Is that one even alive?" Brielle nods toward the front.

Archie is full-on horizontal, legs stretched across Jamie's lap, head tipped back, mouth fully open, one arm's dangling limp.

"Trust me, he is," Jamie mutters under his breath.

"Come on," Blake protests leaning out the open door. "We're only five minutes out."

That somehow revives Irina.

"I'm going to assassinate you," she snarls. "Like, properly."

Blake remains unfazed. Not surprising, considering all the shit he's taken tonight.

Allie helps her back toward the car, one hand gripping Irina's waist, the other steadying her by the wrist. Irina's heels are in her hand now. She's barefoot and pissed, which turns out to be a great combo.

Blake opens his arms like he's expecting a reunion. Irina shoves past him so hard he nearly stumbles into the door, then drops straight into Allie's old spot, next to Max.

Allie climbs in right after her slipping into the seat beside her, now the far end. Maxwell exhales, visibly frustrated, as he sinks further into the seat.

Who would've thought? Irina is officially my favorite person in this vehicle.

Rami pulls back onto the road without a word.

Allie leans back, tilts her head, eyes shut like she might be sick too. Probably her blood sugar again.

Max reaches into his pocket, pulls out a lemon candy, leans forward, and slips it into her hand without a word.

She takes it without even opening her eyes. And that—that's an entirely different kind of knife twisting in my gut. Blade's sharper. Goes in cleaner.

How close do you have to be for something that small to look that instinctive? Like it's happened a hundred times before. Like he knows her blood sugar dips when she's stressed. Or that she's only taken the lemon ones since she was twelve because someone once told her they make her hair shinier.

God.

I might be the one who's sick.

"Second, are you okay?"

Brielle grabs my face, turns it toward her.

"Not exactly." The car slows. "I might head—"

I glance out the window.

"Blake, you didn't."

He turns to me, mischief dialed to eleven.

"Oh, I absolutely did."

38
Isadora

THIS CANNOT BE IT.

"TACOMANIA?" I blink up at the flickering sign. "Blake. No."

He's already walking in. A few groans later, we all follow. Greasy air hits me in the face, grilled meat, burnt oil, something sour. There's a broken chair near the door and a guy asleep against the soda machine. Someone's yelling at the cashier about extra cheese.

Blake doesn't stop. He pushes through the swinging kitchen door like he works here.

Jamie looks around. "Where the fuck are we?"

"You'll see," Max says.

"Vintage Dalton mischief. You're welcome," Archie adds, fully awake now, apparently.

We head to the kitchen door. Max and Archie push through those old-school swinging ones, the kind with round windows and brushed steel edges. They creak open side to side.

The kitchen is loud—pans clattering, someone singing off-key in Spanish. It smells like meat and bleach. One of the cooks sees Blake and barely reacts. He nods toward a silver freezer door in the corner. There's a short pause. Then a click. And the door swings open.

What's behind it is dark and weirdly cold. A hallway? No, like a tunnel. Red lights. A humming noise. Music? I blink. The tequila's hitting now. Harder than I thought.

"Come on," Blake calls over his shoulder.

So we do.

We step through, and everything changes.

Suddenly we're in a different place. The lights are low. Red. Loud. The music is all bass, almost too much. I feel it in my chest. The crowd is packed—people everywhere, skin, sweat, drinks in their hands, laughing too loud. There's a bar to the right. A raised platform on the left. I can't see who's DJing. It smells like perfume and something burnt.

I turn, already losing sight of Hadrian and Jamie. Is Brielle here too? Irina's disappeared. I think Blake's at the bar now? Or maybe that's someone else.

Allie touches my arm. "Hey. Want water?"

I shake my head. I think I say no. I'm not sure.

Someone pushes past me. I stumble into Allie and laugh, but it comes out wrong.

I need to sit. Or dance. Or throw up.

Unclear.

"Actually, water would be great," I say, already moving toward the closest empty stool.

We make it there without tripping over anyone, which feels like a win. Allie flags down the bartender. "Can we get four closed waters?"

He's quick. Shaved head, thick chain, bored expression. He slides the bottles toward us.

I open one and down the whole thing without thinking.

"Slow down." Allie grabs it before I can take another sip. "That much that fast'll make you puke. And I swear to God, I love you—really—but I've seen enough throw-up tonight to last me the rest of the decade."

I laugh.

Wrong move.

My stomach turns immediately. Something rises in my throat, but I force it back down. Not happening here.

Allie's eyes shift past me, toward the crowd. Her expression twists. "Oh no. Are you kidding me?"

I glance over my shoulder.

Max and Archie are getting pulled out by security—one by the collar, one by the sleeve. Max is trying to talk his way out of it. Archie just looks delighted.

I sigh. "What the hell did those idiots do now?"

"Stay here," Allie says. "Seriously. Don't move."

She's gone before I can even sit up straighter.

I stare at the second water bottle.

"Whatever she orders tonight, put it on my tab."

I turn. The voice belongs to a guy leaning against the bar. Leather cuff. Standing a little too close.

"I appreciate the gesture." I keep my voice even. "But I have a boyfriend."

It stings, saying that one out loud.

He grins, eyes dragging lazily over me. "I'm not the jealous type."

I let out a laugh. "Oh my god. Does that usually work?"

The last words trail when he leans closer, his breath laced with tequila. It makes the nausea worse.

"Sometimes," he says.

"Yeah," I mutter. "Hard pass."

His smile tightens.

"C'mon," he says, reaching for me.

Suddenly I'm being pulled toward him. I trip forward...

Before I can even process it, another hand appears from behind me. Fast.

The guy jerks backward, yanked by the collar so sharply his feet scrape against the floor. His drink flies from his hand. The glass explodes against the tiles.

"Hands off her."

Did I pass out? Am I dreaming?

I turn.

Nope. That's definitely Leo. Flesh and blood, jaw tight, eyes darker than I've ever seen them.

I blink. The guy blinks.

"Relax, lover boy. Didn't realize she needed a bodyguard."

He glances past Leo. "Or two."

I follow his gaze. Rami's there. Arms crossed. Calm. Watching.

"You've got five seconds," Leo growls. "Apologize. And walk away."

The guy just stares at him. Then at me. His smirk sharpens.

"What is it?" he says lazily. "Daddy issues?"

Leo doesn't move.

"Last chance."

The muscle in his jaw jumps once.

The guy leans closer.

"How many guys like me do you think she's let touch her before you showed up?"

Leo's fist moves before my brain can register it, the sickening crack of bone echoing through the room. Gasps ripple through the crowd as the man stumbles back, clutching his jaw.

Security's already there. They grab the man fast.

"Relax, man!" he shouts, thrashing in their grip. "She was into it!"

They drag him backward through the crowd.

Leo's gaze locks with mine for the briefest heartbeat, and in that little infinity, I let myself fall into those storm-filled eyes you can never unsee, and if you could, trust me, you wouldn't choose to.

Then he turns, walks toward the back door and goes through it too.

My feet won't move, so I just stand there.

"Isadora." Allie's voice snaps behind me, almost out of breath. "What the hell just happened?"

"I—"

The word dies somewhere in my throat.

And then I'm moving. Straight toward the back exit.

39

Leo

I WAS TWELVE THE first time I heard my father give the order.

"Now's the time," he told OG, voice like steel. "Shake him up. Get the rock purged for the market."

I didn't know what it meant, but it sounded serious. Dangerous.

Of course, he wouldn't let me come. Not because he gave a shit about me, but because I was, in his words, just a fucking kid. A liability.

So I went anyway. Crammed myself into the trunk of OG's black Buick, chest tight, barely breathing. The drive was short—ten minutes, maybe less. I shifted, squinting through a sliver of light near the taillight housing. Just enough to see.

A school zone. Kids chasing each other on the sidewalk, backpacks bouncing.

A few moments later, OG stepped out of the car. The second the door clicked shut, I moved, wedged myself through the narrow opening into the back seat, heart pounding so hard I could hear it in my ears.

He was scanning the sidewalk from behind a closed newspaper stand like he was waiting for someone.

Then he went still.

A little girl pedaled toward him. Six. Maybe seven.

When she got close enough, he kicked at her front wheel. She went flying. Hit the pavement hard. Knees, then face. A sob burst out of her as she curled around her wrist.

Something in me split. She couldn't have been older than my younger sister.

Pulse spiking. Breath sharp. I was moving before I even knew it.

I shoved the door open and stepped out of the back seat.

Didn't think. Just ran.

I dropped to my knees beside the girl, hands already reaching out.

But OG yanked me up.

"What the fuck do you think you're doing?"

His grip was iron-tight, breath hot against my ear.

The girl looked up at him—trembling, bleeding.

He stared at her, then at me and groaned so violently she flinched and shut her eyes.

Then he dragged me back to the car, shoved me inside, and we drove off.

My father beat the shit out of me that day. First time. Not the last.

Didn't stop till I couldn't stand.

"Fucking idiot," he spat over and over, like repetition might brand it into my skull.

Guess it's safe to say he succeeded. But I knew I'd done the right thing. Or tried to.

That day was the black marker across my life. Ink bled through every page that followed.

Since then, I've taken beatings for my sisters. My mother. For women I barely knew.

Doesn't matter who they are—guilty, innocent, doesn't matter.

If I'm there, no one lays a fucking hand on them.

So now, as I drive my fist into this asshole's face, it's not just for Isadora.

It's for that kid hidden in the trunk who decided he'd never be scared enough to look away.

But if we're being brutally honest?

I'm mostly doing it for her.

I don't stop. Don't want to.

Knuckles torn. Blood warm. Doesn't matter.

"Leo, please stop. He's not worth it."

Her voice. Soft. Still lands harder than any punch.

My hands go slack. The guy drops, groaning.

I step back, chest heaving. Look at her.

Her eyes meet mine, and I see it. She's scared. Terrified.

And if I'd cared, because I don't. Truly don't, can't, won't. I'd probably pledge to never in my life let her feel that way again.

I nod toward the guards. "Take care of him."

Then I turn to her.

"You okay?"

She doesn't answer.

The back door swings open and slams against the wall. Hadrian barrels through first, eyes blazing.

Allie's right behind him, breathless. Then Brielle, heels clacking.

In a matter of seconds, Blake, a very drunk Irina, and Jamie stumble into the alley, turning the narrow space into a mess of bodies, noise, and confusion.

"What's going on?" Hadrian demands, voice sharp.

"Uhm... I... he—" Isadora stammers, still frozen.

"A man was distressing her," Rami says, stepping out from the shadows by the dumpster, where he's been keeping watch all along.

"Sartori ensured he won't be in a position to do so again."

Hadrian wheels on him. "And why didn't *you* do that?"

Rami doesn't move. Doesn't even blink. "My job is to neutralize threats, not interfere where protection is already active. The situation was under control. Better I stay clear and keep eyes on the perimeter."

Hadrian exhales hard through his nose. His jaw works. I can see him weighing it—anger versus relief, image versus instinct.

Then finally, a clipped nod. "Right."

"Thanks, man," Jamie says, breaking the tension as he steps between them. He puts a steadying hand on Isadora's shoulder. "Is, so sorry we left you alone."

She doesn't answer. Just stares straight ahead, lips parted, arms crossed so tightly it looks like she's holding herself together.

"Pity I wasn't here to catch it on video." Blake shrugs. "Would've made a killer close friends story."

Hadrian exhales sharply. "Speaking of which—we should go before someone *does* recognize us and makes use of *their* phone. I can't afford that kind of press tonight."

"You always look good on camera." Brielle loops her arm through his. "Nothing to worry about."

Blake lets out a dry laugh. "Yeah, better hurry before someone tips the paps again."

Allie shoots Brielle a deep glance, then turns back to Isadora. "Let's go home."

"Yes, let's," she replies.

Everyone starts to turn.

But she doesn't move.

She looks me dead in the eye like I'm one of her books and she's trying to read it. Read me.

"Could you take me home?"

I nod before the question even finishes leaving her mouth.

40
Isadora

THE SAME BARTENDER FROM before hands me a plastic cup full of ice.

"Thanks."

He nods, and I make my way toward the back door where Leo is waiting for me outside.

Everyone's gone now. They all had to take cabs since Rami wouldn't leave me alone and insisted on following us. Irina gave me a look like I'd personally ruined her night while Blake held her straight. Hadrian had to be dragged by Brielle. Allie gave me one of her proud looks. And Jamie was actually the one to call the cabs.

I push the heavy door open.

He's there, leaning against a brick wall across the street.

Dark jeans, a white shirt. The shirt is crisp, fitted at the shoulders and loose around the waist. His hair's a little longer than when I first met him, falling over his forehead now.

He's rolling up his sleeves. One is streaked with small drops of blood. None of it looks fresh. Probably isn't even his.

I've found other guys attractive while being with Milo. I'm not a nun.

And sure, Leo's one of them. No point denying that.

He lifts his head as I approach.

"Here, for your hand," I offer.

He scoffs. "Thanks, but I don't need it."

I reach for his arm anyway. His skin is boiling.

"Your knuckles—"

He pulls away. "Like I said, I'm fine."

He pushes both sleeves higher. The tattoos start at his left hand and run up past his elbow. Near his wrist, a sun is inked in solid black, the rays precise and symmetrical. Above it, wings stretch across the lower part of his forearm. In the center of his arm, a woman's face is framed inside a circular emblem. She looks like a mythological figure—strong features, a crown of leaves around her head. Closer to his elbow, a dragon curls upward, its teeth locked around a chain. Near his bicep, fine-line geometry: sharp angles, dots, and a shape that looks like a polyhedron. There are more symbols higher up. Some writing I can't read.

He clears his throat. "Shall we? Sun'll be up soon."

We start walking toward the main road, and I fumble through my thoughts, trying to find a reason I stayed behind with him, but I'm afraid reason left us hours ago.

We turn the corner, and a black car pulls into view.

"Here," he says.

"This isn't the same car from the Garden Party."

He doesn't answer.

"Why are you driving a car with diplomatic plates?"

They're pale blue with black lettering, featuring a red banner at the top. I learned that fast when I started working at the UN.

"Gift," he says.

I raise a brow. "A gift?"

He opens the door and holds out his hand.

I take it and step into the car. It's even hotter now, somehow. I'll have to find a way to ice him while he's driving.

It smells the same though—leather seats and that same cologne, something woody and deep.

He slides in beside me and starts the engine.

I realize he's never been to my place, so I tap open Google Maps on the screen and type in my address.

A glance back—Rami's already trailing us.

I clear my throat. "Music?"

"Sure."

I open Spotify and scroll through his On Repeat playlist.

First song: "Aria" by Giovanni Allevi.

"Piano?" I ask.

He side-eyes me. Then looks back at the road, and just nods.

I smile. "Figures."

For the first time tonight, he smiles too.

I turn up the volume and let the keys fill the space. And it feels like air after hours underground.

I was never one for classical music. I tend to run from anything wordless. But somehow, someway, right here and now, I get it.

His right hand rests on the center console. I bring the cup of ice closer. Slowly.

He glances at me but doesn't move or say anything.

I press the ice gently to his knuckles.

He flinches—barely—but doesn't pull away.

"Reverie" by Debussy starts playing next.

The city moves past the window in slow, sleepy blurs.

Shutters half-drawn. Streetlights still lit, even though they're not needed anymore. The sky is that in-between color it gets when the sun is minutes away from cracking through, soft gray with a tint of lavender.

The sidewalks are empty except for a few people walking fast with their heads down, coffee cups in hand, jackets pulled tight even though the air's already warming up.

Shops are dark, but the bodegas glow—those are always awake.

An old man leans against the counter reading a paper like time doesn't apply to him.

"What's your favorite song?" I ask.

He shrugs. "I don't have one."

I chuckle. "Of course you do. Everyone does."

He doesn't answer.

"Let me guess... something by Ludovico Einaudi?"

A half smile. "Close. But no."

"So? Let's hear it."

He hesitates, then taps on the screen and types in *sim*.

Simon & Garfunkel – "The Sound of Silence" shows up.

He presses play. The "Concert in Central Park" version fills the car.

"Why this one?"

"Hits different live."

"I meant more like why this song," I press.

Nothing.

I roll down the window.

"Cisza też jest odpowiedzią."

I flick my hand, half a shrug. "It means 'silence is also an answer'. My Polish professor used to say that whenever I couldn't find the right words."

"Czasem odpowiedzi nie potrzebują słów."

I snort. "Figures you'd side with silence." Then I pause, tilting my head. "Wait. You speak Polish?"

"My mother's Polish." Another half-smile and counting.

"Was she born there?"

He shakes his head. "Her parents. They were Jewish. Escaped in the late thirties before it got bad. They passed through Italy on the way to New York. Started from scratch here. Gemstones, mostly."

I tap my fingers against my leg, committing every detail to memory. "So the family business... it's actually your mother's?"

A flicker of something passes across his face.

"Something like that. Used to be anyway."

"Bridge Over Troubled Water" starts playing.

"Are your parents still together?" I ask.

He shakes his head. "Haven't been in years."

"And what about siblings?"

"Three half-sisters. Younger. They live in LA with their mom. I don't see them much."

We fall quiet again. The music carries us for a bit.

"Thanks. For tonight."

He nods, and a short laugh slips out of me.

"What?" he asks.

I shake my head. "Nothing. Just... how we keep running into each other. Never in the best circumstances."

The car slows. I look out the window—we're already on my street.

"Milo didn't come out?"

I blink. "What?"

He keeps his eyes ahead, even though we're barely moving now.

"I figured he'd be glued to your side."

"He had something and couldn't stay long." I pause and weigh my options here. "Why?"

"No reason."

He turns off the engine and the sudden silence makes everything louder. Including my thoughts.

"We... we're not together anymore."

He nods again. I wish he'd stop doing that and just say something. Anything.

A few seconds pass but it feels like centuries.

His hands are still on the wheel. Tight.

"What about you?" I ask, quieter now. "Anyone keeping you up at night?"

He exhales through his nose. Scoffs. "I don't date."

"Like... at all?"

His jaw flexes. He still hasn't looked at me.

I study his profile.

Please. A face like that? He probably has a trail of women all the way to Singapore.

His fingers tap once on the leather, then stop.

Two knocks on the window make me jump.

The cup slips, and the melted ice water splashes straight onto my lap.

"Shit."

I look up.

Allie.

She's standing on the sidewalk, arms planted firmly on her hips, mouth tight.

She steps closer and opens the door on my side.

"Hadrian's waiting for you inside. He wouldn't leave," she says, then mouths, "Sorry."

I turn to Leo. "Thanks again. For the ride too." I swing my legs out and step onto the curb, brushing at the wet spot on my dress, half-hoping he'll say something more.

"Carter-Bello." His voice somewhere between a groan and a question.

I turn back to him. His eyes finally on mine.

"Happy birthday."

Champagne Problems

Jamie

Did everyone make it home OK?

Allie

Is and I did. Not sure Archie will ever be okay again though.

Jamie

Good. Maybe my brother and he will finally stop drinking like they're twenty-year-old Scotsmen.

Allie

One can dream

Jamie

Why is Isa so silent?

Allie

I think the car ride with Sarto left her emotionally comatose.

Jamie

Or repressing feelings the old-fashioned way.

Gross.

I was just getting ready for bed.

Allie

Rookie mistake

Jamie

I rest my case, your honor.

Idiots.

41
Hadrian

Being entirely sober during a night out was instructive.

There's something oddly unsettling about watching everyone else get progressively looser and less coherent while you stay painfully aware of every awkward laugh and slurred word. It's like being stuck inside a funhouse mirror version of your own worst nights. It makes you realize just how pathetic you must've looked all the times *you* were the one three drinks too deep.

The night started off predictably enough. I spent the first half hour making polite conversation with familiar and not-so-familiar faces, all while my head split in two.

Half of me was calculating potential fallout from Brielle's announcement.

The other half was thinking about Allie. And her dress. And the way she looked at me, and then the way she stopped looking at me altogether.

Morning light slices through the curtains. My head isn't pounding, exactly, but it feels tight. Raw at the edges. I reach for my phone before I even sit up and text Marcus, who I assume has been monitoring the situation like a hawk.

How's the trend?

His reply comes before I even block my screen.

Reactions are great. Mostly positive. Don't stress.

I toss the phone onto the duvet and drag myself upright, feet hitting the floor harder than they need to. The apartment is still.

In the bathroom, I splash cold water over my face and brush my teeth, staring blankly at my own reflection. My eyes are bloodshot.

I towel off and head into the kitchen.

Brielle is already up, humming to herself as she makes coffee, her phone glued to her hand. She's smiling—an annoyingly satisfied, cat-that-ate-the-canary kind of smile.

"What are you so happy about?" I ask, sinking onto one of the bar stools and rubbing the sleep from my eyes.

She turns her phone around to show me the screen, her grin widening. "We're trending everywhere. People love it."

I frown, not sure I want to know what *it* is. "Define love."

"They're calling us the next JFK and Jackie O. Or, for the younger crowd, the Obamas. They're eating it up, Hadrian. *Power couple goals,*" she says, tossing in air quotes.

I stare at her. "You're joking."

"Nope. Look." She turns her screen towards me.

One article shows the two of us leaving the venue last night—me in a navy suit, top button undone, hand pressed gently to the small of her back, her in that red slip dress, sleek hair tucked behind one ear.

> **THE SECOND AND THE STORM: Carter-Bello Jr. and "Breezy" Warner Take Center Stage**
> *A political prince and his wildcard heiress walk into a gala. The rest is history.*

Another photo—us laughing, looking too perfectly timed to be candid, champagne flutes raised beneath a string of lights. Truth is, I was laughing at something Blake had said.

> **American Royals 2.0: Hadrian and Brielle Rewrite the Script**
> *Modern love meets legacy politics in this impossibly photogenic pairing.*

I scroll down.

Sparks, Strategy, and Satin: Is This America's New Obsession?
The New Face of the Future: Hadrian Carter-Bello Jr. and Brielle Warner Command the Moment.

My name in serif fonts I've never liked. Hers in gold italics beside it, even less.

I lean back, trying to process it. This is unexpected. And not exactly welcome.

Sure, some buzz is great for the campaign, but it also means more eyes. More questions. Less room to breathe.

Brielle, meanwhile, is absolutely basking in it.

"Hadrian, this is a good thing. People *love* a love story. And we're giving them one. You're the dashing, idealistic politician. I'm the glamorous, unpredictable wildcard. It's perfect."

Perfect.

Right. Because nothing says stability like having your personal life dissected by millions before you've made it to Congress.

I grab the coffee she's poured for me and take a long sip, trying to ignore the sinking feeling in my gut.

"Yeah," I say finally, forcing a smile. "Perfect."

My phone buzzes on the counter. Marcus.

Actually... we may need to strategize. It's bigger than I anticipated.

We need to capitalize on this momentum.

Part of me suddenly wants to crawl back into bed and pretend none of this is happening.

Who am I kidding? All parts of me do.

Especially the one that knows Allie will read this.

Like I've done more times than I can bring myself to admit, I shove the thought of Allie into an even deeper corner of my mind—bury it beneath headlines and headlines and more headlines—because I don't have the margin for it. Not mentally. Not emotionally. Not today.

I head to the bathroom to take a shower and get ready to head to Second Front before Marcus floods my phone with texts.

Steam curls around the mirror as I step under the water, letting it pound against the back of my neck like it might knock the noise out of me.

A few minutes later, I hear the door open behind me. Then the soft rustle of fabric, a pause, and the glass swings open.

Brielle steps in without asking, without hesitation—like it's the most natural thing in the world. Her skin is already dewy from the heat, hair piled into a loose knot, eyes harsh even when they're soft.

She looks flawless. Effortlessly so. She wraps her arms around me from behind, pressing against my back.

"You're tense," she says, lips brushing my shoulder. "Let me help."

I reach for the shampoo instead. "I'm gonna be late."

She hums, unconvinced, running her hands slowly over my chest. "Just five minutes."

I turn slightly, just enough to meet her eyes without letting the moment stretch.

"Not today, Brielle."

She pulls back a little—not hurt, exactly, just... calculating. We both understand the arrangement.

"Alright," she says finally, cool as ever. She kisses the back of my neck anyway, then steps out without another word, leaving wet footprints across the marble.

I exhale and tilt my head back under the water, letting it scald.

For a moment, I just stand there, fists clenched, forehead against the tile, eyes shut like maybe I can disappear into the steam. But it doesn't work. It never does.

Eventually, I shut the water off and step out, towel slung low around my waist. The mirror's already fogged over. Fitting.

I dress quickly—black tee, charcoal slacks, the same watch I've worn since college—methodical, automatic. Armor. As I head back into the bedroom, Brielle's still in bed, propped against a pile of pillows, scrolling with that absent-minded, morning-after glow.

"You're heading out?" she asks without looking up.

"Yeah. Second Front."

She pauses her scrolling. "See you tonight?"

I hesitate. Then shrug, casual. "Can't tonight. I'll text you."

A beat of silence. She doesn't push. Just nods once and goes back to her screen.

I grab my helmet off the console table by the door and step out.

The sunlight slams into me like a camera flash—hot, invasive, unwelcome. I pull the sunglasses lower over my eyes and start walking, then stop.

Shit.

Just down the street, crouched behind a neighbor's hedge and a silver van, they wait—paparazzi. Three, maybe four. Cameras up. Lenses gleam like rifles in the morning light.

Guess they had the wrong address. Not anymore.

I pick up the pace, walking quickly until I reach the curb, then crouch to unlock my bike. Helmet tucked under one arm, fingers fumbling at the latch, trying to stay calm. *Just get out.*

"Hadrian! Over here!"

Click. Flash. Click.

"Is it serious with Brielle?"

"Did you spend the night together?"

"Are you in love?"

The chain finally comes loose. My hands are slick with sweat, but I move fast, throwing one leg over the seat, sunglasses already down, sliding the helmet on like a mask.

"Was last night a soft launch or a real one?"

I start pedaling.

"Hadrian—are the engagement rumors true?"

That one almost makes me flinch.

I pull into the street without looking back.

Pretty sure I break some kind of record—because a few minutes later, I'm outside Second Front, parking fast, locking up the bike like it's muscle memory. I keep my head down and move fast, slipping inside before anyone has time to recognize me.

As I make my way upstairs, I fish out my phone and type a quick message to Brielle.

Paps are outside now. Be careful.

Please. You're talking to a pro

Not sure how she'll manage to avoid the cameras, but I'm sure she's experienced enough to figure it out.

Marcus is waiting for me as soon as I walk in.

"You're trending." He looks up from his tablet. "Nation-fucking-wide."

42

Isadora

I GUESS IT'S TRUE what they say about hangovers getting worse in your late twenties—though I'm barely twenty-six, and it already feels like I'm living inside one.

It's been forty-eight hours since Double Day, and my skull still pulses like a cracked bell.

I'm curled up on the sofa, laptop teetering on my knees, a forgotten mug of tea going cold beside me. The screen in front of me is blank except for a blinking cursor that feels increasingly smug each time it reappears. I've been stuck on the same sentence for nearly an hour, gnawing at it like a loose thread.

Translating isn't just converting words. I know you know this, but people forget. They think it's a swap, a trade. This for that, meaning for meaning. But language doesn't barter cleanly.

Sometimes you stay loyal to the original, faithful in every beat and comma. Other times, you have to trespass. You break it open, step inside, and rebuild the feeling in another tongue. You make it sound like it was always meant to live there.

It depends on everything. Tone. Rhythm. Cultural ghosts. The way a phrase bends when it lands in a new mouth.

Romance, especially, wants softness and flow, something that slips under the reader's skin before they notice it's there. But it still has to ache like the original.

And this quote—this one is haunting me.

I whisper it aloud in Spanish, letting it bloom in my mouth.

"*Hay amores que no buscan completarte, sino desarmarte. Que no te llenan, sino que te vacían de todo lo que no sos, para que puedas encontrarte a vos misma y empezar de nuevo.*"

It's brutal in the gentlest way. Like a confession spoken at midnight, barefoot in the kitchen. It's not just about love. It's about surrender.

About someone seeing you so deeply, they strip away everything you thought you had to be.

The literal translation feels clunky:

"There are loves that don't seek to complete you, but to dismantle you. That don't fill you, but empty you of everything you are not, so you can find yourself and start over."

It works. Technically. But it doesn't *wound.*

I try again:

"Some loves don't exist to complete you but to undo you. They peel away everything you're not, so that you might find yourself, and start anew."

Closer. There's breath in it now.

I lean back into the cushions, eyes tracing the cracks in the ceiling. This is the tightrope I was so afraid to walk—between honesty and beauty, between someone else's voice and mine.

Sometimes all it takes to change everything is underestimating a single word.

Like in 1945, when the Allied forces issued an ultimatum to Japan, the response included the word *mokusatsu*. It can mean "withholding comment." It can also mean "treating with silent contempt." It was translated as contempt. The climate was already volatile. Public sentiment didn't wait to clarify. Some historians even argue that interpretation contributed to escalation before Hiroshima. All this to say, words travel through charged air. And under that kind of pressure, even a small tilt can become irreversible.

A door clicks open down the hall. Allie appears in the doorway holding a vase that looks like a sea creature sculpted during a particularly surreal hallucination—ceramic, pale, with absurd little gold feet and what might be a smirk near the rim. It's part art, part threat. Very Allie.

She stares at it. Then at the dining table. Then back at the vase like it's said something offensive.

"Struggling?" I ask.

"A bit," she says, not looking away from the vase. "But nothing I can't figure out."

"That, I don't doubt."

She comes back with two lemonades, the glasses sweating in her hands. She passes one to me, then sinks onto the couch beside me.

She leans in, glancing at the screen.

"That's beautiful," she says, almost under her breath.

"It is," I nod. "Also a nightmare to translate."

She laughs. "Well, I don't speak a word of Spanish, but that reads like it was written in English to begin with. And it hits."

I let out a breath, sinking back a little. "Thanks."

She fidgets, flicking her thumb along the rim of her glass.

"Have you talked to Hadrian?" she asks, then pauses. "You know, since the whole... Leo drop-off slash brotherly intervention we never properly unpacked."

I uncross, then recross my legs. "Nope. Not in the mood for another 'call Milo' monologue."

She tucks her legs underneath her. "I think he just wants you to be okay. In his own gruff, emotionally stunted way. And safe."

"Well, his idea of 'okay' and mine clearly don't match. And as for being safe—I've got Rami."

"And apparently Leo," she mutters into her straw.

I roll my eyes. "He was just being decent."

"Mm. I doubt the guy who got turned into a chew toy would call it 'decent.'"

I laugh, hand flying to my mouth. "God, you're right. That poor guy."

"No sympathy here," she grins. "Maybe now he'll think twice before being a creep."

"Actually," she says, swirling her lemonade. "Kind of refreshing, honestly."

I squint at her. "What do you mean?"

She shrugs. "Remember that guy at Coachella? The one who flipped when you told him not to wipe his greasy fingers on Milo's shirt?"

The image snaps into place. "Yes. Rami did that pressure-point thing and the guy's whole face collapsed."

We both burst out laughing.

"And then he came back to apologize."

"Right! I forgot about that."

"But he didn't apologize to *you,*" she says, more serious now. "Just to Milo. For touching his shirt or whatever."

I nod slowly, the memory shifting shades. "Yeah... you were so pissed."

"I was pissed at *Milo.* He just stood there. Said 'no worries' and moved on. Didn't even ask for the guy to make an apology to you."

My mouth opens. Closes again.

She watches me for a beat. "It was nice. What Leo did. No second-guessing. No PR spin. Just—he saw something wasn't right and stepped in."

"Is there a hidden message buried in there somewhere?" I ask, narrowing my eyes.

She stands, already halfway to retreat. "Nope. Just a casual, completely objective bystander observation."

I chuckle. "Uh-huh. That sounds *exactly* like you."

She glances back, a grin playing at her lips. "Good luck with that."

I raise a brow.

"I mean the book," she adds.

I roll my eyes at her, though she doesn't see it—she's already walking away.

"Actually—" She spins around. "What are you wearing tonight?"

"Was thinking maybe the nude—"

"Immediately no," she cuts in. I blink at her, wide-eyed.

"Enough with the nudes and the beiges."

"What about the ecrus?" I tease.

"Forget the ecrus too. We're wearing red tonight. We're being bold."

Then she winks—yes, winks at me—and disappears down the hall.

43

Leo

I STOP SHORT AS the doors slide open.

Two Dobermans sit just a few steps ahead, perfectly still, perfectly alert. Sleek, dark, unnervingly symmetrical. No barking. Just watching, eyes locked on me.

One rises—not rushing, but with purpose. A low, guttural sound hums from its chest.

I don't move. I meet its gaze, steady. Let it feel my stillness. Let it second-guess the move it hasn't made yet.

It works. The dog pauses, unsure.

"Belladonna. Vesper. Sit."

Blake's voice cuts across the room.

"Don't worry," he adds, lifting a glass to his lips. "They only attack on Irina's command."

"Not worried," I say, stepping past the Dobermans without breaking stride.

Blake is draped over an armchair, barefoot, sleeves rolled up, cards scattered on the table between him, Hadrian, Max, and Archie. There's jazz leaking from the walls themselves.

"Irina says she doesn't feel safe in America," Blake explains. "She had them brought in from Germany and takes them everywhere now. You should've seen everyone's faces at Carbone last night. I think one kid actually fainted."

Max snorts in amusement.

Just beyond them, the balcony doors are open, sheer curtains stirring in the breeze.

Isadora's out there. In a red dress—loose enough to keep you guessing, short enough to show her legs. Her hair's down, long and a little wild from the wind, and fuck if I don't stop cold just to take her in.

Jamie sketches with quick, practiced flicks of his wrist. Allie's curled into the corner of the built-in bench, watching. Isadora's half-turned, elbow on the railing, a glass dangling from her fingers as she stares out at the dark horizon. She hasn't seen me yet.

I catch movement at the far end of the apartment—the kitchen, dimly lit and too quiet. Irina's in there alone slicing a mango with precision.

"You in, Sartori? Cards are hot tonight," Blake calls from behind me.

"Yeah, in a second."

Time's running out. I need to do this now.

I step into the kitchen, and leave the door ajar behind me. She doesn't look up.

"We were wondering how long it'd take you to make a move."

I don't react.

"We?"

She places the blade down, glances up. "My father and I, of course. We've been curious for months now. I figured dropping diamonds into the conversation the other night might do the trick. But nothing."

She tilts her head, watching me. There's something off. This isn't Irina. Can't be.

Same face. Same hair. Same perfect posture.

But the air's different around her now. Her voice isn't soft, sultry, or bored like usual. It's sharp. Surgical. And her accent... it's clipped. Intentional.

"You're confused," she says lightly. She picks up a mango slice and eats it slowly.

I say nothing.

She steps closer.

"You're used to being the one pulling strings. I get it." She's near enough now I can see the exact angle of the knife mark on the mango. "Not knowing what room you've walked into? Unsettling, isn't it?"

I study her, really study her.

"Here's the deal, Leo. Plain and simple." Her voice doesn't rise. Doesn't need to. "You'll get access to all of my father's corridors. But we have one condition."

"So?" I ask. "What's your price?"

"You know the Lirio Vermelho?"

I nod. "Of course. Your father ran the drop. If I'm not mistaken, he sourced it too."

She rests her hand on the knife handle.

"It's a fake."

My jaw tightens. "No. That's impossible."

"Not exactly," she says, voice like glass. "It was a lower-grade red, yes—but treated using a method so precise, it mimicked the molecular structure of a natural stone. New tech. Experimental, but we still took the risk. Only one lab in the world could tell the difference—and back then, no one was talking."

She leans back slightly, watching me register it.

"But someone, somewhere, changed sides. And now the Belgians know."

Fuck.

This is catastrophic.

The Belgians brokered that diamond on behalf of the Liechtenstein royal family.

That explains everything—why they've been gaining traction so fast, why even the kidnapping of the diplomat's wife didn't move them an inch.

They have Yakov Mikhailov by the throat.

This isn't just bad.

It's *empire-ending* bad.

"Fuck," I mutter.

"We need you to find a real one. We replace the stone, and owe them nothing."

Again, that's impossible," I say. "The Lirio Vermelho was supposed to be the rarest uncut red diamond ever recorded—seven carats of saturated blood-red." I pause. "The only thing that even came close was the Moussaieff, and that was found back in the '90s. Barely crossed five carats."

"There have been whispers the last few days," she almost whispers. "A mine in Brazil. Remote. Unregulated. That kind of rock only surfaces once in a lifetime. If the Belgians get there first—"

She doesn't have to finish the sentence.

"They won't just have leverage," I still say it aloud. "They'll own the whole fucking game."

She nods. "It'd be the end of us."

I breathe out through my nose.

"You and your father have more experience in that region than us. Better contacts. Better reach."

This isn't a twist. It's a whole different game—new board, new rules. And I'm already a thousand moves behind.

"That's our price. Find it and bring it to us. Or get used to watching me auction off my coats while you and your father kiss every eastern corridor goodbye."

And that right there sounds more like the Irina I've known these past few months.

I exhale—long, like it might summon a different solution. One less fucked up. But there's no point. We're cornered. So I steady myself.

"Brazil it is, then."

"Are you finally taking us to your place in Brazil?" Blake's voice cuts in as he steps into the kitchen, and pressure knots low in my ribs. "Fuck yes. It's getting too hot in this city."

"You've got a place there?" Max asks, stepping in too. He pulls open the fridge and grabs a coconut water and some leftover grilled vegetables.

"Yes, he does," Blake answers for me, already grinning. "You promised me back in London we'd go together. What's the name of the island again?"

I glance at Irina. She gives the slightest shrug.

"It's one of those fancy man-name islands," Blake adds, thinking out loud. "Like... Fabrizio or something?"

"Fernando de Noronha," I mutter.

"Yeah, that one." He snaps his fingers.

"We're off-season," Archie says, dropping onto a stool. "No games, no press. I'm in." He throws a look at Max, who gives a one-shouldered shrug like it's already happening.

Blake turns to Irina, looping an arm around her waist. "What do you say, babe?"

She leans into him. "I say let's do it. I need ocean air. New York's giving me migraines."

"We'll take my jet," Blake offers.

"Jet where?" Jamie walks in, trailed by Allie and Isadora.

"To Brazil," Blake says. "You're coming too. We'll call it a reset."

Jamie raises a brow, glancing from Allie to Isadora to me.

"I'm in."

"Beach and bad decisions?" Allie grins. "Sold." She turns to Isadora.

"Sorry—Marcus needed something." Hadrian's voice comes in behind them as he slips his phone into his pocket. "What'd I miss?"

"We're going to an island in Brazil," Blake announces again. Guess it's real now. "Sartori's taking us."

Hadrian zeroes in on me. "Of course he is."

"What do you say, Second?" Blake goes on. "I'm sure Brielle would love it too, if we're building a guest list."

Hadrian shakes his head. "I can't just disappear into a random island mid-campaign." He turns to leave. "But enjoy yourselves."

Jamie nudges Isadora. "Well?"

Isadora's eyes flick to mine, then back to Jamie. And I have to try really fucking hard to keep mine where they should be.

"I'm on a tight deadline," she says, but it lands more like a question. "Don't think I should either."

Jamie groans. "Bring your laptop. You work better with a view."

"Exactly," Allie adds. "And you love Brazil."

She doesn't answer right away.

Then she looks at me, almost as if she expects me to say something. I don't. I just meet her stare and hold it.

Fuck. Please say no.

She exhales, her posture loosening by a fraction.

"Alright. Let's do it."

Great.

Fucking great.

Exactly what I needed—one more liability in a pile of them.

Just one question: anything else out there about to go to shit?

Because a heads-up would be fucking fantastic for once.

44
Hadrian

I WAKE UP JUST before my alarm goes off, like my mind won't let me rest no matter how much my body begs for it.

So much for a quiet night. I told myself I needed some entertainment, considering everyone's flying off to Brazil or whatever.

Brielle felt like work. I can already see the weight of her expectations when she looks at me, and it just... turns me off, I guess.

I feel drained, but my brain's already racing.

Sleep should be a relief, but it feels like a luxury I can't afford—even though I desperately need it.

The faintest light filters through the window, a soft glow hinting at the sunrise. It's the kind of quiet moment that could feel peaceful if it weren't for the unease in my chest and the familiar tachycardia.

I brace myself before glancing to the other side of the bed.

What was her name again?

Maria? No, that doesn't sound right. Melanie? Or was it Madeline?

Something with an M.

Or—wait. N?

I groan internally, running a hand over my face. M. N. Doesn't matter.

I ease myself out of bed, careful not to disturb her. My feet hit the cold hardwood floor, and I wince. The pounding in my head intensifies.

I make my way to the bathroom, and each step is an effort. The face that greets me in the mirror is a stranger too—bloodshot eyes, stubble that's just past the point of intentional scruff, and dark circles I'll definitely blame on the campaign.

Not entirely untrue.

I need to be at Second Front for the first meeting in thirty minutes, which gives me just enough time for an ice-cold shower to slap some life back into me.

I let the freezing water hit me like penance. It does little to shake the fog from my head, but at least the cold water numbs the pounding. I dry off and lean against the sink for a moment. I rake a hand through my damp hair and sigh.

The folder with the NDA agreements catches my eye where I'd left it on the dresser last night. Signed and tucked away, thank God. It's a necessary evil—Marcus's words—to keep the campaign clean.

There's nothing clean about the ritual.

I flip one open.

Naomi Voss.

Right. That was it.

The name stares back at me, sitting just above the black ink of her signature.

I hate it every time. Not because it's wrong—there's no room for ambiguity in my world—but because it turns intimacy into paperwork.. Like I'm signing away the last scraps of what used to feel natural. But I do it anyway, with a practiced charm and an easy smile, the way I've been trained to handle everything.

Back in the bedroom, Naomi's still asleep, her hair spilling across the pillow like a painting I don't have time to appreciate. The moment is over—was over the minute we fell asleep—and reality waits just beyond the door.

I grab a piece of paper and scrawl a note.

> *Naomi, had to head out early for work. Help yourself to breakfast before you go. I'll call you.*

It won't happen.

It's better this way. No messy goodbyes, no awkward questions. Just the illusion of something left unfinished.

I leave the note on the pillow beside her and slip out of the room. The air in the apartment is thick with her perfume—a bit too sweet for me—blended with the lingering scent of whiskey we spilled on the living room carpet last night.

Outside, the city's not fully awake yet, but it's already warm. That sticky, early heat that settles under your clothes and makes everything feel heavier. I exhale. It doesn't help.

The streets are still quiet, the kind of quiet that should be calming.

But it isn't.

My pulse won't settle. My thoughts won't either. I can't tell if it's the hangover, the residual haze from whatever I took last night, or the suffocating weight of feeling like my life is no longer mine.

I slide into the car—no more biking after the shit show with the paps—and slam the door shut. My hands grip the wheel, fingers digging into the leather. The air feels too thin, my chest too tight.

The phone sits on the passenger seat, taunting me. I stare at it, willing it to stay silent, but also half-hoping it'll buzz and confirm my worst fears.

What if someone saw me?

What if there's a photo? A video?

My name's been trending on and off for the last couple of weeks.

My first instinct is to call Allie. She'd know exactly what to say, how to calm me down, how to make me feel like I'm not falling apart.

But I can't.

Because what would I actually say?

Hey, I slept with a woman whose name I couldn't even remember until I saw it on the NDA, and even though I made an idiot of myself with that paperwork, I'm still losing my shit and thinking of you.

Instead, I grab the phone and dial Marcus. It rings once, twice, and then his voice comes through, groggy and annoyed.

"Second, do you even know what time it is?"

"Marcus," I cut him off. "I need you to check something for me."

"What's going on?"

"Scan everything. Reddit, Twitter, whatever gossip sites you can think of. Make sure there's nothing new about me. No photos, no posts. Nothing."

There's a pause.

"You're being paranoid. Have you slept at all?"

"Just check," I snap. "Please."

He exhales heavily. "Fine. Give me ten minutes."

I hang up and toss the phone onto the seat, the silence in the car suddenly deafening. My hands won't steady. My chest feels like it's caving in, my lungs working overtime to suck in air that doesn't feel like it's there.

I start the car and the engine's growl vibrates through me. I pull out onto the empty street, try to focus on the road, but the paranoia clings to me like a second skin.

The light ahead turns yellow. I should stop, but I don't.

My foot slams the gas instead, the car lurching forward.

A horn blares. Headlights flash in my peripheral vision. I slam the brakes, the seatbelt cutting into my chest as the car screeches to a halt. The other driver swerves, their curses muffled but unmistakable as they speed off.

I sit there, heart pounding, chest heaving, hands gripping the wheel like it's the only thing keeping me tethered to reality.

The phone buzzes. I grab it with shaking hands.

"You're clear," Marcus says, his voice flat. "Nothing's out there."

I close my eyes, leaning my head back against the seat. Relief should come, but it doesn't.

"Thanks," I mutter, my voice barely audible.

"Second," his voice softer now, "you need to get a grip. You're going to burn yourself out."

"Yeah," I say, but it sounds hollow.

I hang up and drop the phone onto the seat, staring out at the empty street. What Marcus doesn't understand is that I'm not burned out. I'm washed away, pulled under by the weight of all the words I want to scream but can't, and the ones I need to keep silent but am forced to push out.

I'm not burned out. I'm fraying.

There are two kinds of people in this world: the ones who see yellow and slow down, and the ones who see yellow and speed up. Not to save a few seconds, not because they're late. Just because.

I'd like to be the first.

I put the car in gear and drive. The city is waking up, the first light of day creeping over the horizon.

But I'm still stuck in the dark.

45
Isadora

THE HELICOPTER BLADES SLOW, their roar dissolving into the sound of waves crashing far below the cliff. I slide my sunglasses back on even though the sun's dipped behind a cloud.

Kathy needed the Ellington jet, so we ended up taking Leo's to Recife. And then a heli out here to the island—something about only cleared helicopters being allowed to land on Fernando de Noronha.

Easily the biggest I've ever been in. Matte black, with soft leather seats arranged in a horseshoe around a champagne bar no one touched. Noise-canceling headsets, cold towels, soft lighting.

Allie and Jamie dozed off as soon as we lifted off. Irina took a million videos for her story. Blake tried to flirt with the flight attendant until Irina stared him down. Rami sat next to me. Max and Archie argued about something crypto-related. Leo was busy being the co-pilot. Which shocked me—but also, somehow, didn't.

All I can say is I'm grateful we didn't have to sail all the way out here—because I would've been as seasick as a Jane Austen heroine crossing the Atlantic for a man.

Which is, for the record, not why I'm here.

We step out, and the humidity hits even harder and more mercilessly than it did in Recife. I feel it instantly: in my skin, my hair, even my lungs. You can see the ocean, but you can smell it too. Taste the salt in the air. Feel it wrap around you, thick and alive.

The only house in view, just beyond where we've landed, rises from the cliffside—a blend of stone and dark wood, carved into the rock like it grew from the island itself. Glass walls catch the last of the light, glowing gold at the edges, half-reflecting the sea behind us. There's something quiet about it. Not showy. Just... certain. Like it's not trying to impress you, and that's exactly why it does.

There's a footpath made of volcanic stone leading from the helipad, half-swallowed by vines and pink hibiscus blooms. I'm already sweating through the back of my linen shirt.

"How hot was *that*," Allie whispers as we start down the path. "A *pilot*, huh?"

I smile at her, rolling my eyes.

Max and Archie are already racing toward the house.

Jamie slips between me and Allie, wrapping an arm around each of our shoulders.

"This will be *epic*," he declares as we get closer to the mystery cliff mansion owned by the world's most emotionally unavailable man.

"Baby, I was just trying to be nice to her," Blake's voice trails up from behind us.

"If I wanted to watch a man fail at flirting," Irina says smoothly, "I'd open TikTok."

Allie snorts. We don't turn around.

We make it to the house, and Leo walks past all of us—shoulders set, pace unbothered. He pauses at a sleek black panel beside the door and leans in. There's a small mechanical click as his eye is scanned, followed by a soft *beep* and a hiss as the front door slides open.

We step through.

Allie gasps.

The interior is cool and open, a long stretch of polished stone and dark timber that draws you in like a held breath. The ceiling lifts high above us, framed in slatted beams that allow sunlight to slice through in gold stripes. A series of linen sofas sit square in the center, surrounding a sunken conversation pit that looks like it was made for confessions.

To the left, a kitchen of matte black counters and brushed metal, anchored by a glass-front wine fridge tall enough to step into. On the right, floor-to-ceiling windows open directly onto the ocean, no railing, just infinity. You could fall into it. You *want* to fall into it.

Art is minimal, black-and-white photography, a single driftwood sculpture in the corner, a stack of books on a floating shelf. Some titles I recognize, all in Portuguese.

Max and Archie look at each other. One beat. Then matching, wicked grins.

They break into a sprint at the exact same time, peeling off shirts mid-run. Shoes fly, pants hit the deck, and they hurl themselves into the pool with perfect synchronicity.

The splash is enormous. The glass-flat water erupts into waves, slapping against the edge like applause.

Irina unzips her dress and lets it fall in a single, fluid motion. No hesitation, no announcement. It pools around her ankles, and she steps out of it. Underneath, she's wearing black lace. High-cut at the hips, barely-there straps, silk panels that leave just enough to the imagination while making it clear imagination isn't strictly necessary.

Her long legs catch the light as she steps forward and kneels by the water, touches it with the tip of her finger.

"Perfect," she murmurs right as she shoots Blake a look.

"I'll second that," Archie echoes under his breath, eyes fixed somewhere between her neck and thighs. Completely shameless.

Blake literally groans. "Baby—"

Before he can finish, she dives. Head first, smooth as glass. I've seen Olympic qualifiers with messier form.

Archie and Max instinctively shift, opening space as she slices through between them, then resurfaces at the far edge.

Even Jamie's mouth is open.

I elbow him.

"What?" he says. "We're not related. Yet."

Allie and I both giggle.

Leo appears in the doorway, followed by a team of house staff rolling in luggage. Three people are assigned to Irina's suitcases alone.

"This is Flor," Leo says, nodding toward a warm-looking woman in white linen. "She'll make sure you're taken care of. Anything you need, just ask."

"*Olá.*" She greets us with a gentle smile. "*Sejam bem-vindos.*"

"*Gracias,*" Jamie offers brightly.

Allie snorts. "That's Spanish, genius."

I lean in. "Say *obrigado.*"

"*Obrigado,*" he repeats, a little sheepish.

Flor's smile widens, eyes crinkling.

"There are enough rooms for everyone to have their own," Leo continues. "Take your pick. The main suite is off limits."

He gestures toward the hallway. "Chef's name is Lucas. He'll prep meals unless you tell him otherwise. If you need to get around the island, Marcelo's the driver."

He starts to turn, already halfway gone.

"Wait—where are *you* going?" Blake calls out.

Leo stops. Turns.

There's a flicker in his expression—tight jaw, stormy eyes that say—scream, even—*stay out of my business*.

But then he smooths it over. Just enough.

"I've got business mainland side," he says. "I'll be back."

46

Hadrian

THE FIRST POLL RESULTS are arriving any minute now, and I'm already on edge.

The room buzzes around me, all elbows and tension. Campaign aides murmur near the monitors, the flicker of incoming data casting shadows over their faces. I don't bother pretending to care about the numbers just yet. My hands won't stay still.

My phone vibrates on the table, but I don't even glance at it. Instead, I stand—figuring this is as good a moment as any to step away.

The toilet is quiet. The kind of stillness I need.

My reflection catches me off guard as I approach the sink. Perfectly polished, Carter-Bello confidence practically stitched into the lapels of my suit. But I know better. I lean against the counter, staring myself down, and pull the vial from my pocket.

A voice in the back of my mind starts up, telling me to stop, to think twice. *You've been doing so well. You don't need it.*

You know what?

Fuck that.

Because well is not something I've been.

And that voice of reason doesn't know what it's like out there. It doesn't understand what it takes to keep this whole machine running.

I uncap the vial. Just a little. Just enough to get through the next hour.

This was never meant to be a pattern.

Still isn't.

But I need the edge. The energy.

I'll quit whenever I want. I've done it before.

It wasn't that hard back then.

It kind of started when I was eighteen.

I could probably pinpoint it to the day I found out about my father's affair. I don't blame him. Not entirely.

I'd come home early from school, skipping practice for some reason I can't even remember now. It was Saturday, just past lunchtime. My mother, Isa, and Allie were out, so the house was quieter than usual. Then I heard voices coming from his study. At first, I thought it was just a meeting. But when I opened the door, there they were—my father and some woman who wasn't my mother, talking way too close to each other.

I froze.

They didn't.

She stood up, and he looked up at me like I was interrupting something important. Like I was the one in the wrong.

"Hadrian, what are you doing here?" My father's voice was calm. Sharp. Unbothered.

"Where's Mom?" I asked. Mine was not.

He didn't answer. Just glanced at his watch like I was wasting his time.

The woman was already slipping past me. I watched her cross the hallway, tugging her coat closed, heels clicking a steady escape toward the front door. She didn't look at me—whether that was shame or just her not giving a damn, I couldn't tell.

I followed her out. Through halls of all the family pictures—my father with my grandfather, my father with the former president. The shame I felt was considerable. But the rage was bigger.

When the door finally shut behind her, I turned back, found him in the living room, and cornered him. My voice shook with anger when I spoke.

"How could you do this to her?"

I remember the knot in my throat like it was yesterday.

He tried to dismiss me. Downplay it, like it wasn't a big deal. But I was beyond reason. The argument escalated fast. Me accusing him of betrayal, him calling me naïve. Said I didn't understand the complexities of marriage.

And then I just knew. I was about to fight my own father.

It got physical. I shoved him, and he shoved back. We were on the floor before either of us stepped back.

When it was over, we were both hovering—chests heaving, hands clenched, glaring at each other like strangers. Or worse. Like two people who'd once been close and had just crossed a line they couldn't come back from. I'd never felt so far from him. So disconnected.

I never stopped either.

My mother wasn't there to witness it, but she saw the aftermath. She found me sitting in the back garden later that night, my knuckles raw and my face flushed with shame and fury and that choking heat in your throat you can't cool down.

She didn't ask what happened. She didn't need to.

A week later, she announced she was going to Argentina to take care of my grandmother. She said it was about family obligations, but I knew better. She needed space—from him, from me, from everything.

Without her, the house felt emptier than ever.

I wanted to keep Isa out of it, so I didn't really talk about it with her either.

My father and I barely spoke after that day. He buried himself in work, and I buried myself in anything that could numb the pain.

Alcohol, coke, pills, poker—you name it. I just needed a break from the uncontrollable rage I felt.

I told myself it didn't hurt. That he didn't hurt me.

My mother came back a year later after my father flew all the way down there for her. I don't know how they managed, but they returned as the picture of happy matrimony, and I was the only one left still angry.

I brush off the memory by taking a quick fix.

Won't hurt.

I have it under control.

There's a knock on the door.

"Kinda busy," I say.

"Polls are out," Marcus shouts from the other side of the door.

I compose myself. Wash my face. Stare at the mirror. Grab the sink a bit harder than I need to.

I have it under control. I always do.

I leave the toilet. Marcus has a big grin on his face.

"They're tight," he says. "But slightly inclined toward you."

That's great news. I smile back. Everyone starts clapping.

Definitely great news, judging by the restless energy crawling under my skin.

Like a live wire, peeled raw, sparking on the floor.

Beside a growing puddle of water.

Allie

Hey

Hey

Is everything okay?

Yes, definitely

What time is it there? Isn't it super late already?

It's only a two-hour difference…

Then it's two a.m.

What are you up to?

We're just having some drinks. You?

Who's we?

Actually, don't answer that.

Can I call you?

Hadrian…

I just need to hear your voice.

I'm sure Brielle's voice must sound just as nice.

Actually, I take that back. Mine definitely has a better sound to it.

Believe me, I know.

47

Leo

I STEP OFF THE chopper and into the heat, my jacket slung over one shoulder. The blades haven't even stilled when I spot the SUV—engine running, windows blacked out, heat lines rising off the hood like smoke.

Fakka leans against it, cigarette hanging from his lips, machete tattoo coiled up his forearm like a warning. I only know him by his street name, Fakka. Comes from *faca*, knife. Fitting, given what he can do with one. He's my in with the kind of men who operate outside systems, men who don't ask for reasons. That's why he's here.

Irina's lead on the diamond came through yesterday. A red stone so vivid it defies classification. Too pure to be real, too large to be handled quietly. It shouldn't exist. And yet, here we are. Buried somewhere in the rot and miracle of Brazil, waiting.

Fakka flicks the cigarette, embers trailing through the air, and climbs into the driver's seat.

"The village is ten minutes out," he says, thumbing the pistol at his hip. "Samuel's not gonna like us showing up uninvited."

"He doesn't have to like it." I slide into the passenger seat. "He just has to talk."

The road spits us out into dirt. It's thick, uneven, gutted from the rain and the weight of vehicles that shouldn't have made it through.

I've been on worse.

Fakka doesn't talk. I don't ask him to.

The village appears in fragments. Rusted roofs, crumpled walls, children barefoot in the dust. Then a man—slim build, wire-rimmed eyes—locks onto our vehicle and starts running.

"*Idiota*," Fakka mutters, already shoving his door open.

I step out slower, more deliberate, watching the way Fakka gains on him like a shadow. He tackles him clean, slams him into the dirt like a rag doll tossed from a height.

"*Porra! Me solta, desgraçado! Filho da puta!*" The words spill fast—anger, let me go, son of a bitch. Or close enough. Fakka drags him upright and pins him against a shack with one arm across the chest.

"The diamond," he growls, voice so low it barely counts as human. "Where is it?"

"*Eu não sei do que você está falando!*" Samuel gasps, eyes wide. I guess he's pretending cluelessness.

Fakka draws a knife. Not fast, slow. Like he wants Samuel to feel every inch of the cold edge against his skin.

"Wrong answer."

Samuel's gaze finds mine. He pleads.

I stay exactly where I am, leaning against a tree, arms folded, unmoved. This isn't my part.

"*Espera! Espera!*" Samuel chokes. "*Eu vou contar! Mas é perigoso. A pedra já foi prometida à família Claveneau. Eles estão a caminho para buscá-la. Vocês nunca vão conseguir deles.*"

Fuck.

I don't catch much, but the name is enough. The Belgians are here.

"Where are they keeping it?" Fakka presses, blade nicking the skin now, red beading up like sweat.

"*Um acampamento, três quilômetros a leste daqui,*" Samuel breathes.

"*Mas vocês não ouviram isso de mim.*"

Good. That sounds close.

Fakka exhales. Then drives the knife into the soft part of his neck, fast and precise. Samuel convulses, blood catching on his tongue as he collapses.

It's not the first time I've watched a man die. And it won't be the last.

Fakka wipes the blade on his jeans like it's nothing, then turns to me.

"Rats don't belong in this business."

"Let's move."

We get into the SUV. Fakka starts driving east.

"Fuck." I hit the glove box in front of me.

"We'll get it," he says, eyes locked on the road.

"We don't have time to be wrong."

My phone buzzes in my pocket. I pull it out. One look at the screen.

Fuck.

"They know we're here," I say.

Fakka presses the gas harder.

I pick up.

"Solange."

"Leone Sartori," she says it like she always does. Like my name tastes good in her mouth.

"To what do I owe this unexpected pleasure?"

She laughs, the sound soft and amused. "Oh, *cher*. Don't we know each other too well to pretend?"

I sigh.

"I thought I'd give you the courtesy," she says. "Before it gets messy."

"Already is."

"You haven't even started to see messy, *cher*. We're too close to owning half the world. You know that feeling. You know what it costs. And you know there's nothing that will stop us now."

I scoff. "Get over yourself, Solange. The dust is mine. Nothing you can do about it."

Another laugh. This one real. "Still so sure of yourself. I missed that. Missed us."

"I didn't."

"Either way, I'm glad I'll get to see you again. Even if it's just to kill you."

South Op - R

Hey. I'm in Brazil.

Need a hand.

Are you around?

Not me. But my people are.

What do you need?

Still got a badge on your side?

Yeah

You in trouble or hunting?

Both. Call you in five.

48

Isadora

A CLANG RINGS OUT from the kitchen—like metal on tile, fast and high-pitched. Followed by the sound of rummaging.

I look at Rami.

He's already rising from the couch in one fluid motion, spine straight, hand instinctively brushing the fabric of his waistband. His eyes sharpen. All softness gone.

He starts moving toward the hallway without looking back.

"Stay put," he says, voice low but clipped.

I don't.

There's the tiniest, almost imperceptible sigh. He doesn't turn around, just flicks two fingers back in a signal—*wait*—but I ignore it.

Everyone else left for a night swim. I stayed back to work on the book I'm translating—tight deadline, and I'm still behind. We're supposed to be alone.

Rami's footfalls are silent, and I try to make mine the same. He reaches the threshold, presses his back to the wall beside the door, waits. One hand gently tests the doorknob. The other hovers near his belt.

I hold my breath.

Then, a quick lean as he peeks through the opening.

His shoulders drop, just slightly. The tension in his neck unwinds.

I step past him before he can stop me.

Leo's there. On the floor. Shirt half undone, a dish towel clenched in one hand, stained with blood. He's trying—badly—to wrap his opposite palm in a bandage, but it's slipping. His eyebrow is split, blood threading down his temple.

"Seriously?"

He looks up.

"I'm fine," he groans.

I walk toward him, unblinking.

There's a fresh cut on his lip too.

"You're clearly not," I say.

I reach down for his hand to get a closer look. He tries to pull it back, but I hold on tighter than I mean to. His eyes flick to mine. One brow lifts.

"Rami," I call, still looking at Leo. "First aid kit."

"It's in the hallway closet," Leo says. "Top shelf. Green case."

"On it."

I move quickly too—towel, freezer, ice.

When I return, I kneel beside him on the cold tile, pressing firmly the frozen towel against his brow.

He flinches.

"Hold it there."

He does.

"Is there a reason behind this sudden aggression?"

I don't answer.

He swears under his breath as I press again, harder than needed.

I pause. Just for a second. Then meet his eyes.

"Is there a reason you have to be so rude all the time?"

His unwounded brow lifts again—higher, somehow, like he's trying to look unimpressed but failing.

I don't wait for him to reply. "First you invite us all here like it's no big deal. Then you vanish for three days. Like we're just... stray dogs you left at the gate. And now I find you bleeding on your own kitchen floor. Which—as previously stated—is not the first time."
He opens his mouth. I don't let him speak.

"You know what else isn't the first time? Me offering to help and you pushing me away like I'm trying to amputate your dignity."

I hear Rami's steps retreat, then the quiet thud of the door as it closes behind him.

"Sorry," he says.

I don't look up.

Instead, I take his hand in mine. Gentler this time. The adrenaline's cooled, but the anger hasn't fully left me. His palm is sliced near the base of his thumb—shallow, but messy. I clean around it with antiseptic, then start wrapping it properly.

Once the hand is done, I move closer, his knees brushing mine, and tilt his chin up with two fingers. I dab at the blood trailing from his brow, then reach for the butterfly strips to close the gash.

"What happened?" I ask. "Was it someone else's honor again?"

He lets out a laugh and his fingers fly to his lip like he regrets it instantly.

"Quiet," I snap, brushing his hand away. "And keep those filthy hands away from the wounds."

"I—"

"No more talking," I cut in. "Not until this is clean."

His eyes narrow slightly, and he just nods. I clean the cut at the corner of his mouth last.

His eyes are on me the whole time. The usual. Steady, dark, unreadable.

"There," I say, pulling back just enough. "You won't die. Not today, at least."

His mouth twitches, barely. Then he stands. I do too.

He's close. Very. Towering over me. And I'm not short—five-seven, maybe a little taller. Still, I barely reach his shoulder.

"Drink?"

"Sure."

He disappears down the hallway. I hear a cabinet open, the clink of a bottle against glass. When he returns, he's holding two tumblers.

He offers me one without a word.

I take it. "Whiskey? I don't—"

"So you can stop pretending you like martinis when you clearly don't."

I give him a confused look, then a half-smile creeps in. "And what makes you think I'll like whiskey?"

"Call it a hunch."

He crosses the room to the far end of the kitchen, where the wide-open window makes the night look almost painted. The ocean beyond it shifts gently in the dark.

I follow him, barefoot across the cool tiles, until we're both perched on the wide ledge of the open window. There's no barrier between us and the night, just salt-heavy air and the rhythmic hush of the ocean folding in on itself.

We sit a few feet apart. Not touching. Not speaking. The kind of quiet that wraps around you.

The moon is black tonight. Just a hollow outline in the sky, like someone forgot to turn it on.

I lean forward, forearms on my knees. "So?" I ask. "What happened?"

He lifts the glass, then stops, pressing two fingers to his mouth in a zipping motion.

I roll my eyes. "Really?"

He just nods once and keeps looking ahead.

The silence stretches. And you can almost touch it, heavy and thick, like velvet soaked in water. And I do want to touch it. Touch him, even. And I have no idea where that's coming from.

I look at him. Let myself look. His profile is sharp even in the half-light. Jaw bruised, a scratch across his temple, lips split and still somehow soft. His eyes are darker than the sky above him, and just as endless. And always, always raining.

Seconds or centuries pass. Then he turns.

His gaze catches mine like a tether pulled tight.

"You're saying a lot with your eyes right now."

I narrow them slightly. But don't look away. There's a storm building in his. There always is. Makes you wonder if they've ever once seen a rainbow.

"And what exactly am I saying?"

He makes a sound—not quite a sigh, not quite a groan. Then he looks away.

It physically hurts. Like pulling a muscle you didn't know you had.

I look away too.

It's become quite clear to me that the storm isn't just in his eyes. It's all around him. In the way his shoulders stiffen when things get too quiet. In the silence he wears like armor.

He's unreachable in every sense a person can be.

Thunder cracks in the distance. And I take a mental snapshot of what's in front of me right now. Impossibly beautiful.

"I can't," he says suddenly. Just above a whisper. Gravel in it.

I turn my head. "You can't what?"

He takes a sip from his glass. Keeps his eyes on the sea.

"You know what."

I take my first sip. Swallow. It's smoother than I expected—warm, with a faint honeyed taste.

"Then don't."

The tension is even thicker now. Almost tangible. And I'm scared to figure out where it's actually coming from.

His bandaged hand rises to my chin deliberately. He lifts it. Makes me look at him.

And now I'm properly terrified. All-encompassingly.

There's something about the way he won't look at you, until he does. Something I can't quite name. Just that it feels completely ungrounded. Unstable. I guess there's no staying steady around someone who has skies for eyes.

A voice in the distance cuts through the rustle of trees, Allie's. Jamie's follows. Then Irina's laugh, light and echoing.

We don't move.

Their voices swell as they climb the hill, rising over the noise in my head, thinning it out, scattering it.

A whistle carries up from the backyard, right beneath the window. I blink. Snap back.

"Well, look who's alive," Blake calls out.

"Isadora!" Jamie shouts. "Come join us at the pool!"

"Are they... up there together?" Archie slurs a bit too loud, though he probably thinks he's whispering. Max snorts, then shushes him.

"Isa?" Allie's voice rings high and clear.

I step down from the ledge, feet finally hitting the floor again.

"Coming!" I call out. And make my way to them.

49

Hadrian

THE TIME BRIELLE AND I spend together is... workable.

In fact, it's disturbingly easy to disappear into it. There's a strange comfort in crossing lines with someone who knows how to keep things discreet.

Brielle's brand of partying is a paradox—wild yet controlled, reckless yet calculated. It's an art form, really, and I've come to admire her mastery of it. She moves through these scenes like a seasoned performer, always knowing when to turn up the heat and when to fade into the shadows. Fits perfectly with my current situation. I could even learn a thing or two from her.

Last night, we partied with the cast of that new Netflix show everyone's raving about. I can't remember the name.

I thought my NDA rituals were over the top, but these people have perfected the art of keeping a party under wraps. Makes me wonder how much of the Hollywood gossip that does leak is intentional.

Our phones were locked with some kind of device that disabled both cameras, front and back. And we all signed something that felt more like a blood oath than an NDA.

Nothing illegal, though. Well, aside from the usual drugs. Just a bunch of high-profile people trying to let loose for a night.

Everyone was nice to us. Not sure if it was because of Brielle, but I wasn't about to question it.

Everything was smooth, and I was already euphoric enough that my usual worries shrank to nothing.

We were chatting with one of the supporting actors—tall, good-looking, the kind of guy who knew it. Brielle, ever the diplomat, was in her element, gassing him up with just enough sincerity to make it feel like truth.

"You were great in episode six," she said, tilting her head. "That scene in the motel? You carried it."

He grinned, bashful but clearly used to this. "Wish the writers saw it that way. I'm basically decorative at this point."

"Oh, please," she purred. "Decorative gets screen time. But you deserve a subplot at least."

He turned to me then, eyes flicking over. "Well, Breezy, if I had *his* face and height, I'd probably have a lead by now."

Brielle didn't miss a beat. "Too bad, love. He's mine. And tragically for you, only into women."

I blinked. Not visibly, I think. Then she glanced at me—barely—and gave the faintest wink.

And I just played along. Maybe it was the alcohol. maybe it was habit. I draped my arm over her shoulders, pulling her close.

"That's right," I said, the words slipping out more naturally than I expected. "Sorry, mate. All taken here."

The guy laughed, raising his hands in mock surrender. "Honestly... you two together? Kind of iconic. Not gonna lie."

"Hadrian, you're zoning out again."

Lydia's voice cuts through my thoughts like a scalpel. My campaign chief is one of those people who's always ten steps ahead of everyone else in the room. It's equal parts impressive and exhausting.

The air in the debate prep room is thick with exhaustion, the kind that settles in your bones after twelve hours of relentless work.

I'd come straight here from the party, stopping only for a quick shower at home. It's nearly eight in the evening now, and my patience is wearing thin.

I sit at the head of the table, a stack of flashcards spread out before me like a losing poker hand. Each card is printed with sanitized, focus-grouped slogans. They're not ideas, they're soundbites, stripped of meaning and designed to offend no one.

"I'm fine," I mutter, flipping a card as if it matters.

The debate is in two days.

"Got a sec?" Marcus asks from the doorway.

"Sure." I stand without hesitation. "Perfect timing," I add under my breath as I pass him.

We step into my office.

"What's up?"

"Remember that interview you promised the reporter?"

I was really hoping that would just... fade away. How naïve of me.

It was after the Garden Party disaster. One particularly stubborn reporter wouldn't budge, even with the police trying to clear the place. Everyone else had backed off. We were all running on fumes, high-profile guests twitchy and exhausted, and this guy had parked himself by the only available back exit like it was the Watergate break-in.

I needed him gone. Fast. And, genius that I am, I offered him a short interview if he agreed to pack up and leave.

Apparently, he took me seriously.

"Their social media manager is downstairs," Marcus continues, eyes still skimming his tablet. "Seems like a kid. Friendly. Their audience doesn't go for anything too heavy."

I sigh, dragging a hand through my hair. "So fluff questions and fake smiles. Got it."

"Think of it as damage control with a side of PR."

I nod once. "Fine. Let's get it over with."

I head downstairs and spot said *kid* waiting by the entrance.

I glance sideways at Marcus. "How old is she?"

He shrugs without looking up from his tablet. I turn back to her.

She's already smiling wide. Chunky sweater, dark hair, nervous energy pouring out of her like static. She practically bounces as we approach.

"Hi! I'm Zoey," she says, voice a touch too loud. "With a *y* at the end. Thanks so much for, like, doing this. I'm such a fan—well, not, like, a *fan fan*, but I follow politics. Sort of. Anyway. Should we head up?"

I offer a polite half-smile. "Nice to meet you, Zoey. Follow me."

Upstairs, Marcus leads us to one of the small conference rooms before peeling off.

Zoey immediately starts fussing with her phone, awkwardly adjusting the camera angle like she's never used a tripod before. She bites her lip, moves the setup to another corner of the table, muttering something about lighting.

"Okay," she says, finally settling across from me, fingers still twitching over the record button. "Just a few casual questions. The kind of stuff that trends. Cool?"

"Cool," I say, leaning back, trying to look like I do this every day.

We run through a couple of warm-ups.

Zoey asks about my favorite pizza place in New York ("Joe's on Carmine, obviously"), my go-to karaoke song ("'Mr. Brightside,' it's a crowd favorite, so I stick with it"), and whether I'd rather fight one horse-sized duck or a hundred duck-sized horses ("One horse-sized duck. At least it's just one problem to deal with").

She giggles, finally settling into the rhythm. "Okay. That was perfect. I think we're ready."

We roll.

The actual interview goes smoothly. I play the part. Keep it light. Smile on cue.

"So, one last thing," she says, her tone shifting, making me snap to attention. "There's been a lot of talk about you and Allegra Montrose. You know—your sister's best friend. People have seen you two together. Alone. Pre-campaign. Some say it's a *thing*. Any truth to that?"

The question hits like a punch to the sternum.

My brain scrambles. *Don't stiffen. Don't flinch.* The camera is still rolling. And if I react wrong, it's already clipped and on TikTok.

I laugh, easy. Lean forward, elbows on the table like I'm in on the joke. "Allie? Yeah, we've hung out. She's Isadora's best friend. It's kind of inevitable. But no—no *thing*. I think people just like a narrative."

Zoey nods slowly, her bubbly energy cooling. Then she pounces.

"Got it. Just clearing the air. But speaking of the Montroses... there's been a lot of controversy around their timber company lately. Word is they've been lobbying *against* a federal bill that would require companies to disclose gender equity data in their hiring practices, especially in rural industries like theirs. Some are saying it's a direct slap in the face to transparency. What's your take?"

I steady my breath and keep my tone level. "I'm not sure where you're getting that, but my focus is—and always has been—on the issues that matter to this district. I've been clear from the beginning: no corporate strings, no big-money influence. My priority is the people."

She studies me for a beat, eyes gleaming, not wide-eyed anymore, but calculating.

"Got it. Thanks for your perspective."

She stops recording, packs up in a practiced blur. Her whole demeanor has shifted—cool, efficient, on mission.

"This is gonna do great," she murmurs, almost to herself. "Thanks again, Hadrian. You're, like, way cooler than I expected."

"Sure," I say. My smile feels glued on.

The second she's gone, I sink into the chair like I've been holding up a collapsing building.

My heart's still racing.

What just happened?

I try to replay the exchange, reassure myself I didn't misstep.

Rule one, stay cool.

Maybe this time I managed, barely.

Rule two, don't escalate.

Rule three, don't ignite.

But how do you find the words *not* to, lately?

There are none in the English dictionary. Trust me, I've searched. They are all inflammable. No matter what I say, how I say it—it's always too little, too much, too something. And this wasn't fluff. There's no such thing as an innocent interview anymore.

This was a landmine, and I walked right into it.

Marcus strolls in, beaming. "That went well. She seemed happy."

"Yeah," I mutter. "Not quite."

50
Isadora

"Can we move here?" Jamie says, settling on the pool's edge right beside where Allie and I are leaning in from the water.

We're all drinking margaritas. And yes, I'm aware of the cliché.

"What a life," Allie says. "I wouldn't be against it."

"Right? I say we just stay. Leo probably wouldn't even notice," Jamie adds, lowering his sunglasses. "I mean, he's barely been around all week."

Allie glances at me.

"Has he said where he's been going?"

I shake my head. "Something work-related, I guess?"

"What kind of work involves fist fighting?" Jamie asks, too casual.

Allie gives him a look.

"I'm just saying. So I know what careers to avoid."

"That was probably not work-related," I say. "Considering it was the middle of the night."

"Maybe he was out with friends," Allie offers, adjusting her bun to keep it from brushing the water.

I shrug. Highly doubtful. He doesn't exactly strike me as someone with a wide circle of international friends.

"Anyway," Jamie continues, "I strongly believe we should stay. No one's really waiting for me back home."

Allie and I exchange a look.

"I kind of miss it," I admit. "New York. My desk. My real computer. This laptop's about to fall apart on me."

Jamie narrows his eyes. "That all you miss?"

"Radio silence since Double Day," I say, acknowledging the center of his question.

"Good," Allie cuts in. "You needed the breather."

"So—last night. What's the plan?" Blake's voice calls from across the pool.

Irina's beside him, glowing in white linen. Max and Archie are kicking a deflated soccer ball dangerously close to the edge.

"There's a party," comes a low voice.

We all turn. Leo's standing just inside the patio doors, barefoot. And shirtless.

"The Halcyon Party."

Jamie sits up straighter. "Wait—*here*?"

Leo nods. Jamie's eyes go wide.

"That's not a party. That's *the* party."

"All right," Allie says. "Elaborate."

Jamie turns to her, already halfway breathless. "It's always somewhere different. A monastery. A yacht. One year it was inside a storm shelter under a decommissioned lighthouse."

Max whistles.

"Forty people max. Real names stripped at the door. You're assigned a new one and that's who you are for the night. No phones. No under twenty-ones. No exceptions."

He pauses. "And then... halfway through the night, they give you the riddle."

"A riddle?" I ask.

"People say it's abstract. A phrase. Or maybe even a symbol."

"And?" Allie says.

Jamie shrugs. "You know as much as I do now."

"How do you get invited to that?" Archie asks.

"Unclear," Jamie says, then turns to Leo, who grabs his phone and starts typing.

"You just do."

He looks up.

"We leave at seven."

By the time we arrive, it's fully dark.

The boat dropped us at a hidden inlet. From there, we switched to open-air Jeeps that climbed into the hills without headlights. Then a narrow trail on foot, each step swallowed by vines and soil and silence. No signs. No flashlights. Just small, pulsing stones buried in the dirt to guide the way—violet and dull gold, like the forest itself had a nervous system.

Then, suddenly, light. The forest around us begins to glow.

Branches bloom with fluorescent orchids in impossible colors—electric indigo, blood orange, pulsing jade. Ferns curl and uncurl with slow motion bioluminescence. The undergrowth gleams faintly like it's been painted with stardust. And above us, the trees stretch into glass, barely visible at first, then all at once. A dome. A greenhouse.

We've entered it without realizing.

Inside, the air is thick with something that isn't mist and isn't smoke but behaves like both. It tastes like lime peel and crushed petals. Somewhere, water drips in a rhythm too slow to be natural. There's no ceiling music—just layered vibrations that thrum through the soles of my feet.

Everything is living. Everything is intentional.

There are no walls. Just silk partitions draped from steel ribs, catching shadows as they sway. Couches are carved into stone slabs. Tables grow out of tree trunks.

Allie gasps and someone brushes past me—barefoot, translucent sleeves, and a face painted with thin stripes of something reflective. I catch a flash of copper in their hand. It's cards. And we each get handed one. Just a single letter. Mine is "R."

There's no bar. Only stations—carved tree trunks draped in silk, half-swallowed by foliage—where silent attendants pour drinks that look like they've been decanted from storm clouds. We walk to the nearest one.

I have no idea what I'm handed. Something in a cut crystal bowl. It's cold. Smoky. Slightly floral.

Allie takes a sip. "What in the potion is this?"

Jamie's already halfway through his.

Blake and Irina are already dancing with a bunch of other people right in the middle of the space.

Max has his hands in his pockets, barely speaking. Archie stands straight, tense, eyes constantly scanning the space, probably for exits. They both look uncomfortable. Like they're not sure they should be here.

And of course, there's Rami. Already found his corner for the night. Arms crossed. Jaw locked.

The music starts to swell, pulsing through the floor like it's being pumped in from under the roots.

Allie leans in. "Is that—"

"Don't say anyone's real name," Jamie warns. "They'll kick you out."

"Yeah, it definitely is," I whisper back.

Max heads straight for Allie. A man on a mission. "Care to make every guy here hate me?" he says, extending a hand.

She rolls her eyes but takes it.

I'm wearing a dress by Nicholas K—cowl neck, drapey silhouette, back slit. It feels like wearing air. Around me, glowing moss. Lanterns hanging from branches. Fog that doesn't move like real fog.

This whole thing feels like a fever dream. A curated hallucination.

And then I see him. Leaning against a marble column overtaken by roots and wild jasmine. Dressed in a black linen set. Drink in hand. Watching me back.

I walk over.

His beard's grown in since we got here.

"Hi, I'm R. Nice to meet you," I say, offering my hand with a crooked smile.

He huffs a quiet laugh, then shows me his own card—also R. "Guess we're on the same team?"

I step in beside him, matching the angle of his lean against the column.

He nods toward the lights. "You enjoying this?"

"Honestly? Yeah. Though my sensory system's on overload."

He takes another sip, noncommittal.

"You're a science guy, right?" I ask.

He arches a brow. "Something like that."

"There's this study," I say, watching his face, "that claims it only takes three minutes of uninterrupted eye contact to fall in love."

He gives me a skeptical look. I pull out my phone, open the timer, and set it to three minutes.

"Ready?" I hit start and then lock my gaze on his.

He blinks. "That's—"

"Don't look away."

The seconds begin to tick. He half smiles and rolls his shoulders back, like he's trying to shake off the tension, but it hangs between us. I know he feels it too.

He leans in just a fraction. "Careful," he says, smile still tugging at his mouth, eyes fixed on mine, "one crack in that poker face and I win."

The urge to flinch almost betrays me. Almost. If I look away, it's over, and not in the way I'm afraid I actually want. So I breathe in, steady myself, and keep my eyes on his. His brows are perfectly still, except for the left one, still slightly arched.

The seconds stretch in that traitorous way only time can. I guess that's what happens when you declare war on it.

He studies me, searching for the fissure. Waiting for me to fold. He thinks I can't hold. I almost enjoy it, the thrill of proving him wrong. Because he is. Right? I know you'd bet on me too.

The timer finally chimes, but neither of us moves. We don't break.

"See?" My voice comes out laced with victory. "I'm not in love with you."

For the first time, I see something move across his whole face and overtake it.

"And you're not with me," I add.

"So what now?"

I shift my weight. "So now we stay in minute two."

His gaze sharpens. Then his eyes flick to my mouth for a split second.

He shakes his head once, like trying to reset something. "I mean it, Carter-Bello. If you're not, you're only fooling yourself."

I give a short, breathy laugh. "You don't think I can pull it off?"

"I know you can't."

"I can do casual."

He scoffs. "Yeah? I bet half the guys here would love to test that theory."

That one stings. But I don't want it to.

I glance away, and spot this guy close by who's been watching me since we arrived. I push off the column and take two deliberate steps toward him.

I don't get to three.

A hand finds my arm and stops me.

He breathes something out, and gently turns me back toward him.

"Alright. You got me. Called my bluff. Smart girl."

His eyes linger on my mouth longer this time. It makes my skin tighten.

"So," he murmurs, "casual?"

"That's what I said." I lean in just slightly. "But I don't beg."

He smiles and steps in closer, still holding my arm, his thumb brushing the inside of my wrist like he owns the pulse under it.

"And I don't share," he says. "Tease them. Spin them in circles. Make it a show, even. But when the night ends..."

A heartbeat.

"You leave with me."

A sound like a chime cuts through the air.

I exhale through the rush in my chest and roll my shoulders back in an attempt to shake off the shivers down my spine.

From between the trees, a masked woman steps forward, fog curling around her like she conjured it. She doesn't speak. Just holds out a tray. One envelope for Leo and one for me.

Mine's heavier than I expect. There's a shape inside, something firm pressing against the paper.

I break the seal.

"Is that... a lanyard?" Leo asks.

"Seems like it."

It's old. Frayed. The laminate clouded and sun-warped.

The name has been blacked out. The photo too.

Printed at the bottom the word **Correspondent**.

In the upper corner, a faded logo. Looks like **FBN**.

Across the back, a red stamp, barely legible: **ARCHIVE – DO NOT REISSUE**.

And in the bottom right corner, a tiny scorch mark.

I have absolutely no clue what this could be or mean. I've never seen this before.

Leo unfolds his card.

He reads it, then turns it just enough for me to see.

"No light to give, yet you see me best when the world forgets its sun. No voice to call, yet I'm the first to answer when night falls."

"The moon?" I try.

He waves the card up.

"...That's it?"

He looks at the card again, then back at me.

"That's their big, world-shattering, brain-melting riddle?"

A pause.

"The moon?"

I blink.

"And an old credential?"

He doesn't move. Just stands there, stunned, like he's been personally betrayed by a piece of stationery.

I burst out laughing. Because I've seen this man walk through rooms like nothing can touch him, and a riddle is what finally gets to him?

"Unbelievable."

I open my eyes. He's one breath away. The laugh catches in my throat, then vanishes.

And I can't not do it.

So I do.

I lean in. So does he.

His mouth meets mine with a steady, deliberate surety. One hand anchors my hip, the other cupping the back of my neck.

My breath stutters. Then his thumb finds the line beneath my chin, drawing me closer without moving me.

He tastes the way he smells. A cool, clean sharpness with a warm edge—mint, yes, but toned down, like breath against winter air. Something unmistakably him that I can finally hold on my tongue.

I grab him too, curl my fingers into his shirt, and let myself sink deeper into it. Into him.

Because right now, here, kissing Leo Sartori in the middle of a glowing forest... *this* is the fever dream.

And if I were being honest—which I'm not, and won't be—I'd say I never want to wake up.

"Hey, lovebirds."

We snap apart.

"Party's over." Archie and Jamie are standing right next to us. Behind them, Allie and Max are giggling. Farther off, I spot Blake and Irina still dancing, except it's just the two of them now.

"What—?"

"Yep." Allie steps toward us. "It's nearly daylight. Most people left a while ago. And the music just stopped, in case you didn't notice."

"Yeah... we should hurry," Jamie adds, glancing around. "Or we'll miss the last Jeep. And I don't know about you guys, but I'm not dying to get stuck in a fluorescent forest any longer than I have to."

Max's grin vanishes from his face. "Fair."

Leo and I glance at each other. He offers me a half smile. And I can't help but half-give him my heart.

Half is fine. Half is still minute two.

"Let's go." He grabs my hand. "I'll have the jet fueled and ready in, let's say... two hours?"

There's a collective groan.

I can't help but laugh. "Come on, everyone. Let's go home."

51
Hadrian

I HEAR THE FRONT door unlock, which means Isadora's here.

She steps into the living room where I'm watching TV and sinks onto the couch beside me.

"Hi, Isa."

"Since when are you into Rally?"

"Since this guy Rino started racing. You'd struggle to find a man who isn't at this point. He's completely revolutionized the sport."

"Is that him?" She gestures toward the screen.

"Yeah."

"God. I imagine women everywhere are about to develop a sudden fascination with Rally, too."

I snort. "Yeah, I guess he's a good-looking fella."

She watches the screen a moment too long before snapping herself out of it.

"How was Brazil?" I ask.

"Hot. And chaotic. As expected."

"Was everyone on their best behavior?"

She glances at me. "You know. Same old trouble. Archie and Max broke a window with a soccer ball. Irina fractured her pinky toe walking through the forest in heels. Blake flirted with the flight attendant."

"Business as usual, then."

She leans back. "Anyway, I assumed you'd be barricaded behind a fortress of flashcards, Lydia trailing after you like a storm cloud."

"Reasonable assumption. But I've realized it's more productive to step away a few hours before I have to speak publicly. At this point, my brain won't absorb anything new. I perform better when I'm clear."

"That makes sense. Would you like me to come with you?"

"Appreciate it, but I think I should handle this one alone."

"I figured you'd say that. Still, it was worth trying." She turns to me, tilts her head. "How are you holding up?"

"I'm fine. I just need to pull through tonight. And then primaries next week. One step at a time."

"Hadrian, you'll be brilliant. I know it's an overused sentiment, but all you need to do is be yourself. The real, caring you is all they need to see to trust you."

"Thanks, Isa."

She smiles. "Have you seen Blake since we got back?"

I shake my head. "Not exactly working with a wide-open calendar."

"Makes sense." She slides both hands under her thighs like she used to when we were kids and she was hiding something.

I narrow my eyes. "Why are you being weird?"

She shrugs, casual. "No reason."

"Isadora." I turn to face her. "Spill."

She hesitates. "Okay, but *you* don't get to be weird."

That alone makes me brace.

"Leo and I—"

"No. Absolutely not."

She blinks. "I didn't even say—"

"Truly. Spare me the details."

"We just kissed!"

I snap. "What part of *no* was unclear?"

"You're impossible."

"I'm simply not interested. Do whatever you want."

She leans back. "Well. That's all then. Just thought you'd rather hear it from me than from Blake. Considering you're not his biggest fan."

I scoff. "I think he's a dick. But I also don't care. You probably *need* someone like him anyway."

She gives me that look, the one that comes right before she gets offended.

"I mean," I add, "you've only been with one guy, and he happens to be the nicest one. Maybe being with someone... difficult will clarify things."

She rolls her eyes. "I just don't get why it always has to be Milo or total despair. I'm not incapable of being alone, you know?"

"Being alone is not *exactly* what you're doing."

She let's out a breath, visibly frustrated. "Listen, Hadrian. I get it. You've always thought it was your job to look out for me. But I'm not twelve anymore. I don't need managing, not by Milo, not by you, and definitely not by Leo." She straightens up. "What is it that you are so worried about anyway? That I'll end up old and unmarried like Aunt Honor?"

I don't answer.

"Honor is one of the most respected judges of her generation. I'd be *lucky* to end up like her."

"That's not what I meant." I pause. Because to be honest, I'm not even sure myself.

I shrug. "You're right. You're more than fine on your own. And you have Rami anyway, so 'alone' is just figurative."

She grins, satisfied.

"Just make sure Dad doesn't find out," I add.

"Yeah. Definitely going to have to bribe Rami."

"He'd never."

She stands and smooths her dress.

"Well, I'll leave you to your elaborate relaxation techniques," she says. "I'll be rooting for you."

I take another look at the debate room. The lights are harsh—hot against my skin—and the air hums with tension. Journalists lean forward, pens poised, while the audience holds still. Campaign staffers murmur at the edges, their eyes darting between the candidates and the real-time reaction monitors glowing just out of view.

"Nowadays, candidates chase quantity, not quality. And a certain sector of our party understands that," says Jonas Mercer, his tone smooth, practiced. "Which is why my fellow contender here, Hadrian Carter-Bello, is getting cozy with companies like the Montrose timber empire. And why moderates like him are gaining traction across key states—scooping up uneducated, rural voters who simply don't grasp the complexity of what's at stake. We are faltering because we waste too much time trying to reason with people who lack the tools to understand us."

I expected this line of attack. After the Zoey incident, I knew it was only a matter of time. So I don't flinch.

The moderator glances up from her notes, expression even. "Mr. Carter-Bello, your response?"

I lean forward slightly, fingers grazing the edge of the podium.

"Aren't we supposed to be the ones standing against elitism?" My voice is steady, but firm. "Against the notion that people's worth is measured by education level or zip code? Since when did we start blaming working-class and rural communities for not fitting into our polished, academic narratives?"

I let that land before continuing, my eyes locking with Mercer's.

"Is it just me, or did my colleague here just imply that the disenfranchised—the very people this party claims to champion—are now the problem? That their lived experiences are irrelevant unless they speak our language, hold our degrees, or think like we do? That's not progressivism. That's moral superiority in a new disguise."

I look around. There's a shift. A ripple through the room. Some stir in their seats. A few brows knit.

The moderator clears her throat, re-centering the moment.

"Mr. Carter-Bello, some have pointed out that your stance on corporate accountability seems at odds with your family's connection to Montrose Timber. What do you say to that?"

I take a breath—just long enough to draw the silence tight—then exhale slowly. My jaw tenses, but only briefly.

"I'm not going to waste your time with details about my family's personal relationships." My voice is clear. Controlled. "What I will say is this: I have no financial or operational ties to Montrose Timber. None. But I'm not interested in moral posturing. I believe in engagement. If I have the chance to challenge corporations like Montrose, I will. Change doesn't happen in echo chambers, it happens face to face. It happens when you sit across from power and demand better."

I let my gaze sweep across the audience—eyes, not cameras.

"At the end of the day, this race isn't about soundbites or guilt by association. It's about you. Your voices. Your trust. And with election day around the corner, the choice is simple: either you believe I mean what I say, or you don't."

Silence. Dense, electric. It holds a beat longer than expected.

Then the clapping starts—scattered at first, unsure. Then building. Gathering momentum until the room fills with it. I don't let myself react, but I feel the shift. The current has turned.

Mercer adjusts in his seat, face carefully composed. The moderator leans toward the mic, waiting for the applause to break.

Mom

Congratulations, Hadrian.

I'm so incredibly proud of you.

That was outstanding.

Your words, your presence, the way you carried yourself. Everything.

The spitting image of Hadrian Senior. Wherever he is, I know he's proud too.

Thanks mom

52

Leo

THE TERRACE AT LUNAFERRO juts out like an extension of the building's spine, suspended above Central Park. The stone platform feels barely anchored to the structure, but it holds. It always does. My father's favorite dining spot in all of New York City, it feels like being on a plane. Above it all.

There's just one table. Long, dressed in white linen, set with heavy crystal and low amber candles. The light is soft, almost golden, flickering off cutlery and half-filled glasses. The plates haven't been cleared.

My father and OG sit at the far end of the table. They're the only ones left from what I can tell has been a long, fruitful dinner.

OG sees me first.

"The man of the night," he says as he lifts his glass. "Hell, the man of the year."

I take my seat at the far end. My father is already halfway through pouring the Château Margaux.

"Is the rock secured?" I ask.

He nods once. "At the agreed time and place." He slides the glass over. "Well done."

OG taps my shoulder. "Seriously—Brazil's not exactly beginner-level. And word is, she didn't make it easy."

I take a sip. Let it settle.

"I pulled some strings."

He lets out a low whistle. "Always the magician."

"It's the most unbelievable stone I've ever seen. Seven carats. Saturated blood-red—no zoning, no clouding, no fluorescence. Flawless table, perfect symmetry, zero visible strain. Type IIa. No nitrogen, no boron. Stones like that don't show up. Not in that color. Not at that size."

"Full-bodied, just the way I like 'em," he adds.

"If the saturation holds under cross-polarized light," my father says, "we're looking at a true Fancy Red. Not purplish. Not brownish. Clean red.

He glances at OG. "Auction houses would tear each other apart for that."

"That they would," I say. "Should I lock in dinner with Yakov Mikhailov?"

Lupo clicks his tongue. "I'll take it from here."

I let out a short laugh. "Right."

When he doesn't smile, my jaw tightens.

"Please tell me you're fucking joking."

"I'm not," he says flatly.

"So I risk everything—my name, my life, for God's sake—to secure a diamond no one even fathomed existed. And now you'll take it from here?"

OG shifts, crosses his legs the other way. Tries not to react.

Lupo opens the silver cigar case, takes his time. Hands one to OG without looking at me.

"Brilliant," I say. "Fucking brilliant. You want to at least tell me what the plan is?"

He lights the cigar with a quick flick of flame. The tip glows red as he exhales.

"We're finalizing the details. You'll be informed when necessary."

I look at OG. He gives the smallest shrug.

"Unbelievable."

I push my chair back. Stand. Stone grinds against stone, slicing through the stillness of the wind up here.

"At the very least," I say, "make sure whoever handles it knows what the fuck they're doing. This is war material they'd be dealing with."

Neither of them replies as I walk away.

There's a stone sitting half a world away that cost three people their lives. A fourth lost their freedom. And soon, it'll sit on someone's chest or finger like they've earned it.

People love to think diamonds are simple. Just shiny rocks. Proof of wealth, love, status. But they're not. They're complicated as hell. And the more you know, the messier they get.

Natural diamonds are pulled from the earth after billions of years buried under pressure. And when they come out, they do so flawed, unpredictable. You can see it in the inclusions—distortions, fractures, marks. Each one is proof it didn't come easy.

Some are clean. Mined right, traded fair, documented.

And then there are blood diamonds. Smuggled out of war zones, bought and sold in silence, paid for in blood. They carry bodies, stories, debts. And if you know what you're holding, you feel it. The weight doesn't come from the carats.

It's a luxury, sure. But mostly, it's a fucking ghost.

Most people don't want to know. They'll spend a fortune on a stone and never ask who bled for it. Ignorance is easier.

Lupo's built an empire on that ignorance.

And if you only believe one thing I say, make it this: he's everywhere. Hospitals. Schools. Campaigns. Churches. His name's stamped on every polished surface from D.C. to the Vatican. Try pulling him out, and the whole thing comes apart. You'd have to burn it down to the foundation.

What, you thought you could become the single biggest diamond dynasty by playing nice? That's cute. Really fucking cute.

My phone buzzes in my pocket as I step into the car.

I glance at the screen. A breath escapes before I can stop it. And I hate that it does.

"Carter-Bello," I answer.

"Are after-dark check-ins part of the two-minute deal?" Isadora says in a sing-song voice.

"You're drunk."

"Who? Me? Nope. Just out with Allie and Jamie. Not drunk. Just... out." She slurs the last word like it's doing all the work.

"Where are you?"

"Oh, you know... out."

"Isadora. Out *where*?"

There's shuffling. Like a hand clumsily covering the mic. Then her laugh spills through the line.

"We're at Apotheke in Chinatown!" Allie calls in the background.

I'm already driving.

"I'm close. Ten minutes. Don't leave."

53
Isadora

THE MUSIC IS LOUD enough to make you lean in, but not enough to make you shout.

Old jazz, I think, but warped. Slower. Stranger. Like someone dug up a dusty record and played it through a bass amp in the dark. Every now and then, a trumpet wails like it's drunk. So are we.

It suits the place. Everything feels a little theatrical. The bartenders wear vests and move like they're on stage. The lights are low, golden.

The crowd is dressed like an editorial spread. And I'm tucked into a booth between the two loudest people I know.

"What do you mean *no sex*?" Jamie asks, confusion coating every syllable.

"I mean that," I say, unfazed. "Also, when exactly was all this sex supposed to happen? We went straight from the party to the jet, and I haven't seen him since we landed in New York."

"You clearly lack imagination." He turns to Allie, seeking backup.

"Hey, I respect the entire spectrum of decisions a woman makes about her body," she says, lifting her glass in salute. "Even if it means abstaining from sex with one of the hottest men in New York."

Jamie snorts into his drink.

"Scratch that. On the East Coast." She pauses—only for effect, not because she's finished.

"Actually—I'll say what everyone's thinking and just go with America. Hollywood can keep their polished pretty boys."

I roll my eyes. "Exactly. That man looks like trouble."

"That just sounds like a rave review," Allie says. "Like he's going to ruin all other men for you. Glory, honestly."

I can't help it, I laugh. "The *point* is, we don't need to overcomplicate this with sex."

"One month," Allie declares, planting her glass down like a gavel. "Thirty days."

"I give her a fortnight," Jamie says confidently. "Tops."

"Wanna put your money where your loud mouth is?"

Jamie's eyes gleam. He turns to her with a mockingly gallant nod. "You're on, Allegra Elizabeth Clementine Montrose."

"Love it when you place bets on my self-control," I say, finishing the last of my whiskey.

I see him before they do. He's already seen us. Seen me.

He approaches us, and how do I explain this to someone who doesn't have actual eyes on him? Which, by the way, makes me feel slightly sorry for you. He walks like someone who doesn't have a worry in the world. Slow. Sure. Measured. But there's something in his eyes that doesn't match the rest. Something colder. Something stuck.

He's wearing a short-sleeved knit polo, cream-colored, the fabric loose-knit and slightly sheer, the collar soft. Below, cream-washed denim sits low on his hips with a brown leather belt.

It's the first time I've seen him in something that isn't black. Or a white shirt.

His skin is gold now, bronzed and warm from Brazil, and his tattooed arm is fully bare. From wrist to bicep, every line visible, its black ink mirroring the darkness of his hair.

He stops right beside us. Allie stands and swaps her spot for the little velvet armchair next to Jamie, and I'm left on the double seat alone.

"Hey," I say, flashing a smile before I can think better of it.

"Carter-Bello," he says, returning it. "Hi, Allie. James." He nods at them.

"Hey, Sarto," says Allie.

"Yo. What's up?" Jamie chimes in.

He slides into the seat beside me—arm to arm, leg to leg.

Jamie lifts the bottle of mezcal. "Want some?"

Leo shakes his head once. "Thanks, but I'm driving."

Then he turns to me. And I try not to mirror him, I really do. But I fail—spectacularly—as I meet the most haunted eyes I've ever seen, just inches from mine.

"Drinking whiskey?" he asks, a smile tugging at his mouth.

I smile back. "Trying something new."

"And how's that been going for you?" he asks.

"Surprisingly well," I say. "You, on the other hand, seem a bit... distressed."

"Just one of those days." He lets a breath out. "You have freckles."

Not a question. Just... a fact.

I let out a quiet laugh. "Yeah. I usually get them in the sun."

His hand lifts, just slightly, like he might touch my face. Then it falls, quiet again, like he thought better of it.

He turns to Allie and Jamie. "Do you guys mind if I steal her for a bit?"

"Absolutely not," Allie says, already grinning.

"Go for it," Jamie adds at the same time, with a little wave of his hand.

"Follow me," he says, already standing up and walking towards the door.

"What's happening?" I ask, catching up.

"The night's young. Still salvageable."

We slip out the side door and into the night.

"Where are we—"

"You'll see," he cuts in.

We walk side by side, strings of red lanterns swaying above us, and they might as well be pieces of someone's heart being dragged along the street.

I'm just glad it's not mine.

It can't be.

No matters of the heart in minute two.

His car is parked just around the corner, tucked beneath a flickering streetlamp. Neither of us says much on the drive, just the sound of the city thinning as we head uptown. Windows down. Air warm. At one point, I glance over and catch him drumming his fingers against the wheel, eyes fixed ahead like he's chasing something only he can see.

The streets begin to shift—less noise, less movement, more air. The buildings grow taller, older, heavier in their silence. We take a left off Fifth, and the lion statues come into view, frozen mid-guard.

We park directly in front of the New York Public Library. The building looms above us, its grand facade bathed in shadows, marble pale against the sky. The fountains are still. The steps are empty.

Leo gets out and walks around to my side, opening the door for me.

I look up at him. "We can't just... break in. Right?"

"Trust me?" he asks.

Already do, I'm afraid.

I just nod and step out of the car.

Behind us, I catch sight of Rami parked a few feet back, headlights off.

I brace myself for the inevitable discussion about whether he should come with us.

I'm already rehearsing the argument in my head. That the library's closed. That there's nothing inside but marble and books. That I'll be ten minutes, fifteen tops.

Turns out there's no need. He stays in the car.

Leo and I walk toward the steps I've climbed a hundred times before, just not when they are empty, and it feels like a completely different place. You can really appreciate the marble glowing faintly under the streetlamps, soft and silver, and each step worn smooth by a century of weight and weather.

Two men in dark suits flank the entrance. Their eyes track us as we approach. One gives a small nod.

Leo nods back as they open the grand doors without a word.

We step inside, and the air shifts—cooler, still, faintly perfumed with old paper and polished wood. Our footsteps echo softly across the marble, swallowed quickly by the silence.

"Here," he says, offering me his hand.

I take it. And as I do, I can almost feel the last bit of good judgment slipping away with it.

He guides me into the Rose Main Reading Room, and the vastness wraps around me instantly. The ceiling soars three stories high. Chandeliers hang like constellations. Rows upon rows of oak tables stretch ahead, each perfectly aligned, their green-glass lamps dimmed to a golden hush. Gold leaf. Stone arches. Dark wood.

The world outside stops existing. Because there's simply no way anything else could right now.

It's not empty in here. It's alive. And it's watching us back.

The sound of our steps changes—slower, rounder, almost reverent. The hush isn't hollow. It's full. Heavy. Sacred.

I stop walking just to take it in. The symmetry. The light. The sheer audacity of how much space has been allowed to simply exist. Untouched.

It feels like walking through the world's consciousness.

He lets out a quiet laugh. When I glance at him, he's already watching me.

"What?" I ask.

He just turns and starts walking toward one of the side alcoves, where the books are older and the air smells more like time than paper.

"Will you ever answer any of my questions?" I ask as we drift through the Philosophy and Literature section. Mahogany shelves. Dust-soft air. Books bound in cloth and leather. Lamps that whisper when you pass too close.

"You get three questions," he says, eyes scanning the spines. "Pick wisely."

"Favorite color."

"Black. It absorbs all wavelengths of light and reflects none."

I raise an eyebrow. "Very poetic."

"Next question."

I think. "If you could have dinner with anyone—alive or dead—who would it be?"

He pauses. Just for a moment. "My father. When he was a kid."

It lands heavier than I expect it to. Like something unspoken almost made it to the surface.

I run my fingers along the shelf and then stop.

"Here it is," I say, pulling out *The Waves* by Virginia Woolf. The spine is softened, the pages loose around the binding.

I open it like I used to ride my bike home from school, by habit.

"I am made and remade continually. Different people draw different words from me," I read aloud, my voice barely above the silence.

I glance up. "Do you think we're shaped by the people we let close?"

He looks away—just slightly—but something tightens in his posture.

"I guess so," he says.

I flip further. Find the one that always stops me.

"I am not one and simple, but complex and many." I pause. "I think that's brave. Writing about being a complex, mutable human in a world that keeps telling us to stick to one thing. Don't you agree?"

He turns back to me. "That's four. And I don't," he says. His voice is even, stormy eyes locked on mine. "Words aren't brave. Doing something about it is."

It's me who doesn't agree now, though I don't say it aloud. I think it's silly, implying words are like feathers in the wind. Because I have known words that have been carved into my bones.

The day I die, make sure to cut me open so you can read them.

54

Leo

THE CLOCK STRIKES MIDNIGHT as we leave the New York Public Library, and fuck.

It couldn't be more fitting.

Marble lions. Moonlight on stone. That echo you only get in places built to outlive us. And her, looking like she walked out of some far-off kingdom.

Yet no princess has anything on Isadora Carter-Bello. Trust me, I've met all of them. They all fall short. Don't even fucking scratch the surface.

The way she looked at that empty library. I could almost hear it. Sense it. See it even. The first crack in the armor.

It made me wonder what it'd be like, to be the kind of guy who ends up with a girl like her.

Same thought I had the first night I saw her.

Hadrian's gala.

My father had just dragged me back in after I tried to sneak out.

She left with Milo not long after.

And I just thought, *of course.* Of course she's with him. That's the kind of guy who gets to walk out with a girl like her.

Makes a man wonder what it'd be like to make it out of this life, the one that gives you everything except someone to share it with.

What it'd be like to flip the axis, burn the script, change course and start heading toward her instead. To believe that somewhere, there's a version of this life where you get to have her. Fully. Where the hand you've been dealt isn't already dead in the draw.

All I have right now is this set-in-stone certainty that overpowers everything. One day, Isadora will make some man feel like the luckiest fool alive. And he'll probably be right. And she'll feel the kind of happy that doesn't second-guess itself.

If I don't trust anything else in this world, I trust that.

She deserves things I can't even fathom giving someone. Things I wasn't made for. Don't have time for. Wouldn't know how to keep. Couldn't. Shouldn't.

She doesn't say anything when we step outside. Just grabs my hand like she's pulling me through time itself.

"Take me home?" she says finally, voice low.

I nod. "Wanna walk?"

She gives me a look. "It's almost an hour."

"Fifty minutes tops."

"What about your car?"

"Let it wait."

She squeezes my hand. "Off we go then."

We head north. Out of the corner of my eye, I catch Rami easing the engine on. Lights off. Trailing us like a ghost.

The streets are bone-quiet. Steam rises from a grate. A cab flies past, its horn blaring in the distance. Shopfronts are shuttered. Galleries dark. A doorman leans against his building smoking something thin. Central Park looms to our left, black and endless.

"Do I get three questions now?" I ask.

She doesn't answer right away. Then nods.

"Favorite color?"

That earns me a smile.

"Depends. Right now? Red. But it changes. It used to be yellow. Definitely not black."

I let out a short laugh. "If you had to live your life twice, what's one thing you'd do both times?"

She looks up like she's searching the sky for the answer.

"Study languages. Just... not for the same reason."

I glance at her, waiting.

"I mean, I enjoy my job," she says, tucking a loose strand of hair behind her ear. "But translating this book I'm working on... it made me realize my love for languages was always about something deeper than politics. Maybe it's even what made politics bearable for me."

She shrugs, eyes on the pavement. "I guess that's a perfect example of how the people closest to you shape the choices you think are yours."

"You don't need a second life for that," I say. "Sounds like you're already doing it."

She looks over at me. Then back ahead.

"I guess so."

A beat.

"Last question. Pick wisely."

"Let me think on it," I say.

We keep walking, the edge of Central Park unspooling beside us—black trees like spires, iron fences casting long, broken shadows on the pavement. It's quiet, but not dead.

Not sure if it's the moonlight or the streetlamps, but her hair's doing that thing again, catching the light. Like a rough brown river when the sun hits it just right and it flickers like it's hiding gold under the surface.

"You're doing it again," she says.

I turn to her.

"Looking while pretending not to be."

I stop and softly pull her to a stop, too. Make her face me.

I meet her gaze head-on. If her hair is the river, her eyes are the whirlpool you want to drown in.

And time—time has to be an illusion, because I swear I feel centuries pass in the space of a single breath.

She steps onto her toes and presses her lips to mine.

It's ruthless, really. How much I enjoy kissing her. The quiet sound she makes when she exhales against my mouth, the way she fits against me like my hands already know where to go.

I pull back before it gets worse. And by worse I mean better. But I regret it immediately. Whatever the fuck this pit in my stomach is must be written all over my face, because a flicker of confusion crosses hers.

Then her phone starts buzzing inside that tiny purse she's carrying and I'm relieved. *Relieved*, can you believe it? What a joke.

She pulls it out. "Als?"

"Isadora Sloane Carter-Bello." Allie's voice comes through loud enough for me to hear. "Care to explain what you're doing walking past Central Park in the middle of the night?"

"Just walking home," she says, already sighing. "Rami's here. Also, stop stalking my live location or I'm unsharing it."

"I *know* Rami's there. I called him first. He refused to 'disclose your whereabouts or companionship,'" Allie says, clearly quoting.

Isadora snorts. "I'll be home soon."

There's a pause.

"Sure, just... should I not be there?"

She blushes. Turns her back to me. Takes a step away, like she needs the distance to answer.

"Allegra. I'll see you soon."

Then hangs up.

The last stretch of the walk flies by.

The streets start narrowing. Cleaner. Quieter. That Upper East hush. Brownstones with polished brass numbers. Ivy crawling up façades. Private entrances framed by lantern light.

She walks a little closer now. Our hands brush every few steps, but neither of us reaches for the other again.

Somewhere above us, a doorman hoses down the sidewalk. Water slicks across the concrete, catching the streetlamp glow like oil.

She slows down as her building comes into view. I do too.

"Last question," I say, breaking the silence. "In minute two, if it was all yours—what do you want from me?"

She blushes again.

I've never seen it before, and now it's twice in one night.

We reach her building. Stop. Face each other.

"Just... to see you," she says.

I raise a brow. "See me how?"

"Like tonight."

I exhale through my nose. "Still don't get it. You know I don't date. So what's the point?"

"There isn't one, I guess."

She breaks eye contact. And I just stand there.

"You don't have to get it. I don't either. We can just... be." Her words trail.

Then she turns toward the door, fetching her keys.

"I'll be here, Leo. And I won't say no if you call. Or if you want to see me."

She glances over her shoulder, grin curving slow. "Unless I'm terribly busy, of course."

I know what I want to say. *You'd never be happy with me. Or safe.* But nothing comes out.

She turns away again. "I don't have any expectations. You don't have to worry about me."

She walks a few steps toward the front door. Then stops. Drops her arms to her sides. Tilts her head up.

"God, I'm so fucking tired of everyone worrying about me. Just—" She exhales, quick and shaky. "I've got it. Okay?"

I rush and step in front of her, blocking the door.

"Hey."

She looks up. Her jaw's tense. So are her hands.

"Heard you," I say. "Crystal clear."

She nods. I kiss her goodbye and walk away. Tell myself not to look back. Still do.

Truth is, I'll stay in minute two as long as she wants me to. Even if I know how it ends.

55
Hadrian

WE SMASHED THE PRIMARIES.

I suspected it after the last debate. The response was solid—not just in the room, but everywhere else that matters. Sure, the negativity's still there, growing louder, uglier. But so is the support. And by far, it's winning.

There's a whole mixed bag of people behind it. Some are legacy voters—my grandfather's old loyalists, now suddenly looking at me like I might be worth something after all. Then you've got the ones who just think I'm the better option compared to the alternative, which... fair enough. And then there are the ones who actually seem to like me.

Or maybe it's me and Brielle they like.

I can't tell.

I don't really care why it's working. I care that it is.

Whatever the reason, I've got a seat at the table. And that's all I ever wanted, to be in the room where something real can change.

Which brings us to tonight.

Temple Bar in NoHo.

We rented it out for the evening—low lighting, jazz low in the speakers, black-and-white in its bones. Just enough people to call it a party, but not enough to make it a headline. No press. No stage. No speeches.

Small win, small gathering.

The real thing's in less than three months. General elections. But tonight—tonight we let our shoulders drop just a little.

I watch Allie from across the room.

She's laughing at something Jamie said, holding her drink with both hands like she always does when she's trying to warm them up. She catches me looking and tilts her head.

I shake mine. Smile back.

Nothing.

Everything.

Blake's trying to talk policy with someone I'm ninety percent sure works in fragrance branding.

And then there's Isa. Who brought Leo, if you can believe it.

Well—technically, her, Allie, Jamie, and Leo all came together.

There's something oddly fitting about them. Not sure how to describe it properly. It's something about the way he moves around her, and how she doesn't react. Like she's used to his shape in her space. That sort of familiarity, when you've known someone's rhythm so long you don't register it anymore.

She lives in a completely different world than mine, doesn't she? Hell, sometimes it feels like another galaxy.

And I think part of me—deep down—envies her.

Because my own galaxy—the one I chose, the one I staked my flag in—is spinning on a different axis now. And every day, it pulls me light-years further from Allie.

I glance at her again. Max is standing close to her now.

I don't even want to know if they're messing around. I really don't think I can handle the idea of it.

I *truly* can't.

But... are they? Do you know?

He casually lifts his arm and rests it over her shoulders.

She flinches. It's subtle. Almost imperceptible. But she still doesn't move away.

And it makes me feel like the smallest man in the world. The way I just want to rip his arm off. Off his body. Off *any* body that gets close to her.

And yet, *I'm* the reason we can't be together. I'm even with someone else.

Smaller still. Shrinking.

I'm a crumbling island, slowly disappearing into the sea. But how do you tell the vast, beautiful ocean that it's the one drowning you?

"Second," Marcus snaps me back. "I'm heading out. All good?"

I nod. "All good. Just spaced out for a second."

He glances around. "Where's Brielle?"

"Doing some sort of press tour for her new movie. I think she's somewhere in Asia right now. Thailand, maybe?"

He nods slowly, then shifts his gaze. "What's going on there?"

I follow his line of sight, straight to Allie.

I narrow my eyes. "What do you mean?"

He scoffs. "Come on, man. I might be glued to my tablet half the day, but I'm not blind. And I've spent enough time around you to know what *that* look means."

My brows pinch. "Enlighten me."

"You're done for," he says, matter-of-fact. "Head over heels for that girl."

Somehow, hearing him say it—just plainly putting it out there—makes my shoulders drop. Just a little. Like I've been holding the weight of it in my chest for so long that having someone else finally see it means I don't have to carry all of it alone anymore.

I don't reply.

He shifts beside me. "Listen. I know this is counterintuitive, considering the two of you getting together would be my actual PR nightmare. And I seriously doubt I should even be saying this." He scratches the back of his neck. "But life's too damn short to look at someone the way you look at her and not do a damn thing about it. That's once-in-a-lifetime, Second. Trust me. I know."

I sigh. "Thanks. But I'm in no place right now. I'll mess it up. And I can't afford to mess it up."

"You'll fuck up the campaign?"

I shake my head, look away. "Her life."

He clicks his tongue. "You're braver than that."

He holds my gaze for a moment, something almost like pity behind it, and raises his glass.

"For what it's worth."

Then he turns and walks away.

Slowly, everyone starts leaving. Allie and Isa leave with Leo. Jamie slips out with Brielle's friend, Lyric. One by one, the space empties. And I follow.

The lights feel too soft now. The music too far away. The air too still.

I realize it's not just me shrinking now. It's the space around me too.

I grab a cab and head home.

The ride is quiet. Just the purr of the tires on pavement and the occasional flicker of streetlights brushing across the glass. I lean my head back. Try to breathe slowly. The driver doesn't speak, which I'm grateful for.

We pass late-night diners. A group of kids in formalwear smoking outside a club. An old man walking his dog like it's the only thing tethering him to the world.

And all I can think is, I built this life. Fought for it. Bled for it. So why does it feel like I'm floating outside of it?

By the time I get home, it's dark. The flat is quiet, but not the comforting kind. It's the kind that reminds you just how alone you are.

I toss my keys onto the counter. I pour a drink. Then I do what I promised I wouldn't.

I sink into the couch like it might hold me together.

The first sip burns. But it's familiar. I chase it with another. Then another.

The line hits a moment later, like someone flipped a switch behind my eyes. My teeth clench. My skin buzzes.

I don't know when I started crying but my face is wet.

And all I can think is how disappointing I am. To myself. But mostly to Grandpa.

A few years back, when we started planning all this, I promised him—swore on my life—I wouldn't do this anymore. No more drugs. No more heavy drinking. No more wasting the years he gave me.

"You should be here," I whisper. But it's filled with rage. "You left me. Alone."

The burn fades into a dull, shapeless warmth. My limbs feel slower. My brain fuzzier.

I throw the glass. It shatters against the wall.

Fuck.

"Fuck!"

The warmth turns to static. The room starts closing in. The air thins. The walls inch closer by the second.

My chest constricts—tight, sharp—like someone cinched a belt just under my ribs.

I can't seem to catch my breath.

My hands tremble as I reach for my phone, but it slips. Clatters to the floor.

I double over as a wave of nausea swells and breaks through me.

My heart is racing—*too fast*, too loud, like a war drum inside my skull. Drowning out every rational thought. Every anchoring thread. I claw at my shirt, trying to loosen it, but it's no use. My skin feels wrong. Too tight. Too hot. Like I'm being suffocated from the inside out.

I manage to grab the phone.

Fumble. Miss the code. Try again.

My fingers aren't working right, but I manage to make the call.

"Allie," I rasp when she picks up. My voice sounds foreign, like it's coming from someone else.

"I think... something's wrong."

She doesn't hesitate. "Where are you?"

"Home."

"I'm on my way."

Time folds in on itself, seconds stretching into hours.

I'm curled up on the floor, my back pressed against the couch, drenched in sweat.

There's a darkness around me now. And it promises stillness. So I let it in. Let myself sink into it.

Even if it's just for a moment of relief.

The door slams open.

"Allie," I croak, barely audible.

She drops to her knees beside me in an instant, her hands on my face, scanning me like she's trying to assess the damage.

"Hadrian, look at me. You're okay. Just breathe with me."

Her voice doesn't move. So I can.

She takes my hand and places it against her chest.

"Feel that? Match my breathing."

I try. I really do. But it's like my lungs have forgotten how to work.

"You've done this before," she says gently. "Remember? You can do it again. I'm here."

Her words pull me back, piece by piece.

I focus on the rise and fall of her chest. On the warmth of her hand over mine.

And slowly, the tightness eases. The drumbeat in my ears dulls to a faint echo.

At some point, I feel her arms beneath mine.

"Come on. Let's get you up."

I don't know how she manages it, but the next thing I know I'm on the sofa, slumped against the cushions. She sits beside me, her hand still resting over mine.

We stay like that for a while. My mind is a haze. My body, heavy and uncooperative. She doesn't rush me. She just stays.

I slowly start to feel human again. I let out a shaky breath and glance at her.

Her face is tired. Her hair a little messy.

"I'm sorry," I say, voice hoarse.

She shakes her head. "Don't. Just—don't." Her voice wavers despite her best effort to steady it.

"You scared the hell out of me."

She looks away, then back again, her eyes glistening. "I should've called an ambulance."

"I'm glad you didn't. That would have been—"

"Please don't ever do that to me again," she cuts in. "Don't make me choose the campaign or freaking optics over you, because I won't. I don't care about this country as much as you do."

The honest-to-God truth is I'd trade it all for you.

But I don't say it. Instead, I glance at her and I see it, clear as a lit match in the dark: the sheer worry on her face. Not pity. Not judgment. Just fear.

"I'm sorry," I say again. And this time, it feels like the truth.

Allie exhales, and her shoulders relax just enough to make space for forgiveness.

"You need to stop running yourself into the ground," she murmurs. "You can't keep doing this to yourself, Hadrian."

I nod, though I'm not sure I believe it yet.

"Allie..." I pause. "Do you think we could go to Bedford?"

Her brow furrows. "What?"

"I need a day off. I just—" I swallow hard. "I just need to be away."

"Hadrian..." she hesitates. "I don't think that's a good idea."

“Please.” My voice cracks, and I don’t even care.
She studies me for what feels like an eternity.
“Fine,” she says quietly.
Relief floods me, so full and fast it nearly knocks me sideways.
I’m a shipwrecked sailor, calling out *land ahoy.*
Allie is land.

56

Isadora

I HAD TO WAKE up at four in the morning yesterday to catch an early flight to Madrid. Only a four-day trip for the NATO Summit.

I love Madrid. I think it's one of my favorite cities in the world—there's something about the way the light spills over terracotta rooftops in the morning, how the air smells faintly of orange blossoms and car exhaust. It's a capital city with all the access and energy of a metropolis, yet it never loses that welcoming, sun-drenched, small-town soul.

Yet, I'm not exactly thrilled to be here this time around. Mainly because I'm here to translate for my father. Which, I'm sure makes me sound like a total brat. But trust me. You'd agree if you were working for him too.

Allie left a couple of hours before I did, only to text me a cryptic message saying she wasn't coming back home that night. There's only one place she willingly stays overnight: Bedford. I checked her live location too, naturally. And I was right. Also a given she's there with Hadrian. So I'm eagerly anticipating my return.

Today was the usual at these events. We spent most of the day at IFEMA, the city's sprawling exhibition venue just outside the center—concrete walls, tight security, oversized NATO flags fluttering in a heatwave breeze. The schedule ran tight, down to the minute, with uniformed aides ushering diplomats and defense leaders like overworked wedding planners. My father is here as a civilian advisor with the Department of Defense. His meetings today were all around something called dual-use goods, so you're probably imagining the thrill of the topics I had to interpret for.

Interoperability and critical materials management. Dual-use goods logistics pipeline oversight. And—oh, right—my favorite: geopolitical risk mitigation in international logistics.

My brain was frayed by the end of it. Not just from the lingo or the twelve cups of mediocre espresso, but from the way my father talks when he's in performance mode. Crisp. Cold. Directed at the room but always indirectly slicing into me. I kept feeling like a ghost in the room—seen, but only as a function. Never as a daughter. Which, I guess, is exactly how he wants it. I'm not too sure he's ever subscribed to the whole blood-before-country idea.

We're staying at the Mandarin Oriental Ritz, which is one of my favorite hotels in the city. It's all vaulted ceilings and soft gold light, like walking into a Goya painting. My room has a little wrought-iron balcony that overlooks El Retiro Park, and the linens smell faintly of lavender and starch. If you haven't been, I truly recommend it. Even if it's just for a drink at *Pictura*, the bar in the hotel. Perfect vibes. Velvet chairs, arched mirrors, and a cocktail list that reads like a poem.

I step into the hotel, bone-tired. My heels feel like knives. My mouth still tastes like bitter coffee. My badge is still looped around my neck, and I don't even bother to take it off.

My phone buzzes as I make a beeline for the elevators, nodding at the doorman, who's definitely the kind that remembers faces and offers polite smiles.

I glance at the screen, and a slow smile pulls at my lips.

It's Leo.

How's Madrid?

He came with me to Hadrian's small celebration.

It was... strangely grounding having him there. Something natural about it, though I'm aware him and me together is the least natural thing ever. I could see it in everyone's faces. Including his.

Afterward, he dropped Allie and me off. And that was kind of it.

But I'm not overthinking it. That's the conclusion I keep landing on every time I spiral or try to logic my way out of this. Maybe it's not smart.

Actually, it's definitely not smart. But when I weigh it against the idea of not getting to know him, not spending time with him at all, I'm certain it's worth it.

So I don't. Overthink, that is. And I just press Call.

He picks up on the second ring.

"Carter-Bello." His voice, to me, is a deep shade of greenish-blue.

"Hey."

"How's Madrid treating you?"

"Madrid's lovely. Boiling hot, but lovely. The Summit... less so. Also, the jet lag might actually finish me off. It's evening here, but my body's fully convinced it's lunchtime and I owe it a cappuccino."

He lets out a soft laugh, and I wish this was the future and I could teleport. Just to see it. The real-time version. White teeth, full lips, and—if I'm lucky—one that reaches his eyes.

"How's home?"

I hesitate before stepping into the elevator, then think better of it. I don't want to lose him to bad reception.

Instead, I cross the lobby and sink into a quiet velvet sofa tucked behind a cluster of palms and marble columns.

"New York? You wouldn't believe it. A whole different world than twenty-four hours ago."

Now it's me who lets out a laugh.

"Idiot," I mutter, still smiling into the speaker.

"So," he says, tone shifting playfully, "any political celebrities graced your day today?"

I lean back into the sofa, letting my head fall against the cushion.

"None I'm fond of. Prime Minister Halbridge was there. I'm telling you, there's something very off about that man."

He lets out a quiet snort, the kind that I know comes with a raised eyebrow.

"As in?"

"As in... I wouldn't trust him with my dry cleaning, let alone a country."

"Trust me..." his voice trails off, amused. "He's harmless."

"You know him?" I ask, waving at a passing waiter in a white jacket. He nods and glides over.

"I do," Leo says. "Nice man. Odd, sure—but in a harmless kind of way."

"One sec," I murmur, pulling the phone slightly away. "Could I have sparkling water, please?"

The waiter nods wordlessly and disappears toward the bar.

"I'm back," I say into the phone.

"When are you back in the city?"

"Day after tomorrow. What... missing me already?"

Silence.

"Hey—kidding. No missing allowed in minute two," I add quickly.

Then the softest sound, half sigh, half groan comes through the line.

The waiter reappears with my sparkling water, sets it down gently, and begins to turn away.

"Excuse me," I call after him. "Shouldn't I sign for this?"

He pauses. "Oh—apologies, Ms. Carter-Bello. I've already put it on your father's tab. Should I not have? I'm so sorry."

"Oh, no, it's fine. I just didn't know he was here."

The waiter gestures discreetly toward a small seating area a few sofas over. I follow the line of his hand and see him.

His back is turned to me, and he's dressed in something different from what he wore earlier. He's sitting with two other men. One of them I recognize from one of the interpreting booths, still wearing the white badge all contractors are given. The other I don't know.

I stand up and start walking toward them.

"Odd," I say under my breath.

"Odd?" Leo echoes through the phone. "That your dad's there? I thought you two went together."

"We did. But he's with another translator."

The man I recognize catches my eye and smiles politely. My father doesn't turn. The one speaking pauses mid-sentence, his hands frozen in midair. Everyone waits.

"*Bonsoir—excuse moi*," I say softly.

My father glances at me like I've just said *fuck you all.*

"I just wanted to say I'm heading up." I meet my father's eyes. "I'll see you tomorrow at six?"

He nods once. "Good night."

I turn on my heel.

"Sorry for the interruption. Please continue," I hear him say behind me.

I don't let my shoulders tense. I don't let myself look back. This is always how it goes with him. He asks for my help, then acts like I've overstepped just by showing up.

"Isadora?" Leo's voice cuts through the line.

"Hey. Sorry—what were you saying?"
"Nothing important. Everything okay?"
"Yeah. Just... long day. Early start tomorrow."
I walk to the elevator and press the button.
"See you Thursday?"
I smile, just barely. "See you Thursday."

57
Hadrian

ALLIE'S IN THE KITCHEN packing lunch while I get the basket ready. It's a late one—closer to an early supper. I slept in longer than I meant to.

We got in late last night and went straight to bed. She took her usual room here. I think there's only been one time she didn't—it was Christmas, years ago, when the Bellos were visiting from Argentina. One of my little cousins said he loved the wallpaper in there—faded wildflowers curling along pale blue vines—and Allie immediately offered her the room. The kid was over the moon. Other than that, it's always been hers.

I head back to the kitchen to grab the cutlery and find her moving through the space like someone who knows it down to the grain of the butcher block, because she does.

The cabinets are pale, brass hardware catching the light. The counters shift between marble and butcher block, worn in places, built to last. The sink faces a wide window with a view of the yard and a flash of lake beyond the trees.

It's not just a kitchen, it's the heart of the house. She's the heart of the house, really.

"Anything else I can help with?" I ask, leaning against the doorframe.

She glances over her shoulder, mid-stir at the stovetop, where something sizzles in the pan—zucchini, maybe peaches too. Her cheeks are a little flushed from the heat, her hair twisted up.

"You already grabbed the blanket?"

"In the basket," I say.

"Then you're good," she replies, flicking off the burner. "I want to eat down by the water before the light changes."

We've spent so many days here like this over the years, but I couldn't tell you when she stopped being just my sister's best friend and became mine. Or when she stopped being just my friend and became something... more.

My mind's still foggy from yesterday, and yet I can't stop trying to make sense of it all. There's just something fundamentally wrong with keeping your distance from the one person who makes you feel closest to yourself.

And please, spare me the words *optics* or *narrative*. Because—hell—I'm starting to think this so-called greater good isn't all that good anymore.

I know life is a series of choices. That sacrifice is part of the deal. I do get that. But how do you even know if the thing you're giving up is the right one?

And while we're at it... would you still choose love, even if it cost you everything else?

To answer that honestly, I think you'd have to know what it feels like to love someone the way Sui Generis sings about in "*Quizás, Porque,*" which is playing softly in the background right now.

Sometimes, I think I wouldn't. Choose it, I mean. And I hate how that sounds. Trust me. I know what that makes me.

But the truth is, there are nights I'd give anything to not feel like I'm being stabbed over and over, only to realize I'm the one holding the knife.

And then there are moments like this. Watching her dance around the place we grew up in. When I let myself imagine it. Us. Together. I can almost taste it. Touch it. Finally within reach.

But then I remember what it would cost me. What it would probably cost her too. And that's what always gets me.

Because I've worn this hat for so long, I don't know who I am without it. And what do I even have to offer if not the shape of a legacy that is mine, but also bigger than myself? Bigger than us?

This life has always been the constant. The roadmap. The one thing that made sense.

Until she did too.

Allie steps out onto the porch with a ceramic platter balanced in her hands—grilled halloumi, blistered cherry tomatoes, zucchini ribbons, and peaches glistening with honey and thyme.

I follow her down the gravel path toward the lake, the basket in one hand, and the light—just beginning to turn gold—spilling out across the water.

I spread out the blanket while she settles beside me, cross-legged, barefoot, the scent of thyme and lemon trailing behind her. She starts arranging the food like she's performing some gentle kind of magic—folding slices of zucchini into delicate coils, scattering mint leaves, opening a linen pouch with a still-warm baguette tucked inside.

I reach straight for the halloumi. It's my all-time favorite. And of course, she knows that.

"Superior," I mutter, mouth full.

She laughs softly, popping a cherry tomato into her mouth. Juice drips down her thumb and she licks it without thinking.

"Remember that summer we tried to make s'mores out here, but Isa kept yelling that the graham crackers were too 'processed' and made us all eat them with sliced figs and dark chocolate instead?"

I start laughing at the memory.

"And you got mad and ran into the lake fully clothed."

"In protest."

"You said—and I quote—'If I can't eat artificial marshmallows, I refuse to live in a society.'"

"Well. I still stand by it."

She grins, shaking her head. "You were so dramatic. Always the showman."

"Were?"

She arches a brow. "You're lucky you've always been just cute enough to get away with it."

A memory flashes. I can't help smiling.

"Remember that other time here when you thought I was cute too?"

She rolls her eyes. "Hadrian."

I let out a laugh. We were probably thirteen and sixteen. Milo and Isa were here. I think Blake must've been too. Maybe even Archie and Max. But I don't remember any of them. Just her.

"You asked me to be your first kiss. God—I'd completely forgotten about that."

It was late. We were down by the dock, skipping stones, our fingers sticky from peaches someone brought down in a bowl. The others were back at the house, I think. She turned to me suddenly, cheeks flushed from the heat, or maybe just from being thirteen and alive.

"I don't want it to be just anyone. You're not just anyone," she said.

I remember how off-guard that took me. Allie had always been *there*—woven into my life in a way I never really questioned. Isa's best friend. The girl who always showed up for birthdays, summer weekends, late-night drives. I'd never seen her as anything else... until that moment. Until she said something no one who felt like family would ever say.

It was like staring at a painting you've seen a hundred times, and then suddenly noticing the brushstrokes. The layers beneath. How much more had always been there.

I shook my head. "No, Als. I won't do that."

I try to pull at the thread of that night, to remember what else we said, how it ended. But all that comes back is the look in her eyes. Big. Blue. Braver than I deserved.

She smiles now, probably at the memory too. "I was so disappointed."

"What excuse did I even give?"

She shakes her head. "No excuse. You just said not to worry about my first kiss. That your grandpa told you it was the last one that mattered."

"Yep," I murmur, swallowing. "That sounds like Grandpa."

She doesn't say anything. Just turns toward the lake.

There's something about her when she's near water. Like something inside her quiets. Like the surface of it reflects whatever she needs to see.

"Want to go for a swim?" I ask.

"Already did. This morning while you were still passed out." She grins. "Maybe tomorrow?"

I nod.

We pack up slowly, not saying much, and head back up the path toward the house. The sky's burning gold now, casting long shadows across the grass. Crickets have started humming low in the distance, and the gravel crunches softly beneath our steps. She walks a few paces ahead, the basket swinging lightly from her hand, her blonde hair loose now and catching the last of the light.

And this is it, isn't it? What life's made of. These little moments. Stolen glances of the girl you've loved for so long, you can't remember when it started. What you do know is there'll be no end to it.

"Movie?" she asks as soon as we step into the house.

"What are we watching?" I ask, already knowing I'll agree to whatever she picks.

She scrolls through the options, her brow furrowed in concentration.

"Something light first. I think we could use a laugh."

She settles on an old silent comedy. Not really my thing—but the way she laughs? That I'd watch on repeat. Full, unfiltered, her head thrown back, eyes crinkling at the corners. At one point, she laughs so hard a tear slips down her cheek. She wipes it away like it's nothing, still caught in the moment. I glance at the screen just often enough, but I'm not paying attention. Not really. I'm letting the sound of her laugh get lodged somewhere permanent. Except it's already there, right next to the sound of the final school bell before summer break.

The credits roll and the room goes dark.

"Okay, now for something I truly believe you need to see," she says, grabbing the remote and finding *Life in the Undergrowth*, narrated by Sir David Attenborough.

"You've mentioned this one before," I murmur, sinking deeper into the couch.

The first episode dives into the lives of invertebrates, starting in the water. Her entire face shifts when it starts. Alien-like larvae float across the screen, translucent and half-formed, trying to become. She's completely still, hanging on every word as Attenborough describes their metamorphosis—the shedding of old forms, the emergence of something new. Again, I watch her more than I watch the screen.

We reach the episode on social insects. Ants. Apparently, they're experts at direction. They count steps, track shadows, memorize light. But when you take one away from the colony, it gets lost. It loses the map. Can't function like it normally would.

That's me, I think. A part of something larger. And removed from it, just adrift.

I glance over and realize she's asleep. Her head tilted just slightly, breathing steadily. The blanket's slipped into her lap. One hand dangles near the edge of the armrest.

And I swear to God—how can a face look like that and still be real?

I've lost count of how many of my friends have mentioned how beautiful Allie is. How many have tried their luck and failed. I used to brush it off. But really looking at her—at what her beauty does—it hits like a punch to the gut. She's the kind of beautiful that would've launched a thousand ships and torched the city. Except this time, it'd actually be for the girl.

And here I am. Frozen. Sitting like an idiot. Too scared to do anything about it. She deserves the whole universe. Except I don't even want space between us.

I hesitate—just for a second—but then I lift her gently into my arms, the way I used to when she and Isa fell asleep in the wrong rooms after too much sugar and too many movies. She stirs but doesn't wake. She settles into the space between my neck and shoulder like it was carved for her. It probably was.

I step into her bedroom and lay her down carefully, pulling the blanket over her shoulders, tucking it in the way I know she likes. My throat's tight for no reason I can explain.

"Good night," I whisper, turning to leave.

"Stay? Just for a little while," she says, barely audible.

No hesitation this time. I pull off my hoodie and climb in beside her, facing her. Our heads level on the same pillow. The room is dark, but I can feel her watching me. Like I'm watching her.

"Thanks for today," I say, voice low.

She doesn't answer right away. Instead, she reaches out, brushing her fingers against my cheek, so softly it hurts. I close my eyes. If I could freeze a moment and live in it for ever, this would be the one. Right here. Right now.

"Good night," she whispers.

"Good night, Als."

And I fall asleep to the sound of her laughter still echoing faintly in my ears.

58
Isadora

HADRIAN IS PICKING ME up from the airport.

It's our little tradition. Whenever either of us flies solo, the other one picks them up. No matter if we're fighting, we still always manage to get the flight details. Him mostly from Rami, me mostly from his calendar he still doesn't know he once accidentally shared with me. I haven't had the heart to tell him. Or maybe I just like knowing I have a backdoor into a part of his life he hasn't locked yet.

I spot the black SUV idling at the curb, hazard lights blinking like a heartbeat.

Hadrian steps out as I approach, sunglasses on, hands in his pockets. He opens the back door for me with a smile on his face.

"Someone's in a good mood," I say, tossing my tote first, then my carry-on, as Hadrian deals with the big suitcase.

I step into the back seat and Hadrian ducks in after me, pulling the door shut just as Rami takes his place behind the wheel.

"You look like hell," Hadrian says, settling in.

"Thanks. It's the twelve-hour flight, the jetlag, and an overload of international trade jargon."

He lets out a low chuckle as we pull away from the terminal. Rami merges smoothly onto the highway. I lean my head back, letting the city blur past the window, then glance sideways at my brother.

"Where to?" Rami asks, catching my gaze in the rearview.

"Scarr's Pizza," Hadrian replies, thumbs tapping away on his phone.

Another tradition—greasy, comforting American food straight after being abroad.

"I think Blake's meeting us there. Something's off with him."

"Irina?"

He shrugs. "Maybe. But it feels heavier than their usual blowups."

"I'm sure it's nothing apocalyptic."

He finishes typing and puts his phone away.

"So... Bedford?" I ask, watching him.

"Right." He exhales. "At least let me hold a slice of pizza before the interrogation starts."

I raise an eyebrow. "Stalling won't save you."

He turns to face me. "Fine. Yes, we went to Bedford. And let me say upfront—nothing happened."

I lift a hand, cutting him off.

"Ground rule number two: no graphic details, ever. I thank you in advance. Now continue."

He grins. "I expect the same courtesy from you."

I narrow my eyes. "That was one time. For science."

"Sure," he says, not bothering to hide the smirk.

"Stop deflecting."

"Fine." He leans back. "I wasn't in a great place that day, and I called her. She came over. Helped me calm down. And all I could think about was Bedford. So we drove up. Stopped at DeCicco for groceries. Went straight to the house. She cooked—brilliantly, as always. We watched a couple of movies. Slept. Next morning, coffee at The Coffee House, then crawled back through city traffic."

He pauses, watching my face.

"Sufficiently detailed?"

I nod slowly. "Detailed, yes. But still missing the most important part. When exactly did you two sit down and talk about what you're doing? You're acting like a couple, while very publicly not being one. Oh, and while dating someone else."

"There was no conversation," he says with a shrug. "Just two people who happen to like each other's company. That's all."

"Hadrian," I say, "what are you doing?"

He sighs. "I don't know. I only know that without her, this whole thing feels unbearable. But with her? It's impossible. Ironic, isn't it? That we had to leave the city to spend time together. Maybe we can only exist outside of New York."

I straighten slightly.

"You know I love you, right? You're one of my favorite people in the universe—because I remain convinced there's life on other planets. But what you just said? That sounded like you're treating her as your mistress. And that's not going to fly—with her or with me. She's also a favorite. My favorite non-blood relative. So we're at an impasse."

"That's not what I meant," he says, visibly frustrated.

"I know," I say. "But words matter. Optics matter. You know that better than anyone." I pause. "Have you talked to your team? Drafted a plan? Tested public sentiment?"

He gives a bitter laugh. "Isa, do you honestly think I haven't gone through every scenario? Her family's businesses have been linked to eleven different scandals in the past five years. *Eleven.* I checked. It doesn't matter that she's not involved or that she doesn't personally support any of it. Public opinion doesn't make space for nuance."

"Fine," I say. "Then what about after the general?"

"Right. Announce the relationship once the public's already trusted me. Perfect."

I exhale. "This is so deeply unfair."

He doesn't answer.

"I get it," I add quietly. "I just refuse to believe that any of this should stand a chance against love."

Still nothing. And that's fine. I let it go. He has enough on his plate, and I'm sure he's already spiraling in a dozen directions inside his own head.

A few minutes later, we're pulling up in front of Scarr's Pizza.

Before I can even reach for the door handle, it swings open.

A hand with tattoos I'm pretty sure I could trace blindfolded slides in to take mine, and my stomach curls.

I take Leo's hand and step out of the car.

That face again. I could probably trace it as well. Paint it. By heart, even.

"Hey."

I immediately blush, and his fingers go straight to my cheek, brushing lightly against the heat there.

"Hope it's okay I'm here. Blake mentioned you'd be stopping by. Something about trashy food after being abroad?"

I smirk. "Something like that. Yeah."

I rise onto my tiptoes and press my lips to his. A car door slams shut, and I pull away.

Hadrian's standing on the other side of the SUV, arms crossed, a slightly annoyed look on his face.

He clears his throat. "Pizza?"

Then he nods toward Leo—without really meeting his eyes—and walks past us.

I shoot Leo a complicit look as we fall into step behind him.

Hadrian pulls out his phone, glancing back at us.

"It's Blake," he mutters, then picks up. "Hey."

I turn to Leo, watching his expression as he tracks my brother. I find myself studying his face for any remnants of the old fights I've seen him walk out of. Nothing. Not a single scar.

Must be nice. I still have a faint mark above my right eyebrow from when I was, what, seven? Eight?

Hadrian's pace slows, and we catch up beside him. He stops short. His eyes widen, a crease forming between his brows.

"I'll be there," he says, voice tightening. "Don't do anything. Just—wait for me."

His words trail off, and I step closer.

"What happened?"

He puts his phone away. "Not sure. Irina's gone."

I frown. "Gone where?"

"I don't know. He just said she's gone. Apparently left her phone behind too."

I cross my arms. "Okay... yeah, that's dramatic—even for her."

Hadrian turns to Leo. "Do you mind staying with her? She needs greasy food after a long-haul flight or she'll get hangry."

I roll my eyes. Nothing but the truth.

I glance at Leo, who's gone still next to me, a shadow flickering across his face. I nudge him gently.

"Yeah," he says, coming back to life. "Sure. No worries."

His hand slides to my waist, guiding me toward the storefront.

I turn to see Hadrian, who's already jumping in a cab.

"Hope everything's fine," I say as we get in line to order.

He doesn't say anything.

"Are you okay?" I ask.

His eyes meet mine and again there's a flicker of something indeterminable. I wonder how long it'll take me to read his tiny eye movements. It's a split of a movement really, as you could see something fly by behind them.

He nods as he slips his arm around my shoulder.

"What are we ordering?"

"Well, let's see. Definitely the—"

"So it's true, then."

A familiar voice cuts in, and my already tight stomach knots harder.

I turn, and there he is. Milo. Eyes wide. Jaw tight. Legs planted like he's bracing for something.

"Milo..." I start, already knowing nothing I say will land right.

"Seriously, Isadora? You're too smart for this shit."

His tone freezes me.

I've seen in-love Milo. Tired Milo. Goofy, turned-on, moody Milo. But this isn't any of those. This is something else entirely.

"Hey, man," Leo says, taking one step forward. "I'd watch my tone if I were you."

Milo snaps taut, his whole body tightening like a spring.

The air shifts. Heads turn. A phone lifts. A girl whispers to her friend.

"You stay the fuck out of this."

That's all it takes. Leo plants himself squarely between us, jaw tight.

"You're protecting her—from *me*?" Milo's voice cracks, disbelieving. He shakes his head, lets out one hollow laugh. "She should be protected from *you*."

He leans, catching my eyes around Leo's shoulder.

"Please tell me you're just sleeping with him. Getting it out of your system. Because I'd get it."

Leo's fists clench. I open my mouth, but nothing comes out.

"Oh my god. Please, Isadora. Tell me that's all this is. Please tell me you're not dumb enough to fall for a guy like him."

I see Leo shift his stance—weight forward, shoulders rigid.

"Again." He doesn't raise his voice. "I'd be *very* careful with your word choice."

Milo doesn't break my gaze. "He'll break your heart, Scout." His voice drops. "You know that, don't you?"

Rami materializes at Milo's side, expression carved from granite.

"Milo," he says, calm as ever. "You're making a scene. Step away, or I'll make you."

I inhale sharply and step out from behind Leo, planting myself between them.

In front of the boy who used to be part of my every day. Who used to be life itself.

I turn, just enough to meet Leo's eyes.

"Leo," I say quietly, "I'll call you later, okay?"

He frowns. Swallows. His jaw flexes once, then again. He takes a slow breath, like he's forcing it down, eyes closing before he nods.

"See you later," he says finally, and walks away. Slow at first, then quicker.

I watch him go. Realize, in this exact moment, that the sight of him walking away from me is quickly becoming my least favorite thing in the world.

I turn back to Milo. "Come with me."

A few seconds later, we're in the backseat, opposite sides. And I can tell now. The distance isn't just physical, it's heavier than that.

"I'm really sorry." He turns toward me, and I toward him. "I just... I couldn't believe it when Archie told me."

Archie. That traitor.

"I thought, there's no way. No way. Guess I was wrong again." He exhales hard. "God, when did I start getting it so wrong with us?" His eyes gloss. A tear slips free.

"Milo. This isn't your fault. What we had, it was the best time of my life. Truly. But even good things, amazing things... they end."

More tears cut down cheeks I've kissed a thousand times. And a part of me—small now, but still alive—aches with the nostalgia of it. Almost like a kid reaching for the security blanket they'd sworn they didn't need anymore.

"Then what happened?" The words tremble out of him.

I shake my head, my own tears spilling. "Nothing happened. That's just it. I think... I think in the end, I didn't know who I was anymore. I still don't. I'm just trying to figure it out."

"Fuck." He says it with the most pained smile I've ever seen. On him. On anyone.

"I'm sorry if that's not—"

"It's not that," he cuts in. "It's just... If you don't know who you are, then who am I supposed to be?"

I reach for his arm, resting on his lap. "You'll figure it out too."

And I hope—pray, even—that both of us will.

"Just promise me something, Scout."

I nod slowly.

"If there's ever a day—by some impossible, lottery-twice-over kind of luck—you wake up and miss me... then promise you'll call me. Right away. No matter what, no matter how long it's been. Just... please."

I give him a smile as I wipe away my tears. "You'll be my first call."

And before you say it, I know. It's selfish. It sounds as though I'm leaving the door cracked, not shut, not open. And that's on me. But the truth is I don't think I'll ever get Milo completely out of my system. I don't have it in me to cut him off, to sever the cord, to block him out.

Because, after all, who are we to say what the future holds?

59

Leo

Something's seriously off.

And I don't just mean Isadora's fucking ex making a scene. Something I truly don't have the time—or the tolerance—for.

I mean with Irina and Yakov.

"It's not the best time," OG says the second the elevator doors slide open to the family lounge at HQ.

His voice already has that warning edge to it. Like I'm supposed to tread lightly.

I step out, jaw locked. "Irina's gone. So you'd better explain what the fuck is going on. Now."

He exhales. Hesitates.

"Are you gonna act like a grown-up? Or get all fired up like a kid?"

"OG," I growl, flat. "I'm not in the mood."

"Just asking. You want a seat at the grown-ups' table, you need to act like one."

I stop walking. Look him dead in the eyes. "Talk."

"Your father broke ties with Mikhailov," he says. "He's not handing over the stone."

He pauses, just long enough for it to sting.

"He's bringing it here instead."

I blink. "Has he lost his fucking mind?"

OG raises both hands, palms out like he's trying to calm a dog.

"The stone has more value with us now. And we can purge it for market. Imagine the sea of opportunity that opens."

I stare at him, trying to mask the sheer panic crawling up the back of my neck like ice water.

"Does he seriously think he can go up against both Yakov and the Claveneau?" My voice is steel now. "He's lost it. He's lost the fucking plot."

I run a hand through my hair, then grab the back of my neck. "And how the hell does he plan to purge a dust of that magnitude in the States?"

OG shrugs. "We have the means. M31 has been activated."

I scoff. "M31."

A ghost name. The line item in the Sartori ledger where most trails ultimately end up. The reset. The baptismal pool. Just a letter and two numbers. No faces.

For all I know, they're operating out of a shack in Hawaii.

"Great," I mutter. "That clears things up."

"It means enough for you to know we're bringing in the big boys."

"So what's he so fucking stressed about then?" I shoot back. "Sounds like he thinks he's got everything under control."

OG glances toward the closed door of one of the offices.

His voice drops.

"Well... let's just say M31 has conditions of its own. And your father's having a hard time reconciling with that."

I shift my weight, pacing once toward the window before turning back.

"I need to talk to him."

"Seriously, Leo. It's not gonna end pretty."

I ignore him. Start toward the door.

He grabs my arm. Halts me.

"Trouble's also brewing down south. One of the land veins."

I turn slightly, brows drawn. "What kind of trouble?"

OG's mouth curves, like he's trying not to laugh. "Some idiot fell in love with the wrong woman."

I stare at him.

"A fucking journalist of all people," he adds, voice coated in disbelief. "Can you believe that? What a fool."

The fact that I can makes me nauseous.

I click my tongue. Point a finger at him. Nothing comes out.

I press a hand to my forehead. Drop it low.

"Fuck!"

My phone buzzes.

Isadora.

Meet me at my place?

On my way

I slide it away.

"I'm out," I say, turning. "Tell him to keep his ego in check. And his eyes open."

"Hey," OG calls after me. "You know nothing touches us here. Not in New York. We're insulated."

A beat.

"But still... watch your back."

I glance at him over my shoulder.

"Always do."

I get to Isadora's place twenty minutes later.

Knock once. It's my first time up here.

She opens the door. No hello. No hesitation. Just grabs me and kisses me. Slow at first. Then rushed. Desperate. She kisses me like she's trying to forget something. And I let her. Because I'm trying to forget everything.

She pulls back, breathless. Her lips still close to mine.

"Hey," she says, half-smiling.

"Hey."

She steps inside and I follow, closing the door behind me.

Her place is exactly what I expected. Lived-in. Soft lighting. A little chaotic, but intentional.

"Anything to drink?" she calls from the kitchen.

"I'm good. Is Allie home?"

"No," she answers, voice trailing off. "She's in Williamsport with her family for the weekend."

She comes back with a glass of water and nods toward the living room.

"Here."

We sit. Her laptop's open on the coffee table, surrounded by notepads, loose pages, a pen tucked behind a thick book spine. Handwritten notes scatter like they're mid-thought. A highlighter left uncapped.

She crosses her leg, turns to face me. Then she grabs my hand, and I could swear I can see her grab all my sins with the other one.

"Sorry about earlier." Her voice slips out.

I shake my head. "You don't have to apologize. It's fine. He's your—"

"I know it's fine," she says quickly. "I know I don't owe you an explanation. But I still want to."

I nod. Just once.

"I broke up with him before Christmas last year. We were apart for a while and then it just kind of... started again. Then we officially split on my birthday." She exhales. "He's never seen me with anyone else. So naturally he was upset. But it's fine now."

Something stirs in my gut. Something ugly. A twisting, unfamiliar heat that makes me look away.

"But that's all," she adds, her voice just a little too bright now. "He's fine."

I let out a dry laugh. She tilts her head, eyes narrowing slightly, confusion flickering across her face.

I click my tongue. "Thing is, I don't think he's entirely wrong."

The words slip out before I can stop them.

Her expression hardens.

"What's that supposed to mean?" There's a colder edge now. And I hate that I put it there.

"What he said. About you ending up hurt." I meet her eyes this time. "He's probably not wrong."

She lets go of my hand like it burnt her. Then leans back, folds into herself, like she's trying to protect something. Then grabs a pillow off the couch and pulls it against her chest.

The distance between us grows, and that thing in my gut twists tighter.

What the fuck is even happening to me?

"Why would I end up hurt?" she asks, voice quiet but loaded. Her big brown whirlpool of eyes don't flinch. "Are you planning on hurting me?"

"That's not the point."

"Then what *is* the point?" She says it like she already knows she won't like the answer.

I sigh, rub my hand over my jaw. "I just don't think I'm the kind of guy you'd—"

"Can you not?" she snaps, cutting me off.

Her voice cracks, and for a second I think she might cry.

But she doesn't. She just holds the pillow tighter.

"Seriously, Leo. Spare me. If you're about to pull the 'I'm not the right guy for you' bullshit, just don't."

She's standing now. Pacing.

"If you're too much of a coward to admit there's something between us, and you'd rather pretend it's about me, then fine. Go. Be a coward somewhere else."

She throws the words like knives, each one a little closer to the bone.

I stand too, but she's already walking away.

"You know where the door is."

She disappears into the hallway.

And I just stand there. Frozen.

I must've gotten the season wrong—thought it was summer.

But the second she told me off, it started snowing.

60

Isadora

I SLAM THE DOOR behind me before I can think twice.

A bit too loud. But it doesn't matter. Nothing does if he's not willing to try. Whatever that looks like. Wherever that takes us.

I pace. I kick off my shoes. I pretend I'm not waiting.

But then the knock comes.

One. Two. Three.

Slow. Sure. Like he already knows I'll open it.

I do.

He's leaning on the doorframe like it's an extension of him. Shirt half-tucked. Hair slightly mussed. That look in his eyes—lazy, unreadable, hungry.

"I don't do apologies," he says.

"Good." I fold my arms, defiant. "Because I don't really do forgiveness."

He steps in slowly, like the air might break if he moves too fast.

"So what do we do, then?"

"Apparently?" I lift a shoulder. "Get on each other's nerves."

I turn away before I say too much. Before I let him see the way my pulse is rioting in my neck.

I walk to the window. Look outside. The sky's heavy with navy. The moon's full tonight, huge and bright and spectacular. It's watching us. Maybe even testing us. And we're about to fail.

When I face him again, his expression has shifted. Softened, just slightly.

"I shouldn't have pulled you away like that," he says. "Wasn't my place."

"Damn right it wasn't."

"But I'm not sorry for looking out for you." His voice dips, edges darkening. I blink once, and he's closer. If I stretched my arm, I could touch him.

"Really?" I ask, stepping in even closer. "That's what this is about?" I lift my chin. "I feel safe. With you."

Something flickers in his eyes. I see something fracture in his restraint. His shoulders ease. His gaze gets heavier, deeper.

"Don't look at me like that," I whisper.

"Like what?"

"Like you already know how this ends."

He studies me for a second too long.

"I do."

And maybe I do too. Maybe I've known since the first time I felt that pinch down my spine when someone said his name. Or the way he started showing up in my thoughts on a Tuesday afternoon—no warning, no reason, just there. Maybe it was the kiss during our walk back from the New York Public Library. The one that felt like putting on glasses for the first time and thinking, *Gosh. This is how bright colors were always meant to be. This is how life is supposed to feel.*

Or maybe it was even earlier. The evening after we first met, when he didn't show up. *Dodged bullet*, I remember thinking. Little did I know, beneath the thin crust of solid rock we live on, something imperceptible had already shifted. The magnetic poles had quietly flipped as the universe recalibrated itself.

Call the geologists, let them know: all this time, it's been him, tilting their compasses and rewriting their coordinates.

I don't remember leaning in. But suddenly, my fingers are on his collar. His are at the back of my neck. And there's no space left—no breath, no line to hold.

And the thing is... I know we're about to cross a line that will bind us in ways neither of us are ready for. But I also know that if he stopped now, I'd still be too far gone.

He stands at the edge of something vast. Something carved by every moment we've spent pretending we weren't already his and mine.

And I know I won't make it. The gap is too wide. The wind too cruel.

But still, I step to the edge.

And I jump.

He walks me backward without a word. One step. Then another. Until my back meets the wall. His forehead presses to mine.

And for a moment, we just breathe each other in—fast, uneven, starved. Like we've both been holding our breath for too long.

His hand cups my jaw. My mouth parts.

"You still feel safe?" he asks, low. Ragged.

I nod. Maybe too fast. Definitely too desperate. But I mean it. Because even now—especially now—I do.

He kisses me again. Slower this time. But no less urgent. Like he's memorizing the shape of this. Of us.

My hands move before I can think—over his chest, under his shirt, tugging at the buttons like they're the only thing keeping me from oxygen.

He lets out the kind of groan that lives in a person's chest. Then lifts me. I wrap around him like I was always meant to.

We don't make it to the bed. Not right away.

The wall. The dresser. The trail of clothes—quiet casualties.

He lays me down like I'm the last soft thing in the world. Like he's terrified of breaking something sacred.

There are words between us, quiet ones. Ones I'll remember in fragments.

Things like *you're mine* and *tell me to stop*.

Things like *never*.

Things like *please*.

And when it happens—when all the space is finally gone—it feels less like the start of something reckless and more like standing in a place I didn't even know existed.

Feet on the ground, head in the sky.

Scratch that. All of me is flying.

And I've never felt more undone.

Or more whole.

61
Hadrian

I'M STAYING AT BLAKE'S new place, not far from mine.

Partly because he's in a weird place—Irina just... vanished. But also because my own flat is swamped with paps.

The Dobermans are here too. Belladonna. Vesper. Irina left them behind like everything else. They seem... off. Not aggressive. Just quiet. Almost depressed. They trail after Blake everywhere he goes. No barking. No tugging. Just shadows. When he sits, they flank him—one on each side, each resting their head on one of his legs like they're holding him together.

As for me, it's the usual buzz. General elections are coming up, and the polls are tight, especially considering the way the new district lines were drawn. The traditional Second is still very conservative, directly at odds with the newly added areas. It's like a boiling pot. The tension is palpable, and everyone's watching to see which way it spills.

The press has been getting increasingly intense. Lydia keeps insisting I go through media training, which I've refused determinedly. I'm not interested in learning how to speak in sanitized, meaningless sound bites. If they're going to tear me apart, I'd rather it be for what I actually said.

Also, Brielle's back. I saw her last night.

Calm down—I only went to tell her we're done. I think she saw it coming. She took it well.

She's great. But it's not fair. Not to her, not to me.

I can say a thousand times that I'm not looking for more, that I want to keep it casual, but the second you've got a mob of teenagers screaming online about how perfect you are together, things get blurry.

Not for me. Emotionally, I'm clear. But yeah... overall, it gets confusing.

Blake's passed out on the couch, thankfully. He hasn't really slept in days—mostly alcohol and coke keeping him going. And it's starting to worry me.

I think I get it now. How being on the other side of addiction can be just as painful. Just as frustrating. Watching someone you love spiral, lose control—and, weirdly, realizing that control might be the only way through it.

I've caught myself trying to fix the little things. Nudging him to clean up his sleeping pattern, eat something decent, follow some kind of rhythm. Tiny acts of routine that, together, might anchor him, help bring him back.

Who would've thought? That liberation isn't in letting go, but in holding on. The demons in your head want you to believe the opposite, that freedom means surrender, that chaos is truth. But it's quite clear to me now. Peace is the greater rebellion.

I'm in the guest room getting dressed when the door swings open.

Blake stands there, looking like he just woke up from the apocalypse.

"Your phone won't stop buzzing. Like, perpetually."

He tosses it over.

"Sorry, probably Marcus or Lydia," I say, catching it.

He grunts and disappears down the hall.

I glance at the screen and the notifications are a waterfall, too fast to read.

Marcus starts calling.

"Marcus, what the hell is going on?"

"Finally," he exhales, and I brace. "Someone followed you. To Bedford. Photos of you and Allie—across the lake—are everywhere."

My pulse spikes.

"What? How?"

"You're not gonna like this."

"I already don't. Speak."

"I was confused at first. The timing didn't add up. No way a paparazzo sits on pictures like that for days. They sell fast, move on."

I start pacing.

"So I did some digging—IP traces, metadata, watermark recon—you know, the usual."

"And?"

"The pictures didn't come from a tabloid photographer. They came from a PI."

I stop cold.

"A PI?"

"I tracked him down. Made a few threats, found some interesting stuff in his private—" He pauses. "Anyway. Got him to give up the name of who hired him."

"Mercer?"

"I wish," he says. "At least then we could spin it. Say it was an overreach by a democracy crusader. But no."

He exhales.

"It was Brielle."

I blink.

"No. I saw her last night. We were fine. We left it on good terms, she seemed okay."

"Second." He pauses. "I love you. You're the smartest guy in the room ninety-nine percent of the time. But right now, you're being an idiot."

"Damn it."

"I'm trying to scrub what I can. But you know how this works. It's out there."

"I'm headed to Second Front. See you in ten."

The building entrance is swarming with paps, and the second I step out of the car, the flashes start. My chest tightens. If they're camping outside both my place and the office, how the hell am I supposed to get a break? There's no air left to breathe in this city.

Marcus appears at the door and rushes down to meet me, shielding me as best he can, murmuring for me to keep my head down and just move. But it's not enough. The crowd is too dense, their voices overlapping, camera lenses practically grazing my face.

They're shouting over each other like vultures at a carcass.

"Hadrian! Any comment on the lake photos?"

"Is the blonde your official girlfriend now?"

"Does the campaign approve of this relationship?"

I push forward, trying to tune it all out. The door is just ahead.

"Hadrian, do you think your grandfather would've approved of your taste in women?"

I stop. Turn slowly.

"Say that again," I say, my voice level.

The guy behind the camera lowers it slightly, clearly thinking he's landed something sharp. "Just asking if Hadrian Senior—given his values—would've supported this... phase of yours."

Marcus steps in, trying to guide me inside, but I don't move.

I take a step forward.

"Second," Marcus whispers, grabbing my arm.

"No. Enough is enough," I cut him off, pulling away.

"Please, do enlighten me. What do you think my grandfather would think of me?" I ask, eyes locked on the pap.

He falters—hesitates. Smart of him.

"Just... that maybe a Montrose isn't the right choice for you."

I exhale sharply through my nose.

"I'll try to give you a respectful answer, considering how disrespectful it was for you to assume what my grandfather would think about me. You don't get to speak for my grandfather. And that applies to all of you," I add, glancing around. But I find no eyes. Just lenses, flashes, and little red lights blinking like target marks.

"You aren't born believing in things. You go through life. You screw up. You figure it out. You build your values, develop a consciousness. Everyone deserves that chance—no matter their last name, or background, or where they were born. If you can't open your mind long enough to understand that, I can try my best to explain it. But you'll still only hear whatever fits the story you already decided to believe."

There's a ripple of silence. Even the flashes pause for half a second.

"So you accept it, then?" Someone calls out.

I breathe out. Tired. More tired than I can put into words. I start to turn away. Marcus watches me like I'm a time bomb ticking down.

But I stop at the door. Turn back.

"Aren't you tired?"

A few mutter. One shrugs. "It's our job."

"Just asking questions."

"People want to know."

"Because I am," I say. "I'm tired of fighting invisible battles that always end up being wars against our own values. Our own morals. I'm exhausted of playing this game where the people we're supposed to represent aren't even at the margins—let alone the center. I'm tired of seeing disappointment on the faces of people who, however tired I may be, are worse off. Always worse off. Lied to. Ignored. Used."

I pause. Let it land.

"The enemy isn't our opposition. It's us. Or at least the part of us that surrendered to the idea that this is it. That there's no better way forward. That the only thing left to do is cancel and harass whoever we don't agree with."

No one says anything for a few seconds.

"Easy to talk about values when you were born with a safety net, don't you think?"

I turn toward the voice. "I do understand that. I've benefited from advantages. I won't deny it. All I can do is promise to listen, to stay aware, and to try to do better."

My jaw tightens as I exhale slowly, grounding myself.

"But I won't feel guilty for falling in love with the most amazing woman—someone any of you would be lucky just to stand in the same room with. And I won't feel guilty for having a grandfather who built something lasting, and actually used his influence to make people's lives better."

I shake my head. "I simply won't act from a place of guilt. But I will act from a place of agency. Of knowing I get to choose what I stand for. And who I stand beside."

I finally exhale, the weight of it lifting as the words leave my chest. There's a strange stillness that follows. Maybe peace, maybe just relief.

"If you're looking for one-right-answer politics, by all means, vote for someone who mirrors that. There are plenty to choose from. I just won't be one of them."

I glance around, and for the first time, I actually meet some eyes. Real ones. Unblinking.

"How's that for a headline?" I say.

Then I push the door open and step inside, without looking back.

62

Isadora

AFTER TWENTY-FOUR HOURS OF not leaving my bed, Leo is finally getting ready to go grab us some food.

"What are you feeling like?" he asks, one hand bracing the edge of the headboard as he gets into his pants.

"Surprise me," I say, pressing a kiss between his shoulder blades.

A small, round, golden object clinks to the floor. It rolls once, then comes to a stop against the rug.

"What's that?" I ask, lying on my side, propped up on one elbow.

He bends, scoops it up quickly, then turns it between his fingers. "My loupe."

He brings it up to one eye and peers through it, examining the tiny lens as if making sure it's still intact.

"What is it for?"

"It's what gemologists use," he says. "To look at stones. Diamonds, mainly. You hold it close—like this—and check for flaws. Clarity. Color. Cut. Inclusions, if there are any."

He holds it out to me, the weight of it sitting in the center of his palm.

I take it, turning it in the light. It's heavier than it looks. Cold, too.

I look through it. Everything narrows, warps, comes into hyperfocus. I can see the weave of the bedsheet, individual fibers that were invisible a second ago.

Then I catch something faintly engraved on the inside, just along the rim. Barely there unless you're looking for it.

"*Dominus lapidis,*" I read aloud. "Master of the stone?"

He nods. "It was a gift."

I give it back to him.

He grabs it and puts it away.

"Alright. Food."

"Wait," I say. "Let me come."

He raises an eyebrow. "You sure?"

I nod. "I want air. And... maybe a place that has bread."

"Carbs. Bold."

"I've earned them."

He gives me a real smile. Full. So full it fills me up too.

I slip into a dress, hoping New York's temperature will be merciful today. I'm kind of craving the crispier air of fall. Something tells me the rest of the year is about to unfold spectacularly.

I reach for my comb. "By the way... we host a gala every year. It's a trust my father created to support underfunded STEM education for women. This year's special—it marks twenty years since it was founded." I meet his eyes through the mirror. "Would you come with me?"

He takes the comb from my hand and runs it gently through my hair.

"Are you sure your father will be happy about that?" he asks.

"I'll deal with him."

He smiles and then kisses the top of my head. "Then I'd be happy to."

I kiss his cheek, still half smiling as we walk out together.

We're barely halfway down the hall when the front door opens right in front of us.

Allie steps in.

Suitcase in one hand. Heart in the other.

Her eyes are red, raw around the edges. The tip of her nose, too. She's been crying, hard.

Leo looks at her, then at me. "Text me later?"

I nod.

He presses a kiss to my forehead.

I open my arms to her without saying a word, and she walks straight into them. The second we touch, sobs rip out of her like something's been torn loose inside.

Over her shoulder, I see Leo grab her suitcase and bring it in. He sets it just inside the hallway, careful not to make a sound.

I mouth *thank you*, and he gives the smallest nod before closing the door behind him.

I guide Allie toward the sofa. Though really, it's more like she melts into it.

I tuck her hair behind her ears, wiping a tear that's still clinging to her cheek.

She exhales like her ribs are finally deflating.

"What happened, Als?"

She looks at me, and her eyes are somehow even shinier now. Bluer.

"I don't belong anywhere." Her voice is small. She rubs at her eyes, but the tears spill over anyway.

"Allie." I lean in. "Look at me."

She glances up.

"What makes you say that?"

"My father," she breathes. "He just... laid into me. Said I'm a disappointment. That I've wasted every opportunity they gave me. And my mom—God—she said she can't even look people at church in the eye anymore. Said she didn't raise me to live alone in a Manhattan apartment, unmarried and with no..." She trails off, but I know what she means.

I blink. "I swear to God, I will physically fight them. Actually, I'll verbally fight them. Right now. I'll call and use words that cut deeper than fists."

She lets out a watery laugh, just for a second. A flicker.

"But Als," I say gently, brushing her hair back again. "You know how they are."

She nods. But then the tears start up again, and she pulls in a shaky breath.

"Yeah. I do. But it's always something. I'm too much of one thing for them and too much of the opposite for everyone here. I don't belong anywhere. No one wants me. Not fully."

I reach for her hand and squeeze it hard.

"You belong here. With me. With Jamie. With the things you pour your soul into—which, let's be honest, is everything you put your mind to. And with Hadrian too. It must've taken him a second, but... it seems like he got there. Right?"

She frowns.

"Allie... have you not been online?"

"Online?" she echoes.

"Didn't Jamie call you? He called me earlier. I told him not to. I figured you'd be home soon and didn't need the extra stress on your last few hours with them. But I assumed he still would."

Confusion travels across her face. "My phone's off."

"Turn it on. Like, right now."

Her eyes widen. She bolts to her bag, grabs her phone, and rushes back to the sofa.

"Isadora, what's happening?"

"Just turn it on," I say, already grinning.

When the screen comes to life, she starts scrolling. I watch the moment it hits her, the exact second her expression shifts.

Her shoulders drop. Her lips part. And then, finally, a real smile. One that reaches all the way to her eyes.

She glances up at me. Breathless. "What is this?"

"Search for the video," I tell her. "Press play."

She does.

"All I can do is promise to listen, to stay aware, and to try to do better."

Hadrian's voice fills the room—low, steady, unmistakably him. There's music layered underneath.

"But I won't feel guilty for falling in love with the most amazing woman—someone any of you would be lucky just to stand in the same room with."

The video cuts out. Silence follows.

She doesn't move. Doesn't even breathe, from the look of her. She just stares, phone clutched in both hands.

And I watch every muscle in her face ripple—hope, disbelief, something like awe.

"Where is he?" she whispers.

"Blake's. As of an hour ago." I smile wide. "Go."

"I will," she says, already standing. "But first—you have a glow. And we both know which one. Are you... happy?"

I smile again, wider. "I am."

She tilts her head. "So we're done pretending he's just a beautiful mistake?"

"Leo's the most un-mistake thing of my life."

Champagne Problems

Jamie

Hello?

Can someone please, for the love of God, give me an update?

No updates as of now.

She went to see him.

Jamie

Sounds promising.

I certainly hope so.

Allie

Guys… what am I doing?

This is stupid.

Jamie

Allegra. Don't be a chicken.

You're already there. Just go inside.

Jamie

You knock on that door. Right now!

Allie

Isadora, stop checking my location.

Gladly

Once you go inside

Allie

I'm not sure I will.

James, stop calling me.

Turning my phone off now.

Bye

63
Hadrian

"You really went off script there, man."

Blake's been scrolling through edits of my outburst with the paps.

I shoot him a look.

"I'm proud of you," he adds, grinning. "Also, would've been nice to know you were in love with her before you broke my nose. At least the punch would've had a love story behind it. Kinda poetic. Kinda sick."

I huff out a laugh. He doesn't. Just sinks deeper into the couch, jaw tight.

"You doing any better?" I ask.

He shrugs, eyes on the ceiling. "I will be. Guess I was in deeper than I thought."

A pause stretches between us. I break it. "Still doesn't sit right. Her just disappearing like that. You think she's okay?"

"I think so, yeah." He nods, slow. "She always said her dad had this plan—like a whole protocol—ready to go if anything ever happened. And nothing *has* happened, right? So maybe they just... left."

I frown. "Then that's selfish. And shady as hell. You're better off without her."

There's a knock on the door.

I glance at Blake. "You expecting someone?"

He shakes his head and heads for the door, stopping short when he opens it, half his face curving into a grin.

"Actually... it's for you."

"For me?"

I get up and step to the door. And I'm done for.

She's just standing there. The most beautiful woman I've ever seen. Eyes full of ocean, mine full of sunshine. That's what she feels like to me—that one summer day at the beach you never wanted to end.

We stand there, facing each other for a few seconds.

We're the same people. But something's shifted. Shoulders lighter. Eyes clearer. My head's actually here.

"Uh... I'll be... anywhere but here," Blake mutters behind me, then slips past her and disappears down the corridor.

But I don't move. Don't take my eyes off her.

I wish I could bottle up this feeling—stash it like contraband, pour it when the ache hits. The kind of drunk only she gives me.

And yeah, that would make me a full-blown alcoholic. Gladly so. Straight. No chaser. Bottoms up.

"Als," I break the silence.

"Hey."

I take a step toward her, but she lifts her hand—soft, not harsh—and presses it lightly against my chest, stopping me.

I glance down at her hand, then back at her, unsure.

"I just need to understand first," she says, steady but soft. "What's changed?"

I can see it in her face. She's here. But her guard is up too.

"My feelings for you haven't." I keep my voice low. "They've just gotten louder. Bigger. If that was even possible."

I rest my hand over hers, still hovering on my chest. Her fingers twitch slightly beneath mine, but she doesn't pull away.

"The crack between us... it wasn't ours. Other people put it there. And I let them."

"It's a fault line, Hadrian," she says softly.

"Then I'll stand on it with you."

I exhale heavily.

"I'm not scared anymore. Not of people's opinions. Not of perception. Not of fucking optics." My voice dips lower. "I'm done with all of that."

I glance down, then meet her eyes again—steady this time, anchored.

"If I can't do this as myself—fully—then I'm not doing it at all."

I shake my head, jaw tightening. "That was always the lesson, wasn't it? Right in front of me. And I kept asking the wrong questions, letting the wrong people shape the answers."

My thumb brushes against her knuckles, slow. "It's not about what it costs me to be me... it's what it costs me *not* to be. And that's you." I swallow hard. "Which is everything."

I step in, just half an inch closer. "And I see that now. I see you."

My hand presses gently over hers. "And I'm not scared."

A beat.

"Or maybe I am." My voice dips. "But only of one thing."

I look at her dead-on. "Being apart from you. That terrifies me, Allie."

She blushes—soft, barely there—but it hits me like a punch to the ribs.

"But... you've got, what? Two months 'til the election," she says quietly.

"I don't care." I shake my head, no hesitation. "I'll turn it around. Hell, I'll tell every voter in the district I'm madly in love with you if that's what it takes. Knock on every damn door, say it myself."

I step even closer, voice low but firm. "I don't like who I am when I choose everything but you."

She opens her mouth like she's about to say something else. But I don't let her.

I don't give myself time to think. I pull her in and kiss her. Like I've been dying to do. Like I've been starving for it.

And she answers with a sound I swear I'll remember for the rest of my life.

Her fingers curl into my shirt. Mine slide down to her hips, pulling her closer, until there's no air between us, just heat and years of restraint snapping in half.

She tugs at me, backing up. I follow.

No stumbles. No second-guessing. Just the two of us moving down the hall like instinct, synced and locked in.

We make it to the bedroom like we're being pulled there by some unseen force, her hand tangled in my shirt, my mouth still on hers.

She bumps into the edge of the bed and I don't stop. Just grab her thighs and lift, set her down like I've done this a hundred times in my head.

She pulls me down with her as she falls back, and suddenly we're tangled in sheets, limbs, and all these feelings I have for her flooding my chest like they've found air for the first time.

She's beneath me, eyes wild, lips swollen, breath sharp.

And fuck me if I don't feel like I've already lost the ground under me.

I want every membrane that separates us to dissolve, so I kiss her frantically while I wonder how it's possible that my body intertwined in hers can make me feel the freest.

I've touched her a hundred times before. A hand at her back. A nudge of knees beneath dinner tables. My jacket over her shoulders at every party where she pretended not to be freezing.

But not like this.

Not with my hand sliding up her spine and her breath hitching like she's never been touched before.

She looks up at me like she's reading every version of me that ever existed. The public one. The broken one. The one I kept just for her.

"You're sure?" I ask.

"I've been sure for years."

Something in me goes quiet. I don't hesitate. I pull her in and kiss her.

The kiss isn't soft. It's not cautious. It's years of unsaid things collapsing into a single second. It's knowing exactly where her mouth belongs and tasting everything I was too much of a coward to ask for.

We lose track of what happens next. The room disappears. My thoughts gone. It's just skin and breath and the sound she makes when I find the spot just below her collarbone that makes her whisper my name like it's something holy.

Her hands are all over me, and I can't stop looking at her. Can't believe I get to.

Because she doesn't just love the ocean—she *is* the whole mass of water covering two-thirds of this planet. And I'd rather drown in her than be washed up on the wrong shore again.

And maybe that's what this is.

Not just sex, but drowning, finally, in the one thing I was always meant to go under for.

She exhales—quiet, trembling—and I press my forehead to hers, both of us holding on like it's the end of the world.

When I push inside her, it doesn't feel like conquering something new.

It feels like coming home.

64

Leo

My father asked me to meet him at The Aman.

I'm almost there.

It's the first time he's agreed to see me in weeks, which hopefully means he's ready to listen.

The private lift descends, mirrored doors sealing shut with a whisper. The ride is smooth, silent, like being lowered into the belly of something illicit. When the doors open, the shift is immediate—darker, richer, hungrier.

Whiskey, ash, and sweat hang in the air. A grand piano plays in the corner. The lighting is low. Leather booths line the walls. Velvet drapes absorb the sound. Glasses clink softly as servers move between tables.

It's a hunting ground. The kind of place where predators wear cufflinks and the prey doesn't realize it's been gutted until the check arrives.

Like the table on my right. Three men, dark suits, zero expression. To anyone else, it'd look like a quiet conversation over mineral water. But not really. One of them keeps his left leg angled just enough to hide the Glock printing through his jacket. The other hasn't touched his drink. And the third keeps checking the entrance, like he's timing something. They're here to close.

I move through the room without slowing. The bartender nods as I pass. I don't return it. My eyes lock on the far booth.

And I stall.

Fucking hell.

He's not alone.

My father is seated with a woman I'd recognize even if all I saw was her silhouette.

Solange.

She laughs at something he's said, that familiar, syrupy sound sliding out of her throat like honey laced with arsenic. I've been on the receiving end of that laugh before, and I'd bleach the memory out of my skull if I could.

My father's gaze shifts. Lands on me. A pause, a blink, the faintest tilt of his chin.

That's my cue.

I approach. Controlled.

"Solange. Lupo." My voice is even as I pull out a chair and slide into the seat beside her.

"Hi, *cher*," she purrs, still looking at him. Not me.

My father flicks a speck of dust off his cuff. "Solange was just filling me in on your little crusade in Brazil. Bold play. Having her picked up by the *Força Nacional*."

I glance at Solange, keeping my face blank even as my pulse spikes.

"Fair is fair," she says nonchalantly. "It was clever." She glances at me now. "Don't worry. I'm not mad. I *did* threaten to kill you, after all. And we both know if it came to that, your jiu-jitsu black belt wouldn't hold up against my Krav Maga."

They share a laugh.

I don't.

"What are you doing here?" I ask. No softness to it.

"Business," my father answers for her.

"Lupo reached out, and my father was enthralled. He sent me to close the deal."

My jaw tightens. "What deal?"

My father takes a sip. "The Claveneau and I have decided to bury the hatchet. We're forming a united front." Solange giggles again. My stomach turns. "They'll run Europe from Belgium. We keep the American side. And we'll split the Asia corridors Mikhailov left behind."

He's lost it.

Is he actually convinced he can trust the Claveneau? We've been at war with them for years. I stole the biggest red diamond in recorded history from them, for fuck's sake. And now he thinks a partnership is on the table?

Solange stands, smoothing her dress. "Excuse me, gentlemen. I need the restroom."

As soon as she disappears, he turns to me.

"Which brings me to why I called you here."

Here it is.

"The Claveneau handed us the lead on a rare blue diamond in Golconda. Old mine. Untouched for decades. Could be even more carats than the one you pulled from Angola." He leans back, glass in hand. "You know the business. Diamonds are only as rare as the next one we find. And this one—this one's big." He taps two fingers once against the table. "Time to get to work. You leave tomorrow. Elara One's on standby."

This is it.

The moment I stop pretending I don't see it for what it is. The life I no longer want to live.

Because she doesn't fucking exist in it.

The Earth has already shifted on its axis. My center of gravity's been rewritten—there's no diamond left to dig out of the dirt. There's just her.

And I'm not risking that.

Not that long, wavy hair or those whirlpool eyes that look at you like you may just be worth it, even when you know better.

I exhale. Except it's not just air leaving my lungs. It's realization. I am utterly and irrevocably fucked. Head over heels. Too late for clean breaks or harmless exits. The cards are down, and I've pulled both the Ace and the Joker. Arrow, straight to the heart.

This isn't another crack in the armor. This is its collapse.

A quiet entropy. The disintegration of every structure I know. And at the center of it is her.

"I want out."

He barks a laugh, guttural, unhinged.

"You want *out*?"

"You heard me. I'm done. The company. The name. The blood money. You. All of it. I'm fucking done."

"You think you get to just walk?"

He leans in, voice like oil on fire.

"This isn't retail, Leone. You don't clock out."

"What—you gonna kill me?" I scoff. "Spare me the theatrics."

He smirks.

Doesn't even try to deny it.

"You know what happens to people on the outside who know too much. We run a fragile operation. Leaks aren't tolerated."

"Then come for me. I fucking dare you. Take your best shot."

I stand.

He straightens too, trying to look unbothered, but fury is written all over his face.

Solange slides back into the booth like nothing's happened.

"Gentlemen," she says evenly. "Let's not do this here."

"I'm leaving."

"Leo." I'm already walking when her voice stops me.

I exhale. Jaw clenched. I turn. Her expression tells me I shouldn't have.

"Isadora Carter-Bello?" Her voice is sweet, sharp. "We don't fraternize with leverage, *Cher*."

My father lets out a low laugh.

My blood spikes.

"She's quite the beauty," he says. Voice like a blade. "Soft. Sweet. The kind you want to ruin just to see what she looks like after. Tell me—have you?"

Solange rolls her eyes.

I stare at him. And for a second, I truly wonder if I'd feel anything at all pulling a trigger.

He lifts a hand. "Relax. Just making conversation. She's a beautiful girl. When do I get to meet her?"

"You won't." My voice is ice. "And if either of you so much as say her name again, we'll have a real fucking problem here."

Solange arches a brow, amused. My father grins, teeth flashing like a knife.

"Touchy."

"No," I say. "Clear."

I take a step back. Steady. Controlled.

"She's not part of this. Never will be. And if you try to drag her in, I'll take that as permission."

A pause. Then I look at Solange dead in the eyes.

"Maybe I'll get the chance to kill you after all."

65
Isadora

"Can I borrow this dress?" Allie asks, already holding one up from the rack in my old bedroom—a sky-blue Oscar de la Renta gown with oversized floral appliqués.

"Well, considering you could have one of my kidneys, yeah—I think a dress is also okay."

She grins and disappears behind the dressing screen.

Allie and I are getting ready for The Andromeda Trust's twentieth anniversary gala from the upstairs suite of the Carter-Bello house. My mother curated a whole collection for me to choose from.

Every September, like clockwork. But this one's different. Because Leo's coming with me.

And Hadrian's going with Allie.

And everything kind of feels right in the world.

I'm wearing a Saint Laurent gown—ivory silk, halter neck, backless with a high slit. I added a white feathered stole and black heels.

I finish my hair—just a soft wave, parted to the side—when the doorbell rings. I bolt downstairs before anyone else can intercept it.

Luckily, my parents are already at the venue, probably making Kathy crazy.

This year's gala is at Oheka Castle, just over an hour outside of Manhattan.

Big names attending tonight. Scientists. Nobel laureates. Former presidents.

I open the door. And there he is.

Leo Sartori.

Wearing a double-breasted black tuxedo with peak lapels and silk trim, perfectly tailored to his frame. Crisp white shirt, black bow tie, polished boots. No smile, just that look.

His dark hair's still damp from the shower, pushed back like he didn't try too hard.

My breath catches.

Maybe it's the stairs. Maybe it's him.

"You're over two hours early," I manage, barely.

"Am I?" he says, eyes lingering on me. "You look... breathtaking."

I blush. He leans in and kisses my forehead. Those are quickly becoming my favorite.

"Thought I'd give your father some time to acclimate to the idea before we head to a very public party."

"He's not here." I grab his hand. "Come."

We walk through the hall. He glances both ways as we pass, then stops in front of a photo—me, on horseback, somewhere sunlit.

"Is that you?" he asks.

"Yep. And that's Vega, my mother's horse. She's retired now."

He just... stares.

"What?" I ask.

"Nothing." He shakes his head. "Nothing. Do you still ride?"

"Not really," I say as we keep walking. His arm slips around my shoulder. "Just when I'm in Argentina."

We go upstairs and into my bedroom, where Allie's at the vanity, doing her makeup.

"Hey, Sarto."

"Hi, Als. How's it going?"

She turns around, her face a little pale.

"Actually... a bit lightheaded. Must be my blood sugar again. I'll go grab some orange juice."

"I'll go," Leo says, already moving.

We both look at him. She smiles.

"Absolutely not. You stay here. Have your moment. I'll be back."

She winks at him and slips out.

Leo scratches the back of his head, then slides both hands into his pockets.

"So..." he says. "I have something for you."

He pulls out a small midnight-blue velvet box and opens it toward me.

Inside is a delicate gold chain with a small charm: the number 222, shaped in soft curves and set with tiny white diamonds.

"That's... so beautiful."

I pick it up gently, leaning in for a closer look.

"Wait. There's more," he says. "But you'll need my loupe to read it."

He pulls his golden loupe from his pocket and hands it to me.

"Here, you hold it like this," he says, guiding my fingers. "Pinch the handle between your thumb and forefinger, then bring it right up to your eye. Close the other one. Now hold the pendant about an inch away."

I do as he says. And there it is—something engraved so small it disappears without the lens.

Just one line, barely visible. *Far past minute two.*

I glance up at him. His eyes are shining.

And suddenly, there isn't a single corner of this room that isn't shining too.

"Thanks," I whisper.

He steps closer. So do I.

He presses his lips on mine and I respond by putting my hands around his neck. And now I'm glowing from the inside out, wondering how the stormiest eyes I've ever seen can make everything feel so unbearably bright.

A throat clears behind us.

We both turn.

Jamie leans against the doorframe, arms crossed, smirking.

"So jealous I might vomit," he says.

"Hi, James."

"Hi back."

He strolls over and peers down at the necklace. "Nice. And very on theme."

Leo and I exchange a look.

Jamie sighs dramatically. "Of course you haven't seen it."

He pulls out his phone. "You're on *E! News.*"

"Who is?" Allie walks in, orange juice in hand.

"Is and Leo." He turns the screen toward us. "Here. Look."

A photo of Leo, caught leaving my building the other morning, fills the screen. Underneath it:

Is Isadora Carter-Bello the diamond Leo Sartori would never sell?

Leo scoffs. Allie, Jamie, and I all turn to him.

"It's just..." He shrugs. "To me, comparing a woman to a diamond is kind of... odd."

I raise a brow, waiting for more.

He shifts his weight. "Diamonds are so rare. I don't think people actually grasp that. Most of the ones in circulation aren't even gem-quality. If you're in lo—"

He stops, stiffens. Hand slips to the back of his neck. "Seeing someone," he adds quickly. "That's everything you see. Everywhere. She's not buried. Or locked away. She's in places you didn't even know people could exist."

He glances at each of us. Then lets out a strained laugh.

"I guess the only time that comparison would make sense is if the setting was Planet 55 Cancri e."

I tilt my head.

"I don't know anything about that, but so cute," Allie says.

"Again, disgustingly jealous," Jamie adds as they both retreat to the vanity.

"Planet 55 Cancri e, huh?" I flash him a smile and wish we were alone right about now.

"Actually, I think I know what you're talking about. Come with me."

He follows me down the hall and into the library.

I head straight to the Hydrae shelf and pull down one of my mother's old planetary guides—*The Exoplanet Atlas: Beyond Our Suns.*

Flipping through the pages, I stop when I find it.

"Here," I say, my finger landing on the image.

A glowing, lava-slicked planet locked in a death-close orbit around its star.

55 Cancri e.

Nicknamed the diamond planet because of its carbon-rich composition—extreme heat and pressure that some think create crystalline layers beneath the molten surface. Located in the constellation Cancer, just 41 light-years away.

I hand him the book. He takes it with both hands and studies the page—eyes narrowed and brow furrowed.

I guess he's right. And I also guess that if I were planet 55 Cancri e, he'd be the Sun-like star I orbit, just 0.015 astronomical units away, while humans call it science.

He closes the book and places it back on the shelf, then starts wandering.

"Why so many books on space?" he asks.

"My mother wanted to be an astrophysicist. She's kind of obsessed with it. Especially the Andromeda galaxy, which is why my father opened the trust in her honor." I nod toward the biggest section of the room. "There."

He walks over, eyes skimming the long shelf. Then he stops. Picks up a book and flips it open.

"M31?"

"Yeah. That's its official designation—Messier 31."

He shuts the book with a loud snap, then turns to me. Something in his face has shifted.

"Isadora... do you remember when you were in Madrid and you saw your dad with two men at the hotel bar?"

I blink. "That's... random. But yeah, I do."

"We were on the phone, and you walked up to them. They were speaking French. What were they saying?"

"What?" I laugh, confused. "Leo, I don't remember that. It was months ago."

His eyes don't leave mine. "It was a number."

Something's wrong. My stomach dips. "What's going on?"

"Nothing," he says too quickly. "Just—trying to piece something together. Please. Think. What number were they saying?"

I search his face and try to follow the thread.

"Wait... actually, yeah. I remember. One of them said *nonante millions.* It caught my attention because that's not how the French say ninety. It's—"

"Belgian," he finishes. His voice is flat.

"Leo... you're pale. What is it?"

He doesn't respond. Just stands there, eyes locked on me, but he's staring through me.

"Leo."

Nothing. Then he blinks, steps forward, and kisses my forehead.

"I'll meet you at the party, okay?"

"What? No. Leo, what's going on?"

"Nothing I can't handle," he says. "Just... trust me, okay? I'll see you soon."

He turns to leave, and I hate it. I hate the sight of him walking away from me. And I hate how much I hate it.

"Leo." I catch his wrist. "Promise me."

He turns, then looks at me for a long time.

"Promise."

66

Hadrian

I OPEN THE DOOR, half-buttoning my sleeve.

Rami stands there.

Not a word. No nod. Just the set of his jaw, the way his eyes scan behind me like he's clearing a room.

"Rami?" My voice scrapes out. "What are you doing here?"

"Hadrian." He steps inside.

My pulse kicks. "Isadora—"

"She's fine."

A pause.

"But I need to talk to you."

He looks around. His gaze brushes over the hallway, toward the kitchen.

"Blake's not here," I say. "And you're scaring the shit out of me. So talk."

He pulls something from behind his back—a thick, weathered envelope, creased and sealed with tape that looks like it's been peeled off and pressed back down again.

"What's that?"

He doesn't meet my eyes. "Before I hand you this... you need to know. She was never truly in danger. I wouldn't have allowed it."

Something about the way he says it makes me sit. Just sit. No decision behind it. My body folds into the dining chair like it's instinct. I pull another one out across from me.

He sits and places the envelope down.

"Have you ever wondered why the Sartoris walk around with no visible security detail?"

I squint. "What?"

Rami doesn't blink. Doesn't move.

"No guards. No cars. No shadows. Just them."

I lean back, tension crawling up my spine. "Hell if I know. Maybe they just think they're untouchable or something. What's that got to do with anything?"

There's barely a shift in his chest. The kind of breath you take before pulling a trigger.

"No." He glances down at the table. "It's because they already have protection. Layers of it."

I wait.

"Every private firm in this city. Off-duty police. Federal contractors. Intelligence officers. Former Navy. Old Guard. New Guard. Whatever you want to call it." He meets my eyes now. "They all work for them."

The air in my throat jams.

"That's not—" I get halfway up. "That's not a thing. That kind of network doesn't exist." I shake my head. "Impossible. That'd mean you—"

I stop.

Small fragments start snapping into place, memory shards turning into puzzle pieces, one after the other. The way Leo leaned in, whispered something to him the night I lost it and hit Blake. The near-invisible nod he gave security the night Isa left with him. All of it, tightening now into a noose.

"The Garden Party."

His silence confirms it.

"You left her alone. During an active kidnapping."

I'm on my feet now, pacing. Heat surges through my chest, my fists, up my neck. My vision pulses once.

Isa told me—when I found her shaking in Sartori's car—that something had felt wrong from the start. That something was missing, the edges too clean. All those high-profile people and not a single black-suited man in sight.

I should've known.

"Hadrian—"

"Five minutes." My voice shakes. "You've got five minutes to explain before I forget how long you've worked for my family."

He nods, slow. Hands clasped loosely in front of him, thumbs brushing.

"There are codes," he says. "Embedded ones. Some are dormant. Most are soft—look the other way, make yourself scarce. The Garden Party was one of those. A quiet stand-down."

I stare at him. My hands are trembling. My breath's gone shallow.

"I never stopped watching her," he adds. "Even when she didn't see it."

I sit again before the nausea takes over. The edge of the table presses into my ribs.

"She was never unprotected."

I nod once. It doesn't mean anything.

"But something changed today."

The envelope sits between us like it's listening.

"A code was triggered," he says. "One I've never seen activated."

My fingers curl around the edge of the table.

"It means war, Hadrian. The kind fought in whispers. Shadows. Deaths that don't make the papers."

I stare at him. The pulse behind my left eye throbs.

"And the worst part is—" He leans in. His voice barely moves the air. "It was only triggered for Lupo."

My jaw locks.

"That means," Rami finishes, "as of today… Leo's unprotected."

He pauses.

"And she's with him."

He meets my eyes. "I'll protect her with my own life. You need to know that. But I don't think I'll be enough—not up against this. Not now. Not once they realize I've gone off-code."

Something cracks in my chest.

I shoot to my feet, grab my keys. "Isadora—I need to—"

"Wait." His voice cuts clean through me.

"There's more."

He rests his hand over the envelope, like what's inside could change everything.

"I'm sorry to do this, Hadrian. But I don't know how much longer I have. And if you're going to protect her, you need to see the whole picture."

"Speak, Rami. Now."

He breathes in once. Just once. Like it might be his last.

"Your father… there's so much you don't know about him."

He slides the envelope forward. Doesn't say another word.

I grab it. Tear the flap open. Fingers fumbling.

I pull the stack out all at once and start skimming through fast. Contracts. Photos. Signatures. Pages stamped with the Andromeda Trust header, again and again. Transfers. Scans. Surveillance stills.

And something else that makes my breath catch like I've been punched where the air doesn't come back.

All this time, I thought I was barricaded in a battlefield, dodging enemy artillery, only to realize I'd been standing in the blast radius of a nuclear bomb all along.

Welcome to ground zero.

And I'm so sorry for dragging you into it.

67

Leo

All this time, it was just fucking there.

I've been driving for hours, choking on how fucking blind I was.

I should've put it together sooner. I got so consumed with the minutiae, I missed the bigger picture entirely.

Which means—fuck. I'm about to be sick.

I storm into my father's office, and the smell of leather mixed with a Cuban makes my stomach tighten.

"What the fuck have you done?"

"What's your problem now?" His tone is dismissive.

"M31?" I start pacing. "Fuck."

I slam my hand against the desk. He doesn't even flinch.

"The Carter-Bello trust. You're using it to clean the blood red diamond," I spit out. "Victor forced you to bring in the Belgians, didn't he?"

"Well, look who's finally catching up. About time, if you ask me," he replies, his voice dripping with indifference.

"Listen to me, you piece of shit. I don't give a damn how deep in bed you were with Victor. But the Carter-Bellos are off-limits now. Do you hear me?"

"Oh, Leone, love makes you predictable, I'm afraid. Also, you're late, as usual. Your girlfriend's brother was just here throwing around threats," he responds casually, clearly amused.

"What the fuck are you talking about? Hadrian was here?" I ask, panic creeping into my voice.

"Yes. He found some documents and pieced it all together. Tried to threaten me, can you believe that? Said he'd expose us if I so much as looked at his family the wrong way. Such a shame, really. You should've seen it, the disappointment written all over his face. The betrayal he carried for his father's actions."

He pauses briefly for a cigar hit.

"He has some balls, I'll tell you that. His father could learn a thing or two from him."

Do you think there are different kinds of punishment for different kinds of sins?

Like, is it the same damnation if you steal as if you kill?

If you take the life of someone you don't even know, does it carry the same weight as tearing apart the one who gave you life?

What's your favorite kind of sin? Loving her, do you reckon?

He finally locks eyes with me. And there it is—that sick, twisted darkness I've spent my life trying to outrun. I see it in myself. It's the same venom, the same jagged edge.

It reminds me of something I learned as a kid, sitting in the corner of this very office: only a diamond can cut another diamond. The hardest substance on earth, unbreakable by anything else. But when it meets its match—when one diamond is used against another—it fractures, splits, shatters into brilliance... or destruction.

That's what this is. He and I. Two forces made of the same unrelenting material, colliding.

The aggression I see in his eyes is my own reflected back at me, sharper and more fucked up because I know exactly how far he's willing to go.

Whatever he's done, it's already in motion.

"What the fuck have you done? Where's OG?" I roar, my voice trembling with rage.

He barely glances up, feigning indifference, and shrugs like this is just another Tuesday.

"Oh, nothing new, really. You know the business. We can't have someone threatening to undo all the hard work we've put in. Sadly, he'll have to pay for his father's sins."

Before he's even finished, I'm already out the door, sprinting toward my car.

My heart is hammering so hard it feels like it might break free from my chest.

My breath comes in shallow gasps, and my vision blurs as I pull out of the driveway, tires screeching against the pavement.

The thought of what might be happening to Isadora and her family claws at my sanity.

My hands are shaking as I grab my phone, barely able to dial her number.

And here's the thing: I've faced death before. I've seen people die, I've walked right up to the edge myself and stared it down.

But the idea of her being hurt? That's a kind of fear I've never known. It makes me wish I'd already died, because living with the weight of this would be unbearable.

She picks up on the third ring.

"Leo, can I call you later? I can't talk right now," she says, her voice tight.

"Isadora, listen to me. I need you to tell me where you are. Now. Right fucking now," I bark, my voice frantic, raw with panic.

"What's going on? Why is everyone being—"

"ISADORA. NOW!" I shout, gripping the wheel so hard my knuckles ache.

"We're on our way to the gala," she says, her voice trembling.

"We? Who's we?" I ask, my voice breaking.

"Hadrian and I. Allie wasn't feeling—"

"Isadora, listen to me. Listen carefully. I need you to call the police. Right now. Tell them you're being followed. Take the next exit you see and park somewhere crowded. Do you hear me? Do it. NOW," I order.

"Followed? Leo, don't be silly. I'll meet you at the—"

She stops mid-sentence.

"HADRIAN, ON YOUR LEFT!"

Then I hear it—the sickening sound of metal colliding, loud and sharp, followed by chaos on the other end of the line.

Have you ever had your worst nightmare play out in real life? Heard your unpaid sins collide with the girl you never meant to love from miles away? Felt that kind of terror?

Soulless, I slam my foot on the accelerator—knowing full well that the only thing that could help her now is a time machine.

68

Isadora

I HAVE A SCAR above my right brow.

I got it when I was around eight. Maybe nine. I was riding back from school alone because Hadrian was sick and had stayed home that day.

On the way, a man—big, ugly man, really, though maybe that's just my memory playing tricks—stepped into the path.

And I went flying.

It felt a lot like now.

That strange, suspended moment when you're up in the air and know the crash is coming.

I was terrified. And alone.

I hit the ground hard. Knees first, just like now—except now it's my whole lower body being crushed.

My face hit the pavement after. Mostly the right side.

Now, it's the airbag. Same pressure. Same ringing in my ear. Only now, I don't feel pain. Not really.

Nothing was on fire back then, not like now. But it might as well have been, considering how scared I was.

A boy helped me. He had dark, stormy eyes.

I ran home after. Left the bike behind. Straight into Hadrian's room.

Hadrian.

I look at him now. I think he's saying my name. Though I'm not sure words mean what they're supposed to mean anymore.

Everything feels... light.

I was crying back then.

I think I should be crying now too.

"What happened?" he asked from his bed. His eyes were tired, the shadows underneath them darker than usual. But the worry, that was clear.

Just like it is now. I wish I could tell him not to worry. I'm not scared now. How could I be? He's here.

"I fell from my bike," I lied as I sat next to him.

I always wanted to be as brave as Hadrian. So flawed, yet so full of bravery.

"Also," I added, "I learned in school today that one day all the stars will die out. And we'll all be left in total darkness."

I look at him now. It's getting darker in here. Even though I can still smell the smoke.

I was so scared back then. Who would protect me from men who knocked little girls off bikes if the whole sky went black?

I'm not scared now. I wish I could tell him.

But again—words... they just don't mean anything right now.

"Isa," he said, half-smiling, "that's a million years away."

"I don't want to be alone if it's dark, Hadrian."

And he looked at me, so serious.

"Isadora," he said. "Should the stars go out, there isn't a darkness in any galaxy that could keep me from finding you."

I smiled. Life had been so generous to me. I was born and he was already there. He had known a whole world before I ever opened my eyes. But I had never known life without him in it.

And I remember thinking how lucky that was. That I would never have to.

Not for the rest of mine.

69

Hadrian

"Isa, please. Stay with me."

I shout as I fight against the seatbelt. It's cutting into my shoulder, holding me in place.

I can't tell how we landed, but the angle's wrong—everything's pressing down in the opposite direction.

My arms are above me. Or below me.

Are we on our side?

No—no, I think... we're upside down.

My arms are drenched. Blood or something else. Both hands shaking.

The pitch in my ears is fading now. In its place, a deep groan.

Metal straining. Something shifting under pressure.

And then a sound, like glass cracking under weight. Somewhere close.

I twist my neck. It stabs fire into my spine.

"Isa, can you hear me?"

She's looking at me, but it's like her eyes can't stay open for long.

"Hey. No. Don't do that. You stay awake, you hear me?"

I try again to unclip my belt, but my fingers are shaking too much.

Something in my ribs—or maybe my spine—feels wrong.

My legs aren't responding. Everything's going heavy.

I hear something outside. Maybe distant voices?

A creak. Then metal groans and yields. Glass shatters behind me.

I cough. Smoke. It's in my lungs now.

Something's burning.

I have to get her out.

"Isa," I say, louder now. "You need to listen to me. We have to move. You need to move."

I reach for her, but I can't even get close.

"Don't fall asleep. Not now. Please."

Another sound, closer this time. Another crash. Something hits my face. Glass.

"Hadrian! Can you hear me?"

Rami. Thank God.

"Rami..." I gasp. "Isadora—"

He climbs in through the wreckage. Moves fast.

I think he presses two fingers to my neck, then looks at my side.

His eyes tighten. He's above me—or below, I can't tell—but I still see it.

"Hadrian, I have to get you out first. You're losing too much blood."

"No. Don't." My voice is shaking. "You take her out. First."

"Hadrian—"

"Listen to me, dammit!" I try to raise my hands. Nothing. "You take her out. Make sure she's okay. Then come for me."

He holds my eyes. Then nods.

"Okay."

He pulls out a cutter and slices through her seatbelt. Lowers her carefully, then lifts her into his arms.

"Is she okay?" I ask.

"Her pulse is strong. I'll be back in one minute. Hold tight."

I try to nod. Don't know if it works.

It's getting quieter.

Not around me, inside me. Like someone's turning the volume down from within.

I hear a voice. Rami? Or someone else? It's muffled now. Too far away.

I blink. I think I do. The light's changing—smoke and movement and shadows—and then... something shifts.

It's not the car. Not the wreck.

It's the way the air feels.

Cooler.

Familiar.

"Hey there, son."

I know that voice.

My eyes move—slow, like they're pushing through water—and he's there. Standing a few feet away.

Grandpa?

Yes. *Grandpa*.

When did he get here?

"You did good," he says, hands in his pockets. "You did more than good."

I try to speak, but my mouth doesn't work. Doesn't need to.

He steps closer.

I guess my legs work now because I'm standing in front of him.

There's something in his eyes. I can't describe it.

Like how I'm feeling. It's like words don't exist for it.

"It's alright now. You can rest."

I want to tell him I didn't fix everything. That Isadora's still in danger. That everything we've worked so hard for is at stake.

A weaker version of fear starts creeping in, and I can feel it—how it pulls me down. Makes my body heavier. Or at least tries to.

Allie. The love of my life. The girl of my dreams.

A small part of me still tries to hold on.

To this life.

The one where she is.

The one where she's waiting for me to come back for her.

But that part of me, it's too small now. And I can't hold onto it anymore. Just the idea of trying hurts.

"She's going to be okay."

His voice cuts right through what's left of my fear and evaporates it.

Grandpa's right. Everything feels smaller now. And yet—somehow—everything's immense.

Especially love. I feel so much of it.

Loving her. I think it saved me.

I can see how heavy it all was—what we carry, what we fight for.

Down there, it never stops pressing on you.

But not here.

If only you could all see it too.

Translations

by Isadora Sloane Carter-Bello

[Originally handwritten - transcription below]

"(...) lloró y tejió, hasta que en la madrugada terminó la colcha y se la echó encima. De nada sirvió. Ni esa noche ni muchas otras mientras vivió logró controlar el frío."

Como Agua Para Chocolate – Laura Esquivel

"(...) she cried and ~~knitted~~ **wove**, until in the early morning when she finished the quilt and threw it over herself. It was of no use. Neither that night nor many others while she lived did she manage to control the ~~cold~~ **chill**.
("cold" is accurate, but "chill" feels truer—it lingers, doesn't it?)

"Se non c'è amore, non solo inaridisce la vita delle persone, ma anche quella delle città."

L'amica geniale – Elena Ferrante

"The lack of love not only withers the lives of people, but also the life of ~~cities~~ **a city**."
(cities → a city. too collective. Naples was the point.)

"Non si muore per amore. Si vive per amare, ed è molto più difficile."

Lettera a un bambino mai nato – Oriana Fallaci

"We do not die for love. We live to love, and that is much more ~~difficult~~ **brutal**."
("brutal" is less poetic, but maybe more honest.)

"Lo terrible del mar, es morir de sed."

Nací Para Esto – Gustavo Cerati

"The terrible thing about the sea is to die of **thirst**."
(The king of impossible metaphors.)

"A la ausencia no hay quien se acostumbre. Otro sol no es tu sol, aunque te alumbre."

Insomnios y duermevelas – Mario Benedetti

"There's no getting used to absence. Another sun is not your sun, even if it ~~shines~~ **glows** on you."
(glows → less neutral. more haunted.)

"El verdadero dolor es indecible. Si puedes hablar de lo que te acongoja estás de suerte: eso significa que no es tan importante. Porque cuando el dolor cae sobre ti sin paliativos, lo primero que te arranca es la palabra."

La ridícula idea de no volver a verte – Rosa Montero

"True pain is unspeakable. If you can talk about what burdens you, you're lucky: it means it's not that ~~important~~ **real**. Because when pain falls on you mercilessly, the first thing it takes is your ~~words~~ **voice**."
(was tempted to use "breath." but that felt like erasing the language too soon.)

"Ce que j'ai eu envie de faire dans ce livre, c'est de sauver quelque chose du temps où l'on ne sera plus jamais."

Les Années – Annie Ernaux

"What I wanted to do in this book was to save something from the time where we will never be ~~again~~ **anymore**."
("again" is hopeful. "anymore" is final.)

"La memoria es frágil y el transcurso de una vida es muy breve y ocurre todo tan deprisa que no alcanzamos a ver la relación entre los acontecimientos."

La casa de los espíritus – Isabel Allende

"Memory is fragile, and the course of a life is so brief and passes so quickly that we fail to see the connections between events."
(maybe we're not meant to.)

"Saudade não tem tradução."

Read in the streets of Rio.

"*Saudade* has no translation."
(but still, I try.)

"Чем темнее ночь, тем ярче звёзды. Чем глубже скорбь, тем ближе Бог."

Attributed to Fyodor Dostoevsky. Widely paraphrased. Spirit faithful; source uncertain.

"The darker the night, the brighter the stars. The deeper the grief, the

closer ~~is~~ **comes** God."
("comes", not "is". like an arrival. or a reckoning.)

"Je me souviens de toi comme d'un rêve dont j'ai été soulagée de me réveiller."

Instagram caption. Source unknown.

"I remember you like a dream."
(Not what it says. But what I needed it to.)

"You always translate better when you're angry."

Hadrian Carter-Bello, in Buenos Aires. After the protest.

(He has a point.)

"No la dejó rota. La dejó lúcida. Lo cual fue peor."

Never published. Found in the margins of a draft.

"He didn't leave her broken. He left her lucid. Which was worse."

"Lo còr a sas rasons que la rason non coneis."

Attributed to Blaise Pascal via Old Occitan / French lineage. Disputed in origin; faithful in spirit.

"The heart has its reasons that reason knows nothing of." (traditional)
"The heart reasons in ways the mind will never map." (scholarly, modernized)
"Some things I chose weren't smart. They were true." (my take – I.S.C.B.)

"Czasem odpowiedzi nie potrzebują słów."

Leo Sartori

"Sometimes answers don't need ~~words~~ **language**."
(language = larger than words. less intimate, more dangerous.)

On language and what slips through the cracks

Some words carry such an intrinsic soul that they defy translation. Take *raison d'être*, for instance—its English equivalent *reason for being* feels functional, almost flat in comparison. It's not that translating these words would diminish their meaning. It's that their essence has traveled through time and across borders, and even when placed in a foreign context, they retain their original beauty. They've been shaped by their journey, but remain whole.

Some other examples include, but are not limited to:

- *déjà vu* (French): the feeling of having lived a moment before
- *fiancé / fiancée* (French): too weighted to just mean "engaged"
- *faux pas* (French): a social misstep, but with sharper edges
- *je ne sais quoi* (French): an indefinable allure
- *vis-à-vis* (French): face-to-face, but often with tension
- *dolce far niente* (Italian): the sweetness of doing nothing
- *alter ego* (Latin): a second self—one that often says the things we don't
- *sobremesa* (Spanish): the space after dinner where no one wants to leave

- *macho* (Spanish): not just manly, but armored in performance

(Some of them get misused. Some of them get tattooed. But the good ones stay intact.)

People are like languages—you can choose to speak them or not. Some, for no apparent reason, pull you in, make you want to spend a lifetime decoding them. But no matter how fluent you become, there will always be words you'll never know. Gaps. Missing meanings. Things you have to guess by context.

Some days, that's enough. But then there are moments when it feels like being trapped in one of those dreams where you open your mouth to scream and nothing comes out—where what we need most is someone who understands the parts of us we don't know how to translate. Someone to fill in the blanks.

So today (May 25th 2019), on my graduation day, that's what I vouch to do.

For the rest of my life.

Or at least try to.

Because as George Steiner implied:

"Every act of translation is an act of betrayal, but the refusal to translate is worse."

—I.S.C.B.

Acknowledgments

This will be a short one.

Mostly because the list of people I trusted enough to share this journey with is short. As in, I can count them on one hand.

So thank you. You know exactly who you are. Your faith in me has, more than once, pulled me through.

And to you, the reader. Whoever you are, wherever you're reading this.

I've been asked what my goal for this book is. It's a simple answer.

As a reader myself, I've always wanted stories that make space. Space to feel everything. To let out whatever needs letting out. To cry. To laugh. To sit with the questions that are hard precisely because they matter.

If these words gave you even a fraction of that, then they've done what they were meant to do.

So thank you for being part of Isadora and Hadrian's story. The rest is yours now.

About Me

I know these are usually written in the third person, but since this is my first book, I thought I'd do it in my own voice.

First things first: B stands for Barbara. I'm originally Argentinian and have lived a bit all over—mostly the U.S., the U.K., and Spain. I hold a business degree and a master's in Environment & Development from the London School of Economics, which sounds very serious and structured and nothing like the inside of my Notes app.

I've been writing for as long as I can remember, mostly in Spanish. This is my first fiction book, and the first I've written entirely in English. Across both languages, my work returns to the same questions: love, identity, and loss.

I love sad films and unsent letters. I tend to be convinced I'm right while still rearranging the lens I look through more often than I'd like to admit. I also have a maltipoo named Taavo, who runs the household with not-so-quiet authority.

This book is the first in The Carter-Bello Hall series (with the door suspiciously cracked open for more, should the story insist). Writing it felt vulnerable, exhilarating, and long overdue.

If you'd like to stay connected—for the occasional exclusive gift (like the wallpaper on the next page, designed by yours truly during one of my many sleepless nights), along with release updates, bonus content, and the pieces that never make it anywhere else—you can find me on Instagram at @b_ramonda and subscribe to my newsletter at www.bramonda.com.

I'm so glad you're here.

Much love,

—B

Tuesday, Feb 17

2:22

www.ingramcontent.com/pod-product-compliance
Lightning Source LLC
LaVergne TN
LVHW100511110826
845146LV00002B/593

* 9 7 9 8 9 9 3 6 7 9 4 2 6 *